WINTER'S REACH

THE REVANCHE CYCLE, BOOK ONE

Craig Schaefer

Demimonde Books

Joliet, Illinois

Copyright © 2014 by Craig Schaefer.

All rights reserved. No part of this publication may be reproduced, distributed or transmitted in any form or by any means, including photocopying, recording, or other electronic or mechanical methods, without the prior written permission of the publisher, except in the case of brief quotations embodied in critical reviews and certain other non-commercial uses permitted by copyright law. For permission requests, write to the publisher, addressed "Attention: Permissions Coordinator," at the address below.

Craig Schaefer / Demimonde Books
2328 E. Lincoln Hwy, #238
New Lenox, IL 60451-9533
www.craigschaeferbooks.com

Publisher's Note: This is a work of fiction. Names, characters, places, and incidents are a product of the author's imagination. Locales and public names are sometimes used for atmospheric purposes. Any resemblance to actual people, living or dead, or to businesses, companies, events, institutions, or locales is completely coincidental.

Cover Design by James T. Egan of Bookfly Design LLC.
Author Photo ©2014 by Karen Forsythe Photography
Book Layout & Design ©2013 - BookDesignTemplates.com

Craig Schaefer / Winter's Reach -- 1st ed.
ISBN 978-0-9903393-6-6

Kelly is my friend, my confidante, and often my inspiration. My work wouldn't be what it is, and I wouldn't be where I am, without her. She's given me gracious permission to play a riff on one of her own creations, as a crucial part of the Revanche Cycle's cast of characters, and I hope I do her justice.

Kelly, this is for you.

Revanche ("rə-ˈvänsh", noun)

1. A political policy, carried out by persons, tribes or nations, to regain territory lost to a rival.

    2. Revenge.

CHAPTER ONE

The family estate reminded Felix of a giant's rotting corpse, laid out under skies smeared a filthy gray.

The sagging columns of Rossini Hall looked like teeth, rotting and yellow and brittle, with chunks of plaster fallen here and there. The grimy windows were eyes gone filmy and dead. Thunder rumbled in the distance. When the rains came, servants would put out buckets and pots to catch leaks before they could drench the mildewed rugs.

Felix took a deep breath and forced himself to trudge across the yellowed lawn and up the pebbled walk. His heavy wool cloak, a hand-me-down from his older brother and the color of wet dirt, engulfed his slim frame. It hung on his shoulders like a crow's pelt, complementing his aquiline nose and narrow chin.

Taviano met him in the musty foyer and took his cloak without a word. The family butler was a walking stick of a man, all knees and elbows with a sparse mop of silver hair. Felix glanced up the hallway, listening to creaking echoes.

"He's pacing again," Felix said.

"For an hour at least," Taviano said. "I'm sure your presence will cheer him up."

"I wish I had your optimism."

The old man smiled, his eyes kind as he hung the cloak on a peg by the door.

"I believe fortunes can be reversed," Taviano said, "and that phoenixes can rise from ashes. If I didn't, I would not be here. The household staff has great faith in the Rossini family, young Master Felix. You should take pride in that."

Felix turned to go, then paused. He looked back at Taviano and took hold of the man's arm.

"It is not pride," he said. "It's responsibility. None of you are losing your jobs, not as long as I'm here. You can count on me."

"You have never let us down before," Taviano said.

There's a first time for everything, Felix thought. His guts churned in knots as he walked down a dark and musty corridor to his father's study. He knocked twice and then let himself in.

Albinus Rossini paced the weathered floorboards. The dying embers of a fire in the hearth silhouetted his stooped form. His cane thumped down with every frail step. He'd been blighted with the Withering Pox two winters ago and had spent the six months after that bedridden while the disease devoured him from the inside out.

Felix gestured toward his father's high-backed chair. "You shouldn't be up."

"Helps me think," Albinus grunted, hobbling past. "I'll walk as long as I've got one good leg obeying me. Your brother sent word. No deal. Not a cent. They will not do business with us as long as the Banco Marchetti has them by the short hairs. There's one more lifeline they've ripped from our hands."

"We have seen worse days," Felix said. His brother's letter, the handwriting immaculate and tight, lay on the desk beside a faded map.

"That's what your brother said, and you're both wrong. Right now, our best hope is an alliance with the Grimaldi family. We'll be a poor cousin with our hat in our hands, but we will *survive*, damn it all. Once you are married—"

"Father," Felix said, but Albinus cut him off with a sharp wave of his hand.

"No arguments. You're twenty-three, well past your prime for marriage, and Aita Grimaldi is two years your senior. People are starting to talk. About *both* of you. This alliance will be good for everyone. Besides, Aita is a fine girl. She'll give me grandsons, I'm sure of it."

Felix bit down against a surge of panic. This was it: his moment to shine or crash and burn. He'd practiced the speech in his wardrobe mirror for hours, but all that preparation felt worthless as he stood there and looked into his father's pox-ravaged face.

"What if I had another way?"

Albinus stopped pacing. "Spit it out."

"Alum," Felix said.

"Don't be cryptic, Son, I've no patience for it. The Banco Marchetti has the contract for the papal alum mines, and the only other source is in the hands of *pagans*. The market is as good as theirs."

"There is another option," Felix said. He led the way to the desk, his father clunking behind, and smoothed out the rumpled map with the flat of his palm. "What do you know about Winter's Reach?"

"It's a Gardener-forsaken shithole. Prison colony turned 'free city', only because it's too much effort to take it back. That's all I need to know. What are you on about, anyway? The Reach's only exports are lumber and sin. They don't have anything else to trade."

Felix beamed, his eyes bright. He tapped his finger against the map, coming down on the jagged sketch of a mountain range. "Only because nobody thought to ask. I checked the records from back when the Reach was still a prison. They built *mines*, Father, right here. Plural. Imperial surveyors said the earth was rich with alum."

Albinus squinted at him. "So why aren't they making money from it?"

"I asked some traders who sail the lumber route. It's a matter of history. See, the mines were a punishment for the condemned. The overseers literally worked the prisoners to death. They carted out more corpses than stone. Now that the Reach is free…well, it's mostly the second and third generations of the original prisoners living there now, and nobody wants anything to do with those tunnels. Old memories die hard. The mines are just sitting fallow, waiting to be tapped."

"As big as the papal mines?" Albinus asked.

"Maybe bigger. If we can forge a trade agreement with the Reach, they're all ours. We can even ship in foreign workers, if the locals won't take the jobs. We can break the Marchettis' stranglehold on the market overnight. They will have to come to the table and treat us as equals."

A polite cough sounded from the doorway. Taviano stood there, holding a tray with a porcelain pot and a pair of cups.

"I thought you gentlemen might do with some refreshment," he said. "Hyssop tea, with a bit of honey."

Felix thanked him and took the tray, clearing a spot for it on the cluttered desk. Albinus stared at the map with something curious in his faded eyes. Something like hope. He didn't speak until the butler left the room.

"They would have to respect us," he said softly.

"More importantly," Felix said, "they would have to *work* with us. This trade deal would restore our good name and our fortunes. Except for what little trickles in from the Caliphate, our two families would jointly control the entire alum market. That means we'd jointly control every market that *depends* on alum. Wool, tanning, medicine, all of it."

Albinus opened his mouth, running his tongue over his yellowed bottom teeth, then closed it again. He shook his head.

"No."

Felix's stomach clenched. "No?"

"Too dangerous. The 'citizens' of the Reach are savages, and it was our people who shackled them and dragged them into the snow to begin with. Not saying they didn't deserve it, but they hate us for a reason. I am not sending one of our agents up there, only to get him disemboweled and hammered onto a spike or worse."

"First of all, it was not 'our' people. It was the Empire—"

"Which we are a part of, like it or not," Albinus said.

"We are Mirenzei. The only difference between us and the people of the Reach is that they *won* their revolution."

Albinus narrowed his eyes and stared at the map like he wanted to rip it in half. "Words of treason, Son. Watch your tone."

"Words of truth. And second, no, I do not want to send one of our agents," Felix said. "I will go myself."

Albinus's head slowly turned. He stared at Felix, silent.

Felix squared his shoulders. "I am the best we have, and you know it. I know how to negotiate. I also know when to take risks and when to walk from the table. Look, this Veruca Barrett woman—their 'mayor', dictator, whatever you might call her—whatever her people are like, I believe she has a head for business. She wouldn't have held onto her throne this long if she didn't. I can convince her. All she has to do is grant us permission to dig. As I said, we can even bring in our own workers. She can just sit back and collect her cut of the profits. It's free money! Who would refuse that?"

Albinus looked long and hard at Felix, as if staring right through him.

"You are determined to go, aren't you?" he said. His raspy voice was suddenly distant, contemplative.

Felix nodded. "This deal will save the Banco Rossini. I can *do* this, Father. I just want your blessing."

"You said *want*. You did not say *need*."

Felix didn't say a word.

Albinus sighed and shook his head. "The answer is no. I will send a letter to Calum and tell him to look into it."

"You will send my brother," Felix said flatly, "but not me. When I am twice the negotiator he is."

"You have a wedding to prepare for."

"Right. But you're happy to send Calum into danger, because *his* wife is barren—"

Albinus slapped Felix across the face. Frail as the old man was, it still stung. Felix bit the inside of his lip, his cheek hot, and the two men stared each other down as Albinus shook with rage.

"Don't you *ever*—" Albinus started to say.

"Don't what? Don't point out the obvious? You didn't care that I put our business ahead of starting a family of my own, not until you realized Calum has been married for four years and he is *never* going to give you a grandson. Ever since you hatched this marriage idea with the Grimaldis, you've left me on the sidelines while sending poor Calum all over the Gardener's creation, far from house and home on jobs *I* should be doing. Don't pretend for a *second* that's not what this is about."

Albinus raised his hand. It trembled, hanging there. Felix didn't flinch.

"If you think hitting me again will make you right," Felix said, his voice calm and cold, "try it and see. It's always worked for you before. Why stop now?"

Albinus lowered his hand. He sagged against the desk, head bowed, staring down at the map. When he finally spoke again, his voice was soft as a church mouse.

"There was a time, Son, when the Rossini family was the toast of all Mirenze and beyond. When I was a boy, when my grandfather still held the family's reins, I could walk down any street in this city and be showered with accolades. We were *kings*. Half the moneylenders in the city wore our livery. When the duke needed to secure a wedding dowry for his daughter, he came to *us*. But they whittled us away, didn't they? Bit by bit, piece by piece, they've whittled us away and now…"

He slumped over. Felix caught him, holding the old man in his arms as Albinus shook silently. When he raised his head again, Felix's shoulder was wet with tears.

"I need to lie down," Albinus rasped. "Just for an hour or two. I'll be all right. I just need to lie down."

Felix took his arm and helped him down the hall, walking wordlessly at his side. He eased his father into bed, the old man's form frail under the heavy furs, and kindled a fire in the bedroom hearth.

He lingered by his father's bedside until he heard faint snoring, then padded out of the room and gently shut the door behind him. Taviano waited for him in the hall. The butler furrowed his brow, nodding toward the door and speaking in a whisper.

"Will he be all right, sir?"

Felix waved him along, walking until they were a good distance away and out of earshot.

"He has good days and bad days," Felix said. "When it's damp out, it's usually a bad day. Makes his leg and his head ache. He'll be all right. Just let him sleep."

"I'll see that he rests. Will you be wanting dinner? I could fix something for you."

Felix shook his head. "No, just my coat. I'm going out for the evening."

"In this weather? It's going to storm."

"I need air. One other thing, Taviano. Tomorrow morning, I'm leaving on a trip. Business. I shouldn't be gone longer than a couple of weeks, three at most. Would you just…look after him, for me?"

"Of course. I will keep a close eye on him. He will not be happy you left, will he?"

Felix shook his head. He smiled, but it didn't touch the sadness in his eyes.

"No," Felix said, "no, he will not, and he will not forgive me anytime soon, but this is how it has to be. I've a job to do."

He donned his cloak and set out into the growing shadows, crossing the dying lawn and walking out through the estate's ironwork gate, as the sun sank behind the churning storm clouds. Lightning flickered in the distance, glowing against the bell towers and crumbling curtain walls of Mirenze. Felix slipped into an alley, following a narrow lane crooked like a dead man's finger, and doubled back along a side street to make sure he wasn't being followed.

If anyone from the estate knew the real reason he stole off at odd moments, or exactly where he was spending his idle hours, his entire plan would be ruined. *Just stay the course,* Felix told himself, *we're almost free.*

CHAPTER TWO

A patchwork knight stood in the tanning yard, like a refugee from some distant and terrible war.

The pale young woman had cobbled together her leathers from five different suits: some studded, some plain, some brown, and some black, all tattered and scuffed up. She wore a dull mail shirt over the clutter and a single dented pauldron strapped to her left shoulder. Her ash-blond hair looked like it had been chopped with a kitchen knife, cropped short and ragged.

"Smell that, Mari?" said the stout man beside her. "Strike me blind and I'd still know this was the right place."

Werner Holst's belly protruded against his cheap farmer's shirt and leather vest, and his skin was chapped and windburned. A pole of tough hickory, long as two arms and thick as his fist, dangled over his shoulder on a leather thong. He rubbed his bulbous nose and pointed across the open yard, where laborers in broad-brimmed straw hats scraped at animal hides stretched over wooden frames. The tannery stood on the far outskirts of Mirenze, far enough to keep the stench at bay, and late afternoon storm clouds gathered over the city's bell towers like smears of oil.

"They soak the hides in piss for a few days," Werner explained. "Softens 'em up so they can scrape off all the fur. Those boys over there, stomping in those troughs like they're crushing wine grapes? That's water mixed with pigeon dung. Walking on the hides for a few hours makes 'em supple."

Mari Renault looked down at her leathers and wrinkled her nose. "Could have gone without knowing that."

"C'mon, I thought you liked learning new things."

A voice boomed at their backs, calling down from the balcony of the tanning house.

"I requested *l'Albanella*," a man called down, bracing his meaty hands on the rough timbers of the balcony rail. He was broad shouldered, with a pug nose and bloodshot eyes. His tunic and hose were spun from cheap linen but clean and cut to his frame, like a rich man trying to pass himself off as working-class.

"Holst the Harrier," Werner said with a nod. "You got him."

"What I've 'got' is a broken old sot and a Terrai bitch who looks like she crawled out of a garbage pile. *L'Albanella* is a giant of a man, seven feet at the shoulder, with jet-black armor and eyes of coal."

"You have been misinformed." Werner pushed his shoulders back. "I am Werner Holst. This is my partner, Mari, and I'll thank you not to throw those kinds of slurs in her direction."

"What slur?" the man said, curling his lips into a sneer. "You mean, 'Terrai'?"

Mari took a step forward, eyes cold, her thin lips pursed in a straight line. Werner's hand shot out and grabbed her forearm. She looked up and spoke in a monotone.

"There was a man who thought to trade on our reputation." She tapped her blunt fingernails against the pauldron on her shoulder. "He will not be doing that anymore. Also, he wasn't that big."

Werner nodded. "You are Terenzio Ruggeri, right? You wanted the best. That's who you've got. Let's talk business."

In reply, Terenzio put his fingers to his lips and let out a shrill whistle. All around the work yard, his men stopped and looked up from their jobs.

"Listen up!" he shouted. He held up a dented silver coin, twisting it between his thumb and forefinger to catch the dying light. "It's bonus time! I've got a shiny scudo for whoever beats these two impostors bloody and tosses 'em out on the street."

A ragged semicircle of men closed in on Werner and Mari. A couple carried hook-ended poles, the kind they used for dragging raw pelts. Others brandished scraping knives. Their eyes lit up with the anticipation of easy coin.

Mari's expression didn't change. She glanced over at Werner and said, "Does this mean he's not hiring us?"

"Some clients are easier to deal with than others," Werner muttered, reaching over his shoulder to unsling his staff and grip it in his calloused hands. They turned outward, standing almost back-to-back, as Mari drew a pair of wooden batons from her belt. One was slightly longer than the other, and she held them loosely by their leather-wrapped handles.

One of the laborers pointed and laughed. "Look out, boys! The rat girl's got a coupla sticks! We're done for!"

"Two against six," Mari whispered. Her eyes, the color of sea glass, darted from man to man. Sizing them up, measuring their speed, their threat, their weapons. Planning.

"Remember the rules," Werner whispered back.

"No killing." She gritted her teeth. "You don't have to remind me every single time."

"Come on, then!" Terenzio shouted down from the balcony. "It's an old man and a guttersnipe! What are you waiting for?"

Werner had stopped counting the stand-offs he'd been in. They were always the same. "Most people," he'd taught Mari, "are afraid of violence. Even if they *think* they're spoiling for a fight, they won't want to make the first move. And that's good. That's how it should be. First thing you wanna do, when you go eye-to-eye and violence is on the table, is find the toughest guy in the room. The alpha dog. You take him down first and take him down fast. That'll put a good scare into his buddies."

On his side of the circle, the alpha was a young buck with a lobster-tail sunburn and a saw-toothed knife. Werner saw hunger in his eyes. When the kid made his move, charging in with his knife hand high,

Werner dragged the tip of his staff along the ground and whipped it upward. A fistful of loose dirt went flying into the kid's face, the knife tumbling as he clawed at his eyes. Werner didn't stop, letting the staff's momentum carry him in a circle turn, twirling the wood in his hands and then driving the butt end straight into another man's stomach.

Where Werner was all controlled movement and precision strikes, Mari leaped into the fray like a feral cat in a back-alley brawl. She ducked under a swinging knife, close enough for the blade to snip one ragged blond hair, then whipped a baton against the knifeman's kidneys. Another worker shrieked as her boot heel slammed against the side of his knee, cartilage tearing, sending him to the dirt in a fetal ball. She grabbed an incoming blade between her batons, twisted her grip, and sent the weapon bouncing away. The unarmed man had half a second's warning before her brutal kick caught him square in the gut, sending him staggering backward, tumbling over the edge of a trough and splashing into the dung water.

That ended it. Battered and bloodied men, save one who had been smart enough to run, squirmed and groaned in the dirt around them. Werner slung his staff across his back and inhaled deeply, searching for a center of calm to lull his pounding heartbeat. He tried to ignore the twinge of fresh pain in the small of his back.

Mari, murder in her eyes, strode over and grabbed the shirt of the man who had taunted her. With the tattered fabric bunched in her hand, she hauled him up to his knees and raised one of her batons high above his head.

"*Mari!*" Werner snapped.

She froze, the baton casting a shadow across the man's terrified face.

"Unbecoming of a knight aspirant," Werner said softly.

Mari curled her lip and shoved the man back to the dirt.

"Lucky," she grunted, pointing the tip of the baton at him.

Terenzio stared down at the carnage from his balcony. His mouth opened and closed, wordlessly, like a fish squirming on a dock.

"It appears," he finally said, "I owe you an apology."

Werner just shrugged and spread his open hands.

"I believe you wanted to talk to us about a job," he said.

"I will be right down," Terenzio said.

#

The three of them walked the edge of the fence, circling the tannery as they talked. If he could even smell the rancid filth in the air, Terenzio showed no signs of caring. *It must burn out after a few years*, Werner thought. *Your nose probably just gives up and dies.*

"You really are Holst the Harrier," Terenzio said. "*L'Albanella* himself. Amazing. The man who captured the Witch of Kettle Sands."

Mari's eyes went hard as flint. Werner quickly moved between them.

"We don't talk about that," he said.

Terenzio shrugged. "As you wish. Now, I think this job is well-suited for—"

"Five scudi," Mari interrupted.

"Pardon?"

She stopped walking.

"Either you ordered your men to attack us," she said slowly. "Or you hired us to give them a sparring lesson. A sparring lesson costs five scudi."

"Fine, fine, I'll add it to your fee—"

"Now," Mari said. "You will pay now, so we can put it behind us."

Terenzio looked at Werner, exasperated. Werner shook his head.

"I'd do as the lady asks," Werner said. "She gets twitchy about unpaid debts."

Terenzio dug into his belt purse and handed over a few tarnished coins. "Here. Happy now?"

"It's not about being happy," Mari said. They started walking again.

"I need you to retrieve someone for me," Terenzio said, "and it is a very delicate situation. Does the name Dante Uccello mean anything to you?"

"I read one of his books," Werner said. "Orator, dabbled in politics. Captain of the militia here in Mirenze for about twelve years. Crossed the Marchetti family too many times, and they pulled some strings, got him slapped with treason charges. Heard he went into exile to escape the noose. Hasn't been seen since."

Terenzio nodded. "Right, except that last part. He has been found. He's in the north, hiding in some frozen hellhole called Winter's Reach."

Mari shot a look at Werner.

"We are familiar with it," he said, his tone hesitant.

"I hoped you would be," Terenzio said. "He has wormed his way into the good graces of the city's mayor, Veruca Barrett. By all accounts, the city is a corrupt, violent madhouse, and she is the grifter-queen of the asylum. She gave Dante a job as her advisor. I need you to go in there and extract him. Alive."

"Before we even talk about how impossible that is," Werner said, "why are *you* offering us the job? You're a merchant guildsman. You don't work for the Banco Marchetti or the city."

"Oh, they'll be hiring their own bounty hunters as soon as they get word of Signore Uccello surfacing, believe me. You will have to be fast if you plan to snatch him out from under their noses. No, I don't want to see Dante hang. Quite the contrary: this is a rescue mission. My name has to stay out of it. *Completely* out of it. Once you have Dante, don't bring him here. Take him to Lerautia—to the villa of Cardinal Marcello Accorsi. He is going to help clear the man's name and fight the treason charges."

Werner shook his head. "Like I said, I read one of his books. Dante Uccello is no friend of the Church, and the feeling's mutual. Why's a cardinal want to help him out? And you still haven't told us what your interest is here."

"My interest is singular," Terenzio said, raising his chin. "Money. This isn't an act of charity. The cardinal and I have a shared investment, and restoring Signore Uccello's good name is a critical part of our plan. He benefits, we benefit, and everyone calls it a good day. More than that, you don't need to know."

"Give us a minute," Werner said and pulled Mari away by her sleeve. They moved a few feet upwind.

"I don't like it," he told her, leaning close. "Too dangerous. Nobody steals from Veruca Barrett and walks away."

"So we don't steal him," Mari said. "We make a deal, something that everybody can live with. It's not like we're dragging him back in chains. I'm tired of living on crumbs, Werner. We need the work."

He stared at his boots.

"There's something else," she said. "What?"

"I don't think it's healthy, you going back to that place."

Mari's hands balled into fists at her sides. "Well, now we *have* to take the job. Because if we pass this up, that means *I'm* holding us back. I'll be fine. I promise."

He studied her face for a moment, then nodded.

"All right. Let's go haggle over the fee."

"He smells like money," Mari said, then paused. "Pigeon shit and money. Mostly pigeon shit. Let's get half in advance. It will be nice to sleep in a proper bed tonight."

CHAPTER THREE

Stathis stroked his half-dozen rings like they were a lover's skin, his fat fingers slipping over every glittering ruby and curve of gold.

"Of course, of course," he told the guests in his foyer, "any friend of Eckhardt's is a friend of mine. You have come a long way to see me!"

The woman standing just inside the door smiled, flashing unusually white teeth. She was on the shorter side, with olive skin and braided black hair, and Stathis's eyes couldn't help but linger on the way her russet dress clung to her curves. The man beside her could have been her brother: there was a certain resemblance in their sharp features and bright brown eyes, though he was tall and gangly. He carried a battered leather satchel, and his hand rested on the woman's shoulder, occasionally giving a tiny squeeze or caress.

"We have indeed," the woman said. "Once Signore Eckhardt told us about your art holdings...well, as we said in our letter of introduction, we curate a private gallery for a *very* passionate collector."

"Very particular about what she likes," the man said. "Very deep pockets, too."

Stathis nodded and led the way deeper into his house, waggling his fingers so his rings would catch the light from the chandelier above. It was a gesture he'd practiced a hundred times, ordering the household staff to stand in this place or that and appraise the level of glimmer, until he was confident he had the perfect flourish to impress any guest.

"Welcome to my home," Stathis said, looking back over his shoulder to make sure they'd noticed. "I'm sorry. I am terrible with names—"

"Vassili," the man said. "This is my partner, Despina."

Stathis beamed. "Given your names...originally from Carcanna, then? We are countrymen! How does the northern night air suit you?"

"'No air so sweet as the breeze over Carcannan waters,'" Despina quoted.

"'And no taste so sweet as the olive nurtured in Carcannan soil,'" Stathis replied. He led them up a sweeping staircase draped in a sapphire blue runner, onto a second-floor landing where an elderly maid scoured the floors on her hands and knees. He stepped around her, nearly kicking her water bucket, and ushered his guests into a long gallery lit by candles in silver sconces. At the far end of the hall, balcony doors stood closed against the autumn night.

Stathis waved his arm across the gallery hall in a grand flourish, inviting his guests to take in the dozens of paintings on the walls. Their gold and silver frames hung in a jumble, lush oils next to charcoal sketches.

"My humble collection. Artworks from every corner of the Empire and beyond. This one right here? My latest acquisition. It's a genuine Kleissos, dated to 977. Now, of course I had to pay a considerable sum for it…"

He paused, waiting for one of his guests to ask how much he'd paid. Neither of them did.

"…a *very* considerable sum," he added, "but it was worth it."

"These are all very lovely," Despina said, "but our patron has something else in mind. Something a little more…exotic?"

Vassili nodded. "Eckhardt said you purchased a certain piece from him, just last month. A very *special* piece."

Stathis pursed his lips, suddenly taciturn. His gaze flitted between his guests.

"I might have *spoken* to Eckhardt something along those lines," he said, choosing every word with care, "but that sort of thing, well, it is unwise to possess such an item. The Church frowns upon it. You…*did* say your patron has deep pockets?"

"The deepest," Vassili said. He patted his satchel. "We are prepared to make a generous offer and take it off your hands, right here and now. That is, if the item is authentic."

Stathis wavered on his feet, torn between his greed and his nerves. Greed won. He held up a finger. "Wait right here."

He scurried back a few minutes later, clutching a sandalwood box in his arms. He unlatched it and lifted the lid as his guests leaned in to see. Inside, a mask carved from bleached bone to resemble the face of a squirrel rested on a bed of black velvet.

"It has been authenticated." Stathis trembled with nervous excitement. "It's the real thing. It belonged to the Witch of Kettle Sands."

Vassili and Despina looked at one another. They nodded in unison. Then they turned their gazes back to Stathis.

"It is dangerous, owning such a thing," Despina said.

"Oh, it's hardly the first piece of contraband to pass through my vault," Stathis said. "I've friends in the constabulary, and they're rewarded not to search my wagons too carefully. When Eckhardt showed me this beauty, well, I just *had* to have it."

"He's so brave," Despina said to Vassili.

Vassili clasped his hands together. "Truly. I'd be afraid of getting cut up, like Eckhardt was."

Stathis blinked.

"You didn't hear?" Despina tilted her head. "It was a terrible thing. Someone chopped him up into teeny-tiny pieces and fed him to his own dogs. While he was still alive."

"I—I had no idea!" Stathis stammered. "Poor Eckhardt! He was a bit of a scoundrel, but a good man at heart. When did it happen? Did they catch the rogue who did it?"

"It happened when we visited him," Vassili said.

"And no," Despina added, "we have not been caught."

The sandalwood box tumbled from Stathis's hands. It bounced on the floor, flipping over, and the bone mask spun a few feet away. Stathis staggered backward, bumping his shoulders against the gallery wall.

Vassili opened his satchel. He took out two pallid masks of his own, handing one to his partner. They put them on at the same time. Despina's mask was styled like a shrike. Her piercing gaze bore through the hunting bird's narrow eye-slits. Vassili's mask was a swirling abstract at first, all squirming lumps and strange curves, until Stathis realized what he was looking at.

Worms, he thought. *It's a mask of worms.*

The house exploded in a cacophony of breaking glass and screams. The noise came from everywhere—the kitchens, the grand staircase, the bedroom wing—as Stathis's household staff met their nightmares.

His butler staggered in through the gallery door, reaching out a desperate hand for help. His eyes bulged from his purple, bloated face as he crashed to his knees. He doubled over, heaving, and a flood of cockroaches poured from his mouth. The fat brown bugs spilled out over his tongue in a blood-flecked stream, scrabbling across the man's convulsing body as he choked to death at Stathis's feet.

"Please," Stathis cried, pressing himself flat against the gallery wall and shaking his head wildly. "I don't want the mask! You—you can take it. Just let me go. I won't tell anyone, I swear it!"

One of the housemaids ran past the open door, shrieking at the top of her lungs. A naked man blistered with tumors came leaping after her, bounding on all fours. He paused in the doorway, turning his toad-shaped mask and wide, mad eyes to regard Stathis. The man's engorged tongue waggled out through a slit in the mask; then he turned and jumped out of sight. A moment later, the maid's screams went silent.

Vassili shook his head. "Sorry. We can't accept your offer. The mask doesn't belong to us."

A roach tried to climb up Stathis's leg. Frantic, he shook his foot to flick it off.

"*Who* then?" Stathis's voice rose, shrill and breaking. "Who does it belong to?"

"*Me,*" said an icy voice that coalesced from the air around him.

The balcony doors blew open on a gust of frozen wind. Autumn leaves rolled in across the polished floors, red and orange and dying. The Owl followed.

A feathered cloak hooded her straight black hair and cascaded down her shoulders, draping her in layer upon layer of tawny down. Eyes that could cut diamonds glared out from behind the pupils of her owl mask, locking on Stathis as she strode across the room.

"Please," Stathis babbled. "I didn't—I didn't know what it was. I didn't even—"

"Quiet," the Owl snapped. She paused, crouching and scooping up the squirrel mask with one velvet-gloved hand. The tips of her fingers glinted in the light; tiny metal points were set into her gloves, the hint of claws.

"She was only thirteen," the Owl said, studying the mask. "Did you know that?"

"W-who?"

The owl mask turned to face him.

"Squirrel. The Witch of Kettle Sands. *My apprentice.*"

Stathis opened his mouth, then closed it. His eyes brimmed with tears.

"I didn't know," he managed to whimper. "I didn't know."

"She was blindsided by a miserable pair of bounty hunters, delivered up for 'trial' bound and gagged, and forbidden from speaking a single word in her own defense for fear she might 'cast a hex upon the magistrate.' In the end, all she could do was scream through her gag while they burned her alive."

"I d-didn't *know.*" A tear trickled down Stathis's pudgy cheek.

"Tell me: where are Werner Holst and Mari Renault?"

"I don't—I don't even know who those people *are*! I'm just an art dealer, that's all—"

"Where," the Owl said, "is the book?"

"What book? There is no book. I just bought the mask, that's all. Eckhardt didn't *have* anything else!"

Despina nodded. "He's telling the truth. We wrung his little friend dry. The mask slipped onto the black market a day after Squirrel was murdered. No book."

"Then the hunters took it for a trophy," the Owl mused. "They must be terribly proud of themselves. So terribly proud."

She paced the gallery floor, cradling the mask in her hand, her feathered cloak sweeping out behind her. Down below the gallery, the last scream of the last servant died at the end of a wet, meaty *thump*.

Stathis turned and pawed at one of the portraits, fumbling for a catch under the gilded frame. It swung on a concealed hinge, revealing a safe set into the wall.

"Wait," he begged. "Wait, I'll show you—"

It took him five tries, but he finally managed to turn the dial properly and unlock the safe. Inside was a smattering of treasures: a ruby necklace, more rings, a fat accounting ledger, and a fatter sack of purple velvet. The sack jangled as he yanked it out and thrust it toward the Owl.

"I have money! See? Gold, good papal gold! You can have it!"

The Owl stopped pacing.

"Of all the things you could offer a witch in exchange for your life," she said. "Knowledge, a service, a boon, something *real*...you promise me pieces of shiny metal. You can't understand. Men like you never do."

"Money is the most real thing there is! Y-you can't survive without money, you can't eat without it!"

Amusement glittered in the Owl's dark eyes.

"Is that so?" she said. "Let us put your claim to the test, shall we? Worm. Shrike. Take him."

Despina snatched the sack of coins from Stathis's hand while Vassili pinned the fat merchant's arms behind his back, wrenching one shoulder so hard it snapped out of joint with a sickening *pop*. When Stathis opened his mouth to scream, Despina grabbed his jaw and forced it wide.

"That's right," the Owl said. "Feed it to him. One coin at a time."

Vassili giggled behind his mask, holding Stathis in an iron grip. Despina echoed the sound as she held a gleaming coin up to the merchant's terrified eyes.

"The great tragedy of your life," Despina said, "is that all these years, you thought you were a real person. Did you seek meaning in your riches or just ephemeral pleasure? Did you learn anything at all?"

"You created nothing," Vassili whispered in Stathis's ear. "You believed in nothing. You were never real. Don't worry, though. My sister and I are here to help. To give you something real in your final moments. To *enlighten* you."

Despina pressed the first coin against Stathis's tongue and pushed it toward the back of his throat.

"If a life of pleasure has taught you nothing," she said, "let's give pain a try."

#

The Owl paced the gallery floor, cradling Squirrel's mask in her hands and gently stroking its cheek with her fingertips. The merchant's agonized choking and sobbing fell away into the background. Torturing the man was pointless, but she knew Worm and Shrike would enjoy it. *Let them have their fun*, she thought.

They had more work to do, after all. Squirrel's book was out there somewhere, in enemy hands. Just like the girl's mask, it needed to come home.

And then, Holst and Renault. The faces of the two bounty hunters were seared into her mind. The memory was fresh as the day she'd spotted them across the Kettle Sands town square, taking their blood money from the mayor. Collecting their precious *silver* while a child burned.

They didn't know what pain was. They couldn't possibly understand how she had felt, standing there helpless, disguised as one of those pathetic cattle while the cursed townspeople cheered her apprentice's death. They couldn't imagine how her heart broke when Squirrel stretched one blackened, peeling arm toward her, begging with ash-flecked tears for help. Help the Owl was powerless to give.

No, Holst and Renault didn't know what pain was.

But she would teach them.

CHAPTER FOUR

The docks of Mirenze were no place for a gentleman, but under the murky moonlight Felix looked like any other eager wanderer out for a night's pleasure. His hand-me-down cloak swallowed him up in warm folds of wool, staving off the chill and the faint mist that clung to the air. The sky still rumbled with the threat of a storm, but it held back its fury for now.

He knew the route by heart. All the way down to the end of Peregrine Street, where tall ships bobbed in the harbor and the moon's glow gleamed off jet-black waters. A mouth harp trilled in the distance, accompanying the muffled, drunken sounds of a sea shanty as a merchant's sloop slipped away from the dock. Not far up the lane, orange lights glowed behind scalloped glass windows. The sign for the Hen and Caber dangled above the door—a ruffled-looking bird painted on clapboard.

A fire's warmth and a jaunty reel of lute song rushed to greet Felix as he stepped inside. He wiped his boots on the muddy thatch mat just inside the door, while his eyes adjusted to the flood of lantern light from every knife-scarred wooden table and bar shelf. The inn's common room was rough but friendly, mostly dockhands coming in to relax and spend their pay after a hard day's hauling. Some of the men played *primiera*, shouting, tossing tarnished coins, and slapping their bad cards down on the ale-stained wood, while others simply got down to the serious business of drinking. Nobody gave Felix a second glance as he made his way to the edge of the crowded room, finding an empty table and a rickety chair to sit in.

A barmaid meandered over. Heavy rouge streaked her shallow cheeks, the color of a sunburn in the lantern light, and Felix could make out the faint ravages of pox scars under the pigment.

"Evening, Zoe," he said with a smile. "How's the pheasant tonight?"

"Oh, you don't want that," she said, leaning in with a theatrical whisper and putting her hand to the side of her mouth. "The cook's been fearsome sick tonight and coughing up a storm back there. How about you let me bring you a hunk of bread from the pantry? It's yesterday's, but it's still perfectly good."

"You are a marvel and a beauty, as always," he said.

"And you've got a devil's tongue, you have. I'll let you-know-who know you're here."

She tapped her finger against the side of her nose, winked, and slipped into the crowd. Felix leaned back in his chair and soaked in the music and the swirl of conversation around him. The anonymity felt as warm as the hearth fire. It was nice to disappear for a while, and try to forget the wolves at the door.

Not much later, as he bit into a crusty chunk of bread, a young woman in a white linen tunic and a heavy apron appeared at the edge of the crowd. Her rust-red hair was done in a braided twist, and she flashed a brilliant smile when she caught his eye. She held up five fingers on one hand, two on the other, and disappeared back behind the bar.

Felix waited seven minutes before he slipped outside.

He strolled around the building, hands in his pockets, and tried to look nonchalant as he glanced over his shoulder. Behind the inn was a narrow alley where the cobblestones glistened under a spray of mist. He was halfway down the passageway when hands darted from a shadowed alcove, grabbing him by the arm and pulling him into the darkness.

His alarm gave way to sudden heat as warm lips pressed against his, hands stroking his shoulders and curling in his hair. He wrapped his arms around the woman's waist and pulled her close.

"Renata," he breathed, kissing at her chin, her throat, whispering her name as the tip of his tongue flicked against her earlobe.

Renata opened his shirt, fingers urgent as she tugged his collar to one side, while his hand slipped beneath her tunic and fumbled at the laces of her thin linen shift. His fingers slid past the laces, sneaking under the filmy fabric, and she bit at his neck as his fingertips caressed the soft curve of her breast.

"Did you talk to him?" she murmured, tugging at his belt. Felix nodded, quickly, bending down to kiss his way along her collarbone. Every touch of her hand burned under his skin, stoking the fires in the pit of his stomach.

"I leave tomorrow," he whispered. "Back in two weeks, no more than three."

Felix's belt clattered to the cobblestones, and her hand slipped inside his leggings. Her slender fingers curled around his hardness and drew a strangled gasp from his throat.

"Renata, we—we shouldn't—"

"What's the matter?" she whispered, giving him a fiery smile as her fingers slowly stroked up and down. "Afraid someone's going to catch the heir to the Banco Rossini fucking a barmaid?"

"No, but—"

She clasped her hand around the back of his neck and squeezed, hard, as she lifted one foot and hooked her leg around his waist.

"Two weeks is a long time without you," she said and guided him inside her.

Then there was no time for words, no room for them, just two lovers clinging to one another and leaning against a crumbling stone wall as they rutted like beasts. Renata bit down hard on his shoulder, her muscles tightening like steel coils as she crescendoed, and he let out a hoarse cry as he followed her over the precipice. They held each other close, sweating, panting, feeling each other's pounding hearts.

"I love you," he whispered.

They sank to the damp cobblestones together, their legs too wobbly to stand.

"Two weeks," he said, "and I save the Banco Rossini. Money, pride, a place at the bargaining table. My brother and my father can run it from there."

"Without you," Renata said.

"Without me," Felix said, "and I can walk away knowing they'll be all right, with my honor intact."

Her fingers curled around his, twining, holding tight.

"Do you think they'll come looking for us?" she asked.

"When they find out I eloped with a 'commoner'? Father will be furious, but Calum will calm him down. He always does, and the money will soothe any open wounds. Besides, let them look. We'll be all the way to Kettle Sands before anyone notices we are gone."

"I heard back from the owner of the Rusted Plow," Renata said. "You wouldn't believe the hoops I'm jumping through to keep my parents in the dark. He agreed to our offer. I'm starting to think we can pull this off."

Felix smiled. "An inn by the shore, someplace peaceful and warm, just for us. You can tend the bar and I can cook. It won't be easy, but we'll make it work."

She looked in his eyes, and her smile faded just a bit.

"Felix?"

"What is it, love?"

"You once told me that there are no sure things when it comes to business," she said.

"You know that as well as I do. You practically run the Hen and Caber yourself, not that your drunkard of a father has ever given you a lick of credit for it."

"What if you fail?" she said.

He looked down at their twined fingers and shrugged.

"If I fail, the only way I can save the family business—and keep my father from dying in a debtor's prison—is by marrying Aita Grimaldi. So that means there is only one possible outcome here."

"What's that?"

He gave her a lopsided smile. "I don't fail."

#

A light rain fell from the midnight sky as Felix returned home. He ducked under the columned porch and let himself into the dark villa, shutting the door behind him as softly as he could. Metallic plinking sounds echoed up the empty halls as raindrops leaked through rotting boards and down the edges of warped window frames, landing in the battered pots and pans that littered the mildewed rugs.

I will never set foot in this house again, he thought. A bitter pain gripped his heart and nearly drove him to his knees.

The door to his father's study hung open, the candles doused, the hearth cold. It brought him back to the day he'd told Albinus about Renata, almost three years ago. Before the pox had shriveled his father's body, when Albinus could still swing a fist strong enough to break his son's lip and loosen a tooth.

Felix remembered standing there in shock, blood running down his chin as Albinus ranted at him.

"Your mother *died* giving *birth* to you, you ungrateful shit! This is how you want to repay her memory? By dragging our family name into the gutter? By making us the laughingstock of the city?"

"I thought you would be happy—" Felix had said.

"Happy? Why? Because my son is fucking a piece of dockside trash? You are a *Rossini*. A nobleman! I'd rather see you *dead* than dirtying yourself with a commoner."

The room was silent now, but he could still hear the fury in the old man's voice, echoing from the worm-eaten wood.

"Well, Father," Felix said to the empty fireplace, touching his bottom lip and reliving the memory of the pain. "It looks like we both get what we want, in a way."

Another man might have stormed out that night, and sometimes Felix wished he'd been that man. Then he'd taken a look at the crumbling villa, the family business on the brink of ruin, and the old man who could be so loving when he wasn't in one of his rages, and left his bags unpacked. Ever since that night he'd had two goals: to steal every minute with Renata he could, and to find a way to reverse the Banco Rossini's fall from grace.

He'd save the business. Save his family. Then he and Renata could disappear.

Felix padded to his bedroom, wincing at every creak of the floorboards. He undressed in the dark and slipped under the piled quilts. They cocooned him in velvety warmth, the dark stirring memories of his lover's touch.

CHAPTER FIVE

Mari woke up screaming.

Werner jumped up from the armchair he'd been sleeping in, feeling a fresh whiplash of pain in his lower back as he loomed over the small rented bed. He knew the routine by heart, keeping a safe distance as she shrieked like a cat with a sliced-off tail and threw wild punches at the air.

The fit passed as suddenly as it began. Mari sat upright, the sheets and her cotton nightgown soaked and freezing. Icy sweat made her bangs cling to her pale brow as she gasped for breath.

"You're awake," Werner said softly. "It's all right. You're awake now."

"*I don't know that*," she hissed. She closed her eyes and shuddered, forcing herself to take deep breaths.

"You're safe," he said, his voice gentle. He still didn't dare come closer. "You're safe, and I'm here, and everything is going to be all right."

She nodded once. Hiccupped. Her shoulders slumped.

"Can I sit down?" Werner asked.

She nodded again. He sat on the edge of the bed, keeping his hands where she could see them.

"You want to talk about it?"

"It was her again," Mari said, not meeting his gaze.

"The witch."

"The *girl*."

"Mari, we've talked about this—"

"That was no witch. That was a child, and we *murdered* her, Werner."

"We did nothing of the kind. Mari. Listen," he said, and now he did take hold of her shoulder. She flinched and yanked away from him. "Listen. *We* did not kill that girl. Witch or not, guilty or not, it was those motherless fools in Kettle Sands who denied her a trial. If we had known what they were going to do…we wouldn't have taken the job. We wouldn't have."

"But we did."

He sighed and looked over at the window of their tiny room. A waxing moon hung low in a blanket of stars. Under their feet, he could still hear the faint but lively commotion coming from the inn's common room. It couldn't have been much past midnight.

"Yeah," he said. "We did. And that was my call to make. My weight to carry, not yours. So let me carry it."

"How? How do you deal with it?"

Werner stretched one of his legs out, leaning forward to rub at his calf. Another sore muscle. He wanted to blame the weather, but that excuse only carried so far.

"When I was a younger man," he said, "I took a bounty on a fugitive killer. I tracked him all the way to the Enoli Islands and found him drinking himself blind in a thatched hut. He pulled a blade on me. Got in a good cut across my arm, too. The bounty was the same, dead or alive, so I finished him off and rode back home with his head in a sack. Easier than dragging a live prisoner for a hundred miles, I figured."

"That's different," Mari said. "He attacked you."

"Let me finish. Turned out, while I was on the trail, his wife found proof that the poor bastard was innocent. He'd been pardoned. If I'd been just a little more careful, if I'd put just a little more effort into the job and brought him back alive, he would be a free man today. Instead I turned his wife into a widow, because it was *easier* that way. Worst, stupidest thing I've done in my entire life, and that is the honest truth."

He rolled up the sleeve of his shirt, showing her the long, jagged scar that ran a fish-belly-white trail down his bicep.

"Every morning, I see this in the mirror. How do I deal with it? I promise to do *better*. To make that man's death *mean* something, so instead of a weight that drags me down, it's a spur to remind me that I owe a debt. My one big debt."

Mari stared at his scar. A trickle of cold sweat dripped down the nape of her neck.

"I don't know how to pay her back," she said softly.

"Why don't you…why don't you pray on it for a while," Werner said. "That always makes you feel better, doesn't it?"

Mari nodded. She slipped out of bed and rummaged in her knapsack, digging out an old pewter brooch. The face of the brooch resembled the craggy circle of a full moon, encircled with a ring of faded glyphs.

"I'll give you some privacy," Werner said, pushing himself to his feet and ignoring the jolts of pain in his calf and his back. "Sounds like the common room is still open. Think I'll go treat myself to a nightcap."

He meandered down the smoky steps to the tavern below. A few diehards still lingered, drunks slumped against wooden tables, dozing in their cups, but the hearth fire was down to the evening's last embers. Werner took a stool at the bar.

"Whiskey," he told the barmaid and laid a few of the coins from Terenzio's down payment on the ale-sticky wood.

"Looks like you need it," Renata told him. She made the coins disappear and wiped down a glass with a wet rag. "Why the long face?"

"A friend of mine is sick. And I don't know if I can help her. Used to think I could, but now…I don't know. She's getting worse."

Renata uncorked a dusky, unlabeled bottle and splashed two fingers of whiskey into a glass.

"You a surgeon or an herb-monger?" she said. "You don't look the type."

"No. She's not that kind of sick." He tapped the side of his head, then tossed back the glass and downed it in a single swig. As soon as he set the glass back down, Renata was there with another pour from the bottle.

"You're not wearing a ring," she said with a casual flick of her eyes. "Lover?"

"Nah. Apprentice. Business partner. Friend. Hurts like hell seeing her in pain. But I'll stand by her, long as it takes. That's what you do. It's just what you do."

Renata took down a second glass and poured a splash of whiskey for herself. She raised the glass, catching the lantern light.

"Here's to love," she said, "and how far we'll go for it."

"To love." Werner clinked his glass against hers. "Sounds like you have someone to care about, too."

Renata smiled, sipping her drink. "My fiancé. Twelve hours on my feet, hair ragged, smelling like smoke and stale beer, and he looks at me like I'm a princess dipped in gold."

"Hang onto that one. Decent men are hard to find."

"You sound like one yourself," she said.

Werner chuckled, but he couldn't keep a trace of sadness from his eyes.

"No, miss, not me. I'm just making up for lost time, trying to set a few things right while my old bones still let me. I owe some people."

"Owe?"

Werner studied his glass. "Debts. I owe a *lot* of debts."

CHAPTER SIX

On the far side of the city, a fist-sized chunk of alum rested on Lodovico Marchetti's desk. Pale starlight streamed through great bay windows and made the white, chalky hunk of stone glisten like a diamond in the rough.

Lodovico leaned forward in his tall leather chair and stroked the stone with gold-ringed fingers. He looked rough himself, burly with tan, weathered skin, and the unkempt shock of auburn hair he'd inherited from his mother. He could have passed for a dockworker if not for his tailored shirt and silken vest.

A voice droned, "—will have to pay for the indulgences for our street-level moneylenders to continue operating into the new year, at fifty scudi per…Vico? Are you even listening?"

Lodovico yanked his hand away from the stone as if it had burnt his fingers.

"You have my undivided attention," he lied.

Simon Koertig leaned against a wall of bookshelves, his polished boots sinking into the plush blue rug. He held a thick, hidebound ledger like another man might hold his infant child and stared at Lodovico over the tops of his horn-rimmed reading glasses. He was a Murgardt expatriate, with wispy blond hair and pale blue eyes.

"It is good to dream of the future," Simon said, "but only once the cows are milked and the eggs brought in from the hen house. Metaphorically speaking."

"Am I that obvious?" Lodovico said, chuckling.

Simon nodded toward the chunk of alum. "I think you were about to put that down your pants. And if you do, I'm leaving."

"For shame." Lodovico feigned shock. "I'm not even married to it! Yet."

"Yet. Well, to spare you from the horrid boredom of listening to me talk, the bottom line is that the Banco Marchetti is flush with cash for the coming quarter. All of our investments and loans are operating right within the bounds of acceptable risk."

"Is that what you call it?" said a voice from the doorway. Sofia Marchetti strode into the room like a force of nature and slammed a fistful of papers down on Lodovico's desk. Her hair had faded to the color of rusty steel wool and the candlelight caught every line on her once-smooth face, but age hadn't stolen one ounce of her ferocity.

Lodovico leaned back in his chair and clasped his hands behind his head. "And good evening to you too, Mother. Have trouble sleeping?"

"Why are you extending Carlo Serafini another line of credit?"

"Goodness," he said, "I don't know. Maybe because he's the pope's son?"

"He's a gambler and a drunk, and he hasn't lifted a finger to repay any of the other loans we've given him."

Lodovico shrugged. "He's a gambler and a drunk today. Next year he's going to be the pope. Doesn't hurt to spend a little money to keep us on his good side."

"This is more than a *little* money," Sofia said, rapping her fingernails on the desk. "And there is no guarantee he's going to take his father's chair. If the College of Cardinals routs him, they'll cut him off and he will die a pauper. We'll never get a bent copper out of him then."

"They won't," Lodovico said. "Trust me. He's a good investment."

Sofia took a step back, catching something in her son's tone. She crossed her arms over her gray evening gown, looking from him to Simon and back.

"You two," she said, "are up to something."

Simon smiled and held up his ledger. "Just running the numbers, ma'am."

"I have some irons in the fire," Lodovico said. "Nothing you need to worry about."

Sofia leaned over the desk toward him. Her voice dropped low, a warning growl.

"If you are running some kind of side project with the bank's money," she said, "without talking to me about it—"

Lodovico held up one hand.

"Mother? With all due respect, Father passed the reins of the Banco Marchetti to *me* when he died. You were given an advisory position as a matter of courtesy. That's all you are obliged to do. Advise. I have heard your advice, and now we're done."

She straightened her back, glowering at him.

"This isn't over," she said.

"For now, it is," Lodovico said. "Now if you'll excuse us, tomorrow morning will be laden with appointments and visitors. If you pass by the kitchens, would you mind popping your head in and checking on the servants? They could use your supervision, I think."

Sofia turned and strode out of the office without another word. Lodovico watched her go, his expression a mask of stone. Simon let out a long, low whistle.

"She is going to be a problem," Lodovico said.

"Almost unquestionably," Simon said with an agreeable nod. "She smells blood in the water, but she can't find a fish to bite. She'll hunt for one until she's fed."

"Then we will *give* her one, something to keep her distracted while we get our work done. Let me think about it. Our little weasel from the Rossini family should be visiting us shortly. Sent a message claiming he had urgent news. That would be a first."

Soon enough, one of the household servants appeared at the door with their guest in tow. Taviano edged his way into the office, head slightly bowed. The Rossinis' butler still wore his shabby funeral black.

"I don't have long," he said, almost stammering. "I don't have any good reason to be out of doors this late, and the cook is a light sleeper."

Lodovico leaned back and waved his hands. "Well! That's good, because I wasn't going to invite you to breakfast. Speak up. *Entertain* us."

"Felix Rossini has found another source for alum."

The smile faded from Lodovico's face. He sat up in his chair, studying the butler. Simon leaned against the bookshelves and listened, silent as a ghost.

"Explain," Lodovico snapped.

"Winter's Reach. They have mines, several of them, that are lying fallow. Felix is heading north, personally. He thinks he can broker a trade agreement between the Reach and the Banco Rossini."

Lodovico and Simon shared a glance. Lodovico looked back to the butler.

"He's leaving soon?"

"Tomorrow morning," Taviano said, nodding quickly. He looked toward the office door and wrung his hands. "He has booked passage on the *Fairwind Muse*, a merchant ship."

Lodovico steepled his fingers. "Driven little scamp, isn't he?"

"He always has been, sir. He thinks this agreement is the key to saving the family business."

"Well, we can't have that, now can we?" Lodovico said with a humorless smile. "Simon, pay the man."

Simon counted out a handful of copper coins from his belt purse. He held them out to Taviano, but he opened his hand at the last second and dropped them to the carpet. The coins fell in a glittering shower, scattering in all directions.

"Oops," he said. "Clumsy of me."

The butler gritted his teeth as he stooped down on all fours to pick up the fallen coins. He shoved himself back up, wincing, and hobbled to the door.

"Thank you," Lodovico called out dryly. "Do come again."

Simon shut the door behind Taviano and locked it.

Lodovico sighed. "Have I mentioned lately how much I despise traitors?"

"It may have come up once or twice," Simon said.

"I realize dealing with these sorts of people is the cost of doing business and staying informed, but I don't have to pretend to enjoy it. So what do you think? Valid threat?"

Simon shrugged. "Entirely possible. I can check the Imperial register and see if there is any record of a mining operation from the penal-colony days."

"No need. I'll take care of it. I have something more important for you. The Rossinis have been on my mind lately. Tiny fish. The Grimaldis are tiny fish too, but if those families are allowed to join forces…well. Piranha are tiny fish, and that's the makings of a swarm."

"I thought we decided the marriage wasn't a serious threat?" Simon said. "We were going to leave the Grimaldis alone until stage two of the plan—"

"It wasn't, and we were. If the Banco Rossini really found a new source of alum, though? That changes things. Felix Rossini is the key to both deals. No Felix, no alum, and no wedding joining their houses."

A faint smile rose to Simon's bloodless lips.

"You're daydreaming again, Vico."

"Perhaps I am," Lodovico said. "Perhaps I am imagining a world where poor, poor Felix Rossini met with a tragic accident in the frozen north, and he never came home again."

"You know me. I *love* making your dreams come true."

Lodovico swung his chair around. He got up and wandered over to the window, looking out at the starry night sky.

"It's a shame, you know. I met him once."

"Felix?" Simon said.

"At the Feast of Saint Scarpa, last autumn. Smart lad. Good head on his shoulders, quick with numbers. I would have been happy to hire him, if his damned old man would just give up and die. I feel badly about this. Still, there is the grand design to think about."

"Can't afford random variables," Simon said.

"No," Lodovico said, "and young Master Rossini is exactly the kind of person who could cause us problems down the line. Best to avoid the risk. Do me a favor, Simon. No playing with your food this time. Make it quick and as painless as you can manage."

Simon set his ledger on the desk. He took off his reading glasses and buffed each lens with his shirtsleeve. His eyes were as dead as a painted puppet.

"I will see," he said, "what I can do."

CHAPTER SEVEN

At first, Amadeo Lagorio thought someone had run riot inside the merchant's villa with a can of brown paint. Rusty splashes covered the floor, the walls, the broken windows, even clinging to the curving stairs in dried rivulets as if a gallon of it had come splashing down the steps. Then the coppery rotten-meat stench hit him, and he knew it wasn't paint.

The crudely severed head of one of the housemaids stared up at him with wide, glassy eyes, tossed into the corner like a discarded toy.

"Why?" Amadeo whispered. "Why did you bring me to this terrible place?"

Gallo Parri, master of the papal guard, was pushing forty and twelve years Amadeo's junior. Where Gallo was barrel-chested, thick-whiskered, and usually boisterous, Amadeo was a slight, retiring man whose gray hair was receding like an evening tide. Gallo glanced over his shoulder at the broken front door that hung open on one twisted hinge.

"It's the constabulary, Father. They won't set foot in the house until it's been checked out by a man of the soil. Can't say I blame 'em. Wherever the Gardener's love went last night, it wasn't in this house. They came to me, begged me to fetch a priest. I told 'em I'd get the best man in the Holy City."

"I'm no exorcist, Gallo. I'm just a parish priest."

The guardsman snorted. "You're the papal confessor. That makes you plenty important enough to deal with…well, whatever we've got here. Look, I don't think anything's going bump in the night. It's just a crime. A damn heinous one, but a crime, committed by human hands and human evil. It would mean a lot to me if you'd just take a look around and give the all clear, so I can put my men to work."

Amadeo took a deep breath and steeled his nerves.

"All right," he said, "but next time we're at the Cloaked Sow, you're buying the drinks. *All* of them."

Gallo smirked and clapped Amadeo's back. "That's the spirit."

Every open doorway in the villa offered a new horror. Household servants smashed to pulp, beaten beyond anything that resembled a human body, or literally torn limb from limb. Gallo pointed to a casement window, smashed in from the outside.

"Figure there were eight, maybe nine killers. They all broke in at once, from all over the house, cutting off the exits. This was planned. Organized."

"Who lived here?" Amadeo said.

"Small-time criminal named Stathis. He wore out his welcome down in Carcanna, so he figured he'd move north and set out his shingle here. He posed as an art dealer, but that was just a cover. He'd smuggle contraband, stolen goods, anything he could get his grubby mitts on. The constabulary never could find the evidence to lock him away. Moot point, now."

Stathis lay slumped against his gallery wall, under a blood-splashed painting of a pastoral countryside. The corpse's eyes were as wide as his mouth, and Amadeo's stomach churned as he realized what was sticking out of his throat.

"One of his fingers," Gallo said, following the priest's gaze, "with a big ruby ring still on it. Think that's what choked him to death, in the end."

Amadeo looked down at the clotted stumps on the dead man's hands.

"Where...where are the rest of his fingers?"

"Some things, Father, don't bear too much speculation."

An empty purple velvet sack lay discarded at the corpse's side. Amadeo carefully stepped over it, turning his attention to the gallery wall. A small safe hid in the wood paneling behind a painting that hung open on its concealed hinges. The safe was empty, save for a fat accounting ledger.

"A robbery, no doubt," Gallo said. "The gang of robbers invaded his home, murdered the household staff, and tortured Stathis until he gave up the safe combination. Then they stole off with his gold and jewels. Simple and straightforward."

Something nagged at Amadeo—something didn't feel quite right. He reached into the safe and pulled out the ledger, cradling it in one arm as he flipped through the pages. The dead smuggler's writing was cramped and most of the entries were in some kind of code, but the purpose of the green-lined parchment was clear enough.

"The people who did this," Amadeo said, "they'd have to be familiar with the criminal underworld, yes? I mean, if they knew Stathis's real business."

"Someone who could do this? Sure. This wasn't anybody's first crime. They would know their way around."

Amadeo showed Gallo the ledger, tracing a long, bony finger down the list of names and prices.

"Then they would know the value of a smuggler's secret ledger, wouldn't they? Look: Stathis kept notes. Detailed notes. A lot of abbreviations and shorthand, but you could probably reconstruct half his client list with this. Why wouldn't they take it with them, for blackmail, or at least to choose their next target? The killers had to have seen it and known what it was, but they left it behind. Why?"

Gallo frowned and took the ledger from him.

"Huh. Good question, Father. Let's flip to the end, see who old Stathis was doing business with lately."

They paged through, slowly, and as they neared the end of the ledger one name caught Amadeo's eye.

"Wait," he said. "Wait, here—"

His finger fell on one entry from two months prior. What he read made his brow furrow.

"Rec'd / Carlo Serafini / 500sc.

"Paid / Dustmen / 500sc."

Gallo looked at Amadeo. "That's a joke. Has to be."

"I don't see the humor."

"Father," Gallo said, "*Carlo Serafini*. Are you telling me the pope's son was doing business with some lowlife Carcannan smuggler?"

Another entry, farther down the page, mirrored the first. Again, Stathis had taken cash from Carlo and passed it on to the "Dustmen" the next day.

"A middleman," Amadeo mused. "Carlo needed to give money to someone, on more than one occasion, and couldn't do it himself."

"But writing out his full name like that? Why not do it in initials, or use a code name, like these 'Dustmen'?"

Amadeo shrugged. "If you were doing illicit business with one of the most powerful men in the Empire, wouldn't *you* want it all laid out in black and white somewhere? You know, in case…"

His gaze slid down to the mutilated corpse on the gallery floor. The color drained from Gallo's ruddy cheeks.

"You're not saying—"

"No," Amadeo said. "Carlo has his…character flaws, we both know that, but he's no murderer. I don't think there's a connection. That said, I still can't let this go."

"Neither can I. So tell me, Father, how do you want to sort this mess? I have a duty to investigate, no matter whose son he is."

"Take the ledger, but keep it quiet for a few days. Let me look into it on my own, discreetly, and see if we can save his family from any unnecessary embarrassment."

Gallo nodded. "That sounds best. And what should I tell the constables?"

"Hmm?"

"About the house."

"Ah." Amadeo nodded. He looked over at the cold hearth and sighed. "Tell them that some evil people did a terrible thing in this house. Tell them that it is their duty—their professional and moral duty—to bring the criminals to justice and that I have complete faith in them. You are right, Gallo. There are no monsters or demons here. Only men."

Gallo gave Stathis's corpse a little nudge with the toe of his boot.

"Think I'd be happier if we could find a monster to blame," he said.

CHAPTER EIGHT

Pennants rippled in a warm breeze down in Mirenze's harbor, seagulls wheeling in a cloudless sky. Cargo ships lined the docks, and stevedores ran up and down the ramps, rolling barrels and toting sacks, hauling cargo in and out from the customs house. Felix walked along the docks with a heavy traveling pack slung over one shoulder, enjoying the sun.

At the end of dock fourteen waited the *Fairwind Muse*, a fat three-masted galleon. Its northern oak planks, sanded and stained, took on a cherry hue in the afternoon light. It flew two flags: the jagged yellow stripes of the Stockwater Company, and the green and black of the Enoli Islands.

Most of the sailors were Enoli themselves, with skin the color of burnt honey and accented voices that flowed like the ocean waves. As Felix approached the lowered gangplank, he could hear a strident voice booming out.

"Step lively, lads, and lash those barrels down! If they go rolling once we push off, your heads'll roll with them! Kimo, flemish up that line before someone trips over it and cracks their skull. Swear to the Tallyman, you'd think this was your first voyage."

Felix waited patiently at the foot of the gangplank, shifting his weight to rest his pack against his hip. The man at the top had shoulders wider than an ox and a freshly shorn head that gleamed in the sunlight. He gestured wildly as he shouted, flashing a tooth of hammered gold. Then he turned, catching sight of Felix, and broke into a broad grin.

"Hail, Captain!" Felix waved. "Permission to come aboard?"

"Granted and gladly!" the Enoli called down.

Felix hustled up the sloping plank, his well-worn boots catching onto the wooden ribs as he stayed mindful of wet spots. He could already feel the slow, gentle sway of the sea challenging his balance. He'd barely made it onboard before the big man swept him into a crushing hug, kissed both of his cheeks, and slapped his back.

"Brother Felix! It's been, what, two years? Too long."

"Captain Iona," Felix said with a bow of his head, "I can't tell you how much this means to me. Finding passage to the Reach on short notice is almost impossible. It's almost like nobody wants to go there."

"I'm glad they don't! Who needs the competition? We bring Mirenzei goods up, we haul lumber down, and I fill my purse at every port of call. Giving you a berth is just a chance to repay an old debt. Hey, Anakoni! Come here, I want you to meet someone."

A lanky Enoli sauntered over in a rolling gait. Fresh rope burns blistered his palms, and his left eye was a different shade of brown than the right. Felix realized it was glass, cheaply made and a little too big for its socket.

"Anakoni's my first mate," Iona said. "Anakoni, this is Felix Rossini. When no one else in this cursed city would give me the time of day, he opened his doors and his purse to me. Felix here is the reason I own the *Fairwind Muse* today, and the reason *you* have a job."

Felix and Anakoni clasped hands, and the sailor gave him a gruff nod. He looked over at Iona and flashed a toothy smile.

"And you're dragging him out to the Reach, Captain? Sour way to repay a man's kindness."

"No kindness involved," Felix said. "Captain Iona had a solid business plan, and I had the capital. That little gamble paid off for both of us."

Iona put his hands on his hips. "And here you are, gambling again. What's so important about Winter's Reach that you have to take the journey yourself?"

"Like you said, I'm gambling again. I'm looking to make a trade deal with Mayor Barrett. You know, if I pull this off, there's going to be a lot of hauling involved. We might need to get you a second ship."

"The first one I needed a loan for," Iona said. "The second one I can buy out of my own pocket. I wish I could promise you a pleasure cruise, brother, but this is a working ship and there's not much in the way of luxury. There's a berth for you down in the officers' cabin and just enough room to squeeze that pack underneath it. Space is cramped, but we'll get you there."

"A safe arrival is all I ask," Felix said. "I'm not afraid to travel rough, and I'm happy to help out anywhere you need me. As long as it doesn't involve climbing that rigging, anyway."

"And I was going to make you our lookout," Iona said with mock dismay. "Oh, just so you're forewarned, you're not my only passenger. I'm ferrying an old bounty hunter from Murgardt and the other, well, she's an odd one, but she keeps to herself."

Felix tilted his head. "She? I thought a woman on a ship is supposed to be bad luck."

"For Mirenzei sailors, surely it would be. They're afraid of their own shadows, and they spill out perfectly good rum for dead men who can't even drink it. Me, I'm Enoli, and to me she's just a paying fare. Silver can *never* be unlucky."

"Those two hunters don't have a single pair of sea legs between them," Anakoni said glumly. "If they puke all over the deck, I'm not cleaning it up."

Iona slapped Felix's back and laughed. "Of course not, Anakoni. Didn't you hear? Our friend Felix said he is willing to help out anywhere we need him! Ah, here's one of our other guests now."

Felix's eyes went wide as Werner ambled up from belowdecks.

"Werner?" He waved. "Is that…? It *is* you!"

"Felix!" the old man called back, beaming.

Captain Iona watched them as Werner embraced Felix. "You two know each other?"

"Werner used to work for my family. Best guardsman we ever had."

"Sure," Werner said, ruffling Felix's hair, "when you were about half as high as you are now."

"And you had half the wrinkles. What's this I hear, you're a bounty hunter these days? I thought you were off soldiering for the Empire."

"Turns out I'm actually good at something, imagine that. We're headed up to the Reach for a little retrieval job."

Felix followed Werner's gaze. At the far end of the deck, oblivious to the sailors hauling crates and lugging rope around her, Mari sat cross-legged next to the railing. She held her pewter brooch in her cupped hands, her eyes lowered and lips moving wordlessly.

"That's, ah, my apprentice, Mari," Werner said. "We've been riding together for a couple of years now. C'mon, let's get out of the way. I want to hear all about what you've been up to. Let's find a place to talk that isn't bouncing so much."

"Werner, the deck is barely moving. We haven't even left the dock yet."

Werner cringed, looking green. "I know. Believe me. I know."

#

They cast off while the sky turned to gold over the spires of Mirenze. The *Fairwind Muse*'s canvas sails billowed as its masts swung to catch the wind, and Felix looked out over the stern to watch his home slide away. Something pulled at his heart, a kind of wistful pain he couldn't put a name to.

Two weeks, Renata, he thought. *Two weeks and we'll be free.*

An hour later, land was just a memory. The *Muse* cut across the open sea, fast and free. Felix forced himself to walk along the deck, breathing deep, getting accustomed to the sway of the boards under his feet and the slow lurch in his stomach. By sundown, when sailors lit hooded lanterns along the ship's length and Captain Iona navigated by a canopy of shimmering stars, Felix had finally found his sea legs. He made his way belowdecks and looked for the galley.

Dinner, as expected, was a fist-sized chunk of hardtack and a matching slab of salted beef. The cook ladled out some grog into a dented tin cup for him; it was only tepid water with a splash of rum for antiseptic purposes. Just enough to taste the alcohol, not enough to enjoy it. Felix collected his bounty and headed back up on deck. He wanted the night air, to taste the salt and feel the breeze ruffling his hair.

The crew took their meals in shifts. Meandering around the deck, biting into the hunk of stringy, boiled beef, Felix eventually found Anakoni and a small knot of sailors by the railing.

"And how's your worm castle, your lordship?" Anakoni said with a nod to Felix's piece of hardtack. Felix bit into the stale biscuit and chewed a mouthful, washing it down with a swig from his cup.

"Thankfully vermin-free," Felix said, "and I've had worse. Next time you're in Mirenze, try the jellied eel at the Galloping Lamb. Better yet, don't. Your guts will thank you."

One of the sailors, a short, gangly man Anakoni had introduced as Kimo, sat on a barrel and swung his legs from side to side.

"The Lamb?" Kimo said. "You think that place is a shithole, just wait until you see what they call a tavern in Winter's Reach. Maybe you can eat like a sailor, but we'll see if you can drink like one."

Felix raised his cup with a smile. "I'll take that challenge. Soon as my business is done, I'll drink to all your health and buy the first round to boot."

Four cups clinked against his, echoed by grunts of approval. One of the other sailors, leaning on the rail, looked his way and asked, "First mate says you've got business with the mayor. That true?"

"That I do. I've got a deal in mind that could make a lot of people very happy."

"Watch your ass anyway," Kimo snorted. "Barrett's crazy as a rat drenched in oil dancing around a candle and daring it to burn her. She'll cut your throat just for kicks."

"She's got a witch, too," Anakoni mumbled through a mouthful of salted beef.

Felix squinted at him. "I'm sorry. Did you say 'witch'?"

"It's true," Kimo said. "I've seen him. Giant bastard, wears a mask of carved bone shaped like a bear's head. One of the old Northmen. They say he can turn you inside out without even touching you."

"I heard milk curdles when he walks past it," one of the other sailors said.

Felix chuckled, but he could hear the twinge of nervousness in his own voice. *Nobody tells stories like a sailor*, he told himself. *You've got nothing to worry about.*

Craving a change of subject, he looked down the lantern-lit deck.

As far from everyone else as she could get on the busy ship, Mari stood by the railing with her fighting sticks in hand. She moved slowly, gracefully, sliding from stance to stance in what looked to Felix like more of a dance than a warrior's drill. One of her arms made a slow-motion glide from high above her head to aim straight out before her, guiding the point of the baton with absolute precision.

"She's a strange one," Anakoni said. "Guess she's some kind of bounty hunter. Doesn't look like much of anything to me, but she had ready silver to pay, and none of the Mirenzei haulers would take a woman on board."

"Last six hours," Kimo said, "she's either been doing…whatever you call that, or kneeling down and praying to a hunk of metal in her coin purse."

Anakoni slapped Kimo's shoulder. "If you've had six hours to watch her, I'm not keeping you busy enough. Don't get any ideas you shouldn't be having, neither. She's the captain's guest."

"No worries there. She looks like a sewer rat and comes off about as friendly. If I stuck it to her, she'd probably bite it off."

"Has anyone tried, maybe, *talking* to her?" Felix said.

Anakoni shook his head. "We're paid to deliver her safe and sound. We're not paid to be nice to her. She's a girl playing at a man's job. What she gets is what she gets."

Felix thanked them for the company and went back belowdecks, headed for the crowded galley. A few minutes later he was topside again, strolling toward Mari with food in hand. He stood there, waiting for her to notice.

Mari slowly lowered her batons, pausing in mid-motion, and turned to face him. She didn't speak.

"I noticed you hadn't eaten," Felix said, holding out the hardtack and beef. "I didn't know if anyone told you they'd opened the galley."

She blinked, frowning, like she couldn't grasp that he was offering the food to her.

"I thought I'd save you the trip," he said.

She took the hunk of salted meat, sniffed it, then tore off a bite.

"Thank you," she mumbled, talking with her mouth full.

"You're from Belle Terre," Felix blurted out.

Mari frowned. "Why?"

"I mean, your name. Mari? That's Terrai, isn't it? And you're pale, like…like they are."

"Yes," she said.

"I'm Felix. Felix Rossini. I'm from Mirenze, so we have something in common."

"We do?"

Felix nodded, smoothing the front of his tunic, feeling like a babbling fool. "Well, the Empire. Neither of our people joined willingly."

Mari took another bite and chewed thoughtfully.

"Your people," she said flatly, "surrendered without spilling a drop of blood and were welcomed with open arms. My people fought to the end and were punished for it. They're still being punished for it."

Felix winced, barely restraining the urge to slap his forehead.

"They say you're a bounty hunter," he said quickly, trying to change the subject.

"That's right."

"Have you been to Winter's Reach before? I guess it's a pretty rough town."

"Once," Mari said.

"That lot's got all kinds of tall tales," he said, nodding over his shoulder with a jerk of his head. "They tried to tell me the mayor's got a witch on her payroll."

Something went dark in Mari's eyes.

"I need to get back to my training now."

Felix nodded, taking a step back. "Right. Sorry. Um, I'll see you around."

She didn't respond, gripping her batons and returning to her stance exactly where she'd left off.

He was ten feet away when she called after him.

"Felix?"

He turned.

"Thank you," she said, "for the food. It was…nice."

Felix gave her an awkward wave, and walked away.

Cursing himself, he nearly bumped into one of the crew in the dark. Only a few of Iona's men weren't from the captain's homeland in the islands, hired piecemeal here and there to replace stragglers and quitters. This must have been one of them, Felix figured, a blond Murgardt with pale blue eyes.

"Sorry," Felix said quickly, "my fault. Still getting used to the roll of the ship, I guess."

Simon Koertig smiled at him and showed his open palms.

"No apologies needed, friend. Every old salt was new once, so they say. You're that banker, no? Felix...?"

"Rossini," he said, and they shook hands.

"I'm Simon. The captain speaks highly of you. Off on business?"

"Hopefully good business. Have you sailed with Captain Iona for long?"

Simon shook his head. "No, no, this is my first run. It's a terrible thing. One of his crewmen was in a barroom brawl that went bad. Took a knife right between his ribs, and nobody even saw the bastard that did it. My old captain just retired, and I was looking for a new crew to sign on with. Funny how one man's loss can be another man's gain."

"You made a smart choice," Felix said. "Iona's tough, but he's a good man and a fair captain."

"It's a good stretch of sea, too. Did you see the dolphins?"

Felix tilted his head. "Dolphins?"

"Mm-hmm. Bottlenoses, entire schools of them. They're all around, out here. Want to see?"

Felix nodded. Simon waved him over toward the ship's railing, in the shadowy gloom between the dangling lanterns.

"If you lean far enough over—" Simon started to say, pointing down toward the water, but he was cut short by Iona's booming voice.

"Brother!" the captain called out. "Been looking everywhere for you! I picked up a bottle of Itrescan brandy in port, and it's demanding to be shared. Far too good for the likes of my mouth alone. Bring your friend Werner, if he's not still puking his guts up in the cargo hold."

Felix smiled and patted Simon's shoulder.

"Sounds like a command I can't refuse," he said with a laugh. "I'd better go. Thanks, though! Maybe tomorrow."

Simon watched him go. He smiled with gritted teeth at Felix's back.

"Right," he said. "Maybe tomorrow."

CHAPTER NINE

Amadeo sat on a marble bench in the shade of an iron tree, watching his friend slowly die.

Pope Benignus sat beside him, looking up at the elaborate sculpture. Sunlight filtered through the tree's black boughs and glistened off leaves sharper than knives. Benignus wore robes of ermine shot through with gold thread, in contrast to Amadeo's plain brown cassock. The amulets at their throats were the same, though, simple imitations of the great dark tree dangling from silver chains.

"I never liked it," Benignus said. The elderly man's eyes seemed hazy, as if he couldn't quite focus.

"Sir?" Amadeo asked, startled out of his thoughts. They'd been sitting in silence for a good ten minutes, just taking in the sun in the garden courtyard. The sandstone walls and ornate archways of the papal manse rose up around them, fencing them in under the noonday sky.

"The tree," Benignus said. "It was my father's idea. He wanted something...strong. Something to show the Gardener's power. A tree that could never blow down, or be chopped down, or grow sick and die. A tree of iron."

The tree was the centerpiece of the gardens. Flowers in every color of the rainbow bloomed around it in spiraling patterns, lifting their faces to the sun. A rustling caught Amadeo's attention. He glanced over to see a squirrel dart into the bushes.

"He forgot," Benignus said, "that a tree of iron can't bloom. Amadeo, would you do something for me?"

The pope stood slowly, and Amadeo quickly rose to help him to his feet.

"I cannot disrespect my father's wishes," Benignus said. "But when I'm gone? Tear that damned thing down. Plant a real tree here. One that bears fruit."

Benignus turned his face from the tree and took Amadeo's arm. They walked together along a pebbled path.

"You aren't going anywhere," Amadeo said. "Not anytime soon."

Benignus laughed, then doubled over as his hoarse chuckle turned into a coughing fit. Amadeo handed him a handkerchief, helping him to press it against his lips. When the fit passed and the pope stood straight once more, Amadeo took the handkerchief back. Blood spattered the white silk. He folded it and tucked it away.

"You are my confessor and aide, Amadeo, not my surgeon. My surgeon has a grimmer outlook and, I hate to say it, a bit more experience than you in these matters."

"I have faith," Amadeo said.

"And faith can move mountains," Benignus said with a gentle smile, "but it usually doesn't grow new lungs for an eighty-year-old man. I've had a good run, but you and I both know my curtain is falling. Best to prepare for it, with as much dignity as I can still muster, than to shake my tiny fist at the heavens."

"Is that why you wanted to walk in the garden? To talk of loss and grief?"

"More practical than that. There have been rumblings in the College of Cardinals."

Amadeo nodded. "I have heard them. There is talk of mounting a succession challenge questioning your son's…moral fitness."

"My beloved friend, you have a talent for putting a pretty face on disasters. I have heard everything they say about Carlo and then some. Most of it nothing but fantasies and lies."

Amadeo didn't say anything for a moment. He thought to the night before and the discovery of the dead merchant's ledger.

No, he thought, *no need to burden him with that.*

Benignus patted his hand. "*Most* of it. I may be losing my vision, but I am far from blind. Carlo has neither the maturity nor the piety that this post demands, but did I, when I stepped into these shoes? I was wild once, too. Your father molded me. Taught me. Cultivated me like the Gardener himself, trimming away my weeds and strengthening my roots."

"Where are you going with this, Bene?"

"The groundswell in the College is the work of a few ambitious schemers. Most of the cardinals are undecided. You are respected, Amadeo. People listen to you. If you make a strong show of support for Carlo—"

Amadeo shook his head. "I'm just a parish priest with a very special job. Nobody's leader."

"Yet the people flock to hear you speak. The cardinals are, whether some of them like to admit it or not, beholden to the people. The problem is Cardinal Accorsi. He's plotting something."

"What do you think he's after?"

"I think," Benignus said, "he wants to be wearing my slippers five minutes after my feet go cold. Accorsi has always been an ambitious viper. The College would not choose him, though, even if he did force through a succession challenge and remove my son from the running. He cannot get the votes. So what does he gain from all this?"

"Perhaps," Amadeo said carefully, "he honestly believes that Carlo isn't the right choice."

"What do you believe, Amadeo?"

Papal guards in white tabards, their chests emblazoned with the silhouette of the iron tree, hauled open the garden doors and stood sharply at attention as Benignus and Amadeo walked inside. Amadeo led his friend down a long vaulted corridor lined with oil paintings, holding his arm.

"I believe that a father's love is unconditional," Amadeo said. It was the kindest answer he could manage.

"And I believe that you can do for Carlo what your father did for me. You can reach him, Amadeo. You can bring out his inner greatness, chisel away his weakness like a sculptor finding a statue inside a shapeless block of marble."

Amadeo smiled sadly as they walked into the audience chamber. A throne of carved ivory stood at the end of a long green rug, flanked by tubs where shrubs and wildflowers grew in beds of rich black loam. Sunlight streamed though arched windows thirty feet above their heads, casting crisscross shafts of light and shadow across the vast chamber. Courtiers, scribes, and minor cardinals flocked to one another in tiny clusters, whispering their petty intrigues. No heads turned as Amadeo helped Benignus into his throne.

"I am as a ghost," the pope said with a wan smile. Amadeo set a small velvet pillow behind Benignus's head.

"You are alive and well," Amadeo said, "and as far as your son goes, I fear you think too highly of me."

"You have such kind words for everyone but yourself. I think...oh, hello."

Amadeo turned his head. A few feet behind him and off to one side, Rimiggiu the Quiet knelt down on one bended knee.

Rimiggiu was a short, swarthy man with a neat black beard, hailing from the southern crescent of Carcanna. He dressed in simple cotton workman's clothes. Most thought him a mute, but Amadeo knew the man could speak. He just preferred not to. He also knew that Rimiggiu was no ordinary servant. He had a special purpose in Benignus's household, just as Amadeo did, but from a decidedly different angle—an angle Benignus took great pains to keep Amadeo isolated from.

Even the Gardener's ambassador needs a spy, Amadeo thought.

Rimiggiu handed Benignus a folded letter. He unfurled it and read it over, holding it inches from his fading eyes.

"Winter's Reach?" he said to Rimiggiu. "You're sure?"

Rimiggiu nodded, his face grave.

"Dante Uccello," Benignus mused. "There's a name I haven't heard in some time."

"The orator?" Amadeo asked. "Wasn't he hanged for treason in Mirenze years ago?"

Benignus folded the letter back up, handing it to Rimiggiu. "Good work. Stay on it."

Rimiggiu bowed deeply and trotted away. Benignus looked back to Amadeo and shook his head.

"Our enemies are playing strange games, my friend."

"Can I help?" Amadeo said.

"No. That kind of work is...not for the honest of heart. Best leave it to a man like Rimiggiu. From you I must ask a far greater, far more important favor."

Amadeo braced himself. He knew what was coming.

"I believe in my son," Benignus said, "and I believe in you. Just as I believe that when I pass on from this world, my enemies will try to sway you, to claim your support for their own ambitions."

"Bene—" Amadeo started to say, but he fell silent from a wave of Benignus's frail hand.

"Swear to me," Benignus said, "that you will support and serve my son, just as you serve me."

"Is my simple word not sufficient?"

"Not for this. For anything else but this. My line must not end in shame. Carlo *must* be pope, and you must be his guide. Swear to me."

Amadeo dug his fingernails into his palms. His mouth went dry, his tongue feeling limp and useless as a dead fish.

"Is it that important to you?" he managed to ask. The light in Benignus's tired eyes, the hope etched on his withered face, was his only answer.

Amadeo walked to the edge of the flowerbed at Benignus's side. A clay pot rested on the edge of the tub, filled with warm water for the plants. He held out his right hand, palm upturned, over a clump of wildflowers, and gripped the pot with his left.

"I swear, by the Gardener's creations, that I will serve Carlo as I serve you. I swear it by the water that gives us life."

He tilted the pot slowly. Water trickled down, splashing his palm, slipping between his fingers to spatter the flowers below.

"I swear it by the soil that grows our sustenance."

He pressed his palm to the dirt, feeling the rich black loam squish against his fingers. An impression of his hand remained when he pulled it away and touched his fingers to his heart.

"And I swear it by this beating heart, may it ever thrive on truth."

Benignus closed his eyes and smiled. He reached out, clumsily, and managed to take hold of Amadeo's wrist.

"You have lifted a burden from my soul, old friend," Benignus said. Amadeo just stood there with a thin smile frozen on his face.

Was the burden a thousand pounds and made of lead? Because I know where it went, Bene.

"I should go," Amadeo said, desperate for fresh air. "You have courtiers to indulge, and I have a sermon to write."

Benignus looked serene as he released Amadeo's wrist. "Yes, yes, of course. You have an entire flock to look after, and I am only one congregant. A terribly needy one at that. Thank you again, Amadeo. You are a good friend to me."

Amadeo stepped back, bowed his head, and turned to leave as a small flock of supplicants swooped in on the ailing pope, flourishing their requests like children hoping for new toys.

#

Amadeo didn't stop walking until he was back out in the garden courtyard feeling the sunlight against his skin. His stomach churned, and he took deep breaths, trying to calm it.

Bene, what have I done? Of all the things to ask of me, why that?

He went back to the tree and sat down on the edge of a bench, resting his head in his hands as he tried to calm down. The sound of trilling laughter drifted across the courtyard and drew his eye.

Benignus had become a father late in his life. Carlo was thirty going on seventeen, and he eschewed priestly robes for a silken vest with slashed sleeves, looking like he was set for a night out on the town. He had his father's coal-black hair—or at least, Amadeo's memory of what his father's hair had looked like long ago—but beyond that the two men couldn't have been more different.

A pair of women clung to Carlo's arms, giggling, draped in forest-green habits. Novices from the Order of the Harvest. Amadeo knew he should get their names, speak with their matron, but he was too tired and disgusted to care. Carlo spotted him, disentangled himself from the women, and waved, grinning like a loon.

"Amadeo! Hey, hey!" he called, dropping into the bench beside him and throwing an arm around Amadeo's shoulder. His breath stank of cheap red wine. The women milled about, giggling and whispering to each other.

"Carlo," Amadeo said flatly. "Enlightening some of the novices, I see."

"Oh, you know. I enlighten them a little, they enlighten me a little, we swap some parables. Hey. Seriously. How's my father?"

"He would be better if you spent a little time with him."

Carlo winced. His arm dropped from Amadeo's shoulder.

"He doesn't need me around," Carlo said, giving another, less confident smile. "He's got you!"

"Every father needs his son."

"Aren't you afraid I'll embarrass him?" He said it jokingly, like a playful challenge, but Amadeo thought he saw something else behind the facade.

"No," Amadeo said. "Because you love him. And he loves you."

The smile faded. Carlo kicked the toe of his shoe into the dirt. His voice was soft.

"My father is going to die, Amadeo."

"In time, yes."

Carlo looked at him, suddenly frantic, almost pleading. "I shouldn't have to *deal* with that."

Amadeo put his hand on the younger man's shoulder.

"What you have to deal with, right now," he said, "is that there is an ailing man in there who very much wants to spend his remaining hours with his son. You can make him proud, Carlo."

"It would help," said a woman's voice at their backs, "if you didn't gallivant around with whores."

Livia, Carlo's sister, stood regal and serene in a black brocade gown. Her charcoal hair was piled on her head in a wave, fixed in place with a silver pin. She looked at the two novices and fluttered an irritated hand.

"Yes. I called you whores. *Leave*."

"Hey!" Carlo snapped, shrugging off Amadeo's hand and standing to face her. "You can't talk to them like that."

Livia arched an eyebrow. "Why? Have you not paid them yet? I'm sorry, my mistake. They're only sluts."

One of the novices ran off with tears brimming in her eyes. Carlo called to her, flailing his arms, chasing her across the garden with the other novice in tow. Amadeo watched them go without a word. Livia dropped into Carlo's seat, sighing like she'd just hauled a sack of bricks across the courtyard.

"A bit harsh," Amadeo said lightly.

"Was I wrong?" she asked.

"I said harsh. Not wrong."

"And *that*," she said, "is the next leader of our Mother Church. Gardener help us all."

"Your father has faith in him," he said.

"And do you?"

He had to think about how to answer that.

"I have faith in your father."

Livia looked him over, her emerald eyes birdlike and keen.

"You have a smudge of dirt on your right hand. And another on your cassock, just over your heart."

Amadeo nodded. "So I do."

She favored him with the ghost of a smile, showing him the smudge of soil on her own right hand.

"Look," she said, "we're twins."

Amadeo chuckled. "He got you too, hmm?"

"'And so I swear to love my brother as I love you, Father,'" Livia recited with a sweet smile, which faded to her usual dour frown in a heartbeat.

"And was that love, just now?"

"My love can be cruel," Livia said. "You know my father is a good man, and a holy man, but he can be a manipulative old bastard too."

"I can't argue that," Amadeo said with a faint smile. "But he believes Carlo is a better choice than anyone the College of Cardinals could bring to the table."

"Hrm. And with that worm Accorsi leading the charge, he might be right. Best choice in a barrel of rotten apples. No matter what, we're all going to bite down on a maggot."

"A disturbing but possibly apt metaphor. You have a talent for those."

Livia swiveled her hips on the bench, curling her legs underneath, to turn toward Amadeo.

"I'm eight years older than Carlo," she said.

"So you are," he agreed.

"If I had been born a man," Livia said, "I'd be the next pope."

"I'm not sure there is much value in that sort of speculation—"

"Tell me something, Confessor. And tell me the truth."

He lifted his chin, catching the look in her eyes. Sharp. Hungry. She made him think of a falcon soaring over a field of mice.

"If I had been the one," Livia said, "would my father have needed to coerce you into an oath to serve me? Or would you kneel down and kiss my ring of your own free will? Would you recognize me as the rightful heir, one worthy of leadership?"

Amadeo looked over at the iron tree, unmoving in the warm breeze.

"I have seen where you go at night," he said.

She crossed her arms over her stomach.

"I have seen you," he said, "garbed in hooded rags, down in the Alms District and the worst parts of the city. Carrying food and medicine for the destitute. I have seen you cradle a leper in your arms as he died."

"No one was supposed to—" she started to say, quaking with barely controlled fury.

"No one else knows. And no one will. I have said nothing to your father. You know how he would react, if he found out his only daughter was putting herself in danger like that."

"The Church is broken," she said. "My father has tried his best, but the cardinals have blocked him at every turn. We have the means to help people, far more than we do, but Gardener forbid we actually *get* it to them. All I can offer is my little service."

"I happen to agree with you. And to answer your question, no. There would have been no coercion. I would have gladly seen you on your father's throne, but that does not change the reality. The reality is that you are a woman. The reality is that canon law doesn't change without a four-fifths majority of the College in favor, and they can't build that much agreement on whether water is wet. The reality is that Carlo will be our next pope and you, as his sister, have the opportunity to bend his ear in ways none of us can."

"So I can graduate from the useless girl," she said, standing up from the bench and smoothing her skirts, "to the slightly less useless girl. Tell me something else, Confessor? If you had the opportunity to change things, to truly change things for the better, for everyone…how valuable would your pledge be then? Would you break your oath to my father, if it meant saving the Church?"

Amadeo looked up at her, surprised, peering into her eyes as if trying to read her mind. He shrugged. "I can't answer that."

"One day," she said, "you might have to."

CHAPTER TEN

Days passed, and the sky turned white as the ocean turned black.

Shipboard life took on a dulling rhythm punctuated by moments of terror. Felix could sit for hours, lulled while the boat swayed on an easy wind, then suddenly feel his stomach clench as a rogue swell lifted the galleon high only to slam it back down on waves that felt hard as stone.

He had to bundle up now when he went topside, swaddled in his brother's cloak. The air was cold as a Mirenzei winter, and twice now he'd seen glimmering snowflakes kiss the billowing sails. Sailors scrubbed the deck night and day with thick chunks of sandstone, fighting the encroaching frost. Felix's alarm grew one morning when he looked out over the bow and saw floes of ice bobbing in the brine.

He found Anakoni on the starboard side, tightening the braces on a massive harpoon gun. He grunted, waved Felix over, and pressed a wrench into his hand.

"Here. While I push down, tighten that brace as far as you can. The wood's wet, makes it hard to get a grip."

The first mate put his body weight against the brace while Felix pulled hard on the wrench, hauling against the bolt until his arms ached.

"Lots of ice in the water," Felix said. "You don't look worried."

"Because I'm not. We've carved our way through fields of ice thicker than a landslide. This time of year, not likely we'll need to. It's only autumn, too early for the nasty stuff."

"But we could still hit those floes."

Anakoni chuckled and shook his head.

"This is the *Fairwind Muse*, brother. She's built for cold weather, and reinforced against a head-on hit. She also has a false keel and bands of iron at the waterline to save us from nipping."

Felix gave the bolt another tug. "Nipping?"

"Nipping's the real danger. That's when two big fields of ice squeeze against a ship from both sides at once. The pressure could crush a lesser ship like an eggshell. Not the *Muse*, though. Her hull's rounded and shaped for leverage."

The first mate held out his hand lengthwise, demonstrating as he explained. "A nip would squeeze our hull and push us up and over, see? Instead of being crushed, we ride the ice and shove it down beneath us. Worst case then is that we capsize, but that hasn't happened yet. Never will, so long as Captain Iona's at the helm."

"So what are the harpoons for? Whaling for meat?"

Anakoni patted the gun, running his palm along the frost-slicked iron curves of its firing tube.

"No," he said, "they're in case the Elder comes."

"Who's the Elder?" Felix said.

Anakoni grinned, flashing dirty teeth. "Not who. *What*. The Elder's haunted these waters for a hundred years or more, never far from the Reach. One trip in ten, it'll come sniffing our way. We load up a skiff with whatever meat we've got left in the ship's stores and set it adrift. It'll take our offering, but we've got the guns just in case. Don't think we could actually *hurt* it, but it'll take a free load of meat over getting stung by a harpoon."

Felix handed him the wrench. "But what *is* it? A shark or something?"

"Our god Ochali, he's a storyteller. Long before man set foot on our islands, he told the stories of birds, and trees, and fish, and they came into being. Well, one day, Old Man Ochali took a nap while he was supposed to be working. Ribeda the Trickster planted a nasty dream in his head and walked away laughing. When Ochali woke up, he found out all of his nightmares had climbed right out of his head, scattering to the four winds, hiding in the dark spaces so he couldn't snatch them back up again. There's no place in the world that's darker than the bottom of the ocean."

"So the Elder is a god's nightmare." Felix arched an eyebrow. "Is that a metaphor or something? I'm trying to understand."

Anakoni spit over the ship's rail. "You don't want to understand. But if the waves start to boil, and you hear the Elder scream…you'll understand plenty."

Kimo slogged past, dragging a huge coil of rope wound over one bent shoulder. He paused to catch his breath and leaned on the rail.

"Believe that," Kimo said. "First time I heard it, I thought the Tallyman had come for me."

"Tallyman?" Felix said. "That's another one of your gods, right? I read something once—"

Both sailors burst out laughing. "He *read* something," Anakoni snorted.

"We tell our stories like Ochali does," Kimo said, "mouth to ear. It's the mainlanders who think they can lock everything up in ink and paper. Here, I'll give you this one for free. When it's your time to die, the Tallyman comes. He always takes the form of whatever you fear most. So when he whispers your name, looming before you, turning your piss to ice and stopping your heart dead, remember this and remember it good: you stand up straight, look him right in the eye, and spit in his face."

Felix blinked. "And if I do, he'll…let me live?"

"Nope," Kimo said, "but when you go to meet your ancestors, they'll all know you've got balls the size of coconuts."

#

With two days left before landfall, Felix had yet to see any sea monsters. There was plenty to look at, though. The *Muse* had swung within sight of land, following the curving coastline from about a mile out.

Misty gray mountains rose up over a snowy forest, the treeline stretching all the way down to the rocky and bramble-choked shore. Ice floes clanked against the galleon's hull, spinning away on black, still waters.

He had seen Mari every day, usually on deck, doing her slow and strange dance with the fighting sticks. Today, though, she was nowhere to be seen. Not until he wandered into the officers' berths and found her sitting cross-legged on the floor.

She cradled a metal emblem in her cupped hands, some kind of rounded pewter brooch, and she sat so still that Felix wasn't sure, at first, if she was still breathing. The berth was empty except for the two of them, and the hustle and bustle of the ship seemed muffled and impossibly far away.

"I'm sorry," he said softly. "I just wanted to get something from my pack. I didn't mean to interrupt."

She looked up. She blinked at him.

"Are you praying?" he asked.

"It's all right," she said. "Was almost finished."

He nodded toward the brooch. "Is that...some kind of Terrai idol?"

For the first time, she quirked a corner of her mouth in the faintest of smiles. She stroked the brooch with her thumb. It looked like a relief image of the moon, encircled with winding and baroque glyphs.

"Is that what they tell you? That we are idol worshipers?"

"I've just heard that your faith is...different," Felix said. "That you worship five hundred goddesses."

Now she did smile, openly and with a faint chuckle.

"No," she said. "We worship the Lady of Five Hundred Names. Same god as you."

He shook his head. "No, no, I'm from Mirenze. Faithful to the Mother Church. I believe in the Gardener."

"And one of the Lady's names," Mari said, "is 'the Gardener.' Same god. Different church."

"Then why not just call him—I mean, call her that?"

"Because sometimes she doesn't feel like gardening."

"Seriously?" Felix asked.

"We are very small," Mari said, "and the divine is very big. Different names, different faces...they help us to understand."

Felix tilted his head, an amused smile on his lips as he studied her.

"What?" she said.

"After a week of traveling," he said, "you have spoken more words, just now, than you have in the entire journey put together."

Mari shrugged. She looked down at the brooch. "I'm not good at talking. So I don't do it much."

"Practice helps. You know, if the pin on that thing is broken, I've probably got the tools to fix it in my pack."

She clutched the brooch tightly. "Not for wearing. This piece has...history. I'm not worthy of wearing it, not yet. I just use it for a beggar's moon."

"What's that?" he asked.

"In my grandmother's day, every family had a shrine in their home with a symbol of the Lady's moon. Some great, some small, some wood, and some gold. The point was to have a place where the family could come together, for her love and guidance to strengthen one and all. Not an idol, you understand? Not a thing to be worshiped, but a symbol to remind us of our obligations to her and to each other."

Felix nodded. "I get it."

"It wasn't enough for the Empire to conquer us. We'd fought too well, shamed their best generals. We had to be humiliated. Every family was made to take their shrine out to the street and smash it to kindling while the Empire's soldiers watched. Only then, you see, could we properly convert to the 'true faith.'"

Felix shook his head. "I...I had no idea. I'm sorry."

"Why? You weren't there."

"Because that's not my faith," he said. "The Gardener I believe in would never want that to happen. It was wrong."

"And that is the difference between a church and a god. How could I be angry at a god for something a church did? Anyway, our faith never died. We couldn't have shrines anymore—too big, too obvious—so we took to carrying tokens with us wherever we travel. Could be anything, so long as it reminds us of the divine. Beggars' moons. 'Moon' for the Lady, and 'beggars' for what your Empire made of us. Bitter little joke. Most Terrai jokes are."

Felix leaned against the bulkhead and crossed his arms.

"I am no fan of the Empire," he said. "We Mirenzei are proud of our heritage, and we haven't forgotten the sting of surrender, but what they did…that's just cruel."

"Life is cruel," Mari said simply. "That's why the Lady gave us weapons, courage, and will. What are you fighting for? Must be something, to bring you into the north."

"It's a business deal—"

"Lie," Mari said.

Felix blinked. She shook her head at him.

"I read people," she said. "I have to, to be good at what I do. I know the kind of man who risks his life for nothing but fistfuls of money. That's not you. Don't lie. Why are you here?"

He didn't answer at first. She watched him, eyes focused and unblinking, until he spoke again.

"I'm engaged."

Her gaze flicked down to his left hand and back up again.

"I thought the Mirenzei wore pledge rings."

"It's a secret. We're going to run off together, start a new life far away from the city. I owe a debt, though. My family business is on the brink of collapse, and if I don't pull this off, my father and my brother's family will lose everything they have."

"Debt?"

"Debt of honor," Felix said. "My family is dead-set against this marriage. They will disown me, they will certainly never speak to me again, but none of that matters. If I abandon them without setting the bank to rights, my father will die in a poorhouse and my brother won't be far behind him. I cannot have that on my conscience. Once I've secured this deal and ensured they've been taken care of, that's when I can leave. Probably sounds idiotic, I know."

Mari shrugged.

"Honor," she said, "is the coin that stays in your pocket when all your silver has been spent. I think you're doing the right thing."

"It's my last chance. If I can't pull this off, the only other option is an arranged marriage with another merchant family. I can't—"

A shadow on the threshold caught his eye. Simon stood there, freezing in mid-step, his gaze flicking between Felix and Mari.

"Sorry," he said, taking a half step back. "Thought the room was empty."

"It's okay," Felix said. "Did you need something?"

"No. No, thank you."

The blond sailor quickly turned and retreated.

"He is a strange one," Felix murmured, watching him go. "Pleasant but strange. Must be hard, getting used to a new ship and crew."

Mari ran her fingertips over the brooch, cradling it in the palm of her hand.

"Felix?" she said. "Would you like to pray with me?"

He looked over at her.

"For strength," she said. "We can pray in her name of the Gardener, if it makes you comfortable."

He slowly nodded. Felix sank down to the floor and crossed his legs, sitting opposite from her.

"I would like that," he said. "I would like that very much."

CHAPTER ELEVEN

Amadeo's eyes burned at the bottom of a salt sea, and his last breath burst from his lungs in a stream of bubbles. He flailed, clawing toward the surface, toward a bobbing ball of light. Something held his ankle fast. He looked down, frantic, to see a rubbery black tentacle curling around his leg. Hundreds of suckers chewed into his flesh, each one a tiny, toothy mouth.

Far below, far beyond where the sun's light could reach, something was coming for him. The water boiled around him, and he thrashed against the tentacle's iron grip as a shape surged out of the darkness. A blob of living shadow, impossibly huge, opening wide to swallow him whole—

Amadeo shot up in bed, sucking down air in a strangled wheeze. Icy sweat soaked through his dressing gown and cotton sheets. He sat stone-still, arms wrapped tightly around his chest, until he caught his breath and dared to move again.

"Stress," he said to the empty bedroom. Even to his own ears it sounded like a lie.

It didn't help that it wasn't his bedroom. The four-poster bed and the wardrobe carved from imported wood, scalloped and polished to a shine, cost more than a year's wages. It had only been a week since he'd moved out of his tiny cottage near the cathedral and into a guest room at the papal mansion, and it didn't feel like home. Still, he needed to be here, close to Benignus. Just another quiet acknowledgment that his friend was living on borrowed time.

His window looked out over the darkened gardens. A sliver of moon hung high in the sky, but Amadeo didn't give his pillow a second glance. Instead, he stripped off his sweat-sodden gown, put on a simple cassock and slippers, and stepped outside.

Even at this hour, he wasn't the only person awake. He gave a friendly nod to a pair of scribes, shuffling past him in the vaulted corridor and clutching heavy books to their chests as if they were smuggling diamonds. The papal guard was reduced but still in force, with one man stationed at every important door to keep a lonely watch over the night.

The dining hall was big enough to feed a small army, lined with communal benches under the light of two great iron chandeliers. The chandeliers hung cold, but the hearth at the end of the hall burned with a small but warming fire.

"Another night owl," Cardinal Accorsi said from his seat by the fire. "Come, join me. I'm starved for intelligent company."

"Cardinal?" Amadeo said, wandering over. "What brings you to the mansion at this hour?"

Marcello Accorsi sighed. His robes of office were wrinkled, and the green stole hung off-kilter on his shoulders. He was cadaverously thin, and liver spots flecked his long hands.

"The College was in congress today. And tonight. And on and on. By the time the inevitable after-meetings were done, I decided I'd just stay here and get a fresh start in the morning instead of going all the way home and back again. Too much on my mind to sleep, I suppose. Do you like hot chocolate?"

He gestured to the silver kettle at his side and a pair of porcelain cups. Amadeo took a seat near him, close to the fire's warm glow.

"That's a good man," Marcello said, pouring him a cup and refreshing his own. The chocolate flowed in a thick, rich cream. "One of the maids was kind enough to fix this for me, but there's more than I can drink, and I hate wasting a perfectly good kettle. So now that you know my tragic story, it's your turn. What is the pope's confessor doing awake, prowling the halls after midnight?"

Amadeo cradled the hot cup in his hands, blowing across the foamy surface of the drink before taking a sip. It still scorched his tongue, but the melted chocolate tasted like spun sugar.

"Bad dreams," he said.

Marcello swirled his cup. "My cousin, he gets those, but worse than most. Night terrors they're called. Where you feel like great stones are pressing your chest, and you can't breathe, can't even move. You know what I'm talking about?"

Amadeo nodded.

"Of course you do," Marcello said. "You know, one night many years ago, when we'd both had a bit too much wine with our supper, the Holy Father confided something in me. He said you have the Sight."

"No, no. The Gardener has granted me skills, but…all natural ones, Cardinal. All mundane."

Marcello raised his eyebrows in mock surprise.

"Oh? The Holy Father told me that when the cathedral in Grenai collapsed, you had dreamed of the earthquake every night for a week before it happened."

Amadeo sipped his chocolate. "*An* earthquake. Not *that* earthquake. It would take a very generous interpreter to make me any kind of a prophet."

"Not the first time it has happened, though," the cardinal said, studying him over the rim of his cup. "Is it? So what did you dream tonight, Confessor?"

Half-remembered images flitted, unbidden and unwanted, through Amadeo's mind. Splintered driftwood, a length of rusty chain drifting down into the abyss, floating and waterlogged corpses. The monster below, waiting, hungry.

"Somewhere there is a ship, coasting along a black and frozen sea," he said, staring into his drink. Then he looked up, meeting Marcello's gaze. "And I woke with the fervent conviction that everyone on that ship is going to die."

The cardinal shifted in his seat. His brow furrowed.

"Do you know anyone at sail right now? Friends? Family?"

Amadeo shook his head.

"Well," Marcello said, "perhaps it is a metaphor. We are, after all, riding this doomed ship into a storm together. It will be a miracle if we survive."

"It's not as bad as all that."

"*Balls* it isn't," the cardinal hissed. He kept his voice low. "You are a learned man, Amadeo. You know as well as I what happens when an empire falls into decadence. Look at the political situation: Emperor Theodosius is a weakling and a buffoon with a fetish for rattling his saber. You have heard his endless talk of crusades and glory, and twenty years of war with Belle Terre wasn't enough to satisfy him. It is only a matter of time before he drags us into battle with the Caliphate."

Amadeo glanced up from his cup. "It's the *Holy* Murgardt Empire, cardinal. The throne looks to us for guidance, not the other way around. There will be no crusade."

"You make my point for me. The Holy Father has spent *decades* keeping that imbecile in check. What happens when Benignus is gone and Carlo takes the papal seat? Do you really think he's capable of keeping the peace? He's not a quarter of the man his father was."

"*Is*," Amadeo said, correcting him gently. "Our pope still lives."

"How much time do you think we have? Months? Weeks? Days? Benignus is a fist of steel in a velvet glove. Carlo…Carlo is a feather pillow soaked in cheap wine. The people are depending on their Mother Church to keep the emperor in check."

Amadeo sat back and lifted his cup. He blew across it slowly, taking his time, savoring a sip.

"Do you ever long for the days," he said softly, "when it wasn't all about politics?"

Marcello narrowed his eyes. "It was *always* about politics. Don't play the fool, Confessor, it doesn't become you. You know that the decisions we make, the policies we press for, the leaders we sway, are part and parcel of our mission as a church. Lives are hanging in the balance. We give voice to the powerless and a shield to the weak."

Amadeo set down his cup.

"Maybe so," he said, "maybe so. These machinations and grand plans are beyond me. I'm just a parish priest with a special job, that's all."

"You're 'just' a priest whom the people love, Amadeo. The College of Cardinals is powerful, but at the end of the night, we can only make laws. You move hearts."

Here it comes, Amadeo thought, clenching and unclenching his fingers against his legs. *The sales pitch.*

"We have been discussing alternatives," Marcello said.

"We?"

"Alternatives to Carlo," the cardinal said, ignoring the question.

"The Holy Father has made his wishes clear."

"The Holy Father won't have to clean up the mess," Marcello said. "Nor will he have to count the corpses if Theodosius the Lesser slips his leash. A strong pope is the only thing that can keep the Empire in line."

"And I suppose you have someone in mind?" Amadeo said.

"Not me, if that's what you're thinking. No, no, I'm at my best behind the curtain. I have come to terms with my own ambitions, and I like standing right where I am."

Amadeo didn't believe that for a heartbeat, but he nodded amiably anyway.

Marcello leaned close, his voice dropping almost to a whisper.

"What I need to know," the cardinal said, "is if we can hope for your support."

"You still haven't told me who 'we' is."

"Concerned and faithful stewards of our Mother Church. Loyal servants who know that the future is far too precarious to be left to chance."

Amadeo stood and stretched, stifling a yawn.

"I, too, am loyal," Amadeo said. "Which means, until he breathes his last, I am loyal to our Pope Benignus. I won't shovel dirt over his grave before he's dead. Cardinal, I respect you, and I respect your concerns, but this is not the time for such talk."

Marcello took a deep breath and nodded, lifting his cup.

"The respect is mutual, Confessor. I know I may not be your idea of a loving child of the Gardener, and my politics may be too hard-edged and coarse for your liking, but understand this: I care for the Church every bit as much as you do. We *can* work together."

"Thank you for the hot chocolate," Amadeo said and took his leave.

Back in his borrowed room, Amadeo shut the door and lit an oil lamp at the bedside. He rummaged through his trunk at the foot of the bed and took out a small, timeworn book. The gold leaf on the cover read *A History of Martyrs*.

Not the most soothing of bedtime reading materials, he supposed, but it was better than going back to sleep. Better than facing that creature in the frozen dark.

CHAPTER TWELVE

Simon Koertig took no pleasure from the act of murder.

That wasn't true, exactly. He took tremendous pleasure from the *art* of murder. Of honing his skills, refining his craft, pursuing his quarry, and staging their perfect and elegant demise. Some murders were quick and brutally simple, others long and drawn-out affairs, but they were all handcrafted and beautiful acts. The relationship between executioner and victim, he believed, was more sacred than the bond between lovers.

That said, Felix was really starting to piss him off.

No, he thought as he knelt on the ship's deck in the blistering cold, scraping down the planks with a chunk of sandstone and feeling the burning ache in his exhausted shoulders. *That's not fair. It's not his fault he's been so bloody hard to kill. Never blame the victim, that's unprofessional.*

The fault belonged to this stinking, cramped, freezing ship and everyone on it. It was hard enough getting close to the man without someone walking in on them, and keeping his cover meant twelve hours a day of back-breaking, bottom-rung scut work. Worse, they were barely a day and a half out from Winter's Reach. He could still kill the Rossini boy inside the city walls, but that meant a whole new level of complication.

Besides, he'd set himself this challenge, and he aimed to succeed. Simon had never assassinated anyone on a boat, and he didn't know when he'd get another chance.

Doing it tonight would be impossible unless he could lure Felix out of the officers' berth. He'd tried taking Felix out while he slept the night before, slipping into the cabin with a dagger up his sleeve. That Terrai woman, sleeping in the next cot over, snapped her eyes open at the first groan of a floorboard under his boot. He'd barely gotten out without her seeing him.

Trying to stave off the relentless, aching monotony of his work, he inventoried his resources. Stiletto. Vial of cyladic plant extract. Garrote. Maybe he could use this weather, arrange an accident—

"*Wake up!*' a voice shouted in his ear, snapping him back to the moment. Captain Iona stood over him, looking down with his hands on his hips.

"Sorry, Captain."

"You call that scraping? Helmsman damn near slipped and broke his neck back there. Put your *back* into it, man!"

Simon bit back his words. He dug his fingernails into the sandstone hard enough to make them ache. The pain helped him to focus as he looked back up at Iona with an obsequious smile.

"My fault, Captain, so sorry. I'll do better."

"See that you do, or there'll be no job waiting for you on the return trip. Not on *my* ship."

As he stormed off, Simon stared daggers at his back.

I'm only getting paid for Rossini, he thought, *but that doesn't mean I can't murder you too. Wish I could murder everyone on this bloody—*

An idea struck him. Blissful, artistic inspiration.

Now his smile was genuine.

CHAPTER THIRTEEN

Lerautia, the Holy City, was built on a hill. At its peak, the White Cathedral perched like a great dove at the edge of a sheer cliff overlooking a dark and winding river as it opened up to the sea. As the streets sloped downward, though, the pristine glow of the city began to fade. The buildings grew more ramshackle, broken-down, huddled together like toothless old men trying to stave off a chill.

Alms District, Amadeo thought with a shake of his head. *Pretty name for a slum.* He went down along the waterfront, draped in a simple brown cotton cassock and carrying a heavy leather-bound book under one arm. It was late afternoon, and the fishing boats were starting to trickle back into port. The fishmongers waited eagerly along the docks, standing behind crudely built carts still offering the remnants of yesterday's catch to anyone too poor to buy fresh.

Amadeo waved a fat black fly away from his face. It buzzed off, joining its brothers at the nearest vendor's cart. The stench of raw fish on the verge of rot hung strong in the moist air, and a sheen of moldy water clung to the cobblestones.

A shrill cheer went up, and a tiny figure hit him from behind, wrapping tight arms around his waist. Amadeo laughed. No matter how well he watched, they always caught him by surprise. One moment he'd be strolling alone in the middle of a quiet lane, and the next he'd be surrounded by the orphans of Salt Alley. Half a dozen grubby upturned faces surrounded him, beaming like he was their own father.

"Didja bring any? Didja bring any?" clamored a boy of maybe eight or nine, clinging to his arm. Amadeo grinned and patted his cassock, looking forgetful.

"Goodness," he said, "I'm not quite sure if I did. This pocket? No, nothing here…maybe this one? No, that's not it. Perhaps…aha!"

They cheered again as he pulled out a fistful of paper-wrapped toffees, and he doled them out to a forest of eager hands. Pilfering candy from the papal kitchens, Amadeo reasoned, was a minor sin when it yielded smiles like those. Besides, he'd been doing it for years, and the cook was kind enough to pretend she didn't notice.

"Here now!" snapped the oldest child, a freckled fourteen-year-old in ratty clothes made of more patches than original fabric. "Ease off, give the man some room. You'll strangle him, like as not!"

Freda had taken on the unofficial job of riding herd over the neighborhood urchins, doing her best to keep them from wandering too far astray. The tired lines under her eyes were too deep, too worn, for a girl's face.

The children backed off immediately, clutching their little treasures. Amadeo patted his book and smiled.

"Well, let's see here," he said, "*now* I suppose you'll be wanting a story as well, hmm?"

He led the way to a nearby stoop where he could sit down, ignoring the cold dampness soaking through his cassock while the children clustered around him. He ruffled through the pages of the book, looking for the spot where he'd left off reading last week. On a whim, though, he jumped a few chapters ahead. Every once in a great while he'd get these little insights, nudges pushing him toward the lesson or advice his congregants most needed to hear, and this felt like one of those moments.

#

"…so was the apprentice a bad man?" asked one of the youngest children, lisping through a gap in her teeth.

Amadeo had read for about half an hour in his slow, strong cadence, flourishing the lines like a storyteller and doing his best to hold his ragged little audience's attention.

"Not at all," he said, closing the book and resting it on his lap, "and that is the most important lesson in the 'Parable of the Lazy Apprentice.' He was very good at his job, but he only did exactly what his master told him to, no more and no less. When problems started to pile up, well, he *could* have fixed them himself, but he just kept following his instructions and turned a blind eye. That let the trouble get worse and worse—"

"Until it was too late," Freda said. She leaned against a nearby wall, arms crossed and one rough shoe pressed back against the brick, keeping a hard eye on the other children.

Amadeo nodded. "The Gardener gave each of us the power to change the world. Maybe just in small ways, but when trouble comes to your neighbors' doorsteps, there's always *something* you can do about it. What might be a tiny thing to you can be a powerful blessing to the person you help. It's not enough to coast through life and think you're being good just because you're following the rules; that was the apprentice's mistake. The Gardener needs all of you to be his hands in the world. To root out weeds and plant new seeds. That takes creativity, and courage, and hard work. And I *know* you can do it."

That was when he realized why he'd picked that story today.

Preacher, heed your own words, he thought.

"Children, I need to be going. I have some work to attend to. Don't worry, I'll be back next week, and I *might* have some more toffees."

He extracted himself from the tangle of hugs as best he could. Freda followed him a short distance away and tugged his sleeve.

"You okay?" she said. "You got a funny look on your face."

He chuckled. "Probably shame. I realized I haven't been following my own advice. Everything all right out here?"

"As all right as it gets. Listen, though. The cold months are coming, and the way things were last year…" Her voice trailed off as she looked back toward the children. "I don't want to bury any more toddlers. Ground's too hard for digging in the cold."

"I know. I know, and I'm sorry. I've been trying to push for the funds for a relief effort, so everyone would at least have a fire to warm up by and one hot meal in their bellies, but the College keeps saying you should all be in the foundling home—"

"They are *not* going to any damn foundling home," Freda snapped, her eyes fierce. "Not *that* damn foundling home. You *know* why."

"I do," he said, holding up an open hand but keeping his distance. He didn't try to touch her, not when she had that look on her face. "It's all bureaucracy. One nest of red tape after another."

"What about the Holy Father? Why won't he help us?"

Amadeo shook his head, feeling helpless. "It's complicated. The pope can only sign off on certain kinds of expenditures, and the cardinals on everything else. It was a compromise to keep any one side…you know, I'm not going to bore you with a history lesson. You're not getting the help you need down here, and I know it. I'm sorry. I'll take another run at my contacts in the College and see where things stand."

He dug into his pocket and came up with a handful of copper coins.

"Here," he said, "in the meantime—"

Freda shook her head. "I earn my own money, don't need your charity. It's the little ones I'm worried about."

And I'm worried about how you're earning your money, he thought. There were only so many job opportunities for a fourteen-year-old girl in the slums.

"And you watch over them," he said. "So please. Take this. Spend it wisely, for them."

She stared at the coins in his hand, calculating, then nodded. She snatched the money up.

"I'll take care of it," she said.

Walking back up the long, shadowy streets in the wake of the setting sun, Amadeo had time alone with his thoughts. Much as he wanted to believe otherwise, Benignus's days were numbered. Once he passed, it would either be Carlo on the throne or someone handpicked by the College of Cardinals.

Bene was a good man, but Amadeo could see the selfishness in his final wish: he wanted to think the best of Carlo, to imagine the reckless and callow youth growing into a seasoned and wise pope. Amadeo wasn't sure if that was even possible, despite his oath to try to make it so. On the other side, the College was just as self-interested. They—or specifically, Cardinal Accorsi and his band of conspirators—would pick a candidate who danced to their tune, someone who wouldn't threaten their control of the Church's purse strings or upset the status quo.

Nobody, in all this mess, was trying to figure out which candidate would be the best for the *people*. Livia was right. The Church was broken.

And I've been the lazy apprentice, Amadeo thought, *sailing along blithely and letting other people decide our fate. Enough of that. It's time to roll up my sleeves and do what I can to help before it's too late.*

The first step, he reasoned, was to have a long talk with Carlo. Amadeo needed to know if he could really afford to uphold his vow to Benignus. The matter of the smuggler's ledger still weighed on his mind.

A four-horse coach stood in the pebbled horseshoe drive outside the papal manse. The livery of the Banco Marchetti emblazoned its polished doors, and twists of gold leaf adorned the black-stained wood. A bored-looking drover sat up on his perch, huddled under a heavy cloak. Amadeo frowned. Representatives from the bank came from Mirenze to visit the court on a regular basis—they held the contract to work the papal alum mines, after all—but this was after business hours, and he hadn't seen a meeting scheduled in Benignus's appointment ledger.

"The Holy Father?" said one of the maids, pulled aside by Amadeo in the gilded foyer. "No, he's sleeping. No visitors, not since three bells."

"But there is a coach outside. Someone from the Banco Marchetti is definitely here."

The maid nodded and pointed up the hall. "Oh, that was for Carlo. They've been in the conference room all afternoon."

His feet moved faster as he paced up the hall, brow furrowed. Why was Carlo meeting with the Marchettis? He didn't have any authority to do business on the Church's behalf. Amadeo almost knocked, coming up on the closed and ivory-inlaid door. Then he caught himself.

Looking in all directions, biting down on his sudden sense of guilt, he crept close and knelt down to press his ear against the keyhole.

"…how we're going to *sell* you," said a gruff voice on the other side. It sounded familiar to Amadeo, but he couldn't quite place it.

"…care what they…" answered Carlo's muffled voice, softer and farther away from the door.

"Because they can still mount a succession challenge. Don't get overconfident, Carlo. Now is the time for you to be on your best behavior. Especially after that idiot Stathis went and got himself killed. Just get your father on board, and I'll do the rest."

Amadeo couldn't make out Carlo's next question. He leaned closer to the door, pressing himself against the wood. The other man's answer came in a lower, harder tone, and it sent a chill down Amadeo's spine.

"…because that much blood won't wash clean."

Chairs scraped back against marbled floors. Amadeo jumped up, padding backward as fast as he could, and looked around to make sure nobody had seen him eavesdropping. He took a deep breath, held it for a moment, and walked forward as the conference room door swung open. He hoped he'd look as if he'd just been strolling along the hallway.

Carlo and Lodovico Marchetti emerged from the conference room in a haze of cigar smoke. Lodovico had his arm around Carlo's shoulder, hugging him like a brother.

"Amadeo!" Carlo said, stopping in his tracks. "You know Vico, right?"

"We've met a couple of times in your father's court," Amadeo said, realizing where he'd heard that voice before. Lodovico gave him a lazy smile, reached out, and pumped his hand in a vice grip.

"C'mon," Carlo told his guest. "I'll see you out."

Carlo walked Lodovico toward the door, leaving the priest behind. Once they were out of sight, Amadeo poked his head into the conference room. The long, rounded table bore overflowing ivory ashtrays and a nearly empty crystal decanter of whiskey but no papers or contracts, nothing to shed light on what they'd been talking about.

Fine, he thought, *I'll go straight to the source.* When Carlo came back inside from sending his visitor off, he found Amadeo waiting for him in the foyer.

"So what was that about?" Amadeo asked, trying to keep his tone lightly curious.

Carlo shrugged anxiously. He twisted his bottom lip like a child who'd been caught with his hand in the cookie jar. "Nothing. Business."

"Carlo, you aren't in your father's seat yet. You don't have the authority to do business on the Church's behalf."

"No, no, not like that. Personal. I needed a loan. Since we already work with the Banco Marchetti, I figured they'd be the people to talk to."

Amadeo tilted his head. "Didn't you already take out a line of credit, just last year?"

"I needed more," Carlo said.

Amadeo recognized the rising whine at the edge of the younger man's voice. He was digging in, going on the defensive. Amadeo fought the urge to sigh and forced a smile instead.

"Well, just be careful. I'm sure they are happy to offer you all the credit you can use, but there's always a heavy bill in the end."

"I've got it under control," Carlo said.

Whatever they'd been talking about, it wasn't another handout for the up-and-coming heir apparent. Lodovico Marchetti's last words echoed in Amadeo's ears as he walked the halls of the papal mansion alone.

...because that much blood won't wash clean.

He made his way toward the apartments in the east wing. As he approached Livia's door, he paused. He heard something strange, a sort of slow, rhythmic thumping echoed by faint and strangled gasps. He knocked, loudly.

The sounds ceased.

A minute later, the doorknob rattled and turned. Livia stood on the threshold of her parlor, backlit in the glow of a hearth fire. She wore a modest white dressing gown with long draping sleeves, as if getting ready for bed, but her hair was still pinned up and coiffed.

"Sorry to disturb you," he said, "but did you know anything about your brother meeting with Lodovico Marchetti?"

Her already-dour expression dropped a few notches. "I expect he needs more money. You're surprised?"

"Well, that's what he said, and it might be so, but..."

He trailed off. *But what?* he thought. She stared at him expectantly, but he realized he didn't have a theory to hang his suspicions on. He felt ridiculous. His gaze drifted. Over on a chair by the fire, something caught his eye. It was a scourge of braided leather with four or five wickedly knotted strands dangling from the whip's handle. The sounds he'd overheard suddenly made sense.

"Mortification of the flesh?" he said. She followed his gaze to the discarded whip but said nothing.

"Livia," Amadeo said, drawing her eyes back to his. "I know it's a Church-sanctioned practice, for a monk at least, but...have a care. Sometimes I worry that you might be demanding too much of yourself."

"We must all do what we can," she said. "Don't you know the 'Parable of the Lazy Apprentice'? You should read it again, if you haven't lately."

An icy finger trailed down the back of Amadeo's neck. It felt like someone was trying to throw that story in his path today. To make sure he was paying attention.

"Oddly enough, I was just sharing it with some of the children down in the Alms District. I think they got something out of it."

"Children are the best listeners," Livia said. "Now, if there's nothing else, I should get back to my studies. I'm working on a special project, and I don't want to lose my focus."

Amadeo nodded. "Of course. Goodnight, Livia."

She shut the door without another word. He heard locks clicking into place, one after another.

Something was wrong here. Whatever Carlo and Lodovico were cooking up together, it wasn't anything good.

"And nobody is going to figure it out and *do* something about it. Nobody but me," he sighed, talking to himself in the empty hall. "Apprentice, get to work."

CHAPTER FOURTEEN

Livia leaned her shoulder against the door, shut her eyes, and let out a pent-up breath. She waited until she heard Amadeo's retreating footsteps before she dared to move again.

She walked across the room, shedding her slippers and feeling the cool floorboards against her bare feet. A chill hung in the air that her modest fire couldn't chase away. On the other side of the bedroom door, lying on the quilt of her four-poster bed, the hateful *thing* waited for her. It was just a book, a slim little folio with black leather covers and cheap parchment pages, but it sang to her like a siren.

Her gaze flicked toward the fireplace. Ten steps. Five to snatch it up, five to throw the book into the flames. That was all it would take. Ten steps and her problems would be over.

And if you could do that, she thought as her stomach churned, *you would have done it two weeks ago when you brought the book home.*

She unfastened the neck of her dressing gown and let it fall to the floor, pooling around her ankles. Naked, her back reddened with throbbing welts, she picked up the scourge and knelt before the fireplace. The crackling flames filled her bright emerald eyes.

"Gardener," she said, "in your infinite wisdom, you forbade us from the artifices of the deceitful and the damned, the poisoner and the witch, that we might not lead ourselves down the road to the Barren Fields. You know that I am your faithful daughter. You know that I will do what I must to save this church, even at the cost of my mortal soul."

She paused, feeling the whip handle in her palm, its leather warmed by the fire's glow.

"Please," she whispered. "Please don't make the price that high."

She swung her arm back with a sudden ferocity, and the braided strands of the scourge slashed across her shoulder blade. She gritted her teeth, eyes squeezing shut against sudden tears.

Purity, she thought.

The second blow, over her opposite shoulder, lashed across a rising welt. It burned like a hot razor slicing into her skin.

Faithfulness, she thought.

The third blow broke the skin, leaving a hair-thin line of blood trickling down the curve of her hip.

Love.

The knotted tails of the whip came down again and again, a staccato rhythm of pain drowning out the world, drowning out everything but the repetition of her mantra, three simple words. *Purity. Faithfulness. Love.*

When it was finally done, there was nothing left of her. Nothing but tear-stained cheeks, a whip-scarred back, and a peaceful emptiness in her heart. The handle of the scourge tumbled from her trembling fingers. She stood slowly, wobbling on exhausted legs, and left tiny blood spatters on the wood behind her as she hobbled into the bedroom. The book was waiting.

One year ago, the villagers of Kettle Sands cried out that they were plagued by a witch. Nothing but mass hysteria, usually, but a pair of bounty hunters had tracked down a likely culprit: a young girl who was immediately put on trial and burned at the stake. It was only later, searching the hovel she'd been squatting in, that a scavenger found the hidden book.

The book ended up in the Black Archives in the vaults of Lerautia's great library, left to rot in the darkness. And that was where Livia had found it. She couldn't say why she'd slipped the book under her skirts and stolen it from the vault, only that she needed it.

It called to her.

"*My book of Secretts (by Squirrel),*" the first page read, with a clumsy blot of ink to fix the misspelling. Whatever the girl's talents as a witch had been, she was barely literate.

Livia turned the pages slowly, feeling lost in a dream. The throbbing pain from her welts pushed away her conscious mind and washed her in lightheaded tranquility. Her fingers found the page she'd left off on.

"*...we lured the cat from the yard with some bits of tuna, and Miss Owl gave me the knife. She showed me how to squeeze it and cut its throte just right, so that she could catch its last yowl in a jar of blue glass. Miss Owl says there's much mischief we can make with a cat's last yowl! But tonight we needed its bloode so I caught it in a bowl and coverd it with lamskin.*

"*Then Miss Owl taut me the Marque of Passage. Draw it above the door in bloode no colder than two hours gone, and those what are asleep inside the house will stay asleep unless frightfully roused. It is this way, she says, that we can come and go as we please after dark and no-one will wake to learn our business. This Marque looks like this:*"

A ritual circle took up half the page, lined with swirling glyphs that made Livia's eyes hurt. It was something primitive, something wild and cruel that evoked images of fires in a nighttime forest glade. Livia traced her fingertip over the circle's lines, following them like a wandering explorer lost in a labyrinth, memorizing their twists and turns.

And she was only a fledgling, Livia thought. *With this kind of power, imagine what I could do*—and then she slammed the book shut, her tranquility broken.

"Tomorrow," she told the book and went off to find a bath. She needed to sluice the dried blood from her back.

CHAPTER FIFTEEN

Felix wasn't cut out for a sailor's life, but he had to admit he'd weathered this voyage pretty well for a land lover. He stood up at the helm of the *Fairwind Muse* while Captain Iona held the ship's great wooden wheel. An icy wind ruffled their hair and billowed the canvas sails.

"Here's the tricky part," Iona said, pointing off toward the coastline. "The Jailer's Teeth. Jagged rocks reaching up from the ocean floor like knives, just waiting to rip an unwary ship from stem to stern."

Felix cupped his hand over his brow and squinted. Here and there, off to starboard, he watched the ice floes bob against tiny dark nubs in the water.

"Most of the rocks are just below the waterline," Iona explained. "No good trying to navigate between them. We'll skirt alongside the whole mess, close but not too close. We'll follow around until we make port tomorrow morning. Until then, I might as well be lashed to this wheel. Too dangerous to trust anyone else with the job."

Felix was silent for a moment, but his curiosity finally overwhelmed his fear of sounding foolish.

"I was talking to some of the crew," he said. "They told me a story about this, ah, sea monster—"

Iona laughed. "The Elder? Oh, he's real enough, but I wouldn't worry. He won't vex us as long as we send out an offering. Besides, if that old bastard hasn't shown up by now, he won't. We're just past his usual hunting ground. Of course, there's always the return trip! So what do you think? Ready to abandon the banker's life and join an honest crew?"

"Oh, I think I'll leave that to hardier souls than mine. I know where my talents lie."

"No shame in that," Iona said. "The sea's a fine lover, but she'll take everything you've got. Speaking of lovers, saw you feeding that pale sewer rat."

"Sewer rat?" Felix raised an eyebrow.

"The Terrai girl. You're not getting sweet on her, are you?"

"I'm sweet on my fiancé back home," Felix said, "and faithful. Mari's just…she's an interesting person. And it's always good to make a new friend."

Iona snorted. "Just as well. She looks like the type who goes for other women, anyway."

"You are a prince among gentlemen, oh captain, my captain," Felix deadpanned with a bow and a flourish. "Huh, look at that. Werner is back on deck. He's giving it another try."

Iona shook his head and smiled. "I'll say this much about him: never seen a man so stricken with seasickness, but I've never seen a man fight it that hard either. Stomach of jelly, will of iron."

"He'll probably put that on his tombstone. I'm going to go check on him. Galley should be open soon. Since you're stuck at the helm, can I bring you back some food?"

"And see," Iona said, "when we took you on board, I was afraid you wouldn't be useful."

Felix wandered down-deck, keeping his feet light on the snow-flecked beams, and gave Werner a wave.

"I see you've returned to walk among the living!"

Werner chuckled, but his face was pale gray. "For now. Another few months of open water and I might actually get my sea legs."

"Bad news: we're making landfall tomorrow. I'm sure you're crushed."

"Devastated," Werner said.

They walked together, strolling along the side of the ship, watching the snowy wilderness glide by.

"I was talking to Mari—"

"Talking?" Werner said. "She actually *talked* to you? Like, more than please and thank you? That's...that's a good sign."

Felix glanced over his shoulder. Mari was up toward the bow, practicing with her batons, well out of earshot. He leaned a little closer.

"What's her story, anyway?"

Werner didn't answer at first. His hand slid across the ship's railing, fingers tensing.

"Found her in Winter's Reach. When you talk to her, what words come to mind? If you had to describe her in a nutshell."

Felix shrugged. "Controlled. Devout. Taciturn, maybe. The girl's practically a monk."

Werner looked up at the gently falling snow and took a deep breath as tiny flakes turned to water on his cheeks.

"Met her in a tavern. Some drunken sot grabbed her rump as she walked by. She spun and threw a punch—"

"Not unreasonable," Felix said.

"—then she smashed a bottle over his head, knocked him to the floor, and stomped on his skull until it cracked like an eggshell."

Felix stopped walking.

"Mari's father was an aristocrat in Belle Terre," Werner said. "He was supplying the resistance, or they said he was, anyway. When Mari was six years old, Imperial soldiers dragged the entire family out onto the lawn. They beat her father to death in front of her. Broke every bone in his body with an iron bar, making sure to keep him alive and screaming until they felt like letting him die. Then it was her mother's turn, and what they did to her...her father was the lucky one. That girl has *seen* things, Felix."

Felix stared at him. He looked back up toward the bow, watching Mari move in slow motion. A picture of restrained serenity.

"The years after that weren't any kinder to her. When I met her in the Reach, she was feral. Rabid. What you see now, Felix, isn't what I saw then. She was this...this bottomless pit of rage and hate."

Felix's voice was soft. "What did you do, Werner?"

"I...civilized her. Like rehabilitating a fighting dog. Slowly, carefully, I won her trust. Then I set about teaching her a new way to live. Taught her to honor her religion, her heritage, just...in a safer way. Did you see that brooch she carries around?"

"Her beggar's moon, sure," Felix said. "What of it?"

"It belonged to a Terrai knight. See, the *one* thing Mari remembers of her father, besides watching him die, was when he'd read to her from this big book of fairy tales. Stories about valiant knights and chivalry. Honor and justice. She jumbles these things together in her brain. It's the only happy memory she has, from a time when life made sense. When it was fair."

"Werner." Felix stared at him. "What did you *do*?"

"I plucked that brooch off a dead knight's corpse," Werner said, "after I ran three feet of steel through his gut. Course, she doesn't know that. Mari's gotten it in her head that the 'holy order' it belonged to is still out there, somewhere, and if she lives up to their ideals, they'll find her someday and make her a real knight."

"Gardener's rain. She doesn't know, does she? She doesn't know you fought in the war."

Werner loomed over Felix, suddenly furious.

"No," he hissed, "and you'll not say a damn word about it! Far as she knows, I went straight from your family's employ to hunting bounties for a living, and it needs to stay that way for *both* our sakes. It'd destroy her if she knew."

"Why are you doing this, Werner?"

Werner turned his back on Felix. He leaned against the railing with both hands, looking out toward the distant mountains.

"You can't understand what it was like out there. The Terrai weren't some oppressed, noble people being picked on by the big, bad Empire—"

"Murgardt *did* invade them."

"Yeah. Empires do that. Your people at least had the good sense to save themselves. The Terrai poisoned their own wells and salted their own fields just to spite us, and that was only the start of it. I remember my first time out as an officer, greener than green, leading my men up a merchant road. Ragmen, far as the eye could see. You know what a ragman is?"

Felix shook his head, mute.

"They'd take a prisoner of war and skin him alive. Then they'd drape the skin back on the body and impale him on a pole. Ragman. If you got taken captive by the Terrai, that was the *best* thing that could happen to you. Every man in my squad carried a mercy knife, so they could slit their own throats if we got overrun."

"I don't see what this—" Felix started to say.

"The Terrai were slavers. During the Plague Summer, they deliberately infected their slaves with the Blistering Fever and set them loose, aiming them right toward our forces. Eventually my squad had a crossbowman whose only job was to shoot down any refugees in sight before they reached us, because we couldn't tell the difference between the genuine escapees and the infected ones. Even escaped prisoners of war. Even our own men."

Werner turned back toward Felix. His face was chiseled from stone, and his eyes seemed focused on something a thousand miles away.

"We didn't call them the Terrai," he said. "We called them the Wolves in the West, because that's what they were to us. Feral animals. That made it easier, see. Easier to fight savagery with savagery. Easier to justify grinding an entire nation to dust under our boots, because 'they had it coming.' By the end of the war, we were just *like* them."

"And Mari?"

Werner leaned against the railing and sighed.

"I saw her in that tavern and said to myself, '*This* is my legacy.' This feral, fucked-up, broken girl. What happened to her was done under *my* flag. In *my* motherland's name. That's on me. So I decided to fix her."

"Fix her," Felix echoed.

"There's an herb, a root that grows in the desert. The Caliphate feeds it to their elite soldiers. Makes their minds…pliable, to help with their training."

"You drugged her? You drugged her and you brainwashed her."

"I *civilized* her, like I said. For her own good." Werner shrugged. "So maybe what she believes ain't exactly real history. So maybe she thinks if she lives up to some made-up creed, the heroes from her father's fairy tales will show up and make her a real knight. Who's it hurting?"

"*Her.* It's a lie, Werner. This isn't…this isn't *right.* And you're not the man you used to be, if you think it is."

Werner shot another furtive glance toward the bow, making certain she couldn't hear them. He leaned in close, murmuring in Felix's ear.

"None of us, *none* of us who fought our way out of that nightmare came back the way we used to be. As for Mari, I gave her something to believe in and ideals to live for. More important, I taught her to take all that anger and hide it away, to shove it deep down inside and never, *ever* let it out."

Felix watched as Mari took a step forward. Her boot slid on the damp deck, breaking her concentration and throwing off her rhythm. Her placid expression suddenly turned to utter fury, and she whipped her arms down, sheathing her batons and squeezing her hands into fists. She closed her eyes and took a long, ragged breath, steadying herself, mouthing the words of a prayer until the serenity returned.

"Best hope she keeps believing," Werner said softly. "Because the rage bottled up in that girl's heart could burn the whole world down."

CHAPTER SIXTEEN

"There was a time," Basilio Grimaldi said as he trudged down a cramped stone tunnel, "when we didn't have to hide like rats just to meet."

His hair, gray and receding, was slicked back in a widow's peak. A heavy mantle hung across his shoulders, joined with a hammered brass clasp at his shoulder. At his side, Terenzio Ruggeri grunted in agreement. Basilio tried not to wrinkle his nose. The tannery master bathed in cheap perfume, cloyingly sweet, but it didn't conceal the stink of dung that clung to him like a sheen of sweat.

Beyond a pair of oaken doors, casks as tall as a man filled warehouse racks from floor to vaulted ceiling. A stained ramp rose up to a pair of wooden vats for pressing fresh olive oil. At the heart of the room stood an oval table with nine high-backed chairs. The rest of the guests were already there.

In the old days, under an ice-blue flag, the Council of Nine had been the unofficial rulers of Mirenze. Each man on the Council was hand-picked from the city's elite families, captains of industry and finance. They charted the city's rise and measured its steps to greatness.

Now the city's colors were black and gold, and the Council had to meet in a dusty warehouse, far from the eyes of Imperial watchdogs who believed they'd been disbanded long ago.

This is still our city, Basilio thought, exchanging handshakes and gruff nods as he took his seat at the table. *My city.*

"Let's get started," Costantini said. The old man was stringy and lean, like a twist of overcooked beef. "First things first, a bit of unpleasant rumor. Dante Uccello has poked his head out of his hole. Allegedly, he's up in Winter's Reach."

Did Terenzio's hands tense on the table? Basilio silently noted the man's reaction.

"Not our problem," Terenzio said quickly. *Too quickly*, Basilio thought. *Interesting*.

"The treason charges stand," said another of the Nine.

"Charges," Costantini said, "we only levied as a make-peace for the Marchetti family."

"Exactly," grunted the man across the table from Basilio. "There's no profit in going after Uccello. If the Marchettis want their revenge so badly, let them hire their own bounty hunters."

Basilio watched as the table easily came to agreement. He couldn't resist tweaking the situation a bit, just to see how Terenzio would react.

"We have to remember," Basilio offered, "that while the Marchetti family is not a part of our…austere gathering, not anymore, they still wield considerable influence in this city. If we don't make at least a token attempt at capturing Signore Uccello, we could earn their ire."

"Uccello is—" Terenzio started to say, then paused. The tannery master took a halting breath and tried again. "*If* Uccello is in the Reach and out of hiding, he's almost certainly found himself a position in the government there. Sending bounty hunters operating under Mirenzei sanction would be a dangerous provocation. That's reason enough not to get involved."

Basilio smiled thinly as the table quickly swung back into accord and the issue was set aside. He nodded toward the one empty chair.

"We should discuss our vacancy. Signore Leone was a fine man and representative, but his spirit—Gardener grant him rest—cannot vote. It is high time that our humble council was back to its full strength."

Terenzio raised his hand. "Before we do, I have one new matter to raise. An opportunity. Half of you gentlemen, like myself, own businesses that require a steady supply of alum in the manufacturing process."

"And we pay out the damn nose to the Banco Marchetti for the privilege," one of the Nine grumbled.

Terenzio's eyes went sharp. "How would you like to break their backs?"

That got everyone's attention.

"We all know that the Banco Marchetti has a stranglehold on the alum market, thanks to their friends in the Church," the tannery master said, "but the papal mines aren't the only source. Look east. The Oerran Caliphate is rich with alum, and they're eager for Mirenzei silver. I'm launching a new trading company—"

"Hold on," Costantini said, scowling. "You're forgetting something, or conveniently leaving it out. The easterners are heathens, which I personally couldn't give two squirts of rat shit about, but it's a poison pill. The instant the Banco Marchetti feels like they're losing market share, Lodovico will pull the same trick his old man did decades ago. He'll put pressure on the Church, and the next thing you know, we'll be hearing sermons from every pulpit about the 'sins of buying pagan alum' as opposed to the good and faithful kind that says its prayers every night. I don't care how good a deal the Caliphate can offer us. I'm not fighting the pope."

A murmur of agreement spread across the table, but Terenzio shut it down with a wave of his hand.

"What if I could guarantee that you won't have to?" he said.

Costantini slouched back in his chair. "Explain."

"I have some pieces in play. More than that I can't share, but I'll do better than promise a return. I'll back your stakes. I will cover, personally, out of my family coffers, every last scudo you invest in this project plus a guaranteed five percent return. If anything goes wrong, if the expedition fails for any reason at all, you get your money back plus five percent just for your good faith and friendship. Now what do you say to that?"

What they say, Basilio thought wryly as a commotion erupted all around the table, *is 'Take my money, please.'* A sure thing was hard to come by, and the families of the Council were old and honored, but that didn't always mean wealthy.

He should know. He was blackmailing three of them.

#

The Grimaldi family crest adorned sandstone gateposts in hammered brass. The crest depicted a dragon rampant, the scaled beast clutching the world in its claw. Basilio gave it a passing glance and a contented smile as his coach rattled through the open iron gate and up the pebbled drive to his countryside villa.

The sweet strains of a violin echoed through the cold halls. Basilio followed the sound, making his way past stone-faced servants in black livery who stood still as statues. The music grew louder as he approached the door to the banquet hall, where the tan marble floor was polished to a mirror sheen.

Aita Grimaldi danced as she played her violin, cradling the delicate instrument in the crook of her arm while she spun across the floor in lazy circles. Her eyes were closed, and a wave of platinum blond hair shone in the light from the chandelier. Basilio leaned against the doorway and crossed his arms, watching. *She looks like an angel*, he thought. *A dreaming angel.*

She played one last, lilting chord, a strain that echoed with loneliness and regret, and ended her song. Basilio uncrossed his arms and clapped his hands slowly. The echoes of his applause rippled across the room. Aita's eyes snapped open and her brow furrowed.

"A beautiful piece, my dear."

"I didn't play it for *you*," Aita said.

Basilio sighed. "You're still angry."

"You say that as if there's some reason I wouldn't be. As if there's some reason I *ever* wouldn't be."

"You're twenty-five, Aita. Your mother and I were married at sixteen. People are starting to talk—"

"Then let them," Aita said.

"A woman your age should already be married and with children, and Felix Rossini is a perfectly fine match. I've met the man. He's got a good head on his shoulders, and his family's banking connections will help our business grow."

"Oh? The business I'm not allowed to have any part of? That business?"

Basilio spread his hands. "Aita, that is not your place. You are a fine, healthy young woman. You should be raising a family, not fooling with wool merchants and accounting ledgers."

She pointed the tip of her violin bow at him.

"'Wool.' Please. I know what we really do for a living, Father. And you know I know it. So let's not pretend."

"Then you know why it's no place for a woman." His eyes darkened. "My word is final, Aita. You will marry Felix Rossini, you will cement this alliance, and you will learn to be happy about it. All your life I have given you everything, everything you could possibly want. You *will* give me this."

She replied by cradling her violin, turning her back to him, and playing a new song. A faster piece, almost discordant. Basilio stood in the doorway and listened for a while, waiting to see if she'd turn around. She didn't.

Hassan the Barber waited for him in the hallway. Frowning, Basilio waved a hand, beckoning him along. He had a sudden distaste for his daughter's music.

Hassan was tall, falcon-eyed, and dark as chiseled basalt, an exile from the Oerran Caliphate. He'd been a raider once, boss of a bandit gang, until he'd tried to plunder one of the Grimaldi family's caravans. Basilio made him a better offer. The Mirenzei knew raw talent when he saw it.

"Bad time for bad news?" Hassan's voice was a basso rumble.

"How long have we worked together? The faster I know about a problem, the faster I can solve it. I want sugarcoatings on my biscotti, not on my information."

"The Rossini boy is gone."

"Gone? Gone where? Gone fishing?"

"Gone north," Hassan said. "He boarded a merchant ship bound for Winter's Reach. We're not certain why."

"With or without that peasant girl he's been rutting with?"

"Without. She's still in Mirenze."

Basilio waved a dismissive hand as they walked.

"He'll be back, then," he said. "Just the same, keep an eye on the girl. What was her name?"

"Renata Nicchi."

"Renata," Basilio echoed, his lips curling like he'd bitten into a rotten apple. "Gutter trash. He actually thinks he's going to run away with her. Isn't that precious?"

"I can solve that problem with one little cut."

Basilio shook his head. "No. I want the girl alive for now. Alive and under my thumb, she's leverage. Dead, she's nothing. Felix is as headstrong and rebellious as my daughter, but there is one crucial difference. I have ways to *hurt* Felix. He'll do as he's told, once I've explained the facts of life to him."

"There is something else," Hassan said. "Confirmation. The Rossinis' butler is a spy for Lodovico Marchetti. We've seen him coming and going from the estate."

"Vico. There's one we should have sliced out of the picture years ago. I told the Council, you never kill a man and leave his son alive. A boy with a tombstone for a father grows up wanting one thing and one thing only: blood for blood. I should know."

"As far as we know, he believes his father's death was a suicide."

"And if he ever learns the truth," Basilio said, "Lodovico Marchetti is going to be a serious problem. Let's make sure that doesn't happen."

CHAPTER SEVENTEEN

Down in the galley of the *Fairwind Muse*, the cook stood lethargically over a boiling pot, ladling out the last of the ship's stores to a line of hungry sailors. Felix waited along with them, getting a raised eyebrow when he asked for three servings.

"Not for *me*," Felix said.

Once he explained where the food was going, the cook sent him on his way with three hunks of boiled beef and three stale fistfuls of hardtack precariously piled on a dented plate. His first stop was back at the helm, where Iona took a serving off his hands.

Felix bit into a chunk of beef, chewing thoughtfully as he went looking for Mari. She wasn't hard to find, still out on the deck and practicing her fighting forms even as stray snowflakes left wet spatters on her face and patchwork armor. Her only concession to the cold was a heavy woolen cloak with a ragged hem, like something she'd fished from a noblewoman's trash.

"Bad news," Felix said. "This is the last shipboard food we'll get until the return trip. Just think: you're actually going to have to eat real, hot meals in a genuine inn. Can you endure it?"

"The horror," Mari deadpanned, sheathing her batons. She took a chunk of beef from Felix's platter and lifted it to her mouth. She was about to take a bite when a strangled sound turned her head.

A sailor staggered up the gangway from belowdecks, blue-faced and choking. He took three steps and collapsed onto the deck, twitching, white foam leaking from his puffy lips and nose. Mari's gaze darted to Felix, her eyes hard as stone.

"Did you eat *any* of that?" she snapped. "The food! Did you eat it?"

"Two bites, but what—"

She lunged at him and knocked the platter from his hands. It clanged to the deck, hardtack scattering, as she grabbed Felix by the scruff of the neck and dragged him to the side of the ship. He was still trying to protest when she bent him over the railing and rammed two of her fingers down his throat. His guts lurched and he vomited, spewing what little he'd eaten down into the black waters. She held him there, her grip merciless and hard as iron, until nothing was left in his stomach but a trickle of bile.

He wheezed for breath when she finally pulled her fingers out, and she turned to flick the slimy filth from her hand.

Felix looked up toward the helm and shouted, just in time to see Captain Iona slump against the ship's wheel. The weight of his corpse spun the wheel hard to starboard and held it there, his arm tangled. The *Fairwind Muse* groaned and keeled hard, sailing straight for the coastline.

"Someone poisoned the ship's mess," Felix gasped, his throat burning. "What kind of crazy bastard would—"

"Survive now, talk later." Mari dropped into a crouch and looked in all directions, as if expecting an attack.

Felix felt icy hands squeezing his heart as a sailor, tossed by the sudden keel and losing his grip, tumbled from the rigging twenty feet above. The man landed hard and cracked his skull open on the icy deck, twitching and releasing his last rattling breath mere feet from where they stood. Shouts rose up from the lower decks, mingled with terrible choking sounds. The crewmen who hadn't eaten yet were running around in a blind panic, trying to help the fallen.

Then they hit the Jailer's Teeth.

The ship slammed into the rocks. Timbers buckled and snapped under the force of the waves, and the ocean roared as a hatchway below the waterline caved in. Suddenly Felix was off his feet and sliding, tumbling toward the railing while the *Fairwind Muse* listed violently to one side. Mari caught his hand and pulled him up, both of them barely keeping their footing on the tilting deck.

"The skiffs," Felix said, pointing. "We'll get off that way!"

They found Anakoni at the bow, working to loose one of the bound skiffs from its ropes. The long rowboat swayed dangerously off the edge of the ship, high above the water and ice. He waved them over.

"Flywheel's jammed," he shouted. "Help me!"

Across the deck, another trio of survivors worked to lower a second skiff. The *Muse* continued its slow list, taking on water and bound for its grave beneath the black ocean. Felix looked up and saw a few men still clinging to the masts, struggling to chop through the sail lines and keep the wind from pushing the ship any farther onto the treacherous rocks. They couldn't save the *Muse* from going down, but they could stave off its death long enough to get another few survivors off the boat.

Mari and Anakoni gave the ropes one desperate yank, and the flywheel spun free. They watched as the skiff slid down the side of the ship and landed with a splash in the water below. Felix unfurled a rolled-up rope ladder, just long enough to reach the waiting boat.

Werner fought his way up from belowdecks, climbing over corpses and leaning against the tilting walls. He ran to join them, eyes wide with horror.

"Thank the Gardener I was too sick to eat," he gasped. "It's madness down there. Half the crew dead or dying."

Felix clambered down the rope ladder, trying to ignore the ship's groaning and the splintering cracks of its wooden bones. The skiff wobbled under his feet, but he held on to the ladder and kept the boat from drifting away from the *Muse*. Mari was next, gripping the sides of the rope ladder and half sliding her way down, skinning her palms raw but saving a few precious seconds. One of the other three skiffs had already hit the water, and a couple sailors were paddling toward shore with all their might.

As Anakoni and Werner climbed down to join them, the sea began to boil. Not with heat but with raw movement, as if a fistful of worms had woken up at the bottom of a water glass, churning and straining toward the surface.

The first mate landed in the skiff, and his eyes went wide with terror. "*Elder!*" he screamed up to the other survivors. "*Elder!* Abandon ship *now!*"

Something rumbled up from beneath the waves. It was a sound like nothing Felix had heard before, like a single droning note being played underwater on some massive instrument. Anakoni took up one set of oars and thrust the other at Felix.

"Row, damn you!" Anakoni shouted. "Row or we're all dead!"

Felix didn't need the prompting. He shoved the oars into the water and threw his back into it, struggling to keep up with the first mate's frantic paddling.

Icy water sprayed across Felix's face as the sea erupted. A black, rubbery tentacle, at least thirty feet long and thick as a tree trunk, soared up from under the waves and lashed at the *Muse*'s railing. More tentacles, more than he could count, bubbled and boiled up to latch onto the dying ship and dig into every seam and broken plank, tugging viciously. One of the men still clinging to the ship's mast fell free, plummeting down to the water. He surfaced long enough to take a single sputtering breath— and then a tentacle whipped around his head and hauled him under.

One of the skiffs, laden with twelve men and barely floating above the waterline, was a good twenty feet closer to shore. A gasp caught in Felix's throat as a fat tentacle slashed up from the waves and came down across the middle of the skiff, crushing a sailor's spine and tearing the boat in half.

"Steer that way!" Felix said. "We can pick up the survivors!"

"They're already lost," Anakoni said, shaking his head. "Just keep going for shore."

In the blink of an eye, Mari drew one of her fighting batons and swung it at his windpipe, stopping a quarter inch from impact. Anakoni flinched.

"We have to *try*," she said through gritted teeth. "*Steer.*"

Men clung to the wreckage, kicking and batting with their oars at the questing tentacles. Felix immediately recognized Simon. The blond Murgardt was still alive and fighting, clutching a chunk of driftwood and slapping a curling tentacle back down under the water.

"My ankle!" one of the sailors screamed. "It's got my—" And then he was gone, hauled into the black. Felix's skiff closed in, passing a struggling man who'd been knocked from the wreckage. Mari and Werner quickly reached over the side and hauled him in. It was Kimo, soaking wet and cold as the grave.

Another sailor went down as the sea sprouted one blubbery black tendril after another. They brought the skiff as close as they dared, and Felix cupped his hands and shouted out.

"Simon! Over here! *Jump!*"

Simon steeled himself and took a deep breath, leaping from the floating wreckage and hurling himself over a tentacle as it whipped furiously at the frigid air. He landed five feet from the skiff, plunging into the water, and swam hard and fast. They dragged him in, resting him on his back inside the rocking boat as he gasped for air.

Out of twelve men, only Kimo and Simon had survived. The rest were lost beneath the waves and the tentacles hammered the floating debris looking for more, trying to sate their endless hunger.

As they rowed for shore, Felix looked back. He wished he hadn't. Nothing was left of the *Fairwind Muse* but its bow and masthead, slowly dragged inch by inch under the merciless waters. Some sixty feet back, the third skiff followed in their wake, its crew paddling as fast as they could to catch up. The fourth was nowhere to be seen.

The sea boiled around the third skiff, even more ferociously than before. Waves buffeted the craft, and Felix fought to keep their own boat steady. A rumbling sound filled the air, mingled with that distant and horrible trumpeting.

"Something's coming," Mari whispered.

Then the sea exploded, and Felix learned what a god's nightmares looked like.

A beak rose up from the water in a tidal eruption of sea spray and thunder. It was at least fifty feet across, gaping wide and swallowing the third skiff whole. Scab-like barnacles and white fungus covered its cracked chitin. The beak reared up, triumphant, and at its apex it unleashed a deafening, screeching cry to the heavens.

His muscles strained and his breath was raw, but he couldn't stop rowing. Not now, not with that horror still hunting and hungry.

How much of it is still under the water, he thought. *Oh Gardener, how big IS it?*

The rocky shoreline was twenty feet away and closing fast. Then fifteen, then ten, and blood roared in Felix's ears as he shut his eyes and poured his last reserves of strength into paddling, pushing past his breaking point. The skiff bumped against the shore, and Mari put her hands under his arms, dragging him up and away from the boat as Anakoni and Werner did the same for Kimo and Simon.

The shore was a rocky bramble glistening with ice, barren and cold. Fifteen feet inland they all tumbled to the frost, sitting sprawled on the stony ground, watching as the tentacles dragged the last few feet of the *Muse* to its doom. Then the sea was quiet once more, glowing black in the setting sun.

No one said a word. One hundred and twenty-two men had put out to sea on the *Fairwind Muse*. Only six people made it back to shore. A moment of silence felt like the right thing to do.

"When we dropped the skiffs," Kimo breathed, his voice a whisper, "the Elder thought we were making an offering. We *called* it."

Anakoni glared at the water. His one good eye narrowed to a razor slit.

"We wouldn't have had to, if some bastard hadn't tried to murder us all. Why would he do that?" He looked to Felix, Werner, and Mari, furious. "Was it you? Or you? Nobody had any reason to hurt our ship. The only thing different about this voyage was the three of *you*. One of you is responsible for this!"

"Easy," Mari said, a gentle edge of warning in her voice.

"Don't tell me easy! Don't tell me—" Anakoni froze, pressing his hand to his face, letting out a choking sob. When he spoke again, he'd lost all of his fight. "My captain is dead. My friends are *dead*. I just want to know why."

"We survived," Simon said vacantly, giving Felix a lingering and empty-eyed gaze. "That's the important thing."

He's in shock, Felix thought. *I guess we all are.*

"Anakoni," Mari said, "how far are we from Winter's Reach?"

"By foot? A day's hard hiking, if we're lucky and find the forest road."

She nodded over at Kimo, who trembled and stared at the sea, clutching his knees to his chest.

"He's cold-sick and soaking wet, and Simon is almost as bad. They won't make it, not like this. We need to build a camp and get a fire started."

Felix pushed himself to his feet and staggered off into the tree line with the other survivors, looking for a clearing and some tinder to burn. The arctic night was coming fast, and he could feel the cold sinking into his bones.

CHAPTER EIGHTEEN

The architect of Lerautia's White Cathedral had a dream of a great dove descending to land upon the Holy City. Vast alabaster curves formed the building's outstretched wings, "feathered" with scalloped tiles, and a smooth arc stretching out over the columned doors symbolized its craning neck. Long overdue renovations were underway inside, with scaffolding filling the basilica from the mosaic-tiled floor to the long stained-glass windows that loomed fifty feet above the congregation's heads. Still, services went on, and the workmen dutifully shuffled out most nights and mornings so the banging of hammers and the rattling of saws could yield to the exquisite song of the *castrati* choir.

Tonight, the lilting hymns couldn't move Amadeo's heart. Standing behind a pulpit draped in green velvet, he went through the motions, offering the bread and proclaiming the virtues—all the ritual gestures he'd made a thousand times before, but he didn't *feel* them. Still, as always, a crowd of upturned faces awaited him on the cathedral steps long after the service had ended.

"Father!" one of the congregants called out. A farmer, by the cut of his ragged clothes, clutching a fat-cheeked baby in his outstretched arms. "Bless our son? He's had the croup."

Amadeo smiled and fished a slim flask of oil from his cassock. He unscrewed it and waved the man over.

"Of course, of course," he said, dabbing a dot of oil on the child's head and murmuring a quick prayer. He leaned in and kissed the baby's brow on the spot he'd anointed. "If he doesn't get better soon, take him to Dr. D'Antonio on the Via del Popolo. Tell him I sent you."

A plump woman in a well-worn apron bustled up and pressed a round tin into his hands.

"Father," she said, "last apple pie of the season, and I had to bring it to you. I remembered how much you loved them last year."

Amadeo grinned. "Ah, Luisa, you are an angel. Take note, everyone: the Gardener provides. And when the Gardener needs a little extra help, he calls on Luisa's bakery."

"Father?" piped up a young boy of twelve or so, barely audible over a chorus of polite chuckles. Amadeo got down on one knee to talk to him eye to eye.

"Yes, son?"

"Is the pope really dying?"

The chuckles faded. Amadeo took a moment to consider his response and nodded. He reached out and gently held the boy's shoulder.

"Yes, son, he is. Everyone has their time. That will be a *long* time coming for you, but Pope Benignus has spent many good decades tilling the earth here, and he's getting tired. For now, just celebrate the days he has left with us. That's what he wants."

"Who do you think is going to be next on the throne?" called out a man from the back of the crowd. "They're saying the College of Cardinals doesn't want Carlo. They say he's not fit."

Amadeo patted the boy's shoulder and stood. A faint murmur went up around him, and he waved his hands to quiet it down.

"Please, everyone. Times like this are uncertain. I can't know the future any more than you do, but rumors don't help anyone. All I can ask is that you trust the Church, and trust me. The right candidate, whoever it is, will surely be—"

His voice trailed off as the crowd turned, looking to the left. A thunderous tramping sound, iron marching on stone, echoed toward them. Two horsemen rounded the corner, then another pair, then another, the procession continuing without end. The riders wore fluted plate, and blankets in black and gold draped their stallions, the colors of the Holy Murgardt Empire.

It was a military procession. As they tromped past the cathedral steps in perfect unison, Amadeo counted perhaps fifty riders in all. Veteran knights, with eyes of ice. *They're headed toward the papal mansion*, he realized.

All eyes were back on him, and every one of them carried an unspoken question.

"Perhaps an ambassador from the west," Amadeo said, "coming to pay his respects. If you'll pardon me, I should go and see if they need any help."

The scene at the estate, once he finally extricated himself from the crowd and set off, was chaos. Horses milled across the lawns and stamped through flowerbeds while the frantic servants tried to find a place to put them. Soldiers from the papal guard were enmeshed in arm-flailing shouting matches with the estate clerks, the Murgardt newcomers, and anyone else who would listen.

"Father! Father Lagorio!" a voice boomed. Amadeo turned to see Gallo Parri, captain of the guard, descending on him like a maddened bull. The man's whiskers twitched, and he clutched a sheaf of papers in one hand, crumpling them in his fist. "Father, you have to talk to these people! You have to bring them to reason—"

"Wait! Gallo, wait. Slow down. What's going on?"

Gallo loomed over him. He unfurled the rumpled papers and held them up so Amadeo could read.

"We're being reassigned," Gallo said.

"Who is?"

"*All of us!* The entire papal guard! Look at this," he said, ruffling the papers. "Me and three of my best men? Being dispatched to guard a monastery in the Carcannan Mountains. Why does a monastery in the mountains need a four-man security team? Are bandits coming to steal their hymnals? Another one of my men is being sent to a nunnery four hundred miles away. He's supposed to guard a building he can't set foot inside!"

"Wait," Amadeo said, "the *entire* papal guard? Who is going to watch the estate? Not the city constabulary."

Gallo pointed toward a pack of knights hovering by the estate doors and wearing grim faces.

"Those Murgardt pissants. The high and mighty emperor wants to pay a visit, and he only trusts his own men. So we're being replaced until he goes home, which could be *months* if he decides to stay the winter."

Amadeo shook his head. "That's insane. The emperor doesn't get to make those decisions. Look, Gallo...I'll do what I can. Don't be in too much of a hurry to leave town, all right? See if you can hold your men back for a day or two, just in case I can fix this."

"Oh," Gallo said, glowering, "and here I was with my bags all packed and eager to go. But if you're going to *insist*, I suppose I can drag my heels a bit."

Amadeo strode toward the front doors of the mansion. He was almost to the steps when a pike chopped the air just in front of his face, blocking his way. He could see his startled reflection in the finely polished steel.

"Identify yourself," a Murgardt said. Two others lingered nearby, eying Amadeo with barely concealed disdain.

"Father Amadeo Lagorio, the papal confessor. Identify *your*self."

The pike slowly slid back as the soldier stood it upright at his side.

"Kappel, of the Holy Order of St. Friedrich. Sir."

"Who is your commanding officer and where can I find him?"

"That would be Knight-Captain Weiss," the soldier said. "He's inside."

"Then so am I," Amadeo said, walking past him and pulling open the great double doors. It took him a moment to recognize the strange heat simmering in the pit of his stomach. Anger.

More arguments inside, more frantic servants trying to find quarters for fifty unexpected guests, more furious guards stomping out with sacks slung over their shoulders. Amadeo didn't find the mysterious Knight-

Captain Weiss, but he did find Carlo, sitting alone in the dining room and giving bedroom eyes to a glass of wine.

"Oh hey!" he said, waving to Amadeo and tossing back a swallow. "C'mon, join me in a glass."

"I think you've had enough already. What's going on here? Where did these soldiers come from?"

"Knights," Carlo corrected him, holding up a shaky finger. "Order of St. Friedrich. Pedigreed. Very distinguished."

"And why are they replacing your father's personal guard? Did Bene approve this?"

"Of course he did! Emperor Theodosius wants to come out and pay his last respects to the old man, maybe stay for a few weeks. And you know, the guy's a little jumpy. So we thought he'd feel more comfortable, all things considered, if he was surrounded by his own people."

"'We' meaning who?" Amadeo said. He crossed his arms.

"Just, you know, *people*. I spoke to his people; they spoke to me. It's politics! You don't need to worry about it, okay? Just…do your priest thing, that's what you're good at."

"That's exactly what I'm doing," Amadeo said, turning on his heel.

His next stop was Benignus's suite, but Sister Columba, the elderly woman who served as the pope's maid and nurse, caught him at the doors.

"Please don't wake him," she said, shaking her head under the forest-green wimple that shrouded her head and wrapped under her chin. "He's had a frightfully long day as it is, and his cough is back."

"Sister, do you know anything about these knights? Did Bene approve of this?"

Columba looked up the hall before leaning close to Amadeo. She lowered her voice to a whispering rasp.

"I was in the room when Carlo spoke to him. The Holy Father was half-asleep, and he'd taken his tonic. I tried to tell Carlo, but he wouldn't listen. He talked and talked, and finally I think his father just nodded and scribbled his name on the writ just to make him leave. But he didn't say *anything* about sending the papal guard away. He made it sound like we were just bringing in more guards, not replacing the old ones."

Amadeo nodded, remembering a bit of Carlo's conversation with Lodovico Marchetti. *Just get your father on board, and I'll do the rest.*

"I'll be back in the morning," he told her, and headed down the hall.

He nearly ran into Livia, both of them rounding a corner at once. She looked like she hadn't slept in days.

"I owe you an apology," she said. "I brushed you off last night, when you were telling me about Carlo. I should have paid closer attention."

"We both should have," Amadeo said. He went silent as a stone-faced knight marched past them, patrolling the halls.

"We should talk," they both said at the same time.

Livia led the way to the Remembrance Chapel, a tiny prayer gallery not far from the papal quarters. A few short pews lined up before a wooden carving of the Gardener's Tree and a spread of votive candles in red stained-glass cups. Deep frescoes adorned the walls, depicting the lives of the saints. Amadeo and Livia stood in the gloom together, their faces lit by the faint and flickering candlelight.

"It's Lodovico Marchetti," Amadeo said. "He's scheming with Carlo. Pushing him into something bigger and more ambitious than your brother would ever dream up on his own."

He told her about his visit to the conference room yesterday, relating the snatch of conversation he'd overheard, and watched Livia's expression go more and more grim.

"Gardener's rain. And now my father's guard is gone and we've got fifty armed strangers in our house."

"I told Gallo to hold his men close for as long as he could, but that probably won't buy us much time. The cardinals are reconvening here, too. I can't imagine they won't start squawking when they see Murgardt knights guarding the assembly-hall doors."

Livia paced the chapel, rubbing her chin.

"Maybe that's the point?" she said. "Lodovico wants to make sure Carlo is our next pope. Maybe it's some kind of intimidation play, something to throw the cardinals off-balance."

Amadeo shook his head. "They're the emperor's men. It wouldn't matter unless Theodosius supports Carlo too. From what I hear about the emperor, he's barely cognizant of anything outside his own palace. The one thing I think we can be sure of is that they're not here to hurt your father. To be painfully frank, considering his condition…"

He paused, but Livia finished the thought. "Assassinating a dying man would be pointless, even if I believed Carlo would do it. And no. He's a drunken, lecherous buffoon, but he loves my father as much as I do. So. We have a force of Imperial knights who were obviously brought in to render the papal guard powerless. Logic gives us two possible objectives: intimidation or violence."

"Right," Amadeo said. "We're just missing the who and the why."

Livia stopped pacing. She stood at the chapel's edge, cloaked in shadow, with her back turned to the priest.

"Amadeo," she said after a short silence. "Are we agreed that what's happening here is wrong? That whatever my brother and Lodovico Marchetti are after, it's not something healthy for the Church or its people?"

He nodded slowly. "I think so, yes."

"And right now, I imagine you're thinking about the oath my father begged you to swear. An oath to serve my brother, made on soil and water and your own beating heart."

"That's right," Amadeo said.

She didn't move.

"And you're wondering," she said, "if oathbreakers go to the Barren Fields when they die."

He swallowed. In the stillness, it sounded as loud as an arrow punching through his heart.

"The thought had crossed my mind," he said, "but I don't believe in a god of absolutes. Sometimes you have to commit a sin for the best of reasons. Maybe the Gardener will forgive us. But if he doesn't…maybe it doesn't matter."

Livia didn't say anything. Amadeo saw her hand go up to her face, as if brushing something from her eye. Then she finally turned to face him, walking over to stand at his side before the wooden tree.

"We are resolved, then," she said, "to learn the truth, and to do whatever is necessary to protect the Church and her faithful. *Whatever* is necessary."

She held out her hand, palm down. He reached out, after only a moment's pause, and rested his hand on top of hers.

A faint cough turned their heads. At the end of the pews, just inside the closed chapel door, Rimiggiu the Quiet watched them from the shadows.

They froze. The pope's spy approached, and joined them before the wooden tree. Then he reached out and placed his hand on top of Amadeo's.

"I serve the Holy Father," he said in a soft, sonorous voice. "Sometimes that means doing what I know is best for him, not what he commands."

Amadeo nodded slowly. "Well. Two's a partnership, and three's a conspiracy."

"I call it a good start," Livia said.

CHAPTER NINETEEN

Kimo died in the night.

Without bedrolls or furs or shelter, the survivors of the *Fairwind Muse* were left with fire as their only defense against the murderous cold. They'd taken shifts standing watch by the crackling flames, keeping the fire fed while the others huddled close and gathered their strength. Simon's clothes dried and left him with nothing but a sniffle, but Kimo had spent too much time in the freezing water. They found him at first light, stone dead, staring with glassy eyes at the warmth that came too late to save him.

Anakoni didn't talk much after that. Then again, none of them did.

They reckoned their direction by the morning sun and set off northwest, on a bearing that Anakoni thought would eventually lead them to an old logging road. His instincts were good. After seven hours of slogging through thick woods and ankle-deep snow, they emerged onto a wide road slicing through the forest and pointing the way to Winter's Reach. The snowdrifts still sucked at their boots with every step, but at least they knew they were on the right path. It was also a little warmer outside the shadow of the forest canopy. Not by much, but Simon was thankful for tiny blessings.

You, Simon thought, staring at Felix's back, *are the luckiest bastard in the world.*

Try to shove him overboard? The captain came calling. Try to cut his throat in his sleep or ambush him belowdecks? That feral little Terrai was never more than ten feet away. Try to poison the *entire damned ship*, and he doesn't eat the beef.

Then a genuine sea monster shows up, and he's one of the only survivors.

Simon was privately grateful for that. He would never take credit for another man's kill, even if that 'man' had tentacles and a giant maw. If the Elder had eaten Felix, Simon could never have lived it down. Besides, he'd done a fair job of surviving this whole ordeal himself, and that was something to be happy about.

"Five more hours if we keep a good clip," Anakoni called out, leading the weary pack as they trudged through the snow. Werner rubbed the back of his hand against his wet nose and coughed himself hoarse. The cold had gotten into his lungs, in the night, and sounded like it was settling in for a good long stay.

"I had gifts for the mayor in my pack," Felix said to Mari, the two of them hiking side by side along the logging road. "Just some nice Mirenzei porcelain and silk, something to start us off on the right foot. I hope the Elder chokes on it."

"What will you do?" she said.

"Go in with a handshake and a smile. I can't let anything stop me, not after all of this. At least I saved my coin purse. Shouldn't be too hard to book passage on another ship to get the three of us back home."

"The three of us?" Mari said.

He shrugged. "We've all got a job to do, and it shouldn't take either of us too long. We'd probably save money if you, me, and Werner arranged passage together. Besides, I'd...I'd just feel better if I knew you got home safely."

She nodded, falling silent.

Not happening, Simon thought.

As long as they split up in the city, even for an hour or two, catching Felix alone would be easy enough. Then it was just a matter of getting the job done with any old tools that came to hand, and slipping out before the militia was any the wiser. Easy.

He frowned. *Too easy.*

No, after all this effort, all this trouble, jumping the man in a dark alley and strangling him to death would be *vulgar*. When he went home to write the story in his dead-book, it wouldn't be a chapter to be proud of. Honestly, after all they'd been through together, he *owed* Felix a more dramatic death. It was the professional thing to do. As the miles limped by and the powerless sun crested in a cloudless sky, Simon wove together the threads of a plan.

A few hours later, they came to the first corpse.

"Is that—" Felix started to ask as the cross loomed up ahead, a tall wooden pole with a crossarm at the top. A corpse dangled from the pole, lashed to it at the ankles and wrists. It was hard to tell how long the man had been dead. His naked body was frozen and blue, and the crows had pecked the eyes from his skull. A small board hung from his neck by a length of twine, with the word "THIEF" painted across it in jagged black letters.

"The captain warned you about this place, brother." Anakoni waved his hand at the corpse, curling his fingers in a ritual warding gesture. "It's evil. The Reach changes everyone it touches. Never for the better."

Mari walked right up to the pole, looking innocently curious, and paused to study the corpse's bound wrists and ankles.

"Wrists are skinned," she said, "from struggling. He was alive when they put him up there."

"They let him freeze to death?" Simon asked.

Mari pointed to the splotches on the man's body, from his chest to his withered genitals to his feet. "Frostbite hit here first. They splashed a bucket of water on him. Suffer more that way."

About a mile up the road they found another body, hung like the first, but this one had a board that said "MURDERER."

Two more came soon after that, a man and a woman. The woman was another thief, while the man's crime was "DISRESPECT."

"What exactly," Felix said slowly, squinting as if making sure he was reading it right, "constitutes criminal disrespect in Winter's Reach?"

Mari shrugged. "City was a prison. The people still have prison instincts. Veruca can't afford to let anyone think she's weak, not even for a second. She's in charge only as long as her people fear her. The second she slips, she falls."

"I'll remember that," Felix said.

The road turned toward the icy mountains in the distance, towering jagged slabs of bleak gray stone capped with frozen snow. Then they saw the palisade. A stockade wall of stout wooden stakes harvested from the cedars, thirty feet high and banded with mariner's rope, ringed the city of Winter's Reach. Crumbling stone towers sprouted up here and there behind the wall, and scouts stood vigil with crossbows cradled in their arms. One saw them coming, as they trudged along the snow-choked road, and called something down from his perch.

When they got closer, tall gates set into the palisade rattled open, shoving back the snow. Six hardy men walked out to meet them, garbed in black leathers and tattered soot-stained fur. Heavy maces swung from their belts, and they wore tall wooden shields slung across their backs. The shields were in a style Simon had never seen, cut in a sharply angular shape. He realized, a moment later, that they were cut to look like casket lids.

"Coffin Boys," Mari murmured to Felix. Behind her, Simon perked his ears.

"Who?"

"Mayor's elite. They run the city."

"Don't usually get visitors on foot," called out one of the men. "We heard the Elder caught a little snack near the Jailer's Teeth. You wouldn't happen to be the leftovers, would ya?"

Anakoni held up a hand. "Anakoni Mahelona, first mate of the *Fairwind Muse*. We're all that's left."

"He tossed 'em back," one of the Coffin Boys muttered to a chorus of snickers. "Too shrimpy to eat."

The two groups formed ragged lines in the snow, facing each other outside the city gate. The Boys' leader gave each of the survivors a long once-over.

"I see two sailors," he said, "an old man, a sad excuse for a piece of ass, and a dandy. What's your story, dandy?"

Felix blinked. "I, er...me? I mean...I'm Felix Rossini, of the Banco Rossini. I'm here to speak with the mayor, please."

The leader looked back to his men and grinned. "Aww, he's *polite*. We're gonna have some fun with this one."

"No," Mari said. "You aren't."

The leader tilted his head, walked over, and stood in front of her like a drill sergeant on inspection. He leaned in, his bristled and wind-burnt face inches from hers.

"Did you say something, cupcake?"

"You will go to your mistress," Mari said, "and you will tell her that Mari Renault has returned to Winter's Reach."

Maybe it was the name, maybe it was the steel in her voice, but Simon watched the man's expression change in the space of a breath. He took a slight step back and squared his shoulders, obviously mindful that his men were watching him.

"You know who I am," Mari whispered.

Their eyes locked. He blinked first.

"Welcome to the Reach," he said grudgingly. "Obey the law, and respect our mayor's benevolent rule."

The streets of Winter's Reach, to Simon's eye, weren't planned so much as organically grown. Like a cancer. The rebellious inmates had broken the old stone buildings down to the foundations and stolen bits and chunks to build their new homes, along with logs from the forest. It was a crazy quilt of tangled streets and off-kilter buildings, leaning and ramshackle and falling apart. Dirt roads limned with slick ice ran this way and that, widening and shrinking on a whim, with nothing so much as resembling a street sign or a map in sight.

As for the people, they moved like hungry ghosts through the snow. Most wore hoods, and they all kept their heads down, as though eye contact was a lethal poison. When a pack of Coffin Boys came sauntering down the street—Simon noticed a few women in their ranks, despite the name—beggars vanished from the roadside and ragged curtains whipped across windows.

"I guess this is where we part ways," Felix said. "Anakoni, Simon, I'm sorry. I'm sorry for everything."

Anakoni shook his head, too exhausted for anger. "The sea's a lover, but she likes to bite. And when she bites, you bleed. I just want to go home. I hope you find everything you desire here. But be careful, brother. Remember: Old Man Ochali isn't done telling your story. He doesn't promise any of us a happy ending."

Simon shook Felix's hand. He savored the moment of intimacy. "Good luck."

Anakoni slapped Simon's back and said, "Come with me, down to the docks. I'm hiring on with the first ship that'll take me south, and you should too. You're green, but you're a good sailor. I'll vouch for you."

Simon imagined what it would feel like to slit Anakoni's throat. Then again, there was a certain poetry to leaving one single man from the *Muse*'s crew alive. Anakoni would carry the nightmares of that terrible day for the rest of his life, nightmares Simon had helped to weave. *Yes*, he thought, *I like that. You should live.*

"I'm going to stay on for a while," Simon said. "After that experience…well, I'm wondering if I'm really cut out for the sea. I think I'll talk to the loggers, see if they need another strong back. I might enjoy swinging an ax for a living."

Anakoni arched one eyebrow and shook his head. "You're mad, but if it's really what you want, all blessings to you. I'll say a prayer for you every night. As far as I'm concerned, after what we've been through together, you're my brother until the end of days."

Simon just smiled.

While Felix, Werner, and Mari made arrangements to meet up after their business was done, Simon wandered up the street and ducked around the corner of a clapboard shack. Once they split up, he dogged

Felix's heels, elated when the banker stopped in a roach trap of a tavern for a bite to eat. Simon's own stomach was growling itself into knots, but there was no time to lose. He had resolved to try a new approach, something worthy of a chapter in his dead-book.

Neither his garrote nor his stiletto would do the trick. Instead, he would murder a man with a piece of paper.

CHAPTER TWENTY

The problem with conspiracies, Amadeo thought, *is their habit of growing.* Soon enough it wasn't just Amadeo, Livia, and Rimiggiu the Quiet sharing a three-way pact. Sister Columba twigged to what they were up to—Amadeo didn't think much could slip past her—and immediately pledged her support. With her help, they'd know about every visitor the pope received and every conversation she could eavesdrop on.

"I'm just the old woman who cleans the Holy Father's linens and fetches his meals," she confided with a smile. "Nobody ever notices me. How do you think I know so much?"

Now Amadeo was bringing another conspirator into the fold. As they walked up the pebbled drive to the steps of the papal manse, two of the Murgardt knights moved to stand in their way.

"Father," one said, "we know you, but who's your little friend?"

Amadeo patted Freda's shoulder. The ragged girl glared at the knights like a ferret eying two fingers and deciding which one to bite first.

"Freda's the new washing girl at the cathedral. She's never seen the papal manse, and she's done such a good job working for us, I thought she earned a little tour."

"Not on the approved list," one of the knights said to his partner. "Should we get the captain?"

The other one shook his head. "Nah, you kidding? She's a child. How much trouble could she get into? Go ahead, Father, but keep the girl with you at all times, okay?"

Amadeo smiled and gave them a wave as they passed by.

How much trouble could she get into? They had no idea.

Freda's eyes went wide as saucers as they walked through the mansion's galleries, passing under the gaze of portraits two hundred years older than she was.

"And you *live* here?" she whispered.

"Normally, I live in a cottage near the cathedral. Nothing so grand. I'm just staying here until...well, until the transition."

She ran her fingernail along a picture frame.

"Is this real gold? Gardener's blood, melt this down and you could feed the entire Alms District for weeks."

"Language," Amadeo said. "But you're not wrong."

"So why don't you?"

He shrugged. "It's not mine to melt."

"Whose is it then?" Freda said, looking dubious.

"That's...complicated."

Livia waited for them in the east wing, in a recessed sitting nook that offered a good view down two long corridors.

"Freda," Amadeo said, "this is Livia. She's helping us."

Freda narrowed her eyes. "Wait a second. I know you! You're that lady what comes down to the docks after midnight with bushels of food and medicine. The Lady in Brown. Do you work here too?"

Livia favored her with a rare, soft smile. "Something like that."

"Is he still here?" Amadeo asked.

"No," Livia said. "He left twenty minutes ago. He took a coach into town. No telling how long he'll be out, so we'd best get to it."

Midway down the hall, a gilded door stood firmly shut and locked. Amadeo looked to Freda.

"Think you can do it?"

Freda waved a dismissive hand and dug in her ragged shift for a pair of polished and lacquered fish bones.

"Peh," she said, kneeling down and peering into the keyhole. "I'm embarrassed you can't."

She dug around inside the lock with the two bones, sticking out her tongue and biting down on it while she concentrated. Amadeo heard the old tumblers rattle as he looked up and down the hallway. Livia stood down on one end and pretended to read a book, keeping quiet watch. According to the plan, Rimiggiu would be covering the other approach, and Sister Columba should have already taken up position in the foyer, idly mopping the marble floor as she kept one sharp eye on the front doors.

The lock clicked, and the door to Carlo's private office swung open.

Amadeo ushered Freda inside and closed the door behind them. The afternoon light streamed in through a bay window that looked over the back lawns. Correspondence cluttered Carlo's great mahogany desk, most of it unopened and unread, but he had cleared careful room on the credenza for three bottles of Itrescan brandy. Another crystal decanter of amber liquor, half drained, sat beside a pair of shot glasses.

"So what are we after?" Freda said.

"Good question. Anything about those Murgardt knights, the emperor's visit, and anything that mentions the Banco Marchetti. And anything that looks out of place."

"Right," Freda said, rolling her eyes. "So basically everything. You're lucky you taught me how to read."

Freda riffled through the envelopes on the table while Amadeo searched Carlo's closet. Lots of velvet and brocade, everything custom tailored and fit to perfection. He checked the pockets of Carlo's coats, but his fingers came up with nothing but lint and a couple of stray coppers. He heard one of the desk drawers rattle.

"Is this something?" Freda asked.

Amadeo padded over to join her, trying to keep his footsteps light. She'd found a map in his top drawer, rolled up and heavily marked with annotations in red ink. Amadeo's brow furrowed as he traced the circled spots with his fingertips.

"This is a map of the Church's holdings," he said. "Real estate and the like. Unless I'm mistaken, these big circles here mark out the papal alum mines."

"Why does the Church need real estate?" Freda asked.

"To pay for the gold portrait frames. Now, over here? These are mineral deposits in the Oerran Caliphate. Probably alum, too."

"Rocks," Freda said flatly.

"Not just any rocks. Alum is special. You can make dyes with it, tan leather with it, purify water. It's a key ingredient in pickling and some medicines…it's just a mineral, but entire industries depend on it. These mines here are the only serious source of alum in the Empire. Everything else comes in from the far east by caravan."

Some ink from the other side had soaked through the thin parchment. Amadeo turned over the map. The back was a mess of notes and scribbles inside looping circles and lines, like a web woven by a drunken spider. He paused, lost in thought. Freda tilted her head at him.

"What?"

"It's a list of trade goods." He followed a curving line with his fingertip. "Raw silk, rugs, spices…"

"Rich people stuff," Freda said.

"Specifically rich people stuff imported from the east, and this is a list of licensed trading companies. Then these numbers…I'm not sure what these are."

A folded letter on expensive, creamy vellum lay at the bottom of the desk drawer. The royal seal of Murgardt, painstakingly inked, caught Amadeo's eye. He set the map aside and unfolded the letter.

"'It is his great regret that due to outstanding obligations,'" he started to read aloud, then trailed off.

"What?" Freda said. "What's it say?"

Amadeo's face went ashen.

"That due to outstanding obligations," he said slowly, "the emperor can't possibly come to Lerautia for at least two months. He sends his respect and prayers for the Holy Father's continued health."

"But I thought the whole changing of the guard was because he's on his way," Freda said.

"That's what we were told." Amadeo shook his head at the letter. "But according to this, he's not. Which means the emperor didn't send those knights, if they even *are* knights. And Carlo knows it. The guard has been shoved out, fifty armed men are occupying the papal estate under a false flag, and Carlo *let it happen.*"

A shrill whistle made his head jerk toward the door.

"Put it back just as you found it, quickly!" he said, stashing the letter. Freda folded up the map and slipped it back in the drawer. They ran to the office door, and Amadeo poked his head out, looking left and right. Down the hall, he saw Livia raise her head and look the other way.

"Hello, Brother," she said, a bit louder than she needed to. As she walked up to meet Carlo and slow him down, Amadeo and Freda slipped out, shut the door behind them, and headed the other way.

CHAPTER TWENTY-ONE

Felix knew he stuck out like a sore thumb in Winter's Reach. His skin and hair were too dark for the frozen north, his clothes too expensive for this town. Still, he kept his chin up and ignored the heat from the staring eyes. *You've been in worse places than this*, he told himself, though he knew it was a lie.

The tavern he strolled into didn't even have a name, just a sign over the door with a crudely painted fish and what he thought might have been a hunk of green cheese. The smoky smell of charred halibut wafting through the doorway, though, won out over his better judgment.

The room fell silent as he walked in the door. Dirty faces and hard eyes looked over from a scattering of mismatched tables and chairs, silhouetted in the light from a couple of frosted-over windows. Even inside, Felix could still see his breath gusting out in a curlicue of steam.

He ignored the looks, kept a polite smile on his face, and saddled up to the bar. The stools, like the scattered chairs, had dirty leather skins stretched over the seats to cushion the wood and fight off the cold. The bartender, a stout woman with braided blond hair and a scar notching her bottom lip, made her way over.

"If you're lookin' for paradise," she said, "this ain't it."

"If you've got something I can eat, then it's close enough for me. What kind of coin do you take?"

She shrugged. "Mostly barter and logging-company scrip around here, but we get enough sailors that I'll take any coin that spends."

He dug into his belt pouch and held up two silver scudi.

"What'll this buy me?" he said.

She made the coins disappear. "Best damn meal you ever had, that's what."

She wasn't lying. The fillet was a little too charred, and the tin plate she served it up on was a little too dirty, but it quieted the rumbling in Felix's stomach even as it left a pleasing burn on his tongue. After a week of nothing but hardtack and salted beef, he couldn't imagine a better meal.

"Spicy," he said, nodding at his tarnished fork. "Is that chili pepper?"

"Ground juminweed. Grows like, well, like weeds up here, but it makes a hell of a spice. We like our food hot in these parts. You Imperial?"

"No. Mirenzei."

"Mirenze is part of the Empire," she said dubiously.

"That's not the way we see it."

She chuckled and wiped down a tankard with an oil-spotted rag.

"Hope you didn't come up here because you like the weather," she said.

"I'm hoping for an audience with the mayor. I have a proposal for her, about the old alum mines outside town."

The bartender shook her head. "Huh? This is a logging town, Mirenzei. We don't have any mines here."

His heart skipped a beat.

"Not—not active ones," he said. "But I've read that before…before the Reach was a free city, there were mines here."

"First I've heard of it, but we don't spend a lot of time reading history books around here. I'd ask one of the old-timers, they'd know. You just mind your p's and q's when you talk to Her Honor. Folks don't much like Imperials around here, Mirenzei or otherwise."

"I'll be on my best behavior," he said with a smile.

There was nothing but bones and a bit of burnt gristle on his plate by the time he was done, and the meal lifted his spirits. The bartender's comment about the mines still worried him, but if the mines had been left to rot since the revolution, it made sense that she might not have heard of them.

Maybe we'll be able to hire local workers after all, he thought. *That'll save money, and it certainly won't hurt the economy here. These people could use some opportunities.*

He was too deep in contemplation to notice the tavern going dead quiet, or how the bartender suddenly needed to scurry over and tend to a table on the far end of the room. His first warning that anything was wrong came when a leather glove clamped down on the back of his neck and slammed the side of his head down against the hard wooden bar.

"Hello again, dandy," the leader of the Coffin Boys hissed in his ear.

Rough gloves grabbed his arms and hauled them back. Ice-cold iron burned his wrists as a pair of heavy manacles clamped shut. Head stinging from the blow, he blinked, dazed, as the glove yanked him to sit upright.

"You're making a mistake—" he started to say. Then the backhand hit him, spinning him off the barstool and onto his knees on the frost-licked floorboards. The Boys clustered around him, four in all. Felix felt a trickle of blood leak from the corner of his mouth.

"No mistake," the leader said. "Your pal told us everything. He led us right to your little hidey-hole."

"What pal? What hidey-hole? What are you even—"

One of the men grabbed him by his hair, yanking his head back and forcing him to kneel up straight. Their leader waved a tiny glass flask in front of his eyes. The flask was almost empty, but it still glistened with traces of green liquid.

"That sailor, the Murgardt. He saw what you did. Cyladic toxin. You poisoned everyone on that ship."

Felix's eyes went wide. "What? *No!* It wasn't me! You have to believe me!"

"He saw where you stashed your gear, under a loose rock just inside the gates. This look familiar?"

He held out a long, thin-bladed stiletto and rested it on the bar. Next came a strand of wire with two leather-wrapped wooden handles. It took a second before Felix recognized what it was: an assassin's garrote.

"This is insane," he said. "Those aren't mine. Look, I'm Felix Rossini, of the Banco Rossini. You can check—"

The leader leaned in with a cruel smile.

"I knew you were gonna say that. Know why?"

Felix shook his head, mute. The leader unfurled a piece of water-stained parchment and held it up so Felix could read it.

"You will be traveling under the guise of a banker named Felix Rossini. The real Rossini is vacationing in Itresca, so there's no risk of your ruse being discovered.

"We need you to determine the strength of the Reach's defenses, especially the stockade wall, and their troop numbers. Your service will pave the way for the reclamation of Imperial soil. Fealty and glory!"

"No," Felix said, his heart pounding. "No, this is all...oh *damn* it! Simon, it was fucking *Simon*! Don't you get it? He's the one who wrecked our ship, and now he's setting me up!"

"What do you think, boss?" one of the Boys asked. "Take him out to the logging road, string him up?"

The leader shook his head. "Oh, no. Not this one. Been a long time since we had an Imperial dog to play with. She always comes up with the best punishments for spies."

He leaned in, nose to nose with Felix, and grinned.

"Her Honor is going to want to pass sentence on this one *personally*."

They hauled Felix to his feet and dragged him out into the snow. He trudged along with them, occasionally stumbling on the ice or falling to his knees on the rocks when a hard hand gave him a shove. The men yanked him up just as quickly as he fell, keeping him moving.

A procession waited up the street. Ten or so people, a mixture of men and women dressed in rags and misery, forming a chain gang.

"Hold up!" the leader called. "Got one more for the show!"

Each of the prisoners wore a chain belt around his or her waist, linked through their manacles and passing forward to the belt of the person in front, keeping them together. Felix stood mutely as they chained him up at the end of the line. He felt like he was lost in a nightmare, that this couldn't possibly be happening, but he couldn't will himself to wake up, no matter how hard he tried.

At a shout from the guards, the prisoners trudged forward.

"Where are they taking us?" Felix whispered to the man in front of him.

"Hall of Justice," the man said glumly. "For the show."

"What show?"

The man looked back as far as he could, turning enough for Felix to see his badly beaten face.

"The one where we die."

As they made their way to the center of town, the streets grew more crowded, more energetic. Electric anticipation hung in the air while the sun sank behind the mountains, shrouding the snow-swept city in darkness. Torches ignited here and there and cast a yellow, flickering glow over the eager faces of the locals as they ran ahead of the chain gang.

It wasn't long before Felix saw where everyone was going. It had to be the biggest building in Winter's Reach, a longhouse-style enclave built from stout cedar logs. The guards led the prisoners away from the throng of people jostling to get through the front doors, around the side and down a sharply sloping log-paved ramp.

As they marched through a wide doorway and down a short torch-lined hall, Felix almost dared to hope. If this was the Reach's courthouse, that meant he'd get a chance to talk to a real judge, a *sane* person. He could explain everything, he was sure of it. He just had to keep calm and focus on his breathing.

Breathing got harder when they shoved him into a cage with the other prisoners in the middle of a screaming auditorium.

Edging up to the rusty bars, he craned his neck to see. The cage was down in a shallow pit of sorts, about six feet lower than the rest of the hall. The wooden planks of the pit were knife-scarred and strewn with sawdust and what he hoped wasn't dried blood. All around the pit, the "court" was standing room only. Citizens of the Reach packed the bleachers, standing shoulder to shoulder and leaning against the pit railing to get a look at the new arrivals.

Cordons kept the far end of the hall free of the rabble. An empty throne of black basalt, jagged and crude, sat on a lip overlooking the pit. Behind it, doorways curtained with dangling animal furs led into parts unknown.

As if on cue, from no signal Felix could perceive, the room went silent as the grave.

One of the furs swung aside, and a woman stepped out onto the dais. Her hair was the color of ripe strawberries, under a black top hat that dangled crookedly to one side. She wore patchwork trousers and boots, along with a red-and-white striped blouse and a brass-buttoned vest accentuated with ruffles.

The crowd exploded. Felix almost covered his ears as the citizens hooted and screamed and stomped their feet on the wooden bleachers. The woman flashed a dazzling grin, waved, and walked in front of the throne. Two men took up places behind her, a gaunt Mirenzei with a neat black goatee and a giant of a man wearing a sable robe. A mask of white bone shrouded the giant's features, carved to resemble a bear's head. Felix's shoulders tensed as he remembered Kimo and Anakoni's shipboard tales about the mayor's witch. *One of the old Northmen. They say he can turn you inside out without even touching you.*

"Well, well," the woman called out as the clamor died down. "Look at you! Look at all these smiling, eager faces. I think you boys and girls are hungry for some *justice.*"

She laughed, waiting for another round of cheering to end, and stretched out one languid hand to take in the packed hall.

"You know," she said conversationally, "a man came to me last week, and he said, 'Why don't you declare yourself queen?'"

A shocked murmur rippled through the crowd. "No!" shouted someone in the back.

"I told him," she said, her voice slowly rising, "because I believe in the rule of law. I believe in the principles our great city was founded upon. Equality, unity, freedom!"

She shook her head defiantly and put her hands on her hips as applause broke out like wildfire, rolling through the room and growing fast.

"I am no queen," she said, her fervor growing like a kettle boiling over. "I am no tyrant, no dictator, no would-be *aristocrat* come to lord it over the peasants. No, I am one of you! I am Winter's Reach! *I am Veruca Barrett, Her Honor the FUCKING Mayor, and THIS IS JUSTICE NIGHT!*"

The crowd cheered and stomped hard enough to shake the cage bars. The floorboards jumping under his feet, Felix felt his heart crawl up into his throat.

Nobody here, he realized, was sane. And no one was going to help him.

Veruca tumbled into her throne and twirled one finger in the air. The cage door clanked and swung open. Two of the Coffin Boys strode in, keeping the prisoners at bay with swings of their maces, and grabbed a pair of ragged men. Up on the dais, the gaunt Mirenzei handed the mayor a furled scroll.

"Let's see," Veruca said as she unwound the scroll and gave it a once-over. "We'll start things off with a proper trial. Two men caught red-handed trying to make off with a merchant's coin box. They each say—now, get this, you'll like this part—they each say that the *other* man is the *real* thief, and that they were merely trying to stop the crime like a good citizen."

The Coffin Boys tossed a pair of rusty, dented short swords at the two men's feet. The prisoners picked them up, hesitant, their hands shaking as they clumsily raised the blades to guard themselves.

"One of them must be innocent," Veruca called out. "Let's find out who. *Fight!*"

The prisoners looked at one another, then down at their swords. Their expressions mirrored the sick churning in Felix's guts. Trial by combat was an artifact of the grisly past, outlawed a century ago in Mirenze. Here in the Reach, it was what passed for entertainment.

For a moment, Felix thought they might fight back. Turn on their captors and attack the Coffin Boys guarding the doors out of the pit. They knew it was futile, though. One of them lost his nerve first, raising his sword and charging the other prisoner with a frantic scream. The other man stepped to the side, lashed out with his sword, and sliced his enemy's guts open. The first prisoner went down and the second one pounced, bringing the sword up high and chopping it down again and again as if he were cutting firewood, drenching himself in blood and bile while the audience roared.

The prisoner staggered back. The sword dropped from his hands as he looked down at the other man's mutilated corpse. He fell to his knees and vomited on the sawdust-littered wood.

"That one looks innocent to me," Veruca said. "Let's have another round of applause for the hero of the hour! He's free to go and sin no more. Boys, clear the floor. It's gonna be a *long* night."

After they dragged the corpse out and led the near-catatonic victor to the door, the next prisoner to face judgment was an accused arsonist. No trial by combat for this one, not in a logging town. The guards stripped him of his rags in front of the crowd and left him naked on the floor with his wrists chained to his ankles. One of the guards upended a bucket of something over his squirming body, some kind of grease, as he kicked and thrashed.

Then they opened the side door and let in the wolves.

Felix closed his eyes, rested his forehead against the cell bars, and waited for the screaming to end.

Gardener, I don't ask you for much. I try to be happy with what I have. But I'm praying now. Please, please get me out of this because I don't think I can do it myself.

They dragged off what was left of the arsonist's corpse and scattered more sawdust on the floor to soak up the blood.

Then they came for him.

Two of the Boys grabbed Felix by the arms and hauled him into the center of the arena under hundreds of watchful, bloodthirsty eyes. They unshackled him and stepped away. Veruca gazed down at him from her basalt throne.

"And what do we have here?" Veruca said. "A spy? An Imperial bootlicker, come to take what we have, to topple the way of life we've all fought and bled for?"

Felix tried not to cower as the crowd booed and spat curses, shaking their fists at him. "I'm innocent!" he shouted over the din.

"Oh, he's *innocent*," Veruca deadpanned to the crowd's delight. "Now that's just silly. The pit is where the guilty people go. If you were innocent, you wouldn't be down there, would you? That's simple logic."

Felix shook his head. Adrenaline coursed through his veins, desperation starving out his thoughts.

"*Coward!*" he screamed.

The hall went silent.

"You stand up there, and pass judgment," he stammered, "and have your 'boys' do all the dirty work. How about you come down here and face me yourself?"

Of all the reactions he might have expected, snickering and cruel laughter from the crowd wasn't one of them. Then came the faint rhythmic scraping of feet on the bleachers and the rustle of hundreds of hands lightly clapping in unison.

Veruca looked out across the audience, her mouth agape, one hand pressed to her heart.

"What is this?" she said. "You can't possibly mean…oh, but you do!"

The rhythm grew louder. Scrapes became stomps and the audience's clapping became a three-hit beat in time with the crowd's rising chant.

"*Ve-ru-CA! Ve-ru-CA!*"

"You heartless beasts," she pouted in mock dismay as she rose from her throne. "You can't mean that you want your beloved mayor, your beloved, sweet, fragile flower of a mayor to commit an act of *violence*, do you? Well! I have only one thing to say to *that*."

The crowd hushed. She stretched out the moment, slowly breaking into a grin.

"Have to give the people what they want," she cried and leaped down into the pit as the room shook under a thunderous cheer. She landed in a catlike crouch, stood, and eyed Felix like a hungry lioness who'd spotted a stray gazelle.

"*Knives*," she shouted, and held up her open hand.

Two serrated knives, bone-handled and polished to a deadly sheen, sailed through the air. She caught one, snatching it by the handle and holding it aloft for the crowd's approval. The other knife chunked into the floorboards at Felix's feet.

Veruca sauntered close, lowering her voice into a deadly hiss.

"You know, I might have let you off with a whipping and a brand, and sent you home with your tail between your legs as a message to your bosses. But you challenge *me*? In *my* house? In front of *my* kids? Now I *really* have to hurt you."

"Please," Felix stammered, "you don't understand."

"Pick up the knife, Imperial. Let's give this crowd a show. You wanted me? You've *got* me."

CHAPTER TWENTY-TWO

Livia's rooms, for the time being, had become the heart of the counter-conspiracy. Her walk-in closet—already almost empty, given the little interest she had in expanding her wardrobe—soon sported a small bench for notes, a stool to hold an oil lamp, and a board of cork that Rimiggiu nailed to the stucco wall. Livia scrutinized the board and tacked up a length of blue yarn between a pair of parchment scraps.

"This is Cardinal Accorsi's inner circle," she said, tracing yarn connections as Rimiggiu watched in silence. "Cavalcante has been his man for years, and everyone knows it. I'm pretty sure Accorsi has some dirt on him. De Luca...well, De Luca's an opportunist slug. He votes with the winning team, but there's no real loyalty there. As for Herzog, he's a wild card. He's a distant cousin of the emperor, and his loyalty to the government comes before his loyalty to the Church."

Rimiggiu shook his head. "The real wild card is Dante Uccello. My man in Accorsi's house confirmed that bounty hunters have been sent to Winter's Reach to retrieve him. Accorsi is working with a merchant named Terenzio Ruggeri. Ruggeri is influential in Mirenze. Council of Nine."

"Uccello. I know that name. He was exiled from Mirenze years ago, wasn't he?"

"He spoke out against the Banco Marchetti's influence on Mirenze's government," Rimiggiu said. "Irritated them enough that Lodovico's father pulled strings to get him accused of treason and sent into exile. He's got a noose waiting for him if he ever goes home again."

"Marchetti," Livia mused, staring at the corkboard. "Again. Everything comes back to Lodovico Marchetti. Whatever he's planning with Carlo involves imports from the east, we know that much, but what's

Cardinal Accorsi's angle? Dante Uccello has never been involved in the Church. He doesn't have any familial connections to the College of Cardinals that I know of, and whatever political pull he used to have is long gone. He's washed up."

Out in the parlor, a key rattled in the lock. Livia's shoulders tensed until she heard familiar footsteps and Amadeo's voice.

"It's me," he called out as he came into the bedroom. "We have a problem."

Rimiggiu arched an eyebrow. Amadeo joined them in the closet, lugging a heavy leather-bound book under one arm.

"I know," the priest said, "obviously. But now we have a bigger problem. The Order of St. Friedrich is a consecrated knighthood. Members have to undergo a limited form of seminary training. I was making small talk with one of the knights, trying to get a read on him. He told me that he'd been trained at the Seminary of the Scroll in Kohn, under Father Gruenewald, two years ago. Then I asked another knight the same question. Kohn, under Father Gruenewald, two years ago. Want to guess what the third one I asked told me?"

"It is possible," Rimiggiu said. "Those men may have come into the order together and trained together."

Amadeo opened the book and flipped through the onionskin pages almost fast enough to tear them. He scanned down a row of minuscule type with his fingertip, under a wood block engraving of a monastery.

"It sounded wrong to me. Like they were reciting something they had been told to memorize. I spent the afternoon searching through the papal library, reading up on the Order of St. Friedrich. Know what I found?"

"Something unpleasant?" Livia said.

"Someone didn't do their homework," Amadeo said, pointing to the entry. "Max Gruenewald, senior instructor at the Seminary of the Scroll. Problem is he's dead. Withering Pox got him four years ago. When they cooked up their story, they must have been working with old information."

Livia frowned. "So we have fifty armed men occupying my father's home. They weren't really sent by the emperor—"

"And they're not knights at all," Amadeo said grimly. "They're impostors. I've sent a courier to the order's chapterhouse, but it's all the way out in Stourgardt. We'll be waiting a while for a response. In the meantime, watch yourselves. Oh, and Lodovico just showed up. Sister Columba said he spent all of five minutes with the Holy Father, paid his respects, and then headed straight for Carlo's office."

"Not being very subtle about it," Livia mused. "He must feel safe. What if we make things a little more complicated?"

Rimiggiu tilted his head.

Livia gestured to the corkboard. "We know Cardinal Accorsi has his own scheme brewing, and we know he wants Amadeo's support. Why don't we give it to him?"

"What he wants can't be much better than what Carlo and Lodovico want," Amadeo said. "Besides, there is no chance he'd suddenly believe I want to work with him, after our last discussion on the subject."

"You can sell it. Just go and…well, be honest, in a roundabout way. Express your misgivings about the goings-on around here, and use that to justify your turn of heart. Accorsi can butt heads with Lodovico and my brother, while keeping us out of it. Create enough friction and one of them will give their hand away."

"Making your enemies fight," Rimiggiu said with the faintest of approving smiles. "A time-honored technique."

Livia nodded. "That will also put one of us in Accorsi's inner circle, which should help us to work out *his* game."

Amadeo took a deep breath.

"All right. I'll do it. The College is in session, so I'll try to catch him as soon as they're done with the evening meetings."

For her part, Livia knew how she could learn more about the impostors occupying her father's home. It would have to wait, though, until Rimiggiu and Amadeo left. When it came to certain matters, she was still very much a conspiracy of one.

#

"Miss Owl is very smart," read Squirrel's cramped and uneven handwriting, littered with misspellings. *"She says everywon wears masks all the time, but we are just honest about it. Other people's real faces are hard to see, but there is a trick for that. It is called the Red Looking Glass and it will let you peek behind everyone's mask to see the true person underneathe."*

Livia knelt at her bedside with the book resting on her naked thighs. Trickles of blood ran down her whip-ravaged back. The pain helped her to focus, to hover above the pit of temptation, to stay pure of heart. *Purity. Faithfulness. Love.*

It was such a simple little spell. Some gestures, some words, two drops of blood—the caster's blood, even, not from a sacrifice. Compared to some of the nightmares she'd read about in Squirrel's notebook, it was almost benign.

Almost.

I can't believe I'm even considering this, she scolded herself. *That's exactly how these things begin. Something small, something harmless. Gardener's love, Livia, that's how this Miss Owl got Squirrel started in the first place!*

But still, she wasn't Squirrel, was she? It made her think of a bottle of wine. On her nocturnal visits to the Alms District, she often came across desolate souls forced to the gutter by their craving for the grape. The love of drink took over their lives and drove out everything else. She, on the other hand, could have a glass of wine with dinner and be perfectly content. Livia didn't understand why some people could drink in moderation and others couldn't stop until the bottle was drained to its dregs, but it was undeniably true.

Could it be the same with witchcraft?

I have a genuine need, she told herself, reasoning through it. *A very specific use for this one specific spell. I am not doing it for power or vanity or any selfish reason. This is to help my friends and my faith.*

She reached over and took a sewing needle from the top of her nightstand.

Another thought swam up from the depths of her mind.

You always knew you were going to jump in the water. Otherwise, why spend so much time dangling your toes over it?

She read over the instructions, then reread to be sure. Her heartbeat pounded in her ears.

"Stir yr. blood to the brink to raise the power, while intoning the words. Miss Owl spelled each one for me so that I would get them right."

Livia had gleaned a lot of context from the rest of Squirrel's book. Techniques like how to pitch her voice for an incantation, or the easiest way to "stir the blood." Sitting naked on her bedroom floor, she set down the book and needle and closed her eyes.

She caressed her body in all the places where she liked to be touched. She stroked the curve of her neck and shoulder, the side of her hip, fingers sliding like silken petals across her stomach, nails lightly grazing her thigh. She took her time, stoking the slowly growing fire in her belly, until she was ready. Then she eased her fingertips down, into the valley between her thighs. Livia bit her bottom lip against a sudden surge of pleasure.

She opened her eyes, focused on Miss Owl's words, and began the incantation.

"*Dromadei,*" she whispered, her breath hitching as her fingers hastened. "*Yilcatarius, dromadei fex, dromadei quen isten...*"

The words were nonsense to Livia, but they still swirled inside her heat-fevered mind, taking on invisible but whirling life in the air around her. As her intensity grew, it was as if her voice had taken on the role of a second organ, with every exhalation of breath and every roll of her tongue drawing pleasure as forcefully as her fingers did below.

The words came faster now, rhythmic and driving, spilling from her hungry lips. She came closer to the edge, cresting, burning, then yanked her hand away and snatched up the sewing needle. She struck quick and deep into the pad of her index finger. With her wounded finger dangling above her face and the chant at a crescendo, she leaned her head back and squeezed a drop of blood into each eye.

A wave of power shot through Livia's body like a stroke of lightning and knocked her flat to the floor. Every muscle, every bone, even her blood felt like it was vibrating to the tune of some cosmic dance. When she forced herself up, the room spun around her so fast it sent her stomach lurching. She looked over and caught a glimpse of her reflection in the full-length wardrobe mirror.

Crimson eyes stared back at her.

They weren't just blood-splashed. Her eyes were gone, pupils and irises obliterated under a flat glaze of baleful red like the eyes of some foul insect. A surge of panic washed over her, but it receded just as quickly when an instinct—half thought, half a wordless spiritual understanding—chased it away.

No one will notice. Only you can see.

She moved slowly, like a woman lost in a dream, and dressed with numb and trembling fingers.

She'd gotten drunk once when she was younger. This reminded her of that night, the feeling after three glasses of wine, when everything felt fuzzy around the edges. She didn't think, just watched quietly as she moved through a world turned to the consistency of molasses.

She stepped out of her suite. A wolf stood at the end of the hall.

No, she thought as she choked back a scream. *A man with a wolf's head.*

He stood like a statue, sheathed sword on his hip, draped in the armor of the Order of St. Friedrich. His face, though, was a drooling monstrosity. Half wolf and half man, with jagged teeth jutting from a misshapen snout. His yellow eyes followed her as she approached.

It's just an illusion, she told herself, fighting to keep her shaking legs under control. *It's just a man, not a monster. Walk past him, nod, and smile. Don't let on that anything is wrong.*

"I raped a woman in the streets of Ferlonde," he said as she walked past.

She froze, taking a halting step away, bumping into the wall. He spoke again, and she noticed that his words didn't line up with the movement of his muzzle. The sound was a little too deep, too echoing and off-kilter.

"I cut her throat while she screamed," he said.

"W-*what*?" Livia said, pressing her back to the wall.

The wolf head blinked. "I asked if there was anything I could fetch for you. Are you all right, ma'am? You seem a little pale."

"Just...just a bit of stomach upset," she said. "It's nothing. Thank you."

"If you need anything at all," the wolf said, "let me know. We're here to serve."

More wolves lurked in the scribal hallways, leering as she passed, muzzles rotten and bloody. She wanted to turn back—she'd seen enough—but she knew there was one more truth to witness.

She headed for her brother's office.

Under the veil of the spell, Carlo was a corpulent and tumor-ridden toad with eyes gone glassy and blind. Gold rings dripped from greasy, clutching fingers as he tossed back a swig of wine from a crystal glass. He wheezed and giggled. Across the desk, a hooded cobra in black velvet reached out with razor-nailed fingers.

"Another glass," the serpent hissed in a twisted parody of Lodovico Marchetti's voice.

"I should know better," her brother chortled, and let his guest refill the glass to the top. Wine sloshed across the desk, running to the floor in rivulets and staining the rug.

"You really should," Lodovico agreed, then twisted his head toward the doorway. Carlo followed his gaze with pale, almost sightless eyes.

"Witches burn," Lodovico hissed, a spear of accusation aimed at Livia's heart. Carlo flashed an idiot grin and waved his bloated, stubby arms.

"Sis! Come join us for a drink!"

"No," she said, stumbling backward. "No."

She turned and ran, charging blindly down the hallway with tears welling in her scarlet eyes. She found herself in her father's audience chamber. The throne sat silent and empty, but knots of courtiers and petitioners still gathered and whispered under the towering arches.

Distorted and feral faces turned her way. Leprous fingers clutched at the air, perpetually needy, snatching at anything they could reach. She held her skirts as she ran past them, head bowed, trying to block it all out.

"Miss Livia!" Columba said, grabbing her shoulders as they nearly collided. "You're white as a sheet! What's wrong?"

Inches away, the sister had the face of a desiccated corpse. Livia could see the diseases that ravaged Columba's body in the shape of maggots bristling under her leathery skin, just as she could see every secret hatred and every guilty lust the elderly woman had ever harbored in her heart.

Livia twisted out of her grip, wide-eyed and panicked. "I'm…I'm fine! I'm fine. I just need…I just need to lie down."

She backed away, turned, and ran. She didn't stop running until she was back in her suite with the door shut and locked, leaning against it as if to keep all the nightmares of the world at bay.

Livia fell to her knees and doubled over. She pressed her hands against her eyes as droplets of blood leaked out from between her fingers and spattered the floorboards.

"Miss Owl helped me to work the trick," Squirrel had written at the end of her day's lesson, *"and took me to the marketplace. She said I needed to see the people of this town as they really are, so I would understand things better.*

"I hate them. I hate them all.
"They deserve everything we do to them."

CHAPTER TWENTY-THREE

Mari rubbed Werner's back as he coughed wetly into his fist. She'd taken him straight to an inn that catered to the merchant crowd and paid extra for a room with a hearth and a door that locked. The warmth of a fresh fire chased the endless winter away and put a little color in Werner's ashen cheeks.

"I'll be fine," he said in the wake of another coughing fit. "You know me, I'm a warhorse. Just need to catch my breath."

"I know," she said.

A knock sounded at the door. Mari gestured for Werner to stay by the fire as she got up to answer it. An exhausted-looking courier stood in the hall, dressed in threadbare livery. He gasped like he'd just run two miles in the snow without stopping.

"Her Honor the Mayor will be happy to meet with you," he said, pausing to gulp down a breath. "At her estate, after tonight's show. Your attendance at Justice Night is requested."

"Not interested. I'll be at her home at ten bells."

The courier winced. "She told me you'd say that."

He handed her a folded scrap of parchment. Mari unfolded it and tilted her head at the flowery, graceful script.

If I don't see your cute ass cheering in the bleachers tonight, don't bother coming to my house after. Respect my town's traditions. Hugs and kisses, V.

"Well, of course she has an angle," she told Werner after sending the courier away. "She always does. Maybe she just wants to size us up from a distance. For all she knows, we're here with a contract for *her* head."

"I don't like it," Werner said.

"I have to go. If we want any chance of getting Uccello without a fight, I have to go."

"You mean 'we.'"

"I mean 'I,'" Mari said. "You need to sit by the fire and rest."

"Mari, no. I'm not sending you to deal with that woman alone—"

She stoked the fire, waking up pale embers, and adjusted her belt. Her batons rested lightly on her hips.

"Push yourself and you'll get sicker," she said. "Which means we could be stuck here, if you aren't well enough for the voyage back. I don't *want* to be stuck here. Rest."

"You're not going to take no for an answer, are you?" he said with a faint, tired smile. "Stubborn."

"Learned it from you," Mari said.

By the time she reached the Hall of Justice, the line at the doors snaked halfway around the building. She fell in with the locals, looking as ragged as them in her patchwork leathers and torn cloak, and waited patiently as the line inched its way forward.

Inside, it was standing room only. She worked her way through the crowd to get as close to the lip of the pit as she could, someplace with a clear view of the platform and basalt throne on the opposite side. More specifically, somewhere Veruca could see *her* and know she'd done as the letter commanded.

The crowd exploded as Veruca took the dais, flanked by her attendants. Mari's eyes narrowed, taking in the older Mirenzei with the black goatee. It was Dante Uccello, happily holding the scroll of executions and atrocities out for the mayor's reading pleasure. He didn't take any notice of Mari, but Veruca did, flashing a hungry smile meant just for her. The huge man in the bone mask spotted her too. He stared, unblinking, as though she was the only other person in the room.

With a wince of guilt, she understood why. The Witch of Kettle Sands had worn a mask like his. He knew exactly who she was.

Then the show began, and her silent introspection quickly turned to disgust. She slipped her hand into her pouch and curled her fingers around her brooch, praying over the beggar's moon and trying to tune out the agonized screams with the serenity of purpose.

"And what do we have here?" Veruca said. "A spy?"

Felix?

Her heart sank as she looked down at her traveling companion. Then he called Veruca out, and Mari felt sick. She knew what was coming next.

At the mayor's goading, Felix bent down and tugged his knife free from the floorboards. He held it like a rank amateur, waving it in front of him in a too-tight grip as if it were a magic wand and he was trying to banish an evil spirit. Veruca lunged in, feinted left, spun on one heel, and kicked his hand hard enough to fracture bones. Felix's knife went flying. So did he, hitting the boards on his belly as a second kick buckled one of his legs.

Veruca landed hard on his back with one bent knee and twisted his arm behind him. Mari leaned against the railing, fighting the urge to run to Felix's defense. One look around the room was enough to tell her it was a suicide mission. Forget the Coffin Boys—the crowd itself would tear her to pieces for ruining their fun. She couldn't fight those odds.

Veruca looked up to the audience as she brandished her serrated knife. "You know what the problem with these Imperial dogs is? They just don't *listen!*"

She reached down, grinning like a hyena, and sawed off Felix's left ear. He kicked and screamed, but she pinned him down under her knee as her knife's razor teeth chewed through flesh and cartilage. Felix's agonized howls rang out over the cheers.

Mari's fists clenched.

Veruca rose, keeping one boot firmly planted on Felix's back, pinning him like a bug while he groaned and clutched at the ragged lump of gore where his ear had been. The frenzied crowd shouted and hammered the floorboards with their feet. Veruca looked up, pointed into a random part of the bleachers with the tip of her knife, and hurled the severed ear toward the crowd as a grisly souvenir. An entire wedge of spectators went down in a heap, pummeling each other as they tried to grab hold of it.

"So I guess he won't need *that*," Veruca said. "Now then, it's the people's choice: what comes off next? The other ear? His nose? Or do we go straight for his high-and-mighty Imperial cock?"

"*Enough!*" Mari roared. She leaped over the railing and down into the pit.

The crowd fell silent.

Veruca blinked. She stepped off Felix, walking over to Mari. Felix squirmed on his side, fetal now, his face a contorted mask of pain as his wound gushed blood onto the sawdust.

"Welcome home," Veruca said softly, for Mari's ears alone. "Nice entrance."

"This man is innocent," Mari said. "I sailed here with him. I know him. He's no spy."

"Huh," Veruca said, glancing back at Felix. "Well, that's a letdown. At least it's good theater. What are you doing here, Renault?"

Mari nodded up toward the platform. Dante Uccello looked back down at her. His expression was a blank slate.

"Bounty on Uccello. Not from the Mirenzei. Friends of his in the Church. They want to help clear his name."

Veruca shrugged. "Well, he's mine now. Unless you could do a little something for me first?"

Mari stared at her.

"Captain Zhou," Veruca murmured, "self-styled pirate king. He's shitting up my port and flouting my authority. I don't want to go at him head-on because he's got too many friends who'll come looking for payback. You're nicely deniable, though. Kill him for me?"

"You know I don't take death contracts," Mari said. "I'm a hunter, not an assassin. And before we talk business, I want this man bandaged and set free."

Veruca looked between Mari and Felix. A sly smile curled her lips.

"How about a friendly wager?" she said.

"Name it."

"My kids need a good show. So we fight for it. If you lose, you promise to take care of Zhou for me. You don't have to kill him, just get rid of him. I'm sure he's got a list of bounties as long as my arm, so capture him and sell him to somebody. As long as he becomes someone else's problem, I'm happy. If you win, on the other hand? I'll stand aside and let you take Uccello, with my blessings."

Nothing was ever that simple with Veruca, but Mari held her reservations in check. She looked over at Felix. "And him?"

Veruca shrugged. "I'll have my boys patch him up and put him on the next boat home. That one's on me."

Bracing for the catch, Mari nodded firmly.

"Agreed."

Veruca waved over a pair of guards and whispered instructions. They hauled up Felix by his arms, dragging the pale and groaning man out through the side door. Then the mayor threw out her arms to address the curious, murmuring crowd.

"Boys and girls, have I got a treat for you tonight! You know her, you hate her, some of you are hiding from her right this very minute. It's the prodigal daughter of Winter's Reach, *Mari Renault!*"

Mari stood there, chin raised, as the crowd hurled epithets and abuse from their perches and shook the room with their stomping feet. Veruca waved them into silence.

"Now this lady, she knows the law," Veruca called out. "In a trial by combat, the defendant is allowed to choose a champion. So, standing in for the One-Eared Wonder, tonight you get to see a *real* fighter strut her stuff."

This, they liked better. Mari still didn't move. Her expression was carved from stone.

"Of course, the law is the law. And the law says that if *he* gets a champion, *I* get a champion. Now I want to hear you scream—but not as much as this guy does! Put your hands together for *the Mangler!*"

Veruca ran to the edge of the pit, grabbed a dangling rope, and scurried back up to her platform. The arena door slammed open. The figure that lurched into the pit towered over Mari by a good two feet. Gaunt and deathly pale, he wore only a ragged pair of pants held up with a rope looped around his waist—all the better to show off skin decorated with jagged, wiry tattoos from his forehead to the tips of his toes. He curled back his spiderweb-inked lips to bare a toothless snarl.

The Mangler's weapon of choice, dragging behind him on the floorboards, was an iron-headed sledgehammer.

Should have seen this coming, Mari thought. She rolled her neck and her shoulders, feeling joints pop, and drew her fighting batons as she bounced from foot to foot to loosen up. Above them, Veruca dropped into her throne and clapped her hands in giddy anticipation.

The Mangler's biceps flexed under scarred and tattooed skin as he hefted the hammer with both hands. He let out a feral roar, more animal than man, and charged. He was fast, faster than he had any right to be as he swung the hammer wide. Mari threw herself to the right, hit the ground, and rolled as the brick of iron whistled over her head.

Lots of scarring, Mari thought, her mind racing as she studied the man. *Been in more than his fair share of fights. Not a finesse fighter. Relies on brute strength. Watch his reach.*

The Mangler turned, recovering from his missed swing, and Mari lunged. She lashed a baton across his lower back, aiming for his kidneys. His expression didn't change as he whirled around and slammed the butt of the hammer into her face. One of her bottom teeth cracked and her lip split open, flooding her mouth with the taste of hot blood. She stumbled, blinded by the sudden rush of white-hot pain, and he raised the hammer high. She jumped back just in time. The hammer came thundering down onto the floorboards and buried itself in a pit of splintered wood.

He bent forward, trying to tug the hammer free, and she darted in to take a swing at his head. The baton cracked against his skull, but she might as well have been hitting him with a feather for all the effect it had.

She jogged backward, opening up some distance, and spat blood onto the sawdust.

Offense is his defense, she thought. *All that scarring. Doesn't care if he gets cut up as long as he can beat his opponent down. Eyes slightly dilated, doesn't react to pain...he's been drugged. I could break half his bones and he wouldn't yield.*

She sheathed one of her batons and held the other one loosely, judging distance and speed, making a dozen instinctive calculations all at once. She backed up toward the wall of the pit.

He raised the hammer and ran toward her like a juggernaut of iron doom. She met him halfway. Running toward him at full speed, she waited until he let loose with the hammer, committing to the swing—and threw her legs out, landing with a thump and sliding across the bloody sawdust. Her momentum carried her under the hammer's arc and right past his legs, giving her a split-second window to swing her baton square into his knee. The cartilage of his kneecap made a satisfying crunch under the lacquered wood, and he fell to all fours as his leg gave out.

She didn't waste a second, jumping up and mounting his back. She grabbed the baton with both hands, bringing it over his head and across his neck, then yanking back hard. He flailed and thrashed, trying to throw her off, but she held on with every last ounce of strength. Finally, with a strangled wheeze, the Mangler crashed like a bull with its throat slit.

Mari checked his pulse. She'd only intended to choke him out, not crush his trachea, but she wasn't sure how much damage she'd done. She felt a weak throbbing under her fingertips. Good.

The crowd wasn't sure if they loved her or hated her. Nobody liked seeing a hometown hero lose, but they'd gotten the violence they came for. Under a shower of mingled catcalls and jeers, Mari walked through the side door without a word and left the arena behind.

CHAPTER TWENTY-FOUR

Mari stood on the snowy, dark street outside Veruca's mansion. Orange lights burned behind frost-glazed windows.

This should have been the easy part. Most of the people they hunted had prison bars or a noose waiting for them at the end of the line. Dante Uccello, on the other hand, had friends, warmth, and money in his immediate future.

Of course, Mari thought, *that assumes everyone keeps their hands above the table.*

She knocked on the front door.

Mari expected a servant to answer or maybe one of Veruca's guards. Instead, the door swung open and she found herself looking up at the man in the bear mask. Her stomach clenched.

"Veruca," she said, refusing to make eye contact.

He stood aside and gestured for her to come in. The mayor lived more comfortably than most of her subjects. Mari wondered if, back in the Reach's prison-colony days, this had been the warden's house. Candle sconces lit the hallway, casting shifting shadows across green-and-silver-striped wallpaper. A carpeted runner lined the floorboards, stretching off into the dark. The masked man walked deeper into the house, and Mari followed. He raised one muscular arm, showing ornate knot-work tattoos in winter blue as his sleeve slid back, and pointed to a closed door at the end of the hall.

A strange thumping sound accompanied by the rhythmic creaking of wood echoed from behind Veruca's door. Mari knocked.

"Enter!" Veruca called out, sounding breathless.

The nearly naked man stretched out on the mayor's desk was a bit of a surprise. He wore bits and pieces of his armor, the rest of it strewn across the burgundy carpet. With layered skirts hiked up around her hips, Veruca rode him hard and fast, dragging her fingernails down his chest fiercely enough to leave scarlet welts.

"Close," she hissed, "the *door*, Renault."

Mari closed the door. She stood awkwardly at the edge of the room.

"What are you looking at?" Veruca said. "You want to get in here and make this a proper threesome?"

The man clenched her waist, bucking his hips to meet her rocking, his grunts growing more labored and hoarse.

Mari shook her head. "No."

"Good," Veruca said, slapping the man's chest. "I'm not into girls, and he's going to be useless in about ten seconds."

It only took him five. The mayor sighed as the man let out a strangled gasp, his entire body going rigid and then sagging limply against the desk. She slid off him, smoothed her skirts, and patted his shoulder.

"Well, that did absolutely nothing for me, so great job. Back to work, stud."

Red-faced, the guard gathered up the fallen scraps of clothing and armor, dressing as quickly as he could.

"I'm here for Uccello," Mari said.

"Why are you in such a hurry? We should have a drink, get caught up on old times."

"Uccello," she said.

The guard slipped past her, mouthing an apology. Mari shut the door behind him.

"You seem uncomfortable all of a sudden," Veruca said, languidly stretching her arms above her head. "What, you've never seen a cock before? You're blushing like a schoolgirl."

"Uccello. Please."

Veruca leaned close, craning her neck, making an exaggerated study of Mari's face.

"Are you...? You are! Oh fuck me sideways, the dreaded Mari Renault is a *virgin*. All the time I've known you, how did I never twig to that? Don't you worry, Auntie Veruca's going to fix you up proper. One of my boys, he's hung like a baby carrot and likes to cuddle, but that's what you want for your very first time. Once you're broken in good and proper, I'll throw you a real party. Honestly, it'll be my pleasure. No need to thank me."

"Veruca," Mari said, taking a deep breath, "we had an agreement. I lived up to my end, and I played your little game. Now give me Dante Uccello."

"Can't. I sold him."

Mari blinked.

"You *what?*"

Veruca shrugged, wandering across the office, smart enough to stay out of reach. She paused under an oil portrait of herself, larger than life and framed in hammered copper.

"Sold him. About an hour ago. Well, gave him away, really. I sent Dante to deliver a tribute of gold to Captain Zhou along with a sealed envelope. The letter inside the envelope said 'And also, please keep this one as a slave, with my compliments.'"

"We had a *deal*, Veruca."

She looked wounded. "Which I lived up to. My exact words were that I'd stand aside and let you take Uccello, with my blessings. I never said I'd *give* him to you, or ensure he was somewhere you could easily get at him. Just that I wouldn't *stop* you."

"Zhou," Mari said, "the man you wanted me to kill. The one I would have had to take care of if I'd lost the fight."

"And now you'll probably have to deal with him anyway, given that Dante's locked up on his ship. Funny how that turned out, isn't it?"

Mari seethed, glaring daggers at Veruca. Her hand edged toward the baton on her belt, then pulled away as she counted under her breath and shoved the anger down into the dark pit in her stomach. Veruca shook her head.

"You're upset," she said, seeming almost contrite.

Mari didn't say a word. Veruca leaned back against her desk, splaying her palms on the polished wood.

"I rule a city that cannot be ruled," Veruca said. "Every hour of every day, a sword hangs over my head, suspended by the thinnest of strings. There are wolves at the door, and if I show the slightest weakness, the tiniest crack in my armor, they'll tear me to pieces. Do you know what it's like to live under that kind of pressure?"

"Why are you telling me this?" Mari asked. Veruca pushed away from the desk and sauntered toward her.

"Because I think you understand. Holding onto the reins in this town means using every resource I have. Bread and circuses, fear and discipline, the occasional show of gleeful violence to prove I know how to kick a little ass. That's what I do: find resources and use them. I'm a leader."

"You're a tyrant."

"You say that like it matters. The truth is these savages *want* a dictator. They take comfort in knowing there's a person at the top who has all the answers, someone who's ruthless enough to protect this city against all comers. A leader. You, though? You aren't a leader. You're what every leader needs."

Mari stared at her, silent. Veruca closed the gap between them.

"Do you know what I think, Mari? I think you're a purebred war dog. I think you're happy that way, because you don't know any other way to live. You're a weapon. Finely forged and built for speed." She reached out and trailed the tip of her index finger along Mari's stony jaw. "I can't see a weapon like that and not want to wield it against my enemies. It's just how I am."

"You're reprehensible," Mari said.

Veruca's hand slid down to Mari's shoulder. She leaned close enough that the tips of their noses brushed.

"And you," Veruca whispered before taking a step back, "were the finest of the Coffin Boys."

"That was another life. I'm not...like that anymore. I'm a better person now."

"You're a survivor. Just like me. We could be good for each other, you know. Come work for me. Not in the rank and file, no. Be my enforcer. My right hand. My very own hunting dog. Maybe I'd keep you on a leash. I think you'd enjoy that, wouldn't you?"

"I'm going to get Uccello," Mari said. "And then I'm leaving."

"You'll be back. When you realize there is nowhere else in this world that suits you, that you *need* the Reach, you'll be back. For now, I suppose there's only thing left to say."

Mari glared. Veruca moved up against her, intimate as a lover, brushing her lips against Mari's earlobe.

"Good doggy," she whispered. "Go fetch."

A knock echoed at the door. Veruca stepped away from Mari, turned, and opened it. The giant in the bear mask stood outside, grimly silent.

"Bear," Veruca said.

"Mayor," he replied. "We need to talk. When...*that* leaves."

"I'm leaving now," Mari said. "Oh, Veruca? While you're feeling smug about tricking me, there's something you should know. That man you almost killed really was Felix Rossini, of the Banco Rossini. He was here to make you a deal for the use of your alum mines. He would have poured gold into your pocket for doing absolutely nothing. So that's a nice opportunity you just squandered."

Veruca shook her head, confused. "What alum mines?"

"In the mountains. He told me about the old records, from when the Reach was a prison. They've been left dormant for decades now."

Mari's gaze flicked toward Bear. The fingers of the witch's left hand did a strange, twitching jerk, like a puppeteer making a marionette dance. Veruca rubbed at her temple, wincing, and shook her head again.

"If we had mines here, they wouldn't be dormant. Believe me, I could use the money. Your little friend was mistaken."

"Right," Mari said slowly. "He must have been."

"Good luck out there," Veruca said. "Come back soon."

Bear led Mari out.

Please don't talk to me, she thought on their way to the front door. *Please just don't—*

"So," he rumbled, his hand pausing on the doorknob. "Renault."

She tensed, waiting for the inevitable.

"Hunt any witches lately?" he asked.

"No."

Bear turned to face Mari, standing between her and the door.

"Really?" he said. "Because I hear you're good at it."

"I didn't come here for a fight," she said.

He crossed his beefy arms. "No. You don't like fair fights, do you? You like ambushing thirteen-year-old girls and knocking them out cold."

She grimaced. Shook her head.

"I shouldn't…I shouldn't have taken that job. I didn't realize how it would end. If I could go back and do it all again—"

"You mean you didn't realize she'd get a twenty-minute trial followed by, oh, forty minutes of being slowly roasted to death? A trial where she was bound and gagged, I hear. Wasn't allowed to speak a single word in her own defense."

"No," she said firmly, "I *didn't*. If I'd known how panicked those people were, how desperate they were, I'd never have left a prisoner in their hands. I made a mistake—"

"She was innocent," he said.

The words died in her mouth. She stared up at him, frozen.

"The girl was innocent," he repeated. "Well, not completely. I mean, she did steal Squirrel's mask. Had no idea what she'd found, I imagine. Some kind of curio she could peddle for a handful of silver. If only she could have known, hmm? That she'd be tortured to death for it."

Mari's mouth opened and closed, wordless. Bear tilted his head.

"Oh. But look at you, Renault. You already knew it in your heart, didn't you? You just never had confirmation before. There was always the chance, the tiny chance, that your hands were clean. But now you know for sure."

He leaned in close. His pale blue eyes burned like stars behind his bone mask.

"You are a murderer, Renault. You murdered an innocent child. They did the burning, but you're the one who lit the torches."

He stood up straight.

"So in case you're worried about retaliation," he said, "don't be, because you've never actually harmed a member of my coven. As for Squirrel, well, she left town two days before you even started looking for her. Shall I give her your regards?"

Mari's hands clenched at her sides. Her short nails dug into the meat of her palms, hard enough to leave little ragged half-moon welts.

Bear stood aside. He held open the front door for her, gesturing out into the frozen night.

"Have a safe trip back, Renault. And...happy hunting."

Mari held her back straight and her chin high as she walked away. She made it as far as the end of the street. Out of sight, alone in the snow, she slumped against the wall of a crumbling stone house and buried her face in her hands.

CHAPTER TWENTY-FIVE

By tradition, the College of Cardinals convened in the cavernous underhalls beneath the papal estate. Corridors hived off from the great council auditorium and led to smaller conference rooms, meeting nooks, and baths, all appointed in a gala of ivory, marble, and gold leaf.

Cardinal Accorsi commandeered one of the smaller, more intimate parlors, well off the beaten path. He'd been surprised when Amadeo came to him, requesting a meeting, but there was an urgency in the priest's voice he couldn't deny. Now, as they sat on two divans with a full pot of tea going cold on the table between them, Marcello knew he'd been right to hear him out.

"That's a strong accusation to make," Marcello said evenly. He sat back, keeping a watchful eye on his companion. Every irregular breath, every twitch at the corner of Amadeo's eye, Marcello filed and cataloged with the skill of a lifetime spent reading people's motives. So far, everything the priest had said came across as sincere.

"I'm not making an accusation," Amadeo said, "just telling you what I've uncovered. If you have a rational explanation, believe me, I'd love to hear it. I'd be so happy to be wrong right now."

The steel trap of Marcello's mind turned slowly. Considering, weighing, discarding, and sorting every piece of evidence into neat little bins. Outside, leaden footsteps clunked on the marble as one of the visiting knights made his hourly patrol.

Suddenly, Marcello jumped to his feet and yanked open the parlor door. The knight—a younger man, towheaded and not quite filling out his armor—froze, startled.

"You there," the cardinal said. "Settle a bet for us, would you?"

"We're...not allowed to gamble, sir," the knight said.

"No, no, nothing sinful, just a dispute between friends. One of your colleagues was telling us that a handful of you graduated together from the Seminary of the Scroll in Stourgardt, is that right?"

The knight started to nod, then caught himself. "It's in Kohn, sir."

Marcello slapped his forehead. "Of course! Sorry. You see, I was only there once, about four years ago on a speaking tour. We were just talking about good old Father Gruenewald. Did he ever stop wearing that terrible wig? The big fluffy one that didn't even match his eyebrows?"

The knight relaxed, his expression mirroring Marcello's friendly smile. "No, sir, still wearing it."

"Ah, that poor man. I suppose nobody ever told him how it looked. Let's hope you and I have better friends in our old age, eh?"

"Yes, sir!"

Marcello waved and shut the door. When he turned back to Amadeo, his smile had vanished.

"I knew Gruenewald," he said. "Not intimately, but well enough to know he was a brother of the Eastern tradition. They cut their hair in a tonsure as a mark of their ordination. No wigs. Also, my first little slip about the location of the seminary: I mentioned Stourgardt since that's where his alleged chapterhouse is. You would think he'd find that worthy of comment, if in fact he remembered where he was supposed to hail from."

"You see?" Amadeo said.

"I see an effect, but we're lacking a cause. Was it Carlo and Lodovico's intent to deprive the estate of its proper guard? To place impostors under their control? Or both? Let's assume both. This is about control."

"Or violence."

"Violence *is* control," Marcello said. "They're here for the succession hearings, then. They'll be poised to flex their muscle if we offer a challenge against Carlo's claim to the papacy. How *much* they're willing to flex—and how far they're willing to go—is the real question."

Amadeo knotted his fingers together in his lap, anxiously eyeing the closed door. "How far do you think?"

"I may have a way to determine that. Leave it to me. For now, go back to your duties. I'll contact you when I need you. And...Amadeo? You made the right choice, coming to me with this. Your loyalty will not be forgotten."

#

As he prowled the halls of the estate alone, Marcello tried not to feel insulted. *Instead of trying diplomacy, you bring the makings of a coup? Seriously, Carlo. For shame. Of course, when all you have is a hammer, everything looks like a nail...*

But how far would Carlo and his wealthy patron push if they didn't get their way? Intimidation was one thing—Marcello could rally the cardinals and spin that back against them with the grace of a ballerina—but all bets were off if they had murder on their minds.

By the time he reached the council auditorium, he'd worked out a plan to test their resolve.

Six flights of velvet-cushioned seats curled around a white Verinian marble podium, all illuminated under a great crystal chandelier. Each concentric circle of seats rose up above the ones before it, like some baroque artist's dream of a filigreed soup bowl. The College was between sessions, so only a few green-sashed cardinals and their aides lingered in the chamber.

"Cardinal?" called out a doughy young man in an aide's white cassock, "Sir! Cardinal, sir?"

Marcello flashed a smile and walked over to greet him.

"Goffredo," he said and clasped the young man's arms. The smile disappeared as soon as Marcello pulled him to the side, out of earshot. "Not in public, son. We've talked about this."

"Right," Goffredo said, wincing. "I'm sorry, I know. I was just so excited. I've got information for you!"

Marcello nodded, pretending to believe him. Cardinal Blumenthal controlled a voting bloc almost as big as his own, and Goffredo was his junior aide. For the past month, he'd also been Marcello's pet, feeding him information about Blumenthal's meetings and plans.

That was what Marcello was supposed to think, anyway. In reality, he'd twigged to their game five minutes after Goffredo made the first approach. He'd confirmed his suspicions by sending some secret allies to meet with Blumenthal, then comparing the real conversations to what Goffredo reported back. Blumenthal had the aide relaying absolute garbage, sprinkled with lies intended to steer Marcello down a losing road.

I've played that game myself, Marcello thought. *Problem is you sent an amateur.*

"Time for that later," he told the aide. "You've been doing good work for me, Goffredo. I think it's time I brought you into my full confidence and trusted you with something big."

The poor lad was almost drooling. "I'm ready to help, any way I can. Just name it."

"We can't talk here. It's too dangerous. In town, just off the Via del Rege, there's a small walled garden. Meet me there tonight. Midnight."

Goffredo's head bobbed like a metronome.

Taking his leave, the cardinal stopped into one of the scribal offices and borrowed a sheet of vellum, an envelope, and a quill. He hummed a happy tune as he wrote out a short note, sealed it with a blob of wax, and addressed it with a flourish.

"For Knight-Captain Weiss. Confidential."

The knights were being quartered in the former guards' barracks, a stout wooden fort beside the stables on the east lawn. Too many eyes on it, and too open an approach. Instead Marcello went down to the kitchens and found the young son of one of the cooks.

"And there's another two of these waiting for you when you return," he said, handing the boy the letter and a pair of copper coins. "Just slip it under the door and run back. If anyone asks you who gave you the letter, tell them it was one of the scribes."

He waited patiently for the boy to return. No one had stopped the lad or even noticed him dropping off the letter. So far, so good.

Marcello kept a small flat in the city, a half mile from the papal manse and rented under a false name. It was useful for meeting with people who couldn't, for whatever reason, be seen coming to visit him. After a light supper, he set off into the streets. He walked up a musty stairwell, floorboards creaking under his feet, and jiggled his key in the stiff lock until the tumblers turned.

The decor was minimal. A few cheap wooden chairs and a card table, some spare clothes in a second-hand wardrobe, and a tiny hearth for the winter months. His one concession to luxury was a queen-sized bed with glossy silk sheets the color of a summer storm. He didn't use it quite as often as when he was a younger man, but the memories always put a smile on his face.

The flat also had a lovely view of the walled garden next door. An olive tree stood in the darkness, its branches swaying in a cool night breeze. Marcello pulled a chair up to the window and sat down to wait.

Goffredo came trundling up the Via del Rege, all alone. He craned his neck over his shoulder while he walked, looking as conspicuous as a waterfall in a desert, but at this hour there was no one on the street to notice. Marcello leaned back in his chair, shrouded in shadow.

"You're a little early," he murmured to himself. "Eager boy."

Goffredo walked under a stone arch and stood beneath the spreading boughs of the olive tree. He paced, stuck his hands in his pockets, took them out again, telegraphing his nerves. Marcello didn't budge a muscle. He watched the scene below him like a cat spying on a fat little mouse.

Two men came up the street. They wore shabby tunics and hooded cloaks against the chill, looking like any pair of roughnecks out on the town, but they moved with military precision.

"Here we go," Marcello murmured. "Let's see how serious you gentlemen are."

The letter he'd written to the knights' commander had been short, simple, and to the point: *"I know who you really are. Bring one pound of gold to the garden off the Via del Rege tonight at midnight, or I'll expose you."*

The men swept under the arch and moved in on Goffredo. The doughy young man shook his head, confused, and waved his hands as he spoke. One of the disguised knights shoved him, hard, sending him stumbling back against the trunk of the olive tree. Marcello leaned closer to the window and squinted, trying to read their lips, but it was too dark: all he could make out was their rising anger and Goffredo's panic.

They drew knives and fell upon him. Goffredo went to the ground with a knight's hand clamped over his mouth. He writhed on the grass, kicking and squirming, as they stabbed him again and again. By the time they were done, his chest looked like a bloody chunk of ground beef. They left the knives sticking out of his corpse, wiped off their hands, and left without a word.

"Hmm," Marcello said. "You're *that* serious."

The news wasn't all bad. Goffredo's death would throw Cardinal Blumenthal off-balance for a few days, and it neatly resolved that little irritation. Besides, information was power, and now Marcello knew that the papal manse had been garrisoned by men who were willing to commit murder at the drop of a hat.

"Uncomfortable," he said to the empty room as he pulled his chair back to the card table, "but I'd rather be uncomfortable than ignorant any day."

He threw on a cloak and locked up behind him, setting off into the chilly night. He walked past the garden arch. In the dark, sprawled on the grass, Goffredo's mangled corpse went cold. Marcello didn't give it a second glance.

A pleasant tingle rippled through his bones and quickened his step. There was something irresistible about a good challenge. The imminent danger just added spice. As soon as Dante Uccello was in his hands, he could really get to work.

What's your game, Carlo? Force us at swordpoint to give you the throne? Arrange "accidents" for anyone who looks like they might lodge a challenge?

You have no idea what I've got planned for you.

CHAPTER TWENTY-SIX

The scent of stale incense hung in the air of the cluttered workroom. Moldering books piled high on the rough wooden tables, jostling for space alongside soot-stained brass candlesticks, knives and measuring rods, and bundles of dried herbs from the snowy forests outside Winter's Reach. Bear locked the door and pulled the curtains closed.

He took off his mask and absently rubbed the sweaty blond stubble along his lantern jaw. He knew what he had to do now, and he wasn't looking forward to it. Reporting an act of failure had gotten him exiled to this frozen hell in the first place. At least this time it wasn't *his* failure.

Bear rummaged through the mess, taking his time, and dug out a rabbit-fur pouch. Chips of blood-stained bone rattled into his open palm, each one inscribed with a skeletal rune. He crouched down on the floorboards and threw them like a gambler hoping for a perfect roll.

Adherence to duty leads an innocent toward doom, he thought, frowning as he interpreted the scatter of the runes. *But not the signifier indicating MY duty. Someone else's.*

He scooped the chips up, shook them, and took another toss. *Smile-conceals-dagger. A friend betrays. Tragedy.*

"Like I have any friends out here," he muttered, collecting the chips and putting them back in the pouch. He was too distracted to divine tonight, nothing but gibberish from the runes. Time to quit stalling.

In the middle of the workroom, surrounded by chalk circles etched across the grainy wood, a brass bowl stood upon a low wooden pedestal. Cold, stagnant water filled the basin, with flecks of mold floating on the surface. Bear rolled up his sleeves.

The incantation came to his lips unbidden, rising more from his heart than his memory. He hissed a sibilant litany and held his bare arm out over the bowl. A hundred tiny white lines flecked his frostburned skin under the blue knotwork tattoos, each one the memory of a spell paid for in blood. He raised his white bone-handled knife in the other hand. A raw hunger grew in his belly, surging up, seizing him with almost uncontrollable need.

Then, at the crescendo of the chant, he slashed the knife across his forearm. A quick, shallow cut, just enough to make the blood well up and flow, trickling down into the water. The hunger exploded and was suddenly gone, poured into the magic, leaving him with nothing but a cold emptiness and the pain of the blade.

The water roiled as the blood hit the surface. It swirled in red ribbons, drawing designs that held him transfixed.

"Dire Mother, hear my call," he whispered.

The water turned black. An image rippled under the surface. The vision showed him a chamber of black stone, almost onyx, glistening wetly in torchlight. Bear frowned. The place was right, but where was his coven's mistress?

Slowly, from the side of the image, a bone mask leaned into view. Like his, but carved to resemble an owl. Wide eyes peered from behind the owl's pupils.

"I called to the Dire," he said, "not *you*."

"Bad news," the Owl told him. "I've decided that this is Nobody Gets What They Want Day. The celebration begins now."

"Is this about what happened in Reinsgrad? Are you still angry at me?"

The Owl blinked. "That's silly. I'm not angry at you. I hate you. That's not the same thing at all."

"We have a problem," Bear said. "A man from the Banco Rossini came to see the mayor tonight, asking about the alum mines. We must have missed a survey log or a map somewhere. It's not a local leak. As far as everyone here is concerned, the mines don't exist and never have."

"Could be a problem. Where's the banker now?"

"Gone. Veruca mistook him for an Imperial spy. Sent him home to Mirenze with his tail between his legs, and she cut a piece of him off for good measure. He won't be back."

The Owl raised a gloved finger and wagged it at him. "Don't be shortsighted. Bankers smelling money are like sharks smelling blood. Just less honest about their appetites. You know, you could protect the mines even better with the Brittle Cowl Trick. Oh, but wait. That's a technique from the Third Aerie. You can't use those, can you?"

He gritted his teeth and forced himself to take a deep breath before he answered her.

"You know perfectly well that I can't."

"That won't do! I'll tell you what: to ease the bad feelings between us, I will be *happy* to teach you. Just let me know as soon as you've started menstruating and we can begin."

Up until that moment, Bear had planned to keep the rest of his news close to his hip, hoping for a chance to turn it to his advantage. Now he couldn't resist the chance to ruffle her feathers.

"Something else," he said. "Renault was here."

The Owl fell silent. She stared at him.

Now it was Bear's turn to smile. "She had a bounty on Dante Uccello. Some of his friends in the Church want to take him into safe harbor while they fight his treason charges. Want to hear something funny? I decided to tweak her a little, tried to convince her that Squirrel was just some innocent kid who stole one of our masks and got burned for it. *She already believes it.* I think she's been torturing herself mad over it."

"Then she doesn't have Squirrel's—" the Owl started to say, then caught herself. Her eyes turned to ice behind the mask. "Never mind. She doesn't know what torture is, yet. Where is she now?"

"Going to collect Uccello at the docks. Veruca sold him to some pirates she wants dead. Figures Renault will do the job for free. Want me to chase her down, arrange an accident?"

"No," the Owl said. "Squirrel was my apprentice. Vengeance is my right. No one touches her until I'm ready. As far as the issue with the mines goes, I'm putting Mouse on it. She's already in Mirenze."

"Mouse? She's barely blooded. Why not use Worm and Shrike? They're the best trackers we..." Bear's voice trailed off as he answered his own question. "...because you're going to send them after Renault."

The Owl just blinked at him and tilted her head to one side, as if he'd announced his discovery that water was wet.

"Do you think," he said, "maybe we should put our best people to work on a problem that could affect the entire coven, instead of serving your personal vendetta?"

"No."

He waited, wondering if she was going to follow up with an explanation. She didn't.

"I expect you'll relay all of this to the Dire," he said. "You know, I've been doing really good work out here. And I've learned my lesson. Don't you think it's time I was allowed to come home?"

The Owl threw back her head and let out a screeching cackle. He stood with his fists clenched at his sides, waiting until her hysterical laughter faded into soft, trembling giggles.

"No," she abruptly said and poked her finger at him. The water in the bowl burbled and the image shattered, gone in a heartbeat.

Bear sighed and dug around on his shelves for a roll of gauze to wind around his cut. Dribbles of dried blood caked his wrist and palm, but the sting was gone. His mind kept wandering back to the Owl's one slip.

Then she doesn't have Squirrel's—

What could Renault have that would prove Squirrel was a witch? He almost dropped the gauze as the answer came to him.

Her book of spells.

The Owl assumed Renault had taken the girl's book as a trophy. Obviously she hadn't, which meant writings belonging to the coven were out there somewhere, floating in the wild for anyone to read. Squirrel was the Owl's apprentice. That made her responsible for the cleanup.

Two questions, he thought as his lips curled in a grim smile. *One, how can I use this against her?*

Two, who DOES have the book?

CHAPTER TWENTY-SEVEN

Only a handful of lights still shone in the harbor of Winter's Reach, hooded lanterns dangling from poles at the end of each dock. Trade ships and crab boats slept through the night under the blanket of a gentle, drifting snow.

Mari stood at the end of the boardwalk and looked out at the silhouette of Captain Zhou's galleon, the *Cruel Jest*. Even at this hour, patrols walked the upper deck and kept a sharp watch on the pirate's property. Mari frowned.

They'd see anyone creeping up the gangplank. Swimming around the side of the ship and climbing up the hard way? Not in this cold. Maybe a ruse would work, claiming to be another courier from Veruca. That could get her close enough to strike. If she could take out the sentries on the top deck without raising an alarm...

"There are over eighty pirates on that ship," said a man's cultured voice at her back. Mari spun on her heel. Dante Uccello stood in a patch of scrub, his gaunt frame shrouded in a woolen horseman's cape. He held a light crossbow in his left hand, aimed at her heart.

"Bloodthirsty bastards, too," he said. "Were you really going to take them head-on? I've heard of you, Renault. You've got quite the reputation. I just didn't think you were suicidal."

"I have a duty," Mari said.

"A duty to your purse. How much are the Marchettis paying you?"

"Veruca didn't tell you? I'm not working for them. I was hired by Terenzio Ruggeri to take you to Cardinal Accorsi. He wants to help you. He thinks he can get the treason charges overturned."

Dante chuckled. "Ruggeri's an old friend, but a cardinal? Atheists make few friends in cathedrals, and the Church has never been a great fan of my work. Try again."

"Ruggeri seemed to think," Mari said, "you have some information that he and the cardinal can make money with."

"That sounds marginally more believable."

"You said you've heard of me?"

"I like to know who might be dragging me to the gallows," Dante said. "Besides, Veruca has talked about you once or twice."

"Then you know I don't lie."

"*Everybody* lies," Dante said. The crossbow in his hand held its aim unwaveringly. The steel bolt glistened, wet with snowflakes.

"I don't. My word of honor: I've been hired to bring you to the Holy City, safe and unharmed. All you have to do is hear the cardinal out."

"And if I don't like what he has to say?"

Mari shrugged. "None of my business."

"I'm keeping my weapon," he said.

"Long as you aren't pointing it at me."

"That's fair," he said.

She nodded at the crossbow. "Starting now."

Dante lowered his weapon. He unwound the tension from the bow with a tiny crank and unloaded the bolt.

"One question," Mari said.

"Oh, why aren't I on the boat right now, being buggered by the good captain and his lusty crew?" Dante smiled and reached into his pocket. With a flick of his wrist, he unfurled Veruca's letter to Zhou. "Because I'm not stupid enough to deliver a sealed letter to a man whom the mayor wants dead, roughly twenty minutes after I find out there's a bounty hunter in town come to claim me. Veruca Barrett is the most dangerous woman I've ever met, but she's too impulsive for her own good. She learned nothing from me. As for the coffer of 'tribute' money I was supposed to deliver to Zhou…well, I'll just call it a severance package."

"We should leave," Mari said.

"Agreed. I've worn out my welcome in Winter's Reach. I assume you've arranged transportation?"

"It was eaten."

Dante leaned in, as if he wasn't sure he'd heard her correctly. Then he stroked his neat black goatee as he thought it over. An impish gleam touched his eyes.

"You're a risk-taker by trade," he said. "Up for doing something a little dangerous?"

"Such as?"

Dante looked out across the sleepy harbor.

"We already have passage booked, and the ship leaves in about an hour," he said. "Our new captain just doesn't know it yet."

Mari shrugged. "Let's go get my partner."

#

"If this is a joke," Captain Zhou said, arching one slender black eyebrow, "it's a poor one."

Benegali riches adorned the captain's stateroom, with olive and black silks draping the walls and a tiger-skin rug laid out over the floorboards. Musky incense swirled in the air. Zhou leaned back behind his strategy table, resting wrists heavy with golden bangles on the pitted wood, and stared dubiously at Mari, Werner, and Dante. Behind them, five hard-bitten sailors stood between the new arrivals and the only way out.

"Not in the slightest," Dante said, nodding to the open brass casket on the table. "That payment should be more than adequate to carry us to Verinia. Where, unless I mistake your comings and goings, you'd be headed next anyway."

Zhou stroked his wiry beard, braided into two tails and wound with strips of green silk ribbon.

"Think you're forgetting something," he said.

"Do tell," Dante said, with the air of someone who already saw the question coming.

Zhou dipped his hands into the open casket, letting the silver coins trickle through his fingers like water.

"Veruca was going to give me this money anyway, *and* you along with it."

"Right," Dante said. "And Signorina Renault and Signore Holst were going to kill you and take it all back. Don't forget that part."

The sailors snickered. Zhou gave Mari a long, appraising stare. She stared back, unblinking, until he looked away.

"Maybe yes, maybe no," Zhou said. "That was before you told us the whole plan. So what's to stop us from gutting you all right here and keeping the money?"

One of the sailors moved up behind Mari, grinning. Her eyes flicked to the left as she heard his footsteps, but she didn't move.

"Or we could hang onto 'em for a while," the sailor slurred, his breath rotten with cheap wine. He reached around and groped Mari's breast through her patchwork leathers. "This one could be—"

She spun on one heel and drove her knee up between his legs. As he pitched forward, the breath gusting from his lungs, she grabbed him by the hair and smashed his forehead against the captain's table. Blood spurted and he crumpled to the tiger-skin rug, groaning, cupping his hands over his face.

"No touching," Mari said.

Zhou let out a surprised bark of laughter. His eyes lit up with glee.

"What's to stop you?" Dante said. "Satisfaction."

Zhou nodded. "I'm listening."

"The mayor just tried to have you killed."

"Cost of business," the captain said. "I don't like it, but what can I do?"

"Humiliate her." Dante leaned in, resting his manicured fingernails on the strategy table. "Think about it: her plan's already been derailed, but what could make your survival even sweeter? Take her money as the payment to ferry us to safety. Instead of all of us being her pawns, *none of us will be*."

Zhou slouched back in his chair. He stroked his beard with sharp, dirt-encrusted fingernails.

"That'd tweak her nose," he said.

"She'll be *furious*," Dante said, "and she'll know that we must have told you all about her little murder-by-proxy game. That means she won't dare try it again anytime soon. She doesn't want to attack you in the open, and she won't risk doing it from the shadows. You'll be able to come and go from Winter's Reach as you please."

"An insult she can't avenge," Zhou mused. "Only thing better than putting an enemy in the ground is letting 'em live to hate you. All right. I'm sold. But we take you to Verinia and no farther. And you'll work for your supper. The *Cruel Jest* ain't no damned pleasure cruise."

Dante smiled. "I don't think any of us will have a problem with that."

CHAPTER TWENTY-EIGHT

Felix drifted in and out of consciousness. When he was awake, his world was dark and cold and damp, punctuated by throbbing pain. It felt like the tip of a frozen icepick was driving itself into the lump of mangled tissue that used to be his left ear. Someone had tied a strip of filthy, ragged linen around his head to cover the wound.

He wasn't sure how long he'd floated between drowsy wakefulness and sleep. Nightmares eagerly waited for him in both worlds, wrapping their skeletal arms around him and celebrating his downfall. Awake for the moment, he sat in a dark and icy cargo hold. The ship rose up and dropped hard on a sudden swell of water, making his empty stomach lurch. Dried bile stained Felix's shirt, but he couldn't remember when he'd thrown up. Ropes bound his waist and legs to the bench he'd been abandoned upon, presumably to make sure he didn't tumble over and hurt himself.

A lantern's feeble glow painted the hold flickering yellow as a grizzled man trundled down the steps. He grabbed Felix's jaw and forced his head to one side, tugged up the bandage to look at his wound, nodded, and shoved a mold-spotted chunk of hardtack into Felix's hands.

"Fever's passed," the man said. "You'll live."

"Where am I?" Felix croaked. His throat felt raw.

"Going home. Veruca paid us to ferry you back to Mirenze."

"No," he said, shaking his head weakly. "We have to go back. I have to go back. You don't understand—"

"You ain't welcome in Winter's Reach," the man said, "and you're nothin' but cargo until we make landfall. So be a good piece of cargo and shut the fuck up."

He tromped away. The trapdoor rattled shut behind him, plunging the cargo bay into darkness again.

Mirenze. Without the alum deal. Without anything to show for all his effort.

I'm mutilated, he thought, imagining Renata's horror when she laid eyes on what Veruca had done to him. For the rest of his life, he'd carry the disfigurement she'd carved into him, see the revulsion in the eyes of everyone he met. *Renata…*

And now, his one opportunity lost, there was only one way to save the Banco Rossini and keep his father from dying in a poorhouse.

Marry Aita Grimaldi.

When his spirit broke, it broke quietly. Felix sagged against the ropes and wept softly into his hands. His shoulders trembled in the dark. No one saw, and no one cared.

CHAPTER TWENTY-NINE

Amadeo woke with a scream frozen on his lips. He lay in bed, shaking, cotton sheets soaked in a cold sweat while a rainstorm pounded against the bedroom window.

His dream was a half-remembered phantasmagoria. He'd been following Livia down a hallway with bone-white walls, calling to her as she ran toward a glowing light at the end. Blood slowly guttered down the walls, rolling from the ceiling in thick, drooling rivulets. Livia stopped and turned to face him. Her eyes were blots of crimson.

"You can't save me," she said.

"I'm coming! Don't go," he'd called out. He kept running, but the floor slid backward under his feet with every step, forcing them apart.

"This is just a mask," she said and reached up to tug at the skin under her eye. The skin yielded under her fingernails, tearing to reveal the wet, glistening muscle and bone underneath.

Then he'd fallen, plummeting backward into an empty void. He saw black smoke curling in a cold and cloudless sky above the Holy City, proclaiming the death of a pope.

The image ripped away, swallowed by billowing flames. Three figures, two men and a woman, searched for an escape behind the wall of fire. Burning timbers fell and the ground shook. Amadeo looked up just as a blazing chunk of wood came plummeting down to crush him.

Then he was awake, soothed by the driving rain, trying to sort it all out in the dark. He knelt down beside his bed, shivering in his sweat-soaked nightshirt, clasped his hands tightly, and bowed his head.

"I am your servant," he said to the empty room. "Please, help me to understand the mysteries before me. Help me to protect my flock, to lead and guide them, to…"

Amadeo let his hands fall to his sides and looked up at the ceiling.

"I don't know why you show me these things," he said. "I don't understand what you want me to *do*."

He didn't get an answer. He didn't expect one. Instead, he bathed and changed into a fresh cassock, heading out to greet the morning.

He found Livia in the hall. Dark circles drooped under her eyes, and her normally pristine hair was disheveled. She greeted him with a tired wave. The dream was still fresh in his mind, that image of her bloody gaze and torn face, and he rushed over to check on her.

"Livia?" he said. "Are you all right? You look like you've barely slept."

"Just a bout of insomnia," she said. "I'll be fine."

Livia was good at many things. Lying wasn't one of them. Amadeo pretended to believe her and motioned her closer, looking back to make sure they were alone in the corridor.

"I talked to Cardinal Accorsi," he said. "He believes us about the knights. He says he's going to do some investigating."

"Good. I think we made the right choice. Accorsi is a snake, but we need a snake in our corner right now. I'm going to say good morning to Father. Coming?"

He gamely accompanied her through the papal mansion, making polite small talk when the knights were in earshot. The usual throng of courtiers and aides clustered in the audience chamber, but Benignus's ivory throne sat empty.

Livia clutched at Amadeo's arm. It was a reflex, mirroring the lurching feeling in the pit of his stomach. She yanked her hand away and mumbled an apology. Sister Columba scurried up to them.

"He's too tired to greet visitors today," the elderly woman whispered.

"Is he...?" Amadeo started to ask, then realized he didn't want to finish the question.

"I...don't know when he'll feel well enough to sit in that chair again," Columba said. She left the *or if he ever will* unspoken, but Amadeo could hear it in her voice. "But he's awake right now. And breathing."

"Can we see him?" Livia said.

"*You* aren't *visitors*. You're family," she told them. "Come on, both of you."

Two of the knights stood silently outside Benignus's bedroom. Amadeo fought to keep his face expressionless as he realized how easy it would be for the impostors to murder the helpless pope anytime they wanted.

Of course, he thought bitterly, *they don't have to. Time is the master of assassins.*

The rain hadn't let up. It lashed against the shuttered bedroom windows and left a damp chill in the air. An oil lamp on the pope's bedside table stood in for the morning sun. Dwarfed by his huge four-poster bed and buried in piled comforters, Benignus looked as frail as a sickly child. He raised his head from the pillow, just an inch or so, and curled his lips back in a trembling smile as Livia and Amadeo came into the room. Columba shut the door behind them, staying out in the hallway to guard their privacy.

"Daughter," Benignus said, reaching out his hand. Livia took it in hers, holding it gently. "Where is Carlo? Is he with you?"

Livia and Amadeo shared a glance.

"He stopped by earlier, when you were sleeping," Amadeo said. "He sat by your bedside for a while. He didn't want to disturb your rest."

"So considerate," Benignus said, eager to believe the lie. He looked toward Amadeo, but his eyes didn't seem to hold their focus. "He is a good son."

Out of the corner of his eye, Amadeo saw Livia bite down on her lip.

"He is," Amadeo said. "Is there anything we can get you, Bene? Anything we can do to make you more comfortable?"

"No, no. I just need to take a nap. Just...don't have the energy I used to. Don't worry. I'll be up in no time."

"We'll let you rest," Livia said. She laid her father's hand down by his side and let go. He closed his eyes, still smiling.

Livia stormed out of the room, her skirts swirling around her as she shoved the door open, balling her hands into fists at her sides. Amadeo ran after her.

He caught up with her in the portrait gallery, standing in the shadow of an alcove. Her arms were crossed tight over her chest, her shoulders tensed and chin tucked down, like her entire body was a cork about to explode from a bottle. She kept her eyes squeezed shut.

"Livia—" he started to say.

"Don't," Her voice quavered. "Don't tell me it's going to be all right. Don't you dare."

He reached out towards her, then pulled his hand away.

"I wouldn't lie to you."

"Good," she said.

"You can cry if you need to, you know."

Livia's eyes snapped open. He almost took a step back as she turned her glare upon him. Her eyes boiled with fury, a rage bordering on abject hate.

"I do not need," she said, "to *cry*. My father is dying. My brother is a worthless glutton who's leading this church, *my* church, down the road to ruin. And if I'd been born with a *cock* between my legs, I'd have the power to stop him, instead of being the useless daughter just waiting to be married off to some foreign aristocrat."

"Livia, I—"

Livia held up her hand. "Have you ever considered, for even a moment, the list of things I'm not allowed to do because some bitter old men say so? I can't lead a mass, can't earn the greens of a priest, let alone claim my birthright. My entire life, from the cradle to the grave, is dictated by 'traditions' and rules that *you* aren't subject to. My power was taken away from me the moment I was born a woman. So no, you do *not* get to give me *permission* to *cry*!"

"I'm sorry," Amadeo said, "I didn't mean it like that. Livia, I'm your friend. We're on the same side."

She looked away.

"You are," she said, her voice softer. "You are a good friend, Amadeo. But I'm concerned. Are you really willing to do whatever it takes?"

"Whatever it takes?"

She looked him in the eye.

"Whatever it takes to save this church," she said. "No matter what has to be done."

Amadeo felt a serpent worming its way through his guts. A low and treacherous roiling that set his teeth on edge. Still, he nodded.

"We made a pledge," he said. "I'm with you."

"Good. Now excuse me. I need to be alone."

Amadeo stood aside. She walked away without another word, chin high, eyes hard.

Marcello strolled in from the other side of the gallery, his manner so casual that Amadeo could almost believe he hadn't been eavesdropping.

"You were right," the cardinal said.

"You investigated?"

Marcello nodded. The clomping of steel boots echoed up the corridor as a patrol of knights approached. While they swept through, Marcello clasped his hands behind his back and pretended to study an oil portrait of Benignus's father.

"That piece of artwork I was thinking of buying," he said lightly. "I had it examined by an expert. Turns out it's a counterfeit."

Amadeo stood beside him and nodded, not looking back at the patrolling knights.

"That's a shame," he said. "I was hoping against hope that I was wrong."

"As was I. Still, at least now we can save our money for a better investment."

As soon as the knights were out of earshot, Marcello leaned close, his voice low and urgent.

"Don't let on. Not a hint. These men are killers."

"How do you—" Amadeo blurted loudly, then caught himself and whispered, "how do you know?"

"Best not to ask. The important thing, right now, is that you do nothing without my authorization. What was that conversation with Livia about? I heard her raising her voice."

"Nothing," Amadeo said. "Her father isn't long for the world. She's feeling the pain of it."

"Is she involved in this? Does she know anything?"

Amadeo looked over at Marcello. His instinct was to deny everything, but the cardinal always knew more than he let on. He couldn't risk being caught in a barefaced lie. He couldn't tell the truth about their compact either.

"She has suspicions about her brother and his relationship with Lodovico Marchetti. I've been telling her what I know, which isn't much."

Marcello sighed, looking up at the portrait.

"Livia is…a very headstrong young woman," the cardinal said. "Given to dangerous ideas of independence. She can't help us, only get in our way. Cut her off."

"Cut her off?" Amadeo said.

"Don't tell her anything more. Especially not our business. Simply feign ignorance and change the subject should it come up. Amadeo, we are playing for very high stakes here. I need to know my confidence is well placed. I need to know that you're my man. Mine alone."

Amadeo swallowed hard. Then he nodded.

"I'm your man," he lied.

#

Back in her suite, Livia's scourge lay abandoned on the divan, still flecked with dried specks of her blood from the night before. There was no time for the ritual today. No time for purity. She made a beeline for the chest at the foot of her bed. She burrowed through her linens and dug out Squirrel's notebook.

"Come on," she said, flipping through the pages with reckless abandon. "Tell me how to save him. Tell me how to save them all. Give me what I *need*."

It was useless. There were spells to wither crops, spells to make a corpse dance and bite, but nothing that could rescue a dying man from the ravages of time. Squirrel had been a fledgling, a novice taking her first steps into the shadows.

"*Miss Owl says the strong rule over the weak and that is nature,*" read her fumbling, scrawl, "*and that is why the sheep and cattle forbade our Art, because they cannot master it and we can. They have muscles and swords and money and they call it strength. We have will, and will is true power. Muscles wither, swords rust, money means nothing if all the bankers are dead.*"

Livia flopped back on her bedspread and pressed her knuckles against her forehead, feeling another headache coming on. She had the will, all right. She'd been born with the will to steer a nation. She just didn't know how.

Miss Owl would know what to do, Livia thought. *So would I, if I had power like hers.*

No. Absolutely not. Dabbling was one thing, and you remember how that ended. You have to stop this, Livia. It's unholy. It's wrong.

"And it probably won't even work," she said aloud, marching into her bathroom. It didn't take long to fill her porcelain washbowl and find a straight razor.

She stood in the bathroom her bare feet cold on the tiled floor. A white candle burned on a corner shelf, casting the room in pallid yellow light. She stared into the mirror hanging above her washbowl and held the razor between two fingers, like it was a serpent that might bite her. In the other, she held the notebook open to the lesson where Miss Owl taught Squirrel how to see visions through reflections. *Maybe,* Livia reasoned, *if I focus my mind on my father, the vision will show me how I can save him.*

The incantation was tongue-twisting nonsense, words she fumbled around and tripped over, but the squirming, sibilant cadence drew her in like a fish on a line. Her voice rose as the chant went on, more confident, faltering less, and with it came a gnawing sensation that burrowed down to her very bones. She felt like insects were writhing inside of her, multiplying and breeding, squeezing out every last space and aching to burst from her skin. Then, at the last word, she slashed her forearm with the razor.

Show me what I desire, she thought in a flash.

The sensation burst out on a gust of breath and was gone. She dropped the book as the sharp sting of the cut made her fingers go rigid and her teeth clench. Blood flowed. It dripped into the bowl, over the rim, pattered onto the floor and stained her bare toes. Wincing, Livia turned to the shelves at her back and grabbed a towel. She pressed the fluffy white cloth against the wound and held it tight. Tears of pain and frustration welled up in her eyes.

Stupid, she thought. *Stupid to try this in the first place, even more stupid to think I could possibly—*

"Well, hello there," said a woman's voice, behind her.

Livia's blood froze. In her clenched hand the ivory towel slowly turned crimson, drinking from her cut.

"Don't you want to say hello?" the woman asked.

Livia took a slow, deep breath. Her heart pounded against her rib cage as she turned around.

The Owl peered out from the bloody waters, eyes bright and curious behind her mask of bone.

"H-hello," Livia whispered. Her tongue felt fat and dry in her mouth, her throat parched.

"This is a nice surprise," the Owl said.

"You're Miss Owl," Livia said, fumbling for words.

"Did the mask give it away? Oh, but you know my name, and I don't know yours. That's not fair, is it?"

Livia shook her head and took a step back from the bowl. "I'm sorry. This was a mistake. I shouldn't have done this."

"I think you have something that belongs to me," the Owl said.

"I don't want it," Livia said. "Please—I don't even want it."

"I think you do. Tell me your name. I'd like to visit you. We could chat over tea."

"Gia," Livia stammered. Her mother's name was the first word that came to mind.

The masked figure wagged her gloved finger. The tiny metal talon at the tip gleamed.

"Mm-mm. It's not nice to lie to Miss Owl. Where are you? Looking behind you...that looks like a very pretty bath. Very expensive fixtures. Fine towels. Though you should replace that one on your arm. It's all soaked through."

Livia dropped the bloody towel. It landed with a wet splat on the tile. She grabbed another one from the shelf.

"Have you told anyone that you have Squirrel's notebook?" the Owl asked.

"No! No, never. Nobody knows."

"Good. That's very good. Because if anyone finds out...well, that means you're a witch, doesn't it? And witches burn."

"I am *not* a witch," Livia said. Her face was a pale ghost in the bathroom mirror.

"Tell me your name," the Owl said. Her tone was light, coaxing, but there was nothing friendly in the eyes that shone behind her mask.

Livia shook her head. "I'm sorry. I'm sorry, all right? I didn't mean to bother you. It won't happen again. I promise. I'll just...I'll just lock the book away, and I won't ever even open it—"

"But you don't want that," the Owl said gently. Livia felt her voice catch, as if an invisible hand had squeezed her throat shut.

"Let me make it easy for you," the Owl told her. "I'm going to find you. Then you and I are going to sit down and have a chat about my stolen property and what you've been doing with it. You'll tell me your name then. Or maybe I'll give you a new one. After all, I can't just call you L.S."

Livia blinked. "How…?"

The image in the basin lifted her gloved hand and pointed. Livia followed it to the clean towel pressed against her wound. Her eyes widened at the delicate twist of golden thread in one corner, dangling at the edge of her grip.

"Monogrammed towels," the Owl said. "Very classy. See you soon, L.S."

The image rippled and vanished.

Livia slumped to the blood-spattered floor. She curled her knees up against her chest, her muscles clenched tight as a steel spring, and rolled her head back.

"Don't you cry," she told herself in a ragged, hoarse voice. "Don't you fucking *dare* cry."

CHAPTER THIRTY

The first night on the *Cruel Jest*, sailing south from Winter's Reach and out of Veruca's clutches, was smooth and quiet. The Elder slumbered beneath the black waves. For now, at least, he'd eaten his fill.

The next afternoon, three of Zhou's pirates tried to corner Mari in the galley. One came away with a concussion, another with a fractured jaw and dislocated arm, and the third was smart enough to run. Werner cut him off, stumbling in on the fight, and beat the man half to death with his bare fists. Mari was willing to leave it at that, but Zhou had other ideas. One by one, the three crewmen were bound by their wrists to the mainmast, howling in pain as the first mate lashed their backs bloody with a cat-o'-nine-tails.

"This isn't for your benefit," Zhou said to Mari. He crossed his arms over his silken vest and scowled at the scene. "It's about maintaining discipline on the ship. If they're on shore leave or we've just captured a prize that didn't surrender when we ran up our colors, they can rape anyone they damn well please. *Not* on board, not on duty, and not someone paying me for safe passage. Even an animal knows not to shit where he eats."

After that, the crew didn't even look in her general direction.

Zhou hadn't been kidding about earning their supper. He kept the three of them busy. Mostly scut work, scraping down the frosty decks and scrubbing the ship from end to end, but Mari didn't mind. It was good exercise. By night she would sit out on deck and cradle her brooch in her hand, letting the small beggar's moon guide her thoughts.

"Funny, isn't it?" Dante said. She looked up and shook her head mutely. He pointed at the brooch. "We're being ferried to freedom by a band of remorseless, bloodthirsty killers, and you find time to pray."

Mari shrugged, not seeing the humor.

"So was it your father?" he said. "Or your grandfather?"

"What was?"

Dante crouched down beside her.

"Order of the Autumn Lance," he said. "That brooch you carry around. I recognize it from my military studies. They were wiped out by the Empire, no? I assume it was passed down through your family."

"No. Werner found it on his travels, before we met. He believed it would lead him to its rightful owner. Which...isn't me. Not yet."

"Not yet?"

"When I was a child," Mari said, "all I wanted, more than anything in the world, was to be a knight. All the orders in Belle Terre were disbanded, though. The Empire burned their chapterhouses, drove them underground."

"So you found a more realistic dream," Dante said.

She shook her head.

"I...forgot my dream for a while, but Werner woke me up, reminded me how I used to be. I decided that it didn't matter if the orders were gone. I would live as a knight aspirant anyway. I took the oaths, trained as hard as I could, and set out on my quest. I don't hunt criminals for money. I do it because it's a way to further the cause of justice."

"Wait," Dante said. He curled his legs, sitting down. "Wait a moment. *All* the oaths? You took vows of chastity and poverty, even though you didn't have to and you don't actually answer to anyone but yourself?"

She held up the brooch.

"I am the last squire of the Order of the Autumn Lance," she said. "And someday they'll find me, and I'll earn the right to wear this."

"And if they don't?"

"Then I will live as a knight should, nonetheless. And maybe someone after me will find this brooch on my bones, and they'll be inspired to do the same. *Veritas* is my motto. Truth, above all."

Dante ran his fingers through his hair and let out a faint, nervous chuckle.

"You do realize," he said, "that you're insane."

"Says the man who worked for Veruca Barrett."

The boat swayed gently, canvas sails crackling in a night wind. Dante laughed.

"She's a different kind of crazy. Crazy for money and power, like any politician. *That* I can understand."

"You don't understand principles?" she said.

"I don't understand empty principles or pointless oaths. Wealth can buy you the leverage to achieve your goals. Sex can…well, I don't suppose it'd make you a better knight, but it would likely make you a happier one. I'm a pragmatist."

"I know. I've read your work."

His eyes widened a bit. "You didn't strike me as a student of political philosophy."

"I like to read," Mari said. "Werner gave me one of your books once."

"Then you understand how I could work for a woman like Barrett. She's the leader the Reach needs. Her reign is hard and cruel, but that's nothing compared to the hellish nightmare that city would turn into without her. Between a choice of evils, she's the most palatable."

"A choice of evils still ends in evil."

"Yes," Dante said, "which means absolutely nothing. Politics and morality are apples and parakeets. Leadership involves compromise. Sacrificing principles in the short term to reap a long-term benefit. Taking the seedy vagaries of human nature into account. A true leader must be a tactician first and foremost, cold and calculating."

Mari looked him over. "When you sacrifice your principles, you don't magically get them back at the end of the day."

"There has never been, and never will be, a moral government. The question is whether a government is effective, and whether it is beneficial for its people."

"You don't live up to your own ideals," Mari said.

Dante smiled. "No? How do you figure?"

"You write about utilitarianism and the art of the possible. Working with the people and the resources you have, not the ones you want."

"That's right."

"Yet," she said, "when you were the captain of Mirenze's militia, you fought to have the Marchetti family dislodged from the Council of Nine. One man, crusading against the most powerful family in the city. You had to have known you couldn't win, and you knew they'd retaliate."

Dante ran a finger along his collar, looking wistful for a moment.

"And so they did, hence my current miserable condition. I did it for the city. Luigi Marchetti was both a councilman and the chair of his family bank. I think his son Lodovico has taken over the business since. Luigi was an agitator. Hated the Empire, hated the fact that Mirenze had gone from the greatest city-state in the world to a humble vassal of the holy west."

"Don't most Mirenzei feel that way?" Mari asked.

Dante nodded. "Yes. We are, however, smart enough to shut up and toe the line. Luigi wasn't. I learned through my militia contacts that he was trying to stir up support for a rebellion. It was mad. He would have gotten thousands of people killed. I couldn't expose the truth in public—just the admission that a plot existed would draw down Imperial thunder—so I hammered him on everything else I could find. Banking irregularities, rumors and scandals—half of which I made up out of whole cloth—to keep the heat on him and push the Council to take action."

"And he retaliated by accusing you of treason."

"I miscalculated," Dante said. "I'm not proud of it. I thought I had more friends than I did, and I thought I'd embarrassed the Council of Nine less than I had. So, one night, I was visited by some very somber gentlemen from the government, and we came to an arrangement."

"Arrangement?" Mari said.

"I'd done exactly what I set out to do: wake the Council up and force them to do something about the viper in their midst. I knew there would be consequences. I fully expected to sacrifice my career, but my mistake was thinking it would end with that. They warned me that treason charges would be levied the next morning. They generously gave me the night to pack what belongings I could and flee into exile."

"And Marchetti?"

Dante looked up at the night sky, as if counting the stars.

"Yes. Our arrangement. I would go into exile, never to return to the city I loved, in order to salvage the Council's public reputation. Meanwhile, well…they say Luigi Marchetti was a man haunted by demons. A fortnight after I left Mirenze, he killed himself. Drank four bottles of wine, took a hot bath, and slit his wrists. A tragedy, but with the agitator dead, the city was safe."

Mari ran her thumb over the face of the pewter brooch, thinking it over.

"Suicide," she said flatly.

Dante's smile was almost too faint to see in the dark.

"I received a letter from a dear friend of mine, after the deed was done. Said the hardest part was forcing the first bottle of wine down Luigi's throat. In the end, civic pride, confidence, and order were restored, and life in Mirenze went on."

"With you in exile, branded as a liar and a traitor."

Dante shrugged. "I'm one man. Mirenze is a city of thousands. It was a fair trade."

"Look at that," Mari said, "you have principles after all."

#

The *Cruel Jest* put in at Shepherd Bay, a sleepy Verinian town with a port built for fishing boats. Mari stood out on the deck, marveling at the feel of warm morning sunshine against her cheeks. A crisp wind ruffled her ragged hair and snapped the canvas sails, but after almost two weeks in the north, she barely noticed the chill.

"Can't say I was happy to have you lot on board," Zhou said to her, Werner, and Dante, standing at the edge of the gangplank. "Still, any other way this could have gone, I'd have profited less. Suppose I should thank you for that."

"We all profited," Dante said. "That's my favorite kind of deal."

"Well, we're square now," Zhou said, "so don't expect any special favors if you land in my sights someday. All the same, I won't be looking to cause you no harm. We'll call it a buccaneer's truce."

"What's that?" Werner said. The color was already returning to his cheeks, now that the ship was moored and land was in sight, but he still hadn't completely shaken the cough he'd picked up in the north.

Zhou stuck out his hand. "Peace until it isn't."

"Peace until it isn't," Werner agreed, clasping the pirate's hand and giving it a hard shake.

The town was still waking up as Mari, Werner, and Dante walked down its rolling dirt roads. The scent of warm, fresh-baked bread wafted out from a baker's open window. Dante leaned toward the smell and let out an exaggerated sigh.

"We're stopping there," he said. "We are having fresh bread. And pastries if they have them. With sugar. And tea. Hot tea, with leaves that have never been used before."

"Not used to roughing it?" Mari said.

"There is no virtue in denying oneself pleasure. Asceticism is a cheap substitute for character."

"Discipline makes you strong…" Mari paused, then sniffed at the air. "…but I like pastries."

Happily sated, the trio made their way to a stable at the edge of town. Dante wasted no time in requesting a coach with a trained horseman to take them to Lerautia.

"Less expensive to hire an open wagon and drive it ourselves," Mari said.

"Never you mind," Dante said. "I'm paying. Remember how I opened Veruca's letter to Captain Zhou?"

Mari nodded.

He smiled wanly. "Well, I opened the coffer, too. A few shiny pieces of gold might have found their way into my shoe before we went on board. It's a shame I didn't have more time to plan my escape. I know the combination to Veruca's safe, too. So what's your take on this Cardinal Accorsi fellow? Is he a man of honor?"

"We haven't met," Mari said. "You said Terenzio Ruggeri was an old friend, though."

"In a sense. A greedy man with predictable vices, but he has Mirenze's best interests at heart. You remember the letter I told you about? The one that mentioned forcing wine down Luigi Marchetti's throat the night he 'killed himself'?"

Mari nodded.

Dante put his hands behind his back and stretched, smiling.

"Ruggeri wrote it."

CHAPTER THIRTY-ONE

Sunlight filtered through the dusty curtains over Felix's bedroom window. Back in Rossini Hall, back to the mildewed rugs and leaky roof and walls that groaned with every stiff wind. Felix sat by the window in a rocking chair, with a wool blanket draped across his lap, and stared at nothing in particular.

He thought about getting up and pulling the curtains, so he could at least look at the back lawns. He'd been thinking about doing that, off and on, for the better part of an hour.

Albinus was kind. His father never once said, "I told you so," even if it screamed out from behind his tired eyes. He just welcomed Felix home, called Taviano to draw him a bath, and doddered off to his study to draw up the wedding plans.

Now Felix sat at the window, marinating in his failure, trying to figure out what he could possibly say to Renata. Trying to figure out how he could even face her again.

"Master Felix?" Taviano said. The butler stood on the open threshold, hesitating.

Felix let out a noncommittal murmur. Taviano walked around to the side of his chair, looking between him and the curtained window.

"Would...would you like that opened, sir?"

Another murmur. Taviano pulled the curtain aside, letting Felix look out across a dying yellow lawn wet with morning dew.

"We're all glad you're back," the butler said, "the household staff and I. And we're so sorry the trip didn't go as planned."

Felix tilted his head toward him, giving Taviano his good ear.

"I spoke with the maids," Taviano said, "and they had an idea. It's...not perfect, but they sewed this up for you."

He held out a long strip of crushed velvet in deep ochre, with brass hasps at either end.

"They realized you might not want to be seen in public. Given, that is, your condition. May I?"

Felix nodded. Taviano gently unwound his bandage. Felix felt the butler's fingers jerk with revulsion as he unveiled the scabbed-over ruin of his left ear.

"They made one for each of your good suits," the butler said. He looped the velvet around Felix's head, tucking it behind his good ear and over the wound, clasping it shut at the back. He scurried over to the wardrobe and took out one of Felix's hats, a flat, slouching cap of the same material. He fixed it on Felix's head, then turned the chair to face the full-length mirror.

Felix's look was still odd, jarring, but the twin velvets blended to make it look more like a fashion statement than the aftermath of a crime. The difference between the tailored band and the filthy, blood-stained rags he'd come home wearing was like night and day.

Doesn't make you any less mutilated, he thought.

"I daresay, sir. I think you can pull this off."

Felix chuckled. It sounded like a hitch in his breath. He reached up and patted Taviano's hand.

"Maybe so, old friend," Felix said. "Maybe so."

"I'm going to run my errands. I'll see the cook can make something extra special for dinner tonight for you. You really do need to eat, you know."

Felix nodded. He listened to Taviano's footsteps on the creaking floorboards as he backed away, then walked off down the hall.

Felix stared at his reflection.

It doesn't look so bad, dressed up like this. Maybe I'll start a trend.

His reflection's lips curled in a humorless smile. For the hundredth time he walked backward through the journey, reconstructing every day, every hour, every stray minute in his mind's eye.

Simon was the assassin. Felix was the target. That much was crystal clear. Whatever he'd done to deserve death, it was important enough to poison an entire ship—and then sink it—to make it happen.

And to think we saved that bastard from the wreck, he thought as his hands squeezed the arms of the rocking chair.

All those innocent people, dead. Just to get at him. And when even the Elder didn't swallow him down, Simon played his final hand, using his own tools and poison bottle to point the finger at Felix. Felix hung between guilt and anger, remembering the faces of the dead. If he hadn't taken that ship, the *Fairwind Muse* would still be sailing today.

It's my fault, he thought. *Captain Iona and all his men. They died because of me.*

He knew the *who*. The *why*, that was the unanswerable question. He didn't have any enemies, not the kind that would send a killer to dog his footsteps. He hadn't done anything to deserve that, as far as he knew. The mission, then? A last-ditch effort to stop the Banco Rossini from thriving.

Or, he thought, as a dark cloud brewed behind his eyes, *to stop us from threatening the alum market.*

The Banco Marchetti was the obvious suspect. Felix had met Lodovico Marchetti before, once or twice, and found him likable enough, if a bit of a braggart. He wanted to believe that the man wouldn't mingle business with murder, just as he knew that was a hopelessly naive point of view. You didn't ascend to the lofty heights of a Marchetti without stepping on a few backs along the way.

He'd have to have an inside man, Felix thought, retracing his steps. *I was discreet when I contacted Iona for passage, I didn't write ahead to the Reach. I didn't even tell my father I was going...*

The truth hit Felix like a fist to the gut.

I told Taviano.

Good old Taviano, loyal to the family longer than anyone. My tutor and confidante since I was old enough to walk. The man I trusted more than anyone in the world.

Felix's reflection changed in the mirror. Now he stared back at a face expressing one singular, absolute emotion: rage.

That son of a bitch.

He stood up from the chair.

Misery had been his companion and his shackles since he left the Reach. His failure had haunted him and weighed him down, turning his soul to lead. Now a fire simmered in his stomach, heating that lead red-hot. He couldn't change what Veruca Barrett had done to him. He couldn't change the lost deal or the arranged marriage that would tear him away from the woman he loved.

But he could get revenge.

Felix straightened his velvet cap and adjusted the ear-band, giving his reflection a nod. Then he went looking for his cloak. Before he left the house, he stopped off in his father's office, rummaging through the old man's drawers.

There it was. Second drawer down. A horn-handled hunting knife. It felt good in his hand.

The man who'd sailed to Winter's Reach didn't know the meaning of the word *revenge*. That man would never have dreamed of carrying a weapon, or planning to use it on another human being. But he wasn't that man anymore. He'd lost his ear and his pride in the Reach, but he'd taken something home with him in trade: a dark pounding in his heart that whispered the right path to follow.

He'd track down Taviano, and they'd have a nice long chat. He'd find out exactly who the butler was working for and how much he'd been paid to destroy Felix's life. He'd make Taviano take him to Simon. And then they'd all settle accounts.

It wasn't exactly scripture, but "an ear for an ear" had a nice ring to it.

CHAPTER THIRTY-TWO

Simon Koertig had a smile that wouldn't fade. Even after a week on a dusty merchant ship, working like a dog and feeling his stomach lurch with every swell of the icy waves, nothing could bring him down. He wished he'd been able to stay and see Felix's death in the arena, but watching the arrest from the shadows of the tavern and seeing him protest as the "evidence" was laid out before him had been treat enough. Assassination by government. A masterstroke.

And after all the trouble on that damned ship, he thought as he strolled through the cobblestoned streets of Mirenze, *an epic reversal of fortune. Almost like alchemy. Wait. That's what I should call my book!"The Alchemy of Death"!"The Alchemist of Death"? One or the other.*

The doorman at the Marchetti estate received him with the usual reserved politeness. Simon whistled happily as he made his way down a powder-blue corridor trimmed with white scallops, heading for Lodovico's office. He knocked twice on the closed door and let himself in without waiting for an answer.

"I'm home," he announced, "and your problems are solved."

Lodovico sat behind his desk, reading the morning's broadsheets. A glass of red wine sat at his elbow, drained to the dregs.

"Oh," he said. "Are they?"

Simon shut the door and walked over.

"Wait until I tell you how I finished off the Rossini boy. You'll be amazed."

"Not nearly so amazed," Lodovico said, turning the paper around so Simon could read it, "as I will be at the story of his miraculous resurrection."

Simon leaned in, squinting at the gothic type.

"*...return from parts unknown, but his impending marriage to the very (some say suspiciously) eligible Aita Grimaldi will be the talk of the season. This could mean big things for the ailing Banco Rossini, as they move to stand with their long-time...*"

"No," Simon said, taking a halting step backward. His smile vanished. "No, no, that's not...that's not possible!"

"And yet," Lodovico said flatly. "My man at the docks saw him come home. Somebody took a knife to his ear. Your work? After I explicitly told you I didn't want him to suffer?"

"No. You don't understand. I orchestrated *everything*! He should be dead!"

"Tell me that he at *least* didn't make the alum deal."

Simon shook his head. "There was no deal to make. I asked around while I was looking for a way back home. There aren't any mines in the Reach. Even the old-timers insisted there never were any. Rossini was on a wild goose chase."

Lodovico dropped the papers onto his desk. He held up his empty wineglass and looked at Simon expectantly. Simon blinked, then nodded and walked over to the bar, bringing back an opened bottle.

"I'll consider that a small blessing," Lodovico said, holding out his glass as Simon refilled it. "Did he see you? Does he know your face?"

Simon's grip on the bottle tightened.

"He...may have grounds for suspicion," he said.

"Gardener's blood, Simon, what were you *doing* out there? You've never slipped up like—" Lodovico paused as a knock sounded at the door.

One of the servants poked his head in and cleared his throat. "You have a visitor, sir. Shall I ask him to come back later?"

"No," Lodovico said, "I need a distraction right now. Send him in."

The servant ushered Taviano into the room, then left the three men in silence. The door clicked softly.

"What," Taviano said, his voice quavering, "did you *do*?"

Lodovico sipped his wine. "At what point did I become someone who answers to you?"

"I didn't sell you that information so you could hurt Felix," the elderly butler shouted. "He's been beaten, cut up. He's a shell of the man he used to be—"

"You still haven't answered my question," Lodovico said casually. "And for the record, he wasn't supposed to be *hurt*, just killed. I was very clear on my instructions."

Taviano's jaw trembled. He shook his head, slowly, looking from Lodovico to Simon and back.

"I never meant for anyone to get hurt," he said. "The information I sold you, it was just business. I never imagined you'd do something so monstrous with it."

"Please," Lodovico said, "do yourself a favor and stop lying. You knew that whatever I intended to do with the tidbits you've sold me over the years, it was nothing good for your precious Felix or his family. You're a traitor who sold out the Rossinis for a few extra coppers in your pocket. You're only upset because now, for once in your life, you have to face the consequences. I face them *every day*."

"Then the Gardener have mercy on your soul," Taviano breathed. "But no more. I'm done. I want out."

Simon cradled the wine bottle in his white-knuckled hands. He'd lost none of the desperate fervor in his eyes, feeling the humiliation of his failure more keenly with every passing second.

"You want out," Simon said.

"Was it you that cut him up?" Taviano turned on Simon. "What is *wrong* with you? Why wouldn't you just kill him, if you wanted him dead so badly? Do you *enjoy* hurting people?"

Lodovico leaned back behind his desk. He cradled his glass, rolling the wine around in slow, garnet-colored arcs.

"My friend here," Lodovico said, "is a bit less skilled than I once believed. My apologies."

Simon gritted his teeth.

"You want out," he repeated.

Taviano nodded firmly. "We are through. We'll just…go our separate ways. Don't try to contact me again, or I'll tell the Rossinis everything I've done and throw myself on the mercy of the court. Heavens know I deserve—"

Simon smashed the bottle over Taviano's head. The old man went down in a spray of blood and wine and glass.

"You want out?" Simon screamed as he brandished the broken neck of the bottle. He stood over Taviano and grabbed the butler by his lapels, hauling him up. Then, as the dazed man feebly tried to shove him away, Simon drove the jagged end of the bottle into his neck and chest over and over again, shrieking, "Here's your way out! *Here's your fucking way out!*"

The butler's head lolled to one side, lifeless. Simon suddenly froze, staring into Taviano's glassy, blood-spattered eyes. He blinked. He let go of the lapels. The broken bottle followed, slipping from his fingertips to thump on the rug and leave a curling trail of red droplets, merging with the spreading puddle leaking from the butler's mangled corpse.

"Well," Lodovico said after a moment of silence, "that could have gone better."

"Sorry," Simon said, staring down at the body like he wasn't quite sure if he was the killer. "I've been under a lot of stress lately."

"I see. Feeling better now?"

Simon looked over at Lodovico.

"Some. Once I kill Felix—"

"No," Lodovico said. "You'll do nothing of the kind. Felix Rossini is off-limits. With the alum deal off the table, he's barely a threat. A merger between the Rossinis and the Grimaldis isn't the end of the world, considering the next stage of our plan."

"But I *have* to," Simon said slowly, softly, as if explaining something to a child. "I've never not closed a contract. If he's not dead, it's still open. I can't live with that."

"I'm *rescinding* the contract. Right now, I need you out of sight. You need to go somewhere, take a nice holiday in the islands maybe, and fix…" He paused, then waved at Simon's bloody clothes. "…whatever *this* is. You're my right hand. I need you at your peak for when we make our next move."

"I'm fine," Simon said.

"Simon? You just smashed an elderly man's head in with a very nice bottle of Champs-Montaigne, then stabbed him to death while screaming obscenities. On my carpet."

"Oh," Simon said.

"So you understand why I'm concerned?"

"He had to go. You heard him. He threatened to confess."

"Yes," Lodovico said, "and I would have asked you to kill him. But not on my carpet, and not with a twenty-scudi bottle of wine. Now go to my vault, take out as much money as you need for a lovely time, and go someplace far away for a couple of weeks. Just be ready for the next stage of the plan."

Simon nodded slowly. "All right."

"All right. Good. But first, get rid of the body? Please? And clean the carpet before my mother comes home."

Simon trudged off to the guest rooms, looking for a rug big enough to roll Taviano's corpse up in. His head was a muddle of confused and echoing thoughts. How had everything gone so wrong? He'd snatched victory from the jaws of defeat, gotten all set to write the best chapter yet in his dead-book…and now he was a laughingstock.

Felix. The man was a curse, pure and simple.

The chapter couldn't end this way. It didn't matter what Lodovico wanted, not anymore.

Felix Rossini had to die.

CHAPTER THIRTY-THREE

Renata stared down at the broadsheet. She didn't move, didn't make a sound. Just stared. She'd come back from the market, hauling a small cartload of meat and fish for supper service at the Hen and Caber. The fishmonger had used his copy of the morning's paper to wrap up a big chunk of fresh trout. When Renata unwrapped it, pulling back the knot of twine and peeling away the thin, fish-damp paper, a name in smeared ink caught her eye.

Felix.

Most of the gossip column was too blurry to read, but all she needed was one line.

"...his impending marriage to the very (some say suspiciously) eligible Aita Grimaldi..."

She read it again, hoping she'd misunderstood, or maybe the smeared ink had changed a crucial word or two.

Then she read it again.

And again.

He didn't even tell me he was back in town, she thought.

There was only one reason he wouldn't have come straight to see her, straight to her waiting arms. He'd failed in Winter's Reach.

"Renata?"

The small voice, piping up from the other side of the cluttered kitchen, dragged Renata out of her waking nightmare. The new cook's assistant, Hedy. She was fourteen or fifteen, a thin slip of a girl with bright blond hair and wide, deep eyes that seemed almost too big for her heart-shaped face.

"Are you all right?" Hedy said. "You look..."

"Fine," Renata said. She crumpled the broadsheet in her hands, feeling fish slime smear her calloused fingers. "I'm fine. Afternoon rush isn't long off. Go...go down into the cellar and bring up one of the small casks of Oakman Fifteen, would you? There isn't much left behind the bar."

Hedy nodded obligingly, perpetually cheerful, and vanished down the cellar steps. Leaving Renata alone with her thoughts.

Is this the idea, Felix? Just leave me without a word? Let me find out this way instead?

No. That wasn't the Felix she knew. That wasn't the man she'd fallen in love with. There had to be a reason. She left the kitchen behind, storming out through the swinging doors, out through the tavern and into the street.

She couldn't be here right now. She needed fresh air and time to think.

#

Hedy hummed a happy tune as she bounced down the creaking cellar steps. Then she froze.

Even in the dark, the gloomy, musty cellar didn't scare her. There was nothing hiding in the cobwebs, no goblins lurking among the dusty and quiet racks of kegs and casks. Even still, the second her foot touched the flagstone at the bottom of the stairs, a graveyard chill tingled her spine.

"Hello?" she called out. "Is...is there anyone down here?"

The only sound was a faint rattling from the floorboards overhead.

Hedy took a deep breath, forced herself to smile, and pushed on into the cellar. She walked along the racks, squinting at engraved wood lids and trying to remember where the casks of Oakman Fifteen were kept. Then she rounded a corner and a flurry of feathers flew out of the darkness, ruffling in her face. She jumped back, choking on a scream, and bumped her shoulders against a wall of kegs.

"Boo," the Owl said, straightening her feathered cloak.

"Y-you shouldn't be down here," Hedy stammered.

"Why?"

"Because...because I'm *working*."

"Quit your job," the Owl told her. "You're going to Lerautia, on an errand for me."

Hedy swallowed hard. The girl was frozen where she stood, her fingers pressed back against the rough wooden kegs.

"You can't tell me what to do." Hedy's voice was a high-pitched whisper. "I'm not your apprentice."

Behind her mask, the Owl's voice dripped with amusement. "Mouse. Oh, Mouse, Mouse, Mouse...that's right. You're Fox's student. Where *is* he? Because he's certainly not here. Teaching you. Protecting you. Like he should be. It's not safe. You know what owls do with mice, don't you?"

"H-he had business in Murgardt. He told me to wait, and that he'd be back in a month or two."

"And he left you with a list of goals, I assume. Lessons to study? Milestones to meet? Little ways to challenge yourself?"

Hedy shook her head slowly. "No, he just said to wait, and be quiet, and he'd be back when he could."

Behind the mask, the Owl's eyes narrowed to slits.

"The Fox is your teacher, but I am your elder and you *will* obey me. Travel to Lerautia. I'm looking for a woman. She's wealthy. In her thirties, Verinian breeding, hair dark as mine but she wears it pinned up. Her initials are L.S. Also look for the name Gia. She claimed it as her own, and very quickly, suggesting it's the name of someone close to her heart."

"One woman?" Hedy said. "In the entire city."

"She has a bit of stolen knowledge. She's playing with our art, but has neither the training nor the experience to control it. I suspect she'll light up the city, for those with the eyes to see."

"I'll do my best—"

The Owl lunged at her, gripping Hedy's chin in her gloved hand and pricking her skin with the tiny metallic claws at the ends of her fingertips.

"No," she whispered. "You will succeed and be rewarded. Or you will fail, in which case you will be punished, then sent back out to try all over again, until you *do* succeed. This is a perfectly manageable task. I'll hear no excuses."

Hedy barely dared to breathe. When she managed to find her voice, all she could squeak out was, "Why me?"

"Because you're going to *die*, Mouse. Because your 'teacher' is an imbecile who doesn't deserve his own apprentice, and he's going to get you killed. Because he is *soft*, and he is making *you* soft. Until he returns, you are under my authority. I will test you. I will push you. I will make your life a living hell until you learn how to be a *proper* witch, because *I care enough to do it*!"

The Owl let go of her chin and took a step back. Hedy didn't move a muscle.

"Now tell me: when you arrive in Lerautia, what will you do? Think it out."

Hedy nodded. She bit her bottom lip and took a deep breath, working through it like a puzzle to be solved.

"She's wealthy, so she probably has servants. Servants see everything, and they love to gossip. I'll find work somewhere they congregate. A stall in the marketplace, maybe. Meanwhile I'll start putting together a list of the city's foremost families, looking for S-names. By night I can hunt. I'll use the Charm of the Siren's Echo."

"Clever girl. Be sure to make a friend, too."

"A friend?" Hedy said.

The Owl nodded. "Someone you can use as a patsy, in case anyone sniffs out what you're really up to. You can pin everything on her and disappear."

"And when I find this L.S., what do I do with her?"

"Nothing. You contact me and await my arrival. I assume the Fox has taught you the Marque of Passage?"

Hedy shook her head. "No, he says it's too difficult for me."

The Owl snorted. "It's difficult to *teach*, not difficult to *learn*. Not difficult for a clever girl like you. It should have been one of your first lessons. Find this woman for me, and I'll teach it to you myself. How does that sound? A fair reward?"

Hedy's big eyes lit up, and she smiled. "Oh, yes! I've wanted that one!"

"And now you know how to earn it."

CHAPTER THIRTY-FOUR

"Verinia is a maiden," Dante deadpanned as he craned his neck out the coach window. "And the Holy City is the jewel in her braided hair."

"You don't sound impressed," Werner said. Mari sat on the wooden bench beside him, keeping a dour eye on the opposite window. She hadn't said a word since they'd rumbled into Lerautia's outskirts twenty minutes ago and started the long, circular climb toward the city's heights.

Dante leaned back and grinned. "The heart of the Church, rising above a teeming and desperate slum. What's not to love about that? It's like they wrote one of my books for me. I wonder: on a windy day, when the good Cardinal Accorsi opens his windows, can he smell the trash on the docks?"

"Have to ask him yourself," Werner said with a nod as the horses' clopping hooves slowed to a standstill. "I think we've arrived. Mari?"

"Hmm?" she said, jolted out of her thoughts.

"You can wait outside. If you want."

Mari curled her lip like she'd smelled something foul.

"I'm not afraid of your church," she said. She clambered out of the coach, slamming the door behind her.

"Don't take this the wrong way," Dante said, "but I hope she picks a fight."

Werner just sighed and got out.

The cardinal's red-shingled villa was ringed by an ornate ironwork fence, and a white pebble path wound across a sprawling, immaculate lawn. Dante put his hands on his hips and whistled.

"And the Gardener said, 'Let there be business.' And lo, it was good."

An elderly maid greeted them at the door, ushering them into a parlor where imported woven rugs from the Oerran Caliphate warmed the white marble floors. Bookshelves filled one wall from floor to ceiling, shelves groaning upon the weight of hundreds of musty hardcovers.

They weren't kept waiting for long. Cardinal Accorsi swept in though the doorway, his forest-green stole draped around his neck and his liver-spotted hands open in welcome. He flashed a toothy smile as he descended on Dante.

"Signore Uccello! So glad to see you alive and well. The Gardener has blessed us both."

"I won't say I'm not grateful," Dante said, "but I stopped believing in altruism around the same time I stopped believing in the winter fairies that put presents on your mantle. What's your angle?"

Marcello held up a finger. "A business opportunity. A very unique one, at that. But this is something for your ears alone. You won't mind if I take care of my other guests first?"

He walked past Mari, as if she wasn't there, and handed a heavy purse of black velvet to Werner. He pulled the drawstring and took a peek. Silver coins glinted inside.

"I believe this is everything Signore Ruggeri promised you. Of course, I'll be expecting you to maintain your silence about this entire affair."

"Of course," Werner repeated, weighing the purse in his palm. He nodded his approval.

Dante clasped Werner's shoulders and kissed him on each cheek.

"I won't forget what you've done for me. If I can ever go home again, know that you will always have a friend in Mirenze."

He turned to Mari, paused a moment, then bent at the waist to offer her a courtly bow.

"Mari," Dante said, "I hope you find what you're looking for. I do know that there is *one* true knight of Belle Terre left. It was my great honor to travel with her."

Mari smiled faintly and returned the bow.

"I do believe that concludes our business," Marcello said archly, his gaze swinging between Werner, Mari, and the door. They took the hint. Outside, crossing the manicured lawn while a cool afternoon breeze ruffled their hair, Werner coughed into his fist. Mari shot a concerned look at him.

"Still?" she said.

"I'll be fine. Takes more than a shivery lung to put down an old warhorse like me. Could use something to wet my throat, though. What do you say we head down-city a bit, get out of this rarefied air and find a place to grab a bite?"

They settled on the Rusted Nail, a squat brick tavern on the edge of a great open market square. The tables were packed with a mongrel crowd, merchants and farmers and household servants taking a break from their day's labors, and Werner and Mari squeezed in at the end of the long wooden bar.

"I smell fresh bread," Mari said. "Can we get some?"

Werner patted the velvet purse on his hip, its strings tied to his belt and double-knotted. "Are you kidding me? We can get anything we want. For a month. Maybe two."

He ended up ordering a bread and cheese board, freshly churned butter, and a plate of roasted pheasant. Something about the end of a hunt always gave him a ferocious appetite.

"Two dark ales, whatever the house specialty is," he told the barmaid.

Mari nudged his shoulder and nodded across the room. He followed her gaze and added, "Make that five dark ales. Something strong."

"What are *they* doing here?" Mari said, frowning at the boisterous table in the back.

"Same thing we are? Celebrating a job well done? I'm gonna go pay my respects."

"They're not good people," Mari said flatly.

"We're bounty hunters, Mari. It might come as a shock, but being a good person isn't one of the required skills."

Werner and Butcherman Sykes went way back. They'd served in the same unit for a while, beating back the Terrai, and when the war dried up they'd both turned their hard-earned talents in the same direction. Sykes was lean as a whip and made of gristle, and Werner noticed the old meat cleaver still dangling from his rope belt.

Lydda the Hook, laughing on his left and flashing her gold teeth, looked like she'd just stepped off a pirate ship. Both her hands were just fine; her nickname came from what she did to the unlucky bastards who tried to outrun her. The other man at the table, Pig Iron, Werner only knew in passing. He was squat and bloated with a face that looked like it had met the business end of a meat tenderizer.

Werner held up his tray of tankards. "Somebody order another round?"

"Holst the Harrier!" Sykes shouted with a grin, slapping his palm against the table. "Sit your ass down and share the wealth!"

"Where have you been hiding?" Lydda asked. "And where's Her Ladyship? Finally cut her loose and start making some real money?"

"Over by the bar," Werner said. He sat down and passed out the drinks.

Pig Iron looked over toward Mari, squinted, and licked his fat lips while he raised the tankard to his mouth. "What, she don't wanna be sociable?"

Lydda snorted. "We're not her crowd, Piggy. She's *honorable*. Can't dirty her pristine lady-fingers by drinking with the likes of us."

"The three of you all running together now?" Werner said, trying to change the subject. "When did that happen?"

Sykes clinked his tankard against Werner's and leaned back. "Strength in numbers, old pal. We figured that working together, we could take on tougher jobs for bigger pay. Go after the big fish. In between runs it's pretty easy to, ah, 'supplement our income.'"

"Not *saying* we've waylaid any coaches lately," Lydda added, "but there might be a couple of noble peckerwoods on the Grey Forest Road who got so scared they needed a change of breeches."

"I'd invite you to join the fun, but..." Sykes's voice trailed off as he nodded across the room at Mari. Mari caught the look, narrowed her eyes, and turned away.

"And any other time, I wouldn't miss it for the world," Werner said, not feeling the words. "We just wrapped up a peach of a job, too. Long trip but one damn fine payday—"

"Oh, oh!" Pig Iron interrupted him. "Tell him ours! Ours is better!"

Sykes slurped his ale and chuckled. "You're gonna love this. You ever hear of this Mirenzei blue blood named Dante Uccello?"

Werner's hand clenched the dented tin handle of his tankard.

"I, uh, heard there's a price on his head, and he was sighted up north. You lot headed to Winter's Reach?"

"That's the beauty part!" Sykes said. "He's not in the Reach. He's *here*. This cardinal, some shriveled-up prune named Accorsi, he offered Uccello safe haven. Uccello's here, in town, right this very minute."

Werner narrowed his eyes. "So what's the plan? Don't tell me you're going to attack a cardinal's house. You're a heavy crew, but that's more heat than you want."

"Attack?" Lydda smirked. "Accorsi *hired* us."

Sykes clinked his tankard against hers, sloshing a rivulet of dark ale onto the table.

"I guess Uccello has some information Accorsi wants," Sykes said. "And what he *doesn't* want is the blue blood spouting off to anyone else about it. As soon as he gets what he needs, he's gonna call us in. We drag Uccello just outside town and stick a knife between his ribs. Then we chop off his head and deliver it to Mirenze. Accorsi's paying our full fee, *plus* we get to claim the half bounty for 'capturing' Uccello dead. All for doing damn near nothing! There's no work like easy work."

"Let's hear you top *that* action," Lydda told Werner. "Tell us about your big payday. How'd you do?"

Werner set his ale down. His thoughts raced as fast as his pulse. Taking a deep breath and putting on a big fake smile, he gestured wildly as he spoke.

"Okay, so it was like this. We're hunting this guy, a petty thief who stepped on the wrong toes, and we're chasing him all over Mirenze. Three times, he gives us the slip. We're tired, we're hungry, so we go to this dive by the docks to find some grub. And guess who's walking out the door as we're walking in."

"Dumb luck," Sykes said, chuckling.

"So he just stops, and I just stop, and I realize I've got the door still in my hand. So I swing it right in his face and *bam—*"

Werner swept out his arm in a pantomime. The back of his hand caught his tankard and knocked it over, sloshing dark ale across the lip of the table and onto his lap. He jumped up, cursing, wiping at the spreading stain on his trousers while the other bounty hunters went into hysterics.

"And then he pissed his pants!" Lydda cackled, pointing.

"No, no," Werner said. "*Then* I knocked him out cold on the tavern floor. Damn it, I'll be right back, going to see if the barmaid has a rag. Another round?"

Sykes tossed back the last of his drink. "You're a good man, Werner Holst."

The second Werner turned his back, his smile vanished. He strode to the bar, shouldering his way through the growing crowd, and grabbed Mari's arm as he leaned in toward her.

"We're leaving. *Now.* I'll explain on the way. Get up and casually walk to the door. I'll meet you outside."

She nodded once, curtly, got up, and slipped away. Werner ordered another round of drinks and asked for it to be carried over to the hunters' table. He waited until they were looking the other way, and then he joined Mari out on the street.

"Let's go," he said, walking fast. "It won't be long before they figure out I'm not coming back."

He repeated everything they'd told him. Mari's lips tightened in a straight line.

"How many guards did you count when we dropped Dante off?" she said.

"Two at the front doors, two in the hallways between the front door and the library. We didn't see the whole house, though. I reckon he's got twice that many."

"City militia?"

"Won't be far away," Werner said. "And Accorsi's a cardinal. They'll come running if they hear an alarm, and they'll believe whatever he tells 'em."

"Your hunter friends?"

"Figure we've got a ten-minute head start," he said.

"So," Mari said, "two against eight, three experienced hunters on our heels, and we could end up in a fight with the entire city militia."

Werner nodded. "Sounds about right."

Mari picked up her pace, staring dead ahead.

"I don't like this city anyway. Let's go get our bounty back."

CHAPTER THIRTY-FIVE

Felix found Taviano across the street from the greengrocer's. The sight of a gathering crowd and the sound of murmurs and gasps drew him across the rain-damp cobblestones. He stood up on his toes and peered over onlookers' shoulders to get a better look.

The butler was dead, stabbed and dumped in a blind alley. Someone had taken Felix's revenge for him—and cut off any ties to Taviano's secret master.

"Did anyone see it?" he said. He could barely muster the force to breathe, let alone speak. The wet air had gone thin.

A woman in a calico dress, clutching a wicker shopping basket to her chest, shook her head. "A terrible thing, sir. A terrible thing. I was the first to see him. Just...lyin' there like that. The constables should be here soon enough."

Felix shoved his feelings aside, forcing himself to focus on the grisly sight. No blood on the cobblestones. Taviano's murder had happened somewhere else. Load the body into a coach, pull up to the alley, shove him out when no one was looking...it would have taken no time at all.

His shoulders sagged as he turned and walked away. There didn't seem to be any point in staying. A block later, walking numbly, he realized which way his feet had pointed him.

The Hen and Caber, he thought. *It's time. I've got to face Renata. Show her what Winter's Reach made of me.*

Lost in thought, he barely noticed the black coach rattling alongside him, pulled by a pair of shaggy horses in a slow trot.

"Felix," called a voice from inside. The coach stopped.

The door swung wide, and Basilio Grimaldi gestured toward him. "Get in. We need to talk."

"So," Basilio said as the coach started to roll, "headed for the docks, are we? Bit of an early dinner at the Hen and Caber?"

Sitting on the bench opposite him, Felix felt sick. *How does he know that? WHY does he know that?*

"I'll take your silence as a yes," Basilio said. "Felix, you need to understand something about me. I despise small talk. Straight answers, honesty, the unvarnished truth, these are the traits I admire in a man. You were planning on leaving my daughter standing at the altar, weren't you?"

Felix almost denied it, then caught himself. Half of him had planned to tell Renata it was over. Half had wanted to take her and go, run away together tonight, and damn the consequences.

No. More than half. He'd do whatever it took to save his family, but breaking up with Renata wasn't on the table. Looking back, finally honest with himself, he realized it had *never* been on the table.

He and Renata were going to Kettle Sands and starting their new life together. No matter what.

"No," he told Basilio, finding a quiet confidence. "I would have disappeared long before the wedding, to spare Aita that humiliation. I also intended to write her a personal apology to make sure she knew my leaving wasn't about her."

Basilio nodded. "You are an honorable man, Felix. I like you. Always have. What do you know about the Council of Nine?"

"My grandfather was a member, before the Banco Rossini fell on hard times. They used to advise the Duke of Mirenze, though I'm told the duke was more a puppet than anything else. They basically ran the city."

"We still do, just…more quietly than before. A chair has opened up, a rare occurrence, and I want it filled by a man who will vote exactly how I wish. That man is you."

"Vote how *you* wish," Felix repeated.

"You will marry my daughter, I will use my influence to reverse your family's downfall and make you worthy of the nomination, and you will take your position on the Council as your grandfather's legacy. I will make you a very wealthy man, Felix, and you will show your gratitude by obeying me without question. Is that clear?"

"Not even a little," Felix said, shaking his head. "Why would I do that?"

"I told you. Because I'll make you wealthy. Oh, right. You need more incentive. How about Renata?"

"I can't be with Renata if I marry Aita."

Basilio leaned back. His gaze was cold, reptilian as he studied Felix.

"I'm talking about Renata's continued safety."

Felix blinked. "Signore Grimaldi…are you threatening me?"

"No. I'm threatening her. Listen and understand, as this is very important: Renata is safe so long as you do exactly as you're told. If you disobey, she will be abducted. She will be taken to the basement of a secluded house on the East End, where a number of unfriendly men will spend the next few days doing extremely unpleasant things to her. Then she will be released, possibly missing a tiny piece or two. And this will happen to her again, and again, and *again*, until you learn your place."

Felix stared at him. The coach rumbled along.

His hand was in his belt pouch, fingers closing over the handle of his father's knife before he realized he was doing it.

"Felix," Basilio said softly, glancing down at the pouch, "is that a weapon in your hand?"

Felix nodded. "Yes, Signore Grimaldi. Yes, it is."

"You never struck me as the kind of person who carries a blade."

"I've been to Winter's Reach," Felix said. It felt like the only way he could explain it.

Basilio leaned forward on the bench, closer to him.

"Have you ever taken a man's life, Felix?"

"Not yet," he said.

"The first time," Basilio said, giving him a fatherly smile, "is very difficult. Harder than you think."

"And the second time?"

"Much easier. You understand now, that wool is not my family's only business. Yes?"

"Yes," Felix whispered. The horn hilt of the knife felt smooth against the pad of his thumb.

"Your father. Your brother and his wife. Renata. These are the people who will suffer from now on, if you choose to be foolish. These are the people who will be rewarded, if you choose to cooperate. You're a responsible man. A man of honor. Now prove it to me."

Felix's forced himself to unclench his fingers from the knife, one at a time. Slowly, still staring into Basilio's eyes, he rested his empty hand on his lap.

"I believe," Basilio said, "that one day, we will look back and laugh about this moment. And here's your stop."

He rapped sharply on the roof of the coach. The driver, from his perch above the cab, reined the horses to a stop. Felix opened the door and stepped out onto a street nowhere near the docks. The mist in the air had turned to a light, cold rain. The stump of his ear ached under its velvet wrap.

"Smile," Basilio said from the coach window. "You're about to marry a beautiful woman and come into great wealth. Most people would call this a lucky day."

CHAPTER THIRTY-SIX

"Perhaps the old ducal archive in Mirenze," Dante said. He sat on the velvet sofa in Cardinal Accorsi's library, cradling a cut-crystal glass filled with whiskey in the palm of his hand.

"No, no, we've searched there," Marcello said as he paced the marble floor. "Trace your father's last few years before he died. Think back. Did he keep any spare apartments? Did he have a mistress, perhaps?"

"I'm sure he had five or six. It would help if you would explain exactly what you're looking for."

"Some private correspondence, extremely pri—"

A thundering crash echoed from down the hallway. One of the cardinal's guards ran into the room, wide-eyed and breathless, and slammed the library door shut behind him.

"Sir! That man, the guest from earlier today, he's going on a rampage in the foyer!"

"Werner?" Dante said, looking from the guard to Marcello.

"Rollo's gone out the back," the guard said. "Going to raise the district watch. Stay here. I'll keep you safe."

Shouts sounded behind the library door, punctuated by heavy thuds and the sounds of breaking furniture. The guard drew a thin-bladed rapier from his belt and pressed his back against the door, drenched in panic-sweat.

He shouldn't have been worried about the door.

Mari hit the library window in a sprint, tucking her head down and hitting it at full speed. The glass exploded, spraying glittering shards through the air as she flew into the room, hit the ground, rolled on her shoulder, and came up in a kneeling crouch. One of her batons flung free from her outstretched hand, whipping toward the hapless guard and slamming into his forehead. He crumpled and dropped, out cold.

She jumped up, charged Marcello, and grabbed his collar faster than a viper's bite. Flecks of broken glass hung in her ragged hair, catching the sunlight like diamonds. She shoved the cardinal up against the wall of books, making the shelves rattle, and spoke in a feral growl.

"*You lied.*"

"What's going on?" Dante said, looking between them.

"He was going to kill you once he got what he wanted," Mari snapped. "More hunters coming. Bad people."

"That's—that's," Marcello stammered, "that's preposterous. Just look at her, this girl is clearly deranged."

Dante shook his head. "Perhaps, cardinal, but in my experience, she's the nobler sort of deranged. You, on the other hand? Perfectly sane but not very trustworthy, are you?"

The library door flung open at a kick from Werner's boot. He was red-faced and panting, and fresh blood flecked his tunic and the ends of his fighting staff. None of it appeared to be his.

"Bells ringing out back," he panted. "Constabulary's on the way. We have to go."

Mari shoved Marcello to the floor, stalked across the room, and crouched beside the unconscious guard to pick up her fallen baton. Dante shrugged and downed the rest of his whiskey in one gulp, tossing the glass over his shoulder. It shattered on the floor.

He offered a bow to Marcello and said, "Cardinal, your whiskey was exquisite, but your hospitality was abominable. I shall not be inviting you to Solstice dinner, and you can consider yourself officially removed from my gifting list."

Mari was already gone, clambering out the window and onto the lawn. Dante followed her.

"Perfectly good door back here," Werner called out. Then he sighed, slung his staff over his shoulder, and followed them.

Now they could hear the bells, clanging loudly at the far end of the rolling lawns, calling all swords to defend the cardinal's villa. Dante pointed east, breaking into a run.

"This way, to the stables. I'm sure the good cardinal won't mind lending us a horse or three. Only the best for his guests, after all!"

"Do you know what he wanted?" Werner wheezed, still trying to catch his breath from the fight.

Dante grinned like a wolf. "Not exactly. The important thing is, whatever he's looking for, I know *exactly* where it is."

#

Constables burst into the ruined library, boots crunching on broken glass. Firm, reverent hands hoisted Marcello to his feet and brushed the dirt from his cassock. They asked if he was hurt. He barely heard them. He was a thousand miles away.

Two years of planning. Two years of meticulous research and study, two years of waiting like a trapdoor spider for all the pieces to fall into alignment.

Two years wasted in the blink of an eye.

Dante was supposed to lead him to his father's letters. That was the key to his entire plan. Without them, Marcello had nothing. Worse than nothing: he'd put all of his eggs in one golden basket, and with Benignus at death's door and Carlo about to ascend to the papal throne, he had nothing left to bargain with.

Maybe his plan could still be salvaged. He waved off the constables and poured himself a drink to steady his nerves. Then he dispatched a messenger to the Rusted Nail, where he hoped the ruffians he'd hired would still be waiting for orders. His letter, scribbled in haste and sealed with a rough blob of scarlet wax, went straight to the point: *"Two other hunters in my employ have betrayed me and taken Uccello. They are fleeing the city now. Find them. Kill the hunters. Bring Uccello back alive. Crippled is fine."*

He wasn't hurt, he told the constables, just a little twinge in his shoulder from when he'd fallen to the floor. Had he seen the robbers who broke into his villa? Sadly, no, he had not. The last thing he wanted was for the law to get hold of Dante and hear his side of the story.

After sending everyone away, he stood in his library in silence. Broken glass pooled around his russet slippers. He stared out the broken window, eyes fixed on a distant bell tower.

Carlo's ascension was inevitable. Lodovico Marchetti's backing, the occupation of the papal manse by brigands masquerading as knights...whatever his endgame was, Lodovico was going all-in.

"I need to reposition myself on the chessboard," Marcello mused aloud. "Make sure that whatever happens, I'm in the perfect place to reap an advantage."

The gears of his mind turned with clockwork precision, forging a simple and direct plan: a sacrifice play.

An hour later he sat in the conference room in the papal manse, across the polished mahogany table from Carlo. Alone together in the candlelight, with a pitcher of red wine resting between them. From the smell on his breath, it wasn't Carlo's first of the day.

The rumors are right, Marcello thought. *His drinking is getting worse.* He felt a faint glimmer of optimism.

"Wine?" Carlo said, nodding to the empty cup at Marcello's left hand as he filled his own to the brim.

"No, thank you, but you'll certainly want one. Perhaps two, given what I have to say."

"I was surprised, hearing you wanted to talk to me," Carlo said. His brows knitted. "I thought you didn't like me very much."

Marcello put on his most ingratiating smile. "Carlo, you're still so young. Politics—especially politics in the College of Cardinals—is a viper's nest. Plots within plots. To succeed, you must never let on what you really feel. The truth is I've supported you all along. Given my feuds with your father, though, a public show of support would just breed suspicion. I've allowed people to believe what they will about me, while privately putting good words in the right ears."

Carlo thought for a moment, as far as his wine-fogged brain would allow.

"Guess that makes sense," he said.

"My public veil of disapproval has also ferreted out some potential troublemakers in our midst, people who think they're safe coming to me with their complaints against you. I have some very bad news, Carlo. There's a conspiracy in this house, right under your father's roof."

In the hall outside, a knight's boots clunked heavily against the marble flooring. Carlo shot a nervous glance in the direction of the sound, then pushed himself up in his chair, squaring his shoulders.

"A conspiracy?"

"A conspiracy," Marcello said, nodding grimly, "to dishonor your father's wishes and deprive you of your rightful throne. I wish I didn't have to tell you this, Carlo. You don't know how much it pains my heart—"

"Tell me!" Carlo said, leaning closer.

"Amadeo Lagorio," the cardinal said.

Carlo shook his head. "No. No, that's not right. Amadeo is my friend—"

"It gets worse, dear boy. Your sister is helping him. As well as that mute Rimiggiu, your father's man—"

Carlo looked like he was about to cry. "L-Livia?"

Marcello folded his hands. "She resents that you're Benignus's favorite. She always has. You know that, don't you?"

"She...she has. Nothing I ever do is good enough for her. It's like she *wants* to hate me."

"And Amadeo? Think it over, Carlo. Is he your friend...or hers? Maybe they've been laughing at you all this time. Spying on you. Plotting against you every time your back was turned."

Carlo didn't answer. He didn't have to. The storm clouds brewing behind his eyes told the cardinal what he needed to know. The seeds of betrayal found fertile soil in that drink-addled heart, and Carlo looked like he was waging a war between feeling hurt and feeling furious.

"Search their rooms, have someone follow them quietly. I'm sure you'll find proof in short order," Marcello said. "I'm telling you this, because I want to make sure you know where I stand. I am your friend, Carlo. Your *only* true friend in this house. I'll help you every step of the way, from here to your father's throne and beyond, because I believe in you. That is…if you want my help. You don't have to say yes if you don't want to."

Carlo looked like a true believer in the presence of a living saint.

"I want it," he said softly. "I…I had no idea this was going on. I need your help."

Marcello inclined his head, all benign grace, and reached across the table to clasp Carlo's hand.

"I'm your man," he said.

"What should I do? About Amadeo and Livia?"

Marcello shrugged and pretended to think it over. "Well, Amadeo is the real trouble-maker, isn't he? Livia's not as smart as you are, Carlo. She could never have come up with this on her own. Perhaps keep her under house arrest, locked away until you can marry her off in some favorable alliance. She can still be of use in that manner. Think of her as a valuable piece of property, to be held in safe-keeping until the time is right to make the most of your investment."

"Good. That's a good idea. And Amadeo?"

Marcello sighed. "He's a source of turbulence, in a time when we need clear, calm waters. Denouncing him or exiling him won't work. The people love him too dearly. What else can we do with a turbulent priest, Carlo? Can you think of anything that might…permanently fix our little problem?"

Carlo slouched back in his chair and sipped his wine. The knight's armored boots clopped by in the hallway outside. Carlo's eyes narrowed.

"I think I just did," he said.

Marcello put a few more sweet words in Carlo's ear, kissed him on both cheeks, and took his leave. Sealing Amadeo's fate was a shame, he thought, but it only amounted to a bit of stray housecleaning. The pope's confessor was too popular, his voice too loud among the common rabble. One way or another, he would have become an obstacle to Marcello's long-term ambitions. Best to remove him now and, better yet, let Carlo take the actual risks.

As for Livia, the girl was an annoying nuisance. This would silence her quite nicely. Marcello whistled a happy tune as he strolled out of the papal manse, basking in the sunlight and feeling like things might still be going his way.

CHAPTER THIRTY-SEVEN

Benignus lay under his heavy quilts, still and silent. A crackling fire in the hearth cast a yellow glow across his wrinkled cheek as he slept. Livia sat at his bedside, motionless as her father, watching him dream.

She wanted to say something. It felt like she should, but she didn't know why. Instead, she quietly rose and padded out. *Watching him sleep isn't helping anybody*, she thought, *and neither is fretting away the hours. There has to be something I can DO.*

Down the hallway, the door to her rooms hung open just a crack. Frowning, she let herself in, peering around the dimly lit parlor.

"Amadeo?" she called out, passing through the arch that led to her bedroom. "Rimiggiu?"

Carlo stood with his back to her, in front of the open closet door. He stared at the corkboard on the wall, the lists of names and connections and questions.

"It's true," he said softly.

"Carlo."

"It's true," he repeated, not turning around. "You and Amadeo. You're conspiring against me."

Livia shot a furtive glance at her bed, where she'd hidden Squirrel's notebook under the mattress. The bedsheets looked undisturbed.

She approached him, slowly, uncertain. "Carlo—"

He spun around and lashed a vicious backhand across her face. Livia stumbled backward and fell onto her bed, stunned. Her split lip burned like a wasp sting, and a trickle of blood ran down her chin. He loomed over her, wild-eyed.

"You're in it with him," he said. "Don't deny it!"

"You're drunk," Livia snarled, not daring to move. Under her, she could almost feel the shape of Squirrel's book pressing against her spine. Reminding her just how close she stood to an executioner's pyre.

"You and Amadeo! You're plotting against me. You've *always* been plotting against me!"

"Carlo," she said slowly. "Calm down. Look at what you're doing, brother—"

"*Don't call me brother!*" he roared. "Not after what you've done. The proof is right there, right on the damn wall! You've been sneaking around, plotting to steal my rightful inheritance, to stab our father in the back. You don't deserve to be called a Serafini."

"It's not like that. Carlo, listen, I'm begging you—"

He walked past her bed, not giving her another glance. When he spoke, standing in the doorway between the bedroom and the parlor, he wouldn't meet her gaze.

"Beg all you want," he said softly. "Beg your mirror, because that's the only face you're going to see for a while. You'll stay here. In these rooms. Your meals will be brought to you. You'll stay here until I decide what to do with you. Maybe that'll be tomorrow. Maybe ten years from now. Sit here and rot for all I care. You're no sister of mine."

"You have no authority over me!"

Now he did turn toward her. His face was pallid, caked with a sheen of sweat. Sickly.

"You know," he said, nodding toward the closet. "You know about the knights."

She nodded.

"Then you know," he said, "that inside this house, I have *absolute* authority. Understand this: nobody is going to help you. Nobody is going to save you. Nobody cares about you."

"My friends will come."

He smirked. "Who, like Cardinal Accorsi? He's the one who betrayed you. Oh, or maybe you mean Amadeo?"

He walked away. Just before the door to her rooms slammed shut, she heard his final words.

"He's dead, Livia. Amadeo is dead."

#

Sister Columba was sweeping the foyer when Carlo found her. She could smell the acrid odor on his breath the second he opened his mouth. *Cheap wine,* the elderly woman thought, *and...something else. Something foul. Like a rat crawled into his throat and died there.*

"Sister, good, I was looking for you. Livia is...Livia is ill."

Her eyes went wide. "Ill, sir?"

"It's an illness of the mind. She's very sick. My father has decreed that she should be kept in isolation while we seek a specialist. For her own safety."

We've been found out, Columba thought. She gripped her broom like she was trying to strangle a snake. It was the only thing that could keep her hands from shaking. *Livia's been found out, at least, and he doesn't know I'm helping her.*

"You'll bring her three meals a day," Carlo said, "and a pitcher of water in the morning. Enter her rooms, set down the tray, and leave. You will not speak with her. If she speaks to you, don't answer her. She's been having, um, fits. Violent fits. The doctors say absolute quiet is the best thing to rest her mind."

"I...I'll light a candle for her in the chapel," Columba said. She couldn't unclench her fingers until Carlo was well out of sight.

She made a beeline for the guest rooms. If Livia was in danger, so were the others. No one answered when she knocked at Amadeo's door, and it opened at a touch.

A scrap of paper lay on the bedside table, bearing instructions in a terse, small-lettered hand: *"Found something serious. I know what C. is up to. Too dangerous to discuss here. Meet me at the White Cathedral after dark. -R."*

The paper crumpled in Columba's withered fist. A note from Rimiggiu. There was only one problem, something she recognized because she'd known the terse spy longer than anyone but the Holy Father himself. Something Amadeo couldn't have realized.

It wasn't Rimiggiu's handwriting.

#

At that moment, Rimiggiu the Quiet was out in the winding streets of Lerautia, cloaked by a canopy of stars. He crouched in the shadows under a vaulted arcade, the building's second floor extending out over the first on stout pillars of unpainted wood. He'd received a note of his own, slipped under his bedroom door, and that was when he knew they'd been exposed. The forgery of Amadeo's handwriting, summoning him to a clandestine meeting in the city, was clumsy at best.

He had to trust that Carlo wouldn't hurt his own sister, at least not right away. As for Amadeo, the priest was probably already dead. If not, though, Rimiggiu thought there was a good chance he might slip out of harm's way. Amadeo might be graying and ill-suited for a life of intrigue, but the pope's confessor had more steel in his backbone than he gave himself credit for.

The note was a lure, beckoning Rimiggiu to a lonely house on the edge of the Piazza Colonna, not far from the old curtain wall that cut the district in half and towered high over the rooftops.

Priority one, he thought, creeping around the side of the house, *ambush the ambushers. Keep one alive for questioning. Priority two, evacuate Livia to a safe hiding place, outside the city.*

Priority three, assassinate Carlo Serafini.

Murdering the pope's son would probably buy him a plot of land in the Barren Fields when he died, assuming his deeds hadn't already damned him five times over. So be it. Rimiggiu had pledged his loyalty to Pope Benignus, not to the Gardener, and he'd do what was best for his master. Right now, that meant smashing Carlo's plans and getting Livia to safety.

He chanced a glimpse into a darkened window, staying low. Shapes huddled in the gloom, barely moving. Armed men, at least two of them, right inside the front door. The trap was obvious. They were waiting for him to walk right in, expecting a rendezvous with Amadeo—at which point they'd chop him down before he could draw his knives.

Amateurs, he thought as he crept on by, keeping every movement, every breath, precise and controlled. *Rimiggiu the Quiet never enters by the front door.*

Around the back of the house, a pair of windows looked out from the second floor. One was open, just a crack.

And me, he thought, eying the plaster walls and looking for handholds. He'd slip in through the upstairs window and prowl through the house, picking Carlo's men off one by one. Quick, clean, and easy. Easy, save for whoever was unlucky enough to be the last survivor. That poor soul had a long and painful night ahead of him.

He jumped, hand reaching up to snare a chunk of stone jutting an inch or two from the wall. He swung his legs, building momentum, and the fingers of his other hand dug into a gap in the masonry. Rimiggiu clambered up the side of the house like a venomous spider in the dark, slowly making his way up toward the open window.

Almost there. With the toes of one foot braced in a narrow crack and the other dangling over open space, he stretched to grab the windowsill, curling his fingers around it. Now just to reach up with the other hand, pull himself up with both arms, and tumble up and over—

He never saw the man lurking to one side of the second-floor window, the one holding the ax. He only saw a quicksilver flash of steel, then felt the searing pain as it lopped off four of his fingers in a single stroke.

Suddenly unanchored, Rimiggiu fell, arms flailing, down to the street fifteen feet below. The blood trailed out in glimmering arcs, like liquid rubies in the moonlight. He landed on his back. His shoulder and his hip cracked like twigs against the frigid cobblestones.

His thoughts were consumed in a screaming alarm, an animal frenzy driving him to get away. He rolled onto his belly and dragged himself on his forearms, one agonizing inch at a time, leaving a scarlet slug-trail in his body's wake.

"I bet I can guess what you're thinking," said the man who casually strolled up to him, toting a woodcutter's ax against one shoulder. Rimiggiu recognized him even in a ruffian's leathers and a hood: Weiss, master of the impostor-knights.

"You're thinking," Weiss said, "that between the obvious forgery, the obvious trap, and the fact that we left you one—and only one—way into the house, that you probably should have seen this coming. And you're right. You should have."

Rimiggiu spat up a lungful of blood. He kept dragging himself, forearm over forearm, his glazed eyes fixed on some distant light. Weiss walked alongside him.

"Really? You're still trying to get away? You've got spirit, but the time comes when a man needs to face the facts. It's over. You're done. Here, let me help you with that."

The ax came down with a whistle, straight into Rimiggiu's spine. His mouth opened in a jaw-breaking rictus, a silent breathless scream as his vertebrae cracked in half. Weiss pushed his boot against Rimiggiu's shoulder, rolling him over onto his back.

Rimiggiu's head thumped against the cobblestones, while his limbs hung limp and dead. His eyes rolled back in his skull. Weiss watched him for a minute, curious.

"If it's any consolation," Weiss told him, "you're not half bad. It's just that you're in the spy business, and I'm in the murder business. Oh, one other thing. Carlo Serafini sends his regards."

Then the ax whistled down, one last time, into Rimiggiu's throat.

#

The White Cathedral loomed over the Holy City in the dark, a great alabaster bird of prey. Amadeo shot a furtive glance over his shoulder as he hustled up the pebbled path to the granite front steps, used his private key to unlock the cathedral doors, and slipped inside.

Starlight filtered through the high stained-glass windows, painting the quiet cathedral in shimmering purple and blue. A couple of the windows had been removed for renovation, leaving their stone arches open to the night sky and inviting a crisp fall breeze to whisper in. Scaffolding fifty feet high blanketed the walls, creaking in the draft, waiting for the workmen to return in the morning.

Amadeo crept along the central aisle between the long rows of empty maple pews. His shoes rustled softly against the ceramic tile floor.

"Rimiggiu?" he whispered. The vaulted cathedral caught his low, cautious voice, amplified it, and hurled it back in his face.

"Not exactly," said the man who stepped out from his hiding place behind the altar.

He hadn't even bothered putting on a fresh disguise. It was one of the "knights" from the papal estate, still garbed in his heavy greaves and shining mail shirt, with the Imperial eagle emblazoned on his shoulder in gold and black. He hefted a battle-ax in his hands, a brutal weapon with a long, sweeping blade made for shredding steel.

The cathedral door swung open behind Amadeo. Another pair of knights let themselves in, brandishing swords. The three men flanked him at either end of the aisle, cutting off any hope of escape.

"You've been a bad boy, Father," the axman said. "Sticking your nose where it doesn't belong. Good way to get it chopped off."

The knights advanced on him from both sides. Slowly, taking their time, like they were savoring the smell of his fear. Amadeo held up his hands, looking left and right.

"You're making a terrible mistake," he said. "You don't want to do this."

"Carlo Serafini sends his regards," one of the knights said with a snicker. "His final regards."

Amadeo looked around, frantic. He could try to escape to the side, running through the pews, but where would that get him? They'd corner him either way. He had no weapons and no way out.

No, he thought, his despair turning to a sudden burst of angry fire in his heart. *No, it doesn't end like this. Carlo doesn't get to win. Not like this.*

Looking around the cathedral, a mad idea grabbed hold of him. He couldn't get around the knights, and he couldn't get out through the front door.

But he could go *up*.

Amadeo jumped up onto the nearest pew and ran, his shoes slapping against the polished wooden bench. One of the knights pointed and laughed.

"Where're ya goin', Father? There's no door that way!"

At the farthest edge of the pew he took a mighty leap and threw himself at the scaffolding, catching a wooden support with both hands and hauling himself upward. The scaffold rattled and squeaked, knocking a shower of sawdust onto the tiled floor.

"What are you—" the axman started to say. He shook his head as the knights converged under Amadeo's kicking feet. "Oh, come *on*, Father! Come down from there! You're just going to hurt yourself and die anyway. Tell you what, you come down, lay your head on the pew, and I'll make it quick and easy. One swift chop, you won't feel a thing."

Amadeo's response was a grunt of exertion as he clambered up to the next tier of scaffolding, gripping beams and cross-supports, his arms burning as he climbed.

The axman sighed and looked at the other two knights. "Well? You waiting on an invitation? Get up after him!"

Now it was a race. The knights sheathed their swords and started to climb. Amadeo tried not to look down, the hard cathedral floor growing farther and farther away with every straining inch. Soon he was fifteen feet up, then twenty, but the younger, more limber killers below were closing the gap fast.

Platforms of wooden planks spotted the scaffolding here and there, spots for the artisans to perch as they repaired the fading cathedral frescoes and patched the peeling plaster, but Amadeo refused the temptation to stop and rest. He ignored his burning lungs and aching arms and legs and pushed aside the stabbing twinge in his side as a mistimed jump yanked a muscle taut.

A gauntleted hand grabbed his ankle, yanking hard, almost making him lose his grip on the girders. His fingers clenched and the scaffolding seemed to lean, as if the entire groaning structure was about to come crashing down.

One of the knights grinned up at him. "Gotcha," he said, giving Amadeo's ankle another tug.

Amadeo kicked him in the face. Rotten teeth broke under his heel, and the man instinctively grabbed at his bloody mouth, losing his balance. He teetered backward, arms cartwheeling as he fell down to the cathedral floor. He hit a pew, and his back snapped against the maple with a sickly crack that echoed like a cannon-shot.

"You killed Dieter!" screamed the other knight, not far behind. "You bastard, you killed Dieter!"

Amadeo gritted his teeth and kept climbing.

He pulled himself up onto the top platform just as his arms gave out, quivering like useless jelly. Here, the workmen had been restoring one of the great windows, but their job was only halfway done. An empty stone arch looked out into the starry night sky. Amadeo held his breath as he stepped out onto the ledge.

Barely a foot wide, the ledge encircled the cathedral dome. A gust of cold wind shoved against Amadeo as he made his way across the slick stone, inch by careful inch. The back of the cathedral looked out over a sheer cliff and far below, just a murky snake shadow in the dark, lay the icy waters of the Gabler River where it widened to meet the sea.

"Where now, huh?" shouted the knight as he emerged onto the ledge, barely ten feet away. He drew his sword, holding it tight as he inched his way toward Amadeo. "*Where now?*"

Amadeo realized, with sudden and chilling certainty, that he only had two choices. Skewered on a murderer's sword, or broken and drowned on the river rocks at the end of a very long fall.

Gardener, he thought, clasping his hands before him, *if I must die tonight, so be it. I only ask that you extend your protection over Benignus and Livia. They are good and faithful and true, and deserving of your blessings in this hour of darkness. If I am not to be their protector, then send someone more worthy in my stead.*

"What's with the hands?" the knight demanded, edging ever closer. "Are you *praying*? What, you think the Gardener's gonna come down and save you?"

Amadeo rested his hands at his sides. As a shrill wind washed over him, he felt strangely peaceful. He looked to the knight and shook his head.

"No," he said.

Then he leaned forward, spread his arms, and let the wind take him as he fell from the ledge. Past the cathedral, past the cliff, past the city, down to the waiting darkness and a river grave.

CHAPTER THIRTY-EIGHT

The cardinal's stables provided three strong steeds with dun coats and hooves that crackled like thunder along the old merchant road leading out of Lerautia. Dante led the way, veering off the worn and ancient stone at the first opportunity and guiding Mari and Werner down a dirt path. The Holy City fell away at their backs, but trouble wouldn't be far behind.

As night fell, forest swallowed the dirt road whole. They had to slow down, picking their way through brambles and fallen trees. Eventually they swung down from their saddles and led the horses through, keeping careful hands on the reins.

"The road was better kept, last time I came this way," Dante said, "but that was a long, long time ago. We're almost there."

"You still haven't told us where 'there' is," Werner said. He coughed into his sleeve.

"I smelled something foul as soon as Accorsi began questioning me, and it wasn't his cologne. Didn't think he'd go so far as to have me killed, but he was too eager to know about my father and too reluctant to explain why. My father was a cloth merchant and a man of means. Spent many fine years in the Holy City before commerce drew him to Mirenze. When the cardinal started badgering me about his time in Lerautia, I knew exactly where to look."

The dirt road ended in a clearing. A hunting lodge stood under the starry night sky. The shingles on the roof were broken, the rough-hewn log walls rotting and mold-kissed, and a broken bay window leaned down from a steepled attic.

"Fox End," Dante said, looking up at the house with a strange, cold reverence. "My father's retreat. He'd come here to escape the world. And his family. He only brought me here once, on my seventeenth birthday. It was the first time we'd spoken in over a year. He told me that when he was gone, all this *grandeur* would be mine. And that one day, I would return and find my destiny here."

Werner shook his head at the ruin. "I assume it wasn't a dump back then. So what did you find, when you came back?"

"I never did. In fact, I'd pushed the conversation out of my mind until the good cardinal jogged my memory. My father had been drinking so he was more maudlin than usual when he said it, and I chalked it up to a feeble attempt at impressing me."

"He said your destiny was here, and you never bothered to take a look?"

Dante put his hands on his hips. He stared up at the ruined lodge.

"I wanted *nothing* from him. It's not uncommon for a man of a certain age and certain wealth to take a mistress, but my father was…rampant and indiscreet. Everyone knew about his philandering, the dalliances with noble wives, the whores he'd bring out here for his little holidays. The gossip slid right off his back. No, the shame landed on my mother. And on my brothers. And on me. He'd only married my mother for her dowry in the first place. Seed money for his professional ambitions."

"He dishonored your name," Mari said, nodding like she understood.

"When he died," Dante said, "I sold his business, his properties, everything that carried his stink. I made my own way in the world. I never did sell Fox End, though. I think it pleased me in some petty way, the idea of his pride and joy going to rot."

Werner shrugged and led his horse over to a splintered hitching post, tying off the reins. "Well, let's see what he left for you."

The front door might have been painted nightingale blue once, but the pigment had faded to the color of spoiled milk. The wood warped in its frame, bulging out and wedged fast on its rusted hinges. Werner stood back, took a two-step run, and slammed his boot against the door as hard as he could. It jolted but didn't give.

"Here," Mari said, leading the way to a side window. She turned her face and smashed it open with one of her batons, knocking out the shards of broken glass from the pane until it was safe to swing a leg over the sill and climb inside. Dante saw Werner grit his teeth in pain as he followed, shifting his weight between his feet, but he didn't say anything.

Cobwebs thick as silken veils draped the gloomy parlor. The stench of mildew hung in the air, mildew and animal rot. Dante made his way through the dark to a table, blowing dust from an antique oil lamp. He rummaged in his belt pouch for a thin flask of oil. Soon the lamp ignited, casting a baleful yellow glow across the forgotten lodge. Trash filled the once-grand hearth, choking it shut, and the rotten corpses of rats lay strewn across the broad floorboards.

"My legacy," Dante said.

They rummaged through the cupboards, sending fat black roaches scurrying from the light, and found a second lantern. Werner carried this one with them as they cautiously climbed the creaking staircase to the second floor. A board snapped under Dante's foot and he tumbled back, off-balance. Mari quickly caught him, grabbing his arm and shoulder, holding him steady.

Once he caught his breath, they made their way to the bedrooms. The lantern's glow strobed through open doorways, across broken four-poster beds and once-expensive quilts reduced to rotten tatters. Beady red eyes glared out from the guts of a savaged mattress, and the chittering of rats followed their footsteps.

"If there ever was anything here," Werner said as he poked the tip of his staff into a pile of debris, "the vermin got to it first. Let's hope your father left you something rats don't eat. Like a pile of gold bars, maybe."

At the end of the hall, a rickety ladder led up to the attic trapdoor. Werner gave it a dubious look, but Dante didn't hesitate. One slow rung at a time, resting his full weight on each step before reaching for the next, he climbed up and gave the trapdoor a shove. It lifted, swinging up and over, and fell on its hinges with a dusty *boom* that shook the lodge. He reached down, and Mari passed the lantern up to his outstretched hand.

The lantern's light fell over rotten crates and cobweb curtains. Still Dante pressed deeper into the attic, squinting at the shadows, as the others climbed up behind him. The warped floorboards groaned under their feet, buckling, threatening to snap.

"Not safe up here," Mari murmured. Dante peered around, holding the lantern out before him, then froze. Something caught his eye, a glint of tarnished brass in the dark.

It was a steamer trunk, shoved against one wall and almost out of sight amid the debris. The leather straps that once bound it were rotten, the brass clasps dangling from threads or lying scattered in the dust, but it was still better kept than anything else in the lodge. Dante crouched down on one knee, running a finger across its lacquered lid.

"I remember this," he said. "My father kept curios in here. Keepsakes. The chest was in his office for years, until one day it wasn't. I didn't care to ask where he'd moved it to."

Hinges squealed as he pushed up the lid. Dante's heart sank.

"Empty," he said.

Nothing waited for him in the chest's wooden heart, not so much as a speck of dust. *Some legacy*, he thought.

Something was off, though. He leaned closer, tilted his head, and tried to figure out why the chest seemed strange to him. Something about its dimensions he couldn't put a finger on.

"Well, it was worth a look," Werner said. "We should go. We didn't exactly cover our horses' tracks, and it won't be hard to follow our trail—"

"A moment," Dante said. His heart started to pound as he realized what was wrong: the inside of the chest was too shallow. The bottom, on the inside, was at least three inches higher than the bottom on the outside. He reached in and felt around the seams, fingers pressing against rough wooden joins, trying to find a catch.

With a click, the bottom lid pivoted inward, then rose up on a concealed hinge.

"A secret compartment?" Mari said, leaning over his shoulder to look.

His father hadn't left bars of gold behind. He'd left him letters. Yellowed sheets of folded parchment, envelopes still bearing crumpled bits of sealing wax on their torn flaps. Fistfuls of letters, some in his father's careless hand and some written with a more feminine curve. Dante picked one up at random and was starting to read when a voice bellowed from outside the lodge.

"*Werner! Werner Holst, you get your treacherous ass out here and parley like a man!*"

Werner and Mari darted to the broken bay window. Butcherman Sykes stood alone on the weed-tangled lawn below, holding up a guttering torch to push back the dark.

"To the side!" Werner whispered harshly and quickly moved away from the window. "Lydda and Pig Iron'll be with him, and Lydda's a crack shot with a crossbow. Don't give her a line of sight."

Mari followed his lead. They flanked the window, craning their necks to see as much of the forest clearing as they dared.

"Sorry, Sykes," Werner shouted down. "We went to a lot of trouble to keep this man's head firmly attached to his shoulders, and we'd like to keep it that way. Call it professionalism."

"You're a fine one to talk of professionalism! Your job was done, and you took your pay, Werner. He's our bounty now. I'll make you a deal, for old times' sake. Send Uccello out. We'll take him and leave, and that'll be the end of it."

Under their feet, somewhere in the lodge, a stray floorboard creaked. Mari pointed downward and mouthed, "One's in the house." Werner nodded grimly.

"Can't do that," Werner called back. "The cardinal duped us. Can't let him get away with that. It's a matter of reputation, you understand."

"Reputation, my arse! It's that Terrai bitch, bound around your neck like an anchor. She doesn't even know, does she?"

"Shut up, Sykes!" Werner's gaze flicked between Mari and the window's edge as his face reddened.

"Hey, Renault! You up there? Bet he never told you what he did in the war."

Mari blinked. "War? What's he talking about?"

"Nothing, he's lying," Werner stammered.

"Holst the Harrier," Sykes shouted, "the Terror of Blue Creek. Oh, yeah, we were mates then, tight as drumskin. Comrades-in-arms while we were carving our bloody way across Belle Terre. Did you know, Renault, that your partner there had a necklace of Terrai ears? I won't make excuses. It was just the sort of thing that made sense after a few months on the front lines."

Mari stared into Werner's eyes. Her mouth fell open, but she didn't say a word.

"*Shut up, Sykes!*" Werner bellowed.

"Hey, Renault," Sykes shouted, laughing. "Your mommy and daddy died in the war, didn't they? Who knows, maybe it was Werner there who did the deed. What do you say, old buddy? Did you make that poor girl an orphan? If it wasn't you, it was somebody just like you."

"He's just—he's just trying to confuse you," Werner said, but Dante could hear the desperation in his voice. From the dawning look of horror on her face, so did Mari.

"We'll take care of him for you, Renault. Just leave the lodge. Walk away and leave Werner and the bounty to us. We've got no scores to settle with you."

Something shifted behind Mari's eyes. Her lips tightened, her shoulders slid back.

"I am a knight aspirant of the Order of the Autumn Lance," she shouted down, her voice hard as a diamond, "and Dante Uccello is under my protection. So long as I draw breath, my honor and my weapons will shield him. Take him if you dare!"

Silence.

Then, sounding halfway between bewildered and amused, Sykes shouted back, "See, Werner? This is what you get when you team up with lunatics. All right, Lydda, smoke 'em out."

A crossbow bolt whistled through the air, streaking through the broken window. Its tip, dipped in pitch and lit aflame, trailed sparks like tiny fireflies. The bolt slammed into a ceiling beam, and the flame danced across the dry wood in all directions, reaching out for fuel with ravenous, licking tongues.

"Mari, listen—" Werner started to say.

She drew her batons and turned on her heel.

"Survive now, talk later," she hissed.

CHAPTER THIRTY-NINE

Dante grabbed letters by the fistful, shoving them into his pouch, stuffing them under his vest, anything to save them from the growing fire. Smoke billowed through the attic and stung his watering eyes as the blanket of flames above their heads continued to spread, fast and hungry and hot.

Werner was the first down the ladder, with Mari right on his heels. He only made it halfway before a stout length of chain lashed out of nowhere, wrapped around his ankle, and hauled him down, tearing his grip from the rungs. Werner fell backward, arms flailing, and cracked his head against the floor. He didn't get back up.

Lips curled back in a sudden, feral rage, Mari jumped down through the trapdoor hatch like a falcon plunging toward its prey. She landed in a crouch, the tortured wood groaning under her boots, drew her batons, and lunged. Pig Iron waited in the corner, his leering grin shrouded under the battered full-face helm of a Murgardt infantryman. His tattered leathers were adorned with riveted plates here and there, making him look like some kind of scrapyard golem. He yanked the chain from Werner's ankle and clutched it between his meaty fists.

Mari's batons whipped against his shoulder and hip, clanging off tarnished steel. He laughed and flung out one end of the chain toward her eyes. She lifted a baton to block and the chain spun around it, yanking it from her grip and sending it skidding down the hall.

Dante climbed down, followed by billowing smoke. He dodged clear of the fight, crouched at Werner's side, and pressed his hand to his chest, feeling for a heartbeat. He looked up as Sykes climbed the stairs to the second floor. Standing at the far end of the hallway, he gave Dante a hungry smirk and plucked the meat cleaver from his belt. He slashed the air, spinning the cleaver in his grip, gracefully twirling the wooden handle between his fingers in a practiced dance of murder.

"Don't worry," Sykes said. "Once our boss gets what he needs out of you, we're not takin' *all* of you back to Mirenze. Just your head. Your body can stay a free man."

Pig Iron's chain-wrapped fist cracked against Mari's chin, stunning her and sending her staggering back a step. He got behind her, fast, and wrapped his arms around her in a brutal bear hug that clamped her arms at her sides and squeezed her ribs so hard the air gushed from her burning lungs. As she squirmed in his grip, he dragged her closer to the window at the end of the hall.

Sykes took a run at Dante, cleaver raised above his head. Dante stood up from his crouch, squared his footing, and watched him come. He didn't move an inch, just stood steely-eyed and waited for the blade to fall. At the last possible second he lunged toward Sykes, getting inside his reach, swinging up a forearm to push away his swing and throwing a punch with his other fist that cracked Sykes's nose and left Dante bloody-knuckled.

"I was the captain of the Mirenze militia," Dante roared as he drove his knee up into Sykes's gut, doubling him over. "Did you think I got the job without learning how to *fight?*"

Black spots bloomed in Mari's vision, her air long gone as Pig Iron dragged her to the window. Out in the darkness, by the tree line, she caught the glimmer of steel and understood why. Lydda was aiming her crossbow. With heartbeats before the shot, Mari ducked her head and bit into the back of Pig Iron's ungloved hand. Her teeth chewed into skin and vein, coppery blood pouring down her throat as he howled behind his helmet and loosened his grip. She pivoted, twisting her shoulder and throwing him off-balance, spinning them around just as Lydda's bolt punched through the glass and straight into Pig Iron's back.

The big man dropped to the ground in a spray of broken glass, twitching and thumping his feet as he died. Sykes saw his partner go down just before Dante delivered a lightning-fast rabbit punch to his throat. Choking, eyes tearing up as the roiling smoke from above filled the narrow hall, Sykes turned and ran in a blind panic.

Mari drew in a deep breath only to cough it right back out again. Weak-kneed, she still forced herself to wade through the thickening smoke to Werner's side.

"He's just out cold," Dante said. Mari nodded, coughing again, and got her arms under Werner's shoulders. Dante helped her, and the two of them dragged Werner down the stairs, just ahead of the growing fire. Flames licked the ceiling over their heads, searing the old wood black, and the lodge trembled under their feet.

Out in the clearing, there was no sign of Sykes or Lydda, but Mari wouldn't let Dante stop moving until they were past the weeds and into the forest proper. They laid Werner down behind a clump of tangled brush, stayed low, and watched the shadows. Nothing moved out there, nothing but the yellow glow as the fire devoured Fox End.

"They're long gone," Dante whispered as Werner groaned, coming around. "Cut their losses and ran."

"They'll be back," Mari said. "Did you get the letters?"

Dante nodded, patting his vest. Werner sat up, rubbing the ugly red knot blooming on the back of his head.

"We all right?" he asked Mari. Mari didn't say anything. She stared out into the darkness, frozen in a panther crouch.

Timbers groaned and snapped as the lodge slowly collapsed, a section of blackened roof teetering and crumbling in on itself. Dante had a tiny smile on his lips as he watched it burn.

"They won't be far," Mari said, "and they'll try again. We'll set our horses free. Go through the forest on foot, covering our tracks as we go, staying parallel to the road."

"Mari," Werner said.

She acted like she hadn't heard him. "We'll make camp for the night as soon as we're a safe distance off and I'm sure they're not tracking us."

"Mari."

"In the morning we can choose a new direction," Mari said. "Or just go our separate ways, if that's what we decide."

"Mari!"

She turned her head to glare at Werner. "*What?*"

"Those things Sykes said back there, we should talk about it—"

"I can't talk to you right now," she said flatly, standing up and brushing autumn leaves from her patchwork armor.

She looked up to the canopy of stars, reckoned their direction, and pointed west. Dante followed her as they made their way through the brush, leaves rustling in their wake. Werner trailed a few feet behind.

CHAPTER FORTY

A fever took hold of Benignus in the night, staining his silken sheets with sweat and making his aching joints tremble and clench. His vision was all but gone now, lost in a pearly fog, but a light like the morning sun bloomed before him.

The light, he thought. *The Gardener beckons me. It's time.*

A firm, warm hand held his. He curled his lips back in a pained smile. Amadeo. His faithful friend, true to the end. Of course he would be here.

"Watch," he wheezed, "watch Carlo. Please. Remember...remember your promise."

The hand tightened over his. Reassuring him. The next generation of the Serafini family would hold the papal throne. Hold it and do honor to it. His legacy was assured now. *Carlo will be so good, so strong! They will call him the greatest of leaders, the holiest of men.*

"Livia will help," he rasped, his voice failing him. He needed her here, now. Needed his son here, in his final moments. "Go," he said, pushing the hand away. He meant to say... he wasn't sure what he meant to say. His thoughts slid away like grains of sand in a sieve, and his joints were so cold, but the light was so warm, growing so bright and so very inviting.

#

Carlo stared down at his father in mute horror.

Watch Carlo. Remember your promise.

"It was you," he whispered, still clutching his father's hand as the old man labored to breathe. "It was you putting Amadeo and Livia up to it. You never wanted me to inherit your throne."

His grip tightened on the pope's hand, almost cracking his frail bones.

"Livia will help," Benignus wheezed, squinting up at Carlo but not seeming to see him at all.

"Father," Carlo said, "it's me! *Me*, Carlo! Your son! How could you do this to me? I know I wasn't...I wasn't always the best of sons, but I'm the only one you have! You said you *loved* me!"

Benignus shoved his hand away and rasped, "Go."

Carlo stood there, mouth agape, shaking his head slowly as the old man's head flopped on the pillow, his near-sightless eyes fixed on the flame of the bedside candle.

With one last, rattling gasp, Pope Benignus died.

"To the Barren Fields with you then," Carlo whispered, his lips curling with disgust. "You lost, Father. Your throne *will* be mine. The throne and all that goes with it. When the histories are written, it'll be *my* name they remember, *me* they'll be talking about for generations to come. You're nothing but a footnote."

He stormed out of the room. In the little office outside Benignus's bedchamber, Sister Columba puttered in the linen closet. She looked up at the sound of the door slamming in Carlo's wake. He stopped, glaring at her, and pointed back toward the bedroom.

"He's dead," Carlo snapped. "Deal with the body."

Then he was gone, leaving the elderly woman alone with her sudden tears.

CHAPTER FORTY-ONE

Freda walked the docks in the hour just before dawn, down in the Alms District. The freckled urchin didn't have anywhere else to be, and she loved the way the sky glowed when the morning sun peeked its head up over the sleeping city. Winter's hand hung over the streets. Not long before it would tighten its grip, and there'd be no time for indulgences. She'd have more little ones to bury, she knew, the ones who died from the frost or the hunger. She buried them so no one else would have to.

She walked on the edge of a dock, as close to the brink as she dared, holding her arms out and putting one ragged shoe in front of the other like she was a tightrope walker in the carnival. Down below, the waters were black, reflecting the icy sky. By the edge of the pier the water was choked with trash, discarded boxes and bottles and slops the fishmongers couldn't sell. A rotten odor hung in the air here, clinging to the wet and slimy wood.

Under the dock, a corpse slowly floated by.

A corpse in a priest's cassock.

Freda dropped to her knees on the wood and reached down, grabbing the hem of the cassock in her fingertips and holding fast. A few docks down, sailors were loading a barge with goods for the south. She looked back over her shoulder and screamed for help at the top of her lungs, waving frantically with her free arm. One of the men, a dark and sweaty islander, dropped his crate and ran over. Once he saw the body in the water, he shouted to the others.

Freda bit back a second scream when the sailors hauled the man out of the filthy water and she saw Amadeo's face.

They laid him on his back on the dock. One of the sailors, another islander, waved for room and straddled Amadeo's chest. He shoved down on the priest's ribs, digging calloused fingers in his throat. Freda stood to the side and watched, her hands clamped over her mouth, every muscle in her body tense as a steel cord.

Amadeo's chest spasmed. The sailor rolled him onto his stomach, and Amadeo vomited up a torrent of seawater and blood, spilling across the weathered planks. He coughed, sputtering, and fell limp.

"Is—" Freda said. "Is he—"

"There is more water in his lungs," the sailor said in a thick Enoli accent. "And cold in his bones. With blankets and a fire, he might live."

"Might?"

He shrugged. "Flip a coin."

#

On the far side of a nightmare, Amadeo slowly opened his eyes. The first thing he saw was the light of a crackling fire, warming his cheeks as he nestled under a pile of scratchy blankets woven from cheap, coarse wool. It took a moment for his vision to swim back into focus, but he knew there were faces all around. The first one he saw was Freda's.

"I knew you wouldn't leave us," she whispered.

All around her, the orphans of Salt Alley nodded, with grimy faces and wet eyes. They stood in a dirt-floored cottage, more of a one-room shack with rough timbers overhead and ill-hammered walls, and they weren't alone. Gallo Parri stood at his bedside, the barrel-chested guardsman looking grave and pale.

"They came and got me as soon as you were fished from the drink," he said. "Tell me you had an accident, Amadeo. Tell me you slipped and fell, and this wasn't what I think it was. Comfort my worried mind."

"You know it was no accident," Amadeo said, groaning as he pushed back the blankets and forced himself to stand. His ribs ached with every breath, and his stomach muscles burned. "And I have no comfort to give, not this day. Where is Livia? It's urgent that we—"

He froze, staring out the window of the shack.

Higher up the hill, far away and over the rooftops, he could make out the curve of the dome over the papal estate. And the thick, black curling plume that rose from the chimney there. A chimney only used two times in every generation, to send a message to the world in the form of colored smoke.

"What does it mean?" asked one of the children, standing at his side and following his gaze.

A single tear rolled down Amadeo's cheek. His hands clenched helplessly at his sides.

"It means my friend is dead," Amadeo whispered. "And I wasn't there for him when he needed me most."

The shack door swung open on rusted hinges, and another child led Sister Columba in by the hand. Amadeo swept her into a wordless embrace and held her tightly, pushing away his own tears while she soaked his shoulder with her own. She finally pulled back, wiped the sunken lines of her face with the back of her hand, and took a deep, shuddering breath.

"Livia?" Amadeo said.

"Imprisoned in her rooms. Safe for now. Carlo's gone mad, Father. And Rimiggiu is dead."

"By whose hand?" Gallo demanded, stepping toward them.

"By the 'knights' guarding the papal estate," Amadeo said tiredly. "The same ones who tried to murder me. They're frauds, mercenaries hired by the Banco Marchetti. Lodovico Marchetti and Carlo are plotting together. They aim to seize the throne by any means necessary."

"Cardinal Accorsi betrayed you," Columba said. "I've overheard him talking to Carlo."

Amadeo's hands clenched even harder. "Decided to back the winning team, I'm sure. He offered us up as a sacrifice to weasel his way into Carlo's good graces."

"I have to get back to the estate," Columba said. "It's dangerous for me to leave the grounds at all. Carlo is...you've never seen him like this before, Father. He snarls at every shadow. He's convinced he's surrounded by thieves—"

"But Livia is safe? You're certain?"

Columba nodded and clasped her hands together. "I bring her meals. She's strong. Livia is always strong."

"I know." Amadeo forced his hands to unclench, reached out, and gently squeezed her shoulder. "Best get back before anyone notices you're gone. Keep your head down. I'll send word when I'm ready to move."

"Move?" Columba said. "What are you going to do, Father? Carlo has killers at his beck and call, the resources of the Holy City at his fingertips…soon he'll be pope, and his word will be law. You can't fight him."

Amadeo let go of her shoulder. He turned away and took another step toward the window, looking up at the plume of black smoke. His heart was strangely peaceful as he came to his resolution.

"Benignus was my best friend in the world. I failed him. I *will not* fail his daughter. I swear this. I swear it by water, soil, and sun. No matter what it costs, no matter what it takes, I *will* set Livia free. And I will see Carlo pay for what he's done."

CHAPTER FORTY-TWO

All of Mirenze flooded the streets for the Feast of St. Scarpa. Scarpa was a martyr, his legacy a grim tale of penitence and pain, but all that mattered to most of the city was that he was Mirenzei. He was *their* saint, compared to the hordes of dour-faced Murgardt that looked down from every church fresco, and by the Gardener they'd celebrate his day as they liked. Over the years, the holy occasion had given way to a raucous, merry carnival, an easy excuse for the rabble to shed their inhibitions and their sobriety in one wild, mad night.

Gangs of youths walked the streets in leather masks and brightly colored sashes, declaring themselves the "official and royal army" of their home neighborhoods. When rival gangs met in the streets, the outcome could be anything from ear-blisteringly vulgar but cheerful insult wars to all-out battles with fists, rocks, and branches. On the north bank, packs of self-appointed scholars and troubadours accosted the unwary, demanding gifts of beer and wine. If refused, the empty-handed unfortunates were either subjected to improvised and insulting verse or put through the "learned man's gauntlet," a barrage of questions about Mirenzei history—where errors meant a sacrifice of clothing and dignity.

The upper classes had their own parties, more expensive but no less drunken, celebrating up on feast-hall belvederes, where they could look down on the city below from opulent platforms. That was where Felix found himself that night: on the green and gaily appointed rooftop of the Duke's Bequest, clutching a wine cup in one tense hand as servants lit torches along the ivory-inlaid balustrades to push back the growing shadows. He stood off along the edge of the rooftop, with the other wallflowers, while a few daring couples took to the center of the platform in their finery and danced to a reeling bit of lute song.

On the far side of the rooftop, Aita Grimaldi stood in a gown of spun silver silk, surrounded by a small gaggle of admirers. *My bride-to-be*, Felix thought bitterly and tossed back another swig of red wine. It tasted like ashes in his mouth.

"Hmm?" he said, realizing someone was talking to him. Terenzio, the tannery master, was already half past drunk and slurring his words. He nodded at the sash that wrapped around Felix's head under his cap, covering the stump of his ear.

"I asked if it hurt," Terenzio said.

"Now, or when it happened?"

"Wounds are funny things. One of my men, he did some soldiering years back, helping the Empire beat down those Terrai savages. Got his hand lopped off at the wrist. Funny thing, he says it didn't even hurt when it happened. The next morning, long after they'd burned the stump closed and wrapped it all up neat as a present, *that's* when it started to hurt."

Felix stared at his cup.

"It hurt plenty," he said.

"And yet you returned home, in honor and strength," said Lodovico Marchetti. He approached with a small box in his white-gloved hands. He held it up, showing off the delicately carved sandalwood. "We may be rivals in business, Felix, but courage is something I greatly respect. I've heard the whole story about your little adventure in the frozen north—you know how people talk in this city. Few men have the stones to make a move like you did. I only wish you'd have come to me first. My family investigated that rumor about the alum mines years ago. I could have saved you all that trouble."

Who had the best motive to send an assassin after me? Felix thought as he looked into Lodovico's eyes. *Who benefits most if my family falls?*

You do, Lodovico. You do.

He took Lodovico's hand and gave it a firm, slow shake.

"I wish I had, too. Have you ever been to Winter's Reach?"

Lodovico shook his head. "I haven't, no."

"They say it changes a person."

Lodovico looked into Felix's eyes and hesitated, frozen for a moment. Then he cleared his throat and held out the box in offering.

"A gift. Dried salamander root, from the Oerran Caliphate. Mostly for the relief of joint ache and gout, but it should help speed your recovery along quite nicely."

He leaned in and cupped his hand to one side of his mouth as he added softly, "And if you steep a piece in wine for about half an hour, then drink the wine? It's an experience not to be missed, trust me. You'll thank me later."

"Lodovico, good Lodovico," Terenzio said, nearly spilling his cup as he tried to bow. "Could I steal you away for a moment?"

"Of course. Good seeing you again, Felix. Please, enjoy the gift, and welcome home."

Felix nodded tightly and forced himself to put on a pleasant smile. The second Lodovico's back turned, the smile vanished.

A footman wearing the black-trimmed tunic and crest of the Grimaldi family approached Felix with a decanter of wine. He filled Felix's cup, then reached over with his other hand to press something into Felix's palm. A folded scrap of parchment. Sensing the need to be discreet, Felix edged over to the railing, put his back to the crowd, and hunched his shoulders a little while he unfolded it and read.

"We need to talk. Tonight, midnight, room 8 at the Guildsman's Seat. Tell no one. Come alone."

He looked across the rooftop. Aita stared back at him. She gave one long, slow nod, her eyes grave, then turned away.

#

It took an effort for Lodovico to wear his easygoing smile as Terenzio led him away. He hadn't known what to expect when he'd brought Felix his little make-peace gift. A broken man, maybe. A whipped dog, drowning in failure.

Instead, for a heartbeat—just a heartbeat—he thought Felix might lunge for his throat. A new darkness was hiding behind Felix Rossini's eyes, the kind of darkness that drove a man to extremes.

He knows, he thought, *and if he doesn't know, he suspects. Damn it all, Simon!*

Terenzio threw an arm around Lodovico's shoulder. Lodovico tried not to wrinkle his nose. No matter how much Terenzio scrubbed and perfumed himself, the odor of the tannery still clung to him, buried deep in his pores.

"Just wanted to say, m'boy, you're doing a bang-up job with the Banco Marchetti. Your father would be proud."

"I hope you're not just saying that because you need another line of credit," Lodovico said with a chuckle. He spotted his mother on the edge of the crowd and took the opportunity to politely extract himself from the tannery master's clutches. "Mother! You made it!"

Sofia approached them and gave Lodovico a kiss on each cheek. Her lips were as cold as her eyes. The obligatory show of affection complete, she turned her attention to the other man.

"Terenzio," she said, favoring him with a nod. Terenzio took her hand and bowed, brushing his puffy lips against the backs of her fingers. He inhaled the scent of her perfume like it was a glass of pure springwater, and rose.

"I was just telling your son that I'm sure your husband would be proud, seeing his family thrive so."

"Thank y—" Sofia started to say, but Lodovico cut her off.

"We're not really *thriving* yet, though, are we? Terenzio, I understand there's a vacancy on the Council of Nine."

Terenzio ran a finger along his collar. "That, ah, that is so, yes. But we shouldn't talk of business at a celebration like—"

"I assume that I'm in the running," Lodovico said. "The Marchetti family hasn't been represented on the Council since my father's death. There's hardly anyone in the city better qualified for the post."

"Of course, of course," Terenzio said, nodding quickly. "In fact, I sponsored your nomination myself."

Lying prick, Lodovico thought.

"Excellent," he said. "And do you know when the Council will be making its decision? I assume it's only a formality."

"At our meeting next month. I'll actually be out of the city for a couple of weeks, leaving tomorrow morning. Trade run to Murgardt, sourcing some new suppliers for hides."

You mean the Caliphate, Lodovico thought, *trying to cut me out of the alum market. But I'll smile and nod and pretend I'm the ignorant pawn you think I am.*

You think my father would be proud of me, Terenzio?

You haven't seen anything yet.

#

Felix wasn't coming. That was the fact Renata finally had to face. He'd been back in the city. He'd had every opportunity to come see her at the Hen and Caber or any of the secret nooks they shared, but he hadn't. And if he hadn't by now, he wasn't going to.

That wasn't the Felix she knew.

Something had to be keeping him away, but what? He'd risked his father's anger and the disapproval of "polite society" in the past, and he'd done it with a wink and a laugh. What could have changed? She'd heard rumors about his trip to the Reach—that he'd been hurt, cut up, but she was the last person in the world who would turn him away. He *knew* that.

The servants at Rossini Hall barred her path at the door. Felix was only to have visitors under the strictest supervision and the approval of his father, they said. He had a wedding to plan for, after all.

Renata was trudging off, at a loss for answers, when a matronly woman in a flour-stained apron caught up to her on the walk.

"You're her," the Rossinis' cook said, "aren't you? The one Felix used to sneak out at all hours to see? He doesn't think we know, but...we know."

She nodded simply. "I am."

"Side door. Five minutes."

The cook let her in, shooting a furtive glance over her shoulder, and hustled her through the run-down kitchen to the pantry.

"We have to be quiet. I'll lose my job, or worse, if anyone finds out I helped you, but...oh, miss, there's some terrible trouble afoot."

"Trouble?" Renata's slippers paced across chipped ceramic tiles painted with swirls of deep blue on faded white. "What kind of trouble?"

"Felix hasn't been himself since he came home, but that's not the worst of it. Our head butler, Taviano. The constables found him in an alley. Murdered. Stabbed right through the heart, they say. No one will—"

They heard the rattling of the front door, a brisk slam, and the thumping of footsteps. "Hide!" the cook hissed, pushing Renata into the walk-in pantry. She waited in the dark, still and silent, ears perked.

"—don't have time for dessert," she heard Felix say. "Honestly, I'm grateful, but I have another appointment this evening and I can't be late—"

That was when the cook opened the pantry door, shoved him straight into Renata's arms, and shut it behind him.

Their lips met by surprise. They stayed there deliberately. His arms tightened around her, like a drowning man clinging to a life preserver, and she knew he hadn't abandoned her.

"You can't be here," he whispered. "You're in danger—"

"I'm not afraid of your father, Felix. You never were either. What happened to you? Was it this?"

She reached up, her fingers gently brushing the velvet band over his missing ear.

"*Was* it this?" she said. "Because shame on you, Felix Rossini. You could have come home with worse scars than this, and you'd still be handsome in my eyes."

"It's not...it's not the wound, and it's not my father. It's Basilio Grimaldi, Aita's father. He knows about us, about everything. The wool business is just a front. He's some kind of criminal, and he wants to use my family in a scheme. He told me that if I don't marry Aita and do as he says, he'll hurt my brother, my father...he'll go after *you*, Renata. He said that if I had any contact with you, you'd pay the price for it."

She took a half step back, realization dawning. "That's why you didn't come back to me. You were *protecting* me."

"As best I can. And I always will. Listen, Renata, I'll find a way out of this. We *will* be together. I promised it then and I promise it now. But for right now, I have to play along and find out how powerful Basilio really is. I can't be reckless. There's too much at stake."

He took her hand.

"Renata, I learned something in the Reach. I stood up to someone more powerful than me. I stood up to an entire city. And sure, I lost. I got beaten down. I got a scar to remember it by, but that's not what I learned. What...what I learned is that I *can*. I *can* stand up. I can *fight*. I bled in Winter's Reach, but I didn't die."

"What are you going to do?" she whispered.

"As long as Basilio Grimaldi draws breath, you're not safe. So I'm going to find out what he's capable of, what makes him tick, how to get at him."

"And then?"

"And then," Felix said, "I'm going to kill him."

Renata swallowed hard. She nodded. His eyes were bright and sharp, even in the gloom.

"Aita wants to meet me tonight," he said. "Like father, like daughter. I expect she's got some threats for me too. I'll pretend to be intimidated. For now, I want you to leave Mirenze. It's not safe for you here, not until this is dealt with."

"What? I'm not leaving, Felix. Not if you're in danger. We'll face it together."

"You'd be in more danger than me if you stayed. If something happened to you...Please, I just need to know you're out of his reach."

He kissed her again, breathing her in.

"I'll use some of the money we've saved up," she said. "I'll head to—"

He held up a hand. "Don't tell me. Just in case...just in case Basilio tries to get it out of me. It's safest if not even I know where you went. Once you hear that Basilio is dead, you'll know it's safe to come home."

"I'll meet you here, then."

He shook his head and gently touched his fingers to the bottom of her chin, lifting her face to his.

"No," he said. "Kettle Sands. Our *new* home. I'll meet you there. The plan hasn't changed, Renata, not one bit. We just have to work a little harder to get there."

Renata smiled in the dark.

"I'll meet you on the seashore, then," she whispered.

"Meet you on the seashore," he said and kissed her one last time.

CHAPTER FORTY-THREE

"She's out of control," Bear said, pacing his cluttered workroom. Frost kissed the windows, painting them with ivory spiderwebs.

"I think your perspective is a bit biased," said the slender man in the water's reflection, hovering in the brass bowl. He wore a fox-shaped mask, complete with little bone bristles for whiskers, framed by his groomed and oiled-back silver hair.

"You know what I mean. She's acting like *she's* the Dire Mother. Ordering us around, commandeering coven resources. It's not fair! I make one little mistake in Reinsgrad, and the Dire all but sells me to Veruca damned Barrett so I can keep an eye on some forgotten mine shafts. The Owl *loses* an *apprentice*, and does she even get a slap on the wrist?"

Fox stroked the bristles of his mask. His eyes smiled.

"I love you, brother, but let's be honest. It was hardly a 'little mistake.' And you know exactly what's in those mines. They *need* guarding. Speaking of commandeering resources, I just spoke with Mouse—"

"I know," Bear said. He peeled off a strip of gauze, winding it around a fresh, shallow cut on his tattooed arm. "She told me she was going to send Mouse sniffing around that banker to find out where he learned about the mines."

"Seems she changed her mind on that one. No, Mouse has been sent to Lerautia to hunt for a needle in a haystack. She's supposed to find some woman based on her description and the initials L.S."

"That's ridiculous. You told Mouse to ignore her, right?"

Fox shook his head. He touched his fingers to the mask's muzzle, contemplating.

"No. I told her to go but to report her results to *me*, not to the Owl. I want to know what this is all about."

The memory of their last conversation, the slip of the Owl's tongue, swung sharply into Bear's mind.

"The book," he said. He broke out in a toothy smile. "I don't think Squirrel's notebook was ever recovered. Not long ago, the Owl led an attack on a smuggler's house in Lerautia. I'd bet good silver she thinks the book is floating around on the black market."

"Interesting." Fox's voice had a high, nasal hum. "Who helped her with the attack? Maybe they'll tell us more."

Bear sighed and patted the gauze down on his arm. "Several, but the only brethren who were told anything at all were Shrike and Worm. They won't say anything. They're the Owl's pets; she taught them. They'll do anything for her. Still, what else could it be? Squirrel's book is out there in the wild."

"And if we find it first," Fox mused, "it will be proof positive of the Owl's incompetence. Allowing coven materials to fall into the hands of the cattle…that's a serious offense. With a serious penalty."

"The highest penalty. And we'll move up in the Dire's eyes for exposing her. What do you say, brother? Are we partners in this? We can't lose!"

Fox didn't answer for a moment. His image bobbed in the mold-flecked water, hazy and distant.

"That last part, that's not entirely true. If the Owl finds out what we're about, we'll have her rage to contend with."

"So?" Bear said. The big man slapped his palm against his robed chest with a meaty thud. "Let her come! What are you worried about? She's just one woman."

Fox chuckled and shook his head.

"Ah, my dear, impulsive friend. Do you know why the Owl is the apple of our Dire Mother's eye?"

Bear shrugged. "No, why does it matter?"

"You haven't belonged to the coven as long as some of us. We know the stories. We've seen the aftermath. When the Dire wants someone found, she sends Worm and Shrike. When she wants someone dead...well, at the risk of braggadocio, she usually sends me."

"And?"

"And," Fox said, "when she wants someone destroyed, she sends the Owl."

Bear leaned closer to the brass bowl, looming over the reflection.

"Destroyed?"

"Oh yes," Fox said. "Lives ravaged, *souls* ravaged, dynasties obliterated, and bloodlines burned to ash. When pain is not enough, when *death* is not enough, when the Dire dreams of a river of bitter tears and a wind borne of anguished wails...she sends the Owl. And the Owl enjoys her work. I'll tell you what I believe, old friend. I don't think our Dire Mother keeps the Owl close just to stroke her feathers. I think the Dire is *afraid* of her."

Bear didn't answer right away. When he spoke, he cursed himself for the tremor in his voice.

"I am not afraid," he said.

"Then I will have to be afraid for both of us," Fox said. "Very well. We'll chase the book. See if we can't clip the Owl's wings. But if those great pitiless eyes turn upon us...I'm blaming everything on you. Agreed?"

"Deal," Bear said.

CHAPTER FORTY-FOUR

A tiny fire crackled in a patch of stony dirt, chasing away the night chill. Tangled and gnarled trees rose up around the makeshift campsite, casting shadows like bony fingers grasping at the fire for warmth.

Dante and Werner sat side by side before the fire, sorting the letters Dante had saved from his father's hunting lodge. Mari sat alone on the far side of the fire. She stared into the flames, wordless, unmoving.

Werner had stopped trying to get her to talk to him.

They'd walked through the night and all the next day to shake their hunters, keeping to the woods, moving slow and quiet and only stopping to rest for ten minutes or so at a time. Now, with their bellies rumbling and their trail cold, they'd finally agreed to camp for the night. It was the first chance Dante had to study what his father had hidden away for him to find. He wasn't impressed.

"Love letters," Dante said, his upper lip curled in disgust as he read the perfumed page. "From his mistresses. *This* is my legacy? The old man's rubbing my nose in his indiscretions from beyond the grave. Just one last laugh on the son he never wanted."

He crumpled the letter and tossed it into the fire. It crackled and turned black.

"This one's pretty spicy," Werner said, leaning close to the flames and squinting to read one of his own. "Huh, from G.S. Aren't a few of the others from her?"

"Half of them," Dante said, opening another. "She must have been one of his favorites. And oh, listen to this: *'As my belly swells with child, I think of our time together and regret that I cannot come to you. My husband knows nothing. He is a kindly man, good of heart, and he believes the child to be his.'* Disgusting."

"How about this," Werner said, reading his own. "'*Our son is a bright, healthy boy and already walking on his own! You would be so proud. The other day he climbed into my husband's chair as if it were already his, and the courtiers laughed with such delight.*' Huh. Must be an important family. Nobles, maybe. What's wrong, Dante? You look spooked."

Dante stared into the fire, eyes wide. He couldn't speak. Instead he tore open another letter and read it with haste, then another, then a third, laying them out neatly in the dirt as if drawing a map.

"G.S.," Dante whispered. "All put together, there are enough details, enough evidence spread across these letters to prove it. This is what my father wanted me to find."

"What?" Werner asked, shrugging. "Who's G.S.?"

"Gia Serafini," Dante said slowly. "Pope Benignus's late wife."

Werner looked at the letter in his hands like it might be coated with poison. "You don't mean—"

"Carlo Serafini is my father's son, not Benignus's," Dante said. "Inheritance for the papal throne runs through the male bloodline."

He rested a letter on his lap. When he spoke again, his whisper cut through the darkness like a razor.

"Carlo is a bastard. And Pope Benignus *has* no heir."

"You have to expose him," Mari said. They were the first words she'd spoken in hours.

Werner held up his hands. "Let's not be hasty. This is big, this is…this is really big. Carlo could challenge the legitimacy of the letters. The throne could sit empty for months with the College of Cardinals in full power and no balance on the other side…no matter what happens, this will shake people's faith in the Church for generations to come."

"So?" Mari said.

"So it's *my church*," Werner said. "I don't expect you to care about that, but you have to think about how many people will be hurt—"

"It's the truth," Mari said flatly. "The truth is more important than any church, or anything else made by the hands of man. I wouldn't expect *you* to care about that, but releasing the letters is the only honorable choice."

Dante gathered up the letters and held up one open hand.

"Please," he said, "both of you. I'm hungry, my head hurts, and I need to sleep on it. I'll make my decision in the morning."

"Fine," Mari said. She pushed herself to her feet. "I'm going for a walk."

"Mari!" Werner called. He followed her into the brush, dogging her heels. "Mari, please—"

She spun and faced him, gritting her teeth.

"Please? Like a plea for mercy? Did you hear that often, while you were *butchering my countrymen?*"

"Your countrymen gave as good as they got. You want to know the truth, Mari? The honest, unvarnished truth?"

She curled her arms across her chest and nodded. "I do."

"Truth is it was a war," Werner said. "That's it. Plain and simple. It was a long, brutal slog of a war. Our government said we couldn't retreat. Yours said you couldn't surrender. And while the kings and nobles were worrying about losing face, we were down in the killing fields. We acted like animals—no, we *were* animals. Savages, because that's what you had to become to survive."

"It was the Empire's fault—"

"It wasn't anybody's fault, Mari, but them that gave the orders and never had to spill a drop of their own blood. They never had to spend a single night being eaten alive by mosquitoes and listening to their buddy dying of a rotten gut wound right beside 'em. I can't explain what we did to each other, your people and mine, because we never understood it in the first place. We never understood a damned thing. And for those of us who were lucky enough to come home in the end, we still couldn't figure it out, and it hurt too much to try."

Mari's gaze went distant. Her arms dropped to her sides.

"Why did you lie to me?" she asked softly.

He rubbed his face, his big shoulders clenching as he groped for the right words. "Would you have gone with me if I hadn't? When I met you in the Reach, I saw something...something noble in your heart. Like a flawless diamond covered in dirt. I couldn't leave you there in all that insanity. I couldn't let Veruca Barrett's world take a good, decent girl and turn her into a mad-eyed killer."

"We were both killers."

"Killing's easy," Werner said. "Anybody can be a killer. Becoming a knight, though? That's hard. That's a lifetime job. That's about becoming something greater than yourself. A symbol. A champion. That's what I saw in you. And you see it too. You aren't done becoming yet. I saw..."

His voice trailed off. He shook his head.

"What?" Mari said.

"Nothing. I shouldn't have—"

"Tell me. Or I walk away, and I don't come back."

Werner steeled himself. He shrugged his shoulders.

"I never had a daughter of my own," he said, "but if I did, I'd want her to be just like you."

She stood in the shadows, lips pursed and her gaze fixed on his eyes.

"One rule," she said.

Werner tilted his head.

"From now on, only the truth," she told him. "Even if it's ugly. Even if you think it'll hurt me. Never lie to me again. If you do, we're finished."

"You have my word," he said.

She took a step closer to him.

"I only have two memories of my father. The night he read me stories on his knee and...the next morning. When he died. I don't really know anything about him, I guess. But if I did, if he was still here today...I think I'd want him to be like you."

He pulled her into his arms.

"You and me against the world," he whispered into her hair, his arms wrapped around her shoulders. "Same as it ever was. And we'll do just fine."

#

Dante barely noticed Werner and Mari storming off. He had weightier matters on his mind. Like just how many people would kill to get their hands on his father's letters.

Accorsi's plan is obvious, he thought. *With these, he could have forced Carlo to withdraw his claim to the throne and throw the Serafini family's support at the cardinal's feet. Easy choice between a comfortable retirement on a Church pension or public disgrace and poverty. This would have been a stepping-stone for Accorsi to seize the papacy.*

But Accorsi is only one man, with one ambition. There are dozens like him. And every single one of them, if they knew what I had, would skin me alive to get it.

These weren't letters. They were puppet strings, and a clever man could use them to make the Church dance to whatever tune he desired. With the right incentive, the right threat, the right spot of blackmail, anything was possible. And with leverage on the Church came leverage on the Holy Empire itself.

I have just become, Dante thought, *the most dangerous man in the world. And the most endangered.*

It reminded him of a beloved book from his childhood, a grandmaster's treasury of chess problems. "Survival puzzles," they were called, challenging the student to thread a single chess piece through a gauntlet of deadly traps. One wrong move, the slightest slip, and all was undone.

"I may end up a pawn or a king," Dante said aloud, "but one thing is inarguable. Like it or not, I am most definitely back on the chessboard."

He didn't need to sleep on his decision. He knew what he had to do, or at least the first step.

He had some scribal tools in his belt pouch: a slim vial of squid ink, a bent quill, a scrap of parchment. That was all he needed. Sitting cross-legged by the crackling fire, he set to work.

CHAPTER FORTY-FIVE

Some inns were built for rest and comfort. The Guildsman's Seat was built for pleasure and secrets. It was the sort of place to meet a mistress for a pleasant hour before going home to the family, or for a shady rendezvous with an informant to trade stolen knowledge for coin. As Felix walked through the dimly lit foyer, the room broken into little pockets shielded by cherrywood lattice screens and leafy ferns, he wondered if Taviano had ever come here while he was selling out the Rossini family.

Every time Felix thought of Taviano, he thought of Simon. Every time he thought of Simon, the stump of his ear throbbed.

Room eight stood at the end of a hall lit by bronze candle sconces. The faint strains of a violin, sad and slow, drifted through the dark lacquered wood.

He knocked. The music stopped.

A chain rattled and the door opened a crack. Aita's eye peered through, framed by a dangling golden curl. She recognized him, nodded, and let him inside.

The inn didn't skimp on luxuries. Silk sheets the color of hammered bronze draped a feather bed, bracketed by more wooden lattice screens. Double doors opened onto a veranda, where Felix saw a violin propped up against the ironwork railing.

"Do you play?" he asked.

"Music is my solitary indulgence," she said, closing the door and locking it. She swept past him, beckoning him deeper into the suite, and gestured to an ornate chair in the curving, delicate style of the Benegali east. "Sit, please."

He took a seat. She paced the rug slowly, scrutinizing him.

"You know my father's business?"

"I'm starting to get an impression," Felix said. "He spelled out the consequences of not going along with his plans."

"Mm-hmm. He's not bluffing, in case you're wondering. He never bluffs. Neither do I."

"I got that impression, too. What is this, round two? You can't threaten me more than he already has, Aita."

She stopped pacing.

"I've been told," she said, "by people who put stock in such things, that I'm not unattractive."

"You're beautiful," Felix said with a careless shrug.

"My father has offered you money, social prestige...and me. Most men would jump at the chance."

"A cage with golden bars is still a cage."

Aita's painted lips curled in the faintest of smiles.

"You passed the first test. What's more important, Felix? Money or power?"

He slouched back in the chair. "Power, obviously."

"Why?"

"We're back to the same place we started. Your father will *give* me money, as long as I do what I'm told, when I'm told to do it, and never buck against the reins. Money doesn't set you free. Power, though, that means you can make your own choices. Where are you going with this, Aita?"

"I am my father's daughter. I've spent my lifetime studying him, learning from him...more than he realizes. I'm also a better judge of character. He thinks you're weak. Easily cowed into submission. I know better. Tell me: what do you want, more than anything in the world?"

He didn't have to think about it.

"Her name is Renata," he said, and she nodded in understanding.

"I've heard stories about your trip to Winter's Reach. They say the mayor herself carved your ear off."

"That's right."

"Do you want revenge?" Aita asked. A spark of curiosity glimmered in her eyes.

"Not against her. I don't care about Barrett. She was tricked. I want the assassin who did the tricking, a Murgardt calling himself Simon. And I want the person who sent him."

"You know who it was," she said. It wasn't a question.

"There was only one man who had a motive to sabotage my mission and drive my family under. Lodovico Marchetti. I just can't prove it. Yet."

"And when you have your proof, what will you do then? Will you kill this man?"

Felix looked out the open veranda doors, out to the starry night sky.

"I'll burn his world to the ground."

"Because death is too easy, too good for him," Aita said. "You want him to live long enough to see his legacy in ruins. His plans undone. *Vendetta*."

"That's right."

"I feel the same way," she said, "about my father."

Felix turned, blinking at her.

"My father orchestrates a criminal network from here to Carcanna. His power is absolute. Among the vermin of the underworld, his name is synonymous with terror." She scowled, seething. "That, Felix, is my birthright. The birthright he has *denied* me. He has made it ever so clear that I am nothing but a tool, a convenient pawn to be played in games of marriage and alliance. An empty-headed trophy who will, he steadfastly prays, bear him a grandson who can properly take the reins of his empire when he's ready to retire."

"These are dangerous words," Felix said.

"No, they aren't. Because you won't tell him about this meeting. You won't say a word, because we both want the same thing: Basilio Grimaldi, *broken*. You would have your freedom, and I would have his empire for my own."

Felix folded his hands on his lap. Now it was his turn to study her, reading the fire in her eyes and the steel in her voice.

"It sounds to me," he said, "like you have a plan. What do you want from me, exactly?"

"Pledge yourself to me. Help me to tear my father's works down, from the inside. In return, I will help you to prove Lodovico Marchetti's guilt and find the assassin he sent after you. We'll both enjoy the revenge we're entitled to."

"This sounds dangerous," he said. His tone was curious. It was an observation, not a complaint.

"The most dangerous act you've ever contemplated. We'll be walking a razor wire, Felix. One misstep and we tumble into the fire together. My father reserves the most terrible of fates for those who betray him."

Felix weighed his words carefully, deliberating.

"I was already planning on killing him," he told her.

Aita smiled. "I hoped you'd say that."

He rose from his chair, walked across the rug, and offered her his hand.

"Partners?"

She clasped it, firmly, and looked him in the eye.

"Partners. For now, we play along. Earn my father's trust if you can. Be obedient, but not *too* obedient. He'll expect a tiny bit of resistance. Once we're married and have more leeway to slip away from his watchful gaze—not to mention a natural reason to be alone together—our real work can begin. As for your Renata, send her somewhere outside the city, the farther the better. I know you must ache for her, but it's—"

"For her safety, I know. Already done."

Aita flashed pearly teeth. "Resourceful. We're going to get along just fine. I have a good feeling about this."

Felix walked towards the door. He paused, glancing back. "Out of curiosity, what would you have done if I turned down your offer?"

"Oh, Felix," she said. "You never would have left this room alive."

#

Shrouded by shadow and a light mist of rain, Hassan the Barber stood on the far side of a puddle-spotted street and kept his eyes on the gilded doors of the Guildsman's Seat. Sure enough, there went Aita, alone and unchaperoned. Half an hour later, the Rossini boy came skulking out, shoulders hunched and spending more time watching his back than looking where he was going. No, Felix Rossini was no threat. He didn't have a head for intrigue or the training to know what to do with it. He belonged to a softer world than the one the Grimaldi family trafficked in.

Aita, though, she was a different matter. While her father stayed blissfully, even stubbornly unaware, Hassan had discreetly charted her comings and goings over the past couple of months. Noted her midnight escapes from her bedroom window, and her furtive trips to spy in Basilio's office and pore over his ledgers.

Now she'd drafted her fiancé into her schemes. Interesting. Knowing Aita, she'd throw him to the wolves as soon as he'd played his part, whatever it was. She was as ruthless as her father. That was exactly why Hassan wouldn't say a word to Basilio about any of this.

Hassan had been born to a raiding clan. He'd seized a headman's necklace with the edge of his scimitar and the force of his will. When Basilio Grimaldi first met him, Hassan could smell the opportunity an alliance promised, like spice on the desert wind. He'd learned to play the good and faithful servant. He still had a raider's heart, though, and loyalty was a fool's game.

He imagined Aita and Basilio as two fat merchant caravans, heading straight toward each other on a narrow road. They'd collide, in time, scattering treasure and blood across the sands. In the end, only the vultures would profit.

Hassan was a vulture.

Scheme your little schemes, girl, he thought as a slow, hungry smile rose to his lips. *I'll keep your secret. For now.*

CHAPTER FORTY-SIX

Amadeo and Gallo stood hunched over a map of Lerautia long into the night. Flickering candlelight cast a yellow glow across their faces and the sweaty stubble on Gallo's cheeks.

"An hour or so before dawn, it'll be a skeleton crew," Amadeo said, tapping the map. "Most of the impostor-knights will be sleeping here, in the barracks. Columba said there's two guards stationed outside Livia's door at all hours, though."

"So stealth won't work," Gallo said with a shrug. "We go loud, instead. A distraction. Look, the barracks are on the east side of the manse. One good fire could draw the entire household in that direction. While they're all dealing with the emergency, we slip in, grab Livia and Sister Columba, and make our escape."

Amadeo nodded. "We'll need a cart. Columba can't ride a horse. And we'll need to *leave*. Nowhere in the Holy City will be safe. I say we hire a boat and have it waiting. We'll sail east. Itresca's no friend of the Empire and barely faithful to the Church. I think the king would grant Livia sanctuary just to tweak Carlo's nose."

"Agreed. I love this city like it was my mother, but it's time to move on. Someday, Gardener willing, it'll be worthy of its name once more."

"With the curtain walls between the districts," Amadeo said, tracing his finger along the streets, "we'll have to pass through two gates, here and here, to get to the docks. Any chance the constabulary will help us?"

Gallo snorted. "None. They're all either corrupt or blindly loyal, meaning they'll do whatever Carlo and that rat Accorsi tell them to. Assume they're hostile."

"That means we need to control those gates *before* the rescue, so we can shut them behind us and cut off any pursuers."

"I only have six men left," Gallo mused. "The others all left the city, following their reassignment orders. We need more help, which means we'll need more boats."

"And we'll have them. This is the Alms District, Gallo. Everyone here knows Livia. They just don't know that they know her."

Gallo frowned. "I don't follow."

"Trust me," Amadeo said, patting his back. "Gather your men, and let's go out to the piazza. We're about to make some new friends."

#

Livia perked up every time the door to her suite opened. Sister Columba inevitably puttered in with a tray, eyes downcast, shadowed by a stone-faced knight who barked her into silence if she so much as said a word. Columba would set the tray down on the table by the hearth, turn and leave, and the door would close once more. Sealing Livia in her living tomb.

This time was no different. A meager dinner on the tray, some slices of smoked turkey and a small plate of steamed mussels in some sort of cream sauce. Something caught her eye, though, as she sat down to eat. A tiny corner of parchment poking out from under the plate. Her heartbeat quickened as she slipped the letter out from its hiding place, unfolded it, and began to read.

"*Father Amadeo lives. He and Signore Gallo are planning a rescue. They come tonight, a few hours before sunrise. Have faith, and trust in the Gardener's love.*"

Livia crumpled Columba's note in her hand, suddenly fearful. Not for herself, for them.

They're going to get themselves killed, she thought. *Carlo's mercenaries will chop them to pieces before they even get inside. They're going to die, and it'll be my fault.*

They were fools. Heroes, but fools. There was no way she could help them from here, though, nothing she could do unless...

Her gaze drifted over the threshold into her bedroom. Squirrel's book still rested under the mattress.

They'll die if I don't, she thought.

They'll die tonight.

She took up paper and a quill and wrote a quick note.

"*Brother, now that I've had time to think and reflect on my deeds...how can I tell you how sorry I am? I know how much I've hurt you, how I've broken your heart, and thinking of you in pain just tears me apart. I don't expect your forgiveness. Not now, maybe not for years, but I pray by the Gardener's grace that someday we might reconcile and be siblings once more.*

"*I only ask one thing of you, one small token of grace. Could you send me a pet to keep me company in my rooms? A cat, perhaps, or a bird. Just a small thing, to brighten my hours and hasten my thoughts toward salvation. With penitent love, Livia.*"

She folded the note, and slipped it under her door. She heard one of the knights outside bend down and pick it up, then clank away up the hall to deliver it.

Now it was all up to Carlo.

Not long after, the door opened, and one of the knights marched in carrying a cage of worked iron. Inside, a yellow parakeet warbled from a wooden perch. The knight set the cage in the corner of her room and left without a word.

Livia sat there for a while. Watching the happy little bird. Hating herself. Looking for another way. Not finding one. Two hours passed before she found the resolve to take the next step.

Then she went to fetch two things. Squirrel's book of spells, and one of her knitting needles.

CHAPTER FORTY-SEVEN

Under the light from the crystal chandelier, the concentric rings of the council auditorium were a swamp of tension and stale sweat. The members of the College of Cardinals gathered in cliques and wolf packs, huddling together in soft argument, the room filled with the feuding drone of fifty tired, angry voices.

One man walked alone. Cardinal Accorsi strolled through the gilded chamber, his shoes clicking softly on the pristine marble floors, and just listened. He counted five feeble conspiracies, each backing their own man for the papal throne but waiting for someone else to stand up and formally issue a challenge to Carlo's claim.

The ten knights who stood around the edges of the room, in formal plate and fully armed, might have had something to do with that.

Nobody wanted to say what everyone was thinking: the knights were a threat. A show of muscle, intended to cow the cardinals into rubber-stamping Carlo's ascension. Marcello could tell it wasn't working. They were getting angrier with each passing hour of debate. Not angry enough to risk retaliation, but enough to drag these hearings out forever.

"—nothing says we *have* to vote at all," Marcello overheard Cardinal Cavalcante say to a knot of hangers-on. "Let the bastard stew for a week. A month! When the people see an empty throne and cry out for leadership, that's our chance."

Marcello swooped in with a smile.

"Our chance to look incompetent, you mean. No, friends, we only have one way out of this situation. We need to put Carlo on the throne."

Jaws dropped. "Wait," Cardinal De Luca said, sweat glistening on his double chin. "You've been against Carlo from the beginning. Why the change of heart?"

Just the opening he needed. Marcello raised his voice a bit higher, projecting like a stage actor, as he made the sale.

"Because in a battle with an empty throne, gentlemen, we will *lose*. Do the people know how hard we work, the webs of negotiation and compromise that keep their Mother Church running? No, nor should they! They see a leader. One leader. One leader who, in their eyes, *we* are denying them. A week? A month? They'll be crying out, all right. 'Carlo! Give us Carlo!'"

Cavalcante folded his arms. "Carlo is a drunkard."

"He is. Do the churchgoers in Murgardt know that? In Itresca? In half of Lerautia, his own hometown? No, they do not. Weaknesses can be concealed. Witnesses can be gently encouraged into silence. All the masses know is that he is Benignus's son. Benignus, whom they loved, remember."

Cardinal Herzog wandered over from a neighboring clique, trailed by three of his own sycophants. His bushy eyebrows quirked. "It sounds as if you're advocating putting an unfit man at the helm."

"I do not dispute that he is unfit," Marcello said. "I dispute that it is the helm. Gentlemen, the Church is a mighty engine. Every steeple from here to the Murgardt hinterlands, every priest and pardoner, every faithful follower, is a cog in that machine. And who keeps it running? Who repairs it when it breaks? We do. Benignus was a good man who we all admired, but he was only one man. We benefited from his guidance...but can anyone here say that we *needed* his guidance?"

"The people need a strong leader," De Luca argued. "They need a pope who champions them, who brings the Gardener's light to the world."

Marcello nodded. "And that is a polite way of saying 'figurehead.' Carlo Serafini is weak. But his weakness can be our strength. We can tailor his message, his rule, and *create* the next great pope."

"One who we control," Cavalcante said softly, looking sidelong at Marcello. "Benignus fought us. Carlo will fold."

"Like a losing hand of cards," Marcello said. "We are all men of faith. We all want what is best for the Mother Church and, more importantly, we *know* what is best. We do, don't we?"

He savored the sea of nodding heads. More cardinals had drifted over while he spoke, a crowd building.

"Benignus was the people's pope," Marcello said, "and he had a long reign. Isn't it time for a change? Isn't it time…for *our* pope? A ruler who recognizes the authority of our wisdom?"

"You mean, too drunk and lazy to actually make any decisions of his own," De Luca snorted.

"That is *exactly* what I mean, and I make no apologies for it. Call me crude, but know I'm right. Cast your vote for Carlo, and I guarantee that the purse strings of this holy institution will be placed in your hands, with no questions asked or arguments made. So that you can benefit your homelands and spread the Gardener's light as you see fit."

De Luca and Cavalcante both started arguing at once, a commotion that flooded to every corner of the council hall and led to raised voices roiling like water brought to a seething boil. Marcello stepped back, folded his arms, and smiled. His work was done.

They'd argue until dawn, he knew—some out of principle, some desperately clinging to their hopeless dreams of ascension, some just to show they had a backbone—but with sunrise the arguments would be over, and they'd cast their votes just as he wanted. An honest man was hard to manipulate. A greedy one was child's play.

He had them in the palm of his hand.

CHAPTER FORTY-EIGHT

Cheap pitch-dipped torches guttered and spat black smoke at the edges of the piazza in the Alms District. A crooked well squatted at the heart of the open square, surrounded by concentric rings of muddy and broken cobblestones. Amadeo stood by the well with Gallo and his six loyal men at his back, their chests draped in the white tabards of the papal guard.

Word of their arrival flew like lightning through the slums. The locals came from all around, crowds of dirty faces and hungry eyes, to hear what Amadeo had to say. More faces loomed in the shadows of the lopsided buildings that crowded the piazza, peering out from behind barred windows and rickety wooden slats.

Amadeo took a deep breath and curled his hands, rubbing his fingertips against his moist, clammy palms. He was used to speaking in front of bigger crowds than this from the cathedral pulpit, but never with lives at stake.

"You all know the Lady in Brown," he called out. His voice echoed across the open square. He paused, making eye contact with as many people as he could.

"Yes, you know her. The lady from the high streets who comes down among you by night, in a plain-woven cloak and a mourner's veil. She brings food, medicine, does what she can to help."

More than a few nodding heads. Good. Amadeo spread out his hands and raised his voice.

"Her name is Livia Serafini. She is the daughter of Pope Benignus, and she has been falsely imprisoned."

A murmur rippled through the crowd. Amadeo let it percolate, felt it growing stronger as it gathered steam.

"You all know me, too. I am not a great man. I am not always a good man. But I try to be an honest one. Livia and I had concerns about her brother's fitness for the papal throne. We investigated, discreetly, but we were betrayed. Three assassins sent by Carlo—assassins in the guise of holy knights—attempted to murder me."

The murmurs grew into a slow-building thundercloud. Amadeo felt his palms. They were dry now. Raising his chin, he pushed ahead.

"I was saved by the Gardener's intercession. Not for my own sake, but so that I could continue my service to our Mother Church. Tonight, that service starts with bringing you the truth. Carlo Serafini is a traitor. He has imprisoned Livia inside the papal estate, and I fear what he might have planned for her. The second part of my service is this: I'm going to free her."

He held up one hand, sharply, silencing the growing clamor.

"The entire estate has been compromised. Carlo has hired mercenaries, at least fifty of them, to pose as knights and occupy the grounds. These men are brutal, remorseless killers. I have Maestro Parri of the papal guard and six of his finest soldiers on my side. I won't lie. The odds aren't good. The plan is to rescue Livia and flee by water, to seek sanctuary in Itresca."

"Father," a man near the front of the crowd shouted, "you'll be killed!"

"Maybe so," Amadeo said, "but then…maybe not. Not if our numbers were greater. You all know Livia Serafini. Night after night, she walks among you, helping where she can. Tonight, she's the one who needs help. Will any of you extend your hand?"

The crowd fell into whispers and uncertain silence. Suddenly it was hard for Amadeo to find anyone who would meet his eyes.

"You got us," Freda said, marching up with a pack of her urchins in tow. "The lady's always done right by us, and Salt Alley always pays its debts. We'll stand by you."

A burly man in a soot-stained apron, hair mussed like he'd been dragged out of bed to come hear Amadeo speak, shook his head and stepped up. "Damned if I'm going to sit on my thumbs while a little girl does my job. When my son had the shaking coughs last winter, we couldn't afford the herbs to cure him. The Lady in Brown got us all we needed. Wasn't for her, I might be visiting a grave instead of raising my boy. I'll fight."

A wiry woman with a pox-scarred face shouldered her way to the front of the crowd.

"I almost lost my fishing boat in rain season. Wood rot and I couldn't make enough to keep ahead of the repairs. The lady made sure I had enough coin to stay afloat when the moneylenders all turned me away, and all she'd take in repayment was one fat trout. Only fittin' it's my boat that takes her to freedom now."

Others stepped up, one by one or in pairs, sharing their memories of the Lady in Brown. When all was said and done, some two dozen men and women had pledged their hands—and their lives, if that was what it took—to see her freed.

It would have to be enough.

CHAPTER FORTY-NINE

A pale and pitiless moon loomed over the Holy City. While the College of Cardinals still raged in debate down in the underchambers of the papal manse, the rest of the estate slept. A few impostor-knights trudged across the frost-kissed grass, keeping a halfhearted watch.

At the gatehouse on the Via Sacra, the great boulevard that wound its way through the heart of the city, weary-eyed constables stood a lonely guard over the curtain wall gate. Half a city away and down toward the docks, the gate on the Via del Popolo was no different. The one constable still awake to keep watch barely noticed the long covered wagon rattling out of the Alms District, drawn by a pair of rheumy-eyed horses.

He did notice the pounding on the gatehouse door, though. Grumbling and pushing himself up from his stool, he trudged over and opened it. The constable didn't have time to blink before a beefy fist slammed into his jaw and knocked him flat on his back. The tiny gatehouse flooded with half of Amadeo's small army, their faces masked under hoods of leather or rags of dirty cloth with crude slashes for eye holes. They fell on the sleeping guards with clenched fists and coils of sailor's rope, binding their wrists and stripping away their sword belts.

Amadeo huddled under the wagon canopy with the papal guard. They'd decided that the raid on the estate was too dangerous for anyone but them—and Gallo had to be talked into letting Amadeo come, for that matter. While their new recruits secured the two gatehouses and got the boat ready to leave, they'd handle the rescue.

The wagon parked on the edge of the rolling lawns, just outside the tall iron fence that ringed the papal estate. Gallo's two best climbers scaled the fence and tumbled silently to the grass on the other side. The rest ran, keeping low and quiet, toward the front gate.

The knight in the gatehouse was more alert than the constabulary in the city, but he still hesitated, confused to see two members of the guard strolling toward him. His gaze flicked between the iron trees emblazoned on their ivory tabards, and his brow furrowed.

"What are you lot doing here? I thought you were all reassi—"

One of Gallo's men grappled his arms. The other punched a dagger through the knight's throat and then wrenched it free, tearing open his windpipe. They left him to drown in his own blood, dumping the twitching body and unlocking the gate without a second's pause. Reunited, Gallo pointed to four men, then east, toward the barracks. The other two guardsmen, along with Amadeo, followed him in a long jog along the outer edge of the estate. They kept to the shadows of the fence line as they closed in on the mansion.

There they waited, huddled in the dark, ears perked and waiting for a sign. It came ten minutes later in the form of warm orange light, growing in the distance. Not the sunrise. A fire.

#

Sister Columba took a deep breath as harsh, booming alarm bells rang out in the dark. This was the sign she'd been waiting for.

A pair of knights ran past, nearly knocking her over. "Barracks fire!" one told the other, breathless. "There are two dozen men trapped in there, and Gunther says they're not waking up!"

Columba rounded a corner on her way to Livia's rooms. Another knight sat dozing in a chair, snoring and slumped to one side, oblivious to the world. Columba frowned. Something felt wrong, like an itching in her bones. Or a heaviness in her eyelids, encouraging her to rest, take a short nap right here in the middle of the hallway. She shoved aside the bizarre temptation and flung open Livia's door, eager to deliver her mistress to safety.

Bloody feathers drifted across the hardwood floor. Bloody smears coated Livia's hands. She crouched over a strange and swirling design painted onto the wood at her feet, a symbol that made Columba's eyes water and her heart pound. Livia's head snapped up. She gasped, then rose and snatched a small bag from the chair by her hearth.

"Let's go," she said.

"Livia, you—what did you—"

Livia's eyes blazed as she loomed over the elderly woman.

"Nothing," she hissed. "I did *nothing*."

Then she stormed out, leaving Columba to try to keep up in her wake.

#

Gallo's men had accounted for the spread of the blaze, the direction of the wind—for everything except how fast the impostor-knights would react when the first shouts rang out across the rolling lawns. The four guards were halfway back to rejoining the rest of the team when cold steel suddenly gleamed from the darkness around them. One guardsman doubled over, taking a slash to the gut that spilled his intestines across the mansion's lawn. Another barely got his blade clear of its scabbard before a sweeping ax chopped him open from the slope of his shoulder to his rib cage. The knights moved with practiced finesse, precise and lethal, and seemed to be everywhere and nowhere at once. With numbers and coordination on the knights' side, Gallo's men never had a chance.

On the far side of the lawn, still in hiding, Amadeo saw Gallo grind his teeth. He had to make a split-second decision, doing the hard calculus of war. "We keep to the plan," he whispered sharply, leading the way to the darkened windows of the mansion and leaving the fire team to die.

Livia and Columba met them at the window, and Gallo helped Columba climb over the sill. Amadeo tilted his head, noting the way Columba jerked away when Livia tried to touch her. For as long as he'd known the pope's chambermaid, he'd never seen that look on her face before.

Revulsion, he thought.

Gallo scooped Columba up in his arms. They ran. With heads ducked and hearts pounding, the remnants of the team barreled across the lawns, headed for the gate. The fire grew at their backs, greedy for kindling, dining on the wooden barracks-house. Tendrils of flame casting the grounds in shifting twilight. Amadeo heard a new shout, one aimed in their direction, just before a crossbow bolt whistled past him and punched a hole in another guardsman's back.

The knights came running like a flood of furious ants across the lawn as a few doubled back toward the stables. Amadeo's lungs burned for air as he clambered into the wagon, helping the survivors up, pulling Livia into his arms as she tumbled in. Gallo jumped up onto the driver's perch, snapped the reins, and they were off.

#

"They *what?*" Carlo roared, pacing through the halls like a hungry lion, clutching a half-empty bottle of wine in his sweaty grip.

"Took your sister and the old maid, sir," said the knight who jogged to keep up with him. "The fire was apparently a distraction. Worse, we found something in your sister's room. It looks like she was doing…some kind of witchcraft."

"*Not surprising,*" Carlo spat. "This is war. She's declared war against me, her family, her flesh and blood, her church and faith—"

"Sir? What do you want us to do?"

Carlo's eyebrow twitched. A vein pulsed in his temple.

"I want you to *find her*! She wants to play with fire? Fine. Burn her out. Wherever she's hiding, whoever is stupid enough to grant her sanctuary, burn her out. Burn half the city if you have to."

"Is...is that wise? You haven't been coronated yet, and you could lose the support of—"

Carlo hurled his bottle against the wall. It exploded in a shower of smoked glass. Burgundy wine splashed the plaster and rolled down in gleaming rivulets. He grabbed the knight's collar and yanked him close, bellowing in his face.

"Burn! Her! Out!"

CHAPTER FIFTY

The wagon jolted through the dark streets as Gallo whipped the horses into a stampeding frenzy. Other hoofbeats sounded in the air, though, closing in fast from behind. Stallions with grim-eyed riders out for blood.

"We can't outrun them!" Livia said, squeezing Amadeo's hand as they watched the horsemen close the gap.

"We don't have to beat them to the docks," Amadeo said. "Just to the first gatehouse."

The curtain wall loomed up ahead, carving its twisting way through the district. The portcullis arch stood open and inviting.

Amadeo held his breath as the horsemen closed in. The gap between them and the wagon narrowed to ten feet, then eight, then six, and the lead rider drew his sword.

The wagon shot under the arch just as one of Amadeo's recruits chopped the rope connected to the gatehouse crank. The severed end whipped free and the gate fell with a groan of rusted iron, eight hundred pounds of metal crashing down on the lead rider's skull, impaling him against the broken back of his stallion. Man and beast twitched and bled out on the cobblestones. The other knights reared their horses, drawing up short, and jumped from their saddles to run over and try to lift the gate.

"Don't look—" Amadeo started to say, but Livia waved him away.

"I am not innocent," she said softly.

The second gate at the Via del Popolo rattled down in their wake, a second chance to slow down the steel tide, but Amadeo knew it wouldn't last long. There were other, less direct ways through the city, and now Carlo's mercenaries had a personal motive for revenge.

The fishing boat, *Morning's Glory*, was tied off at the docks and ready to go. A few of the volunteers worked frantically, loading its tiny hold with crates of food and emergency supplies, whatever they could scrounge for the voyage. Amadeo felt a surge of exhilaration as the cart clattered to a stop, and he jumped out. They were actually going to make it. Five minutes and they'd be sailing, far from the city and Carlo's mad grasp.

Then he smelled the smoke and heard the screams carrying over the rooftops. Gallo grabbed his arm and pointed. Down on the far end of the Alms District, flames rose up to lick at the starry sky.

"They're burning it," Gallo said. "They're burning *everything*."

They know, Amadeo thought as icy fingers of dread squeezed his heart. *They know which way we ran, and they know where we recruited help. There's going to be a massacre. And it's my fault.*

"Right," he said, turning to the *Glory*'s captain. "Cast off, right now. Get Livia out of here and as many people as you can pack aboard. Gallo, take your men up and down the docks and start commandeering boats. Fishing boats, barges, rowboats—if it floats, get it ready to launch."

"What are you doing?" Livia said.

"Whatever I can," Amadeo said.

Then he was off and running, his shoes pounding the broken street as he headed straight toward the fires. He hammered on doors and windows along the way, cupping his hands to his mouth and shouting for everyone to evacuate to the docks. A few locals were already out on the street, drawn from their beds by the smell of smoke. They joined in the shouts, racing to get their families or sprinting down side streets, spreading the word.

Amadeo rounded a corner onto the Via Marlane and froze in stark horror. Flames roiled from open windows, and clouds of billowing smoke washed over the corpses that littered the street. Carlo's men were making their way from house to house, kicking in doors, butchering and burning like rabid animals. He'd known they were killers, but to see carnage on this scale, to hear the screams of the survivors as leering mercenaries dragged them into dark alleys for mutilation or worse—

"Hello, hello," said a familiar voice. The axman from the cathedral strode from the smoke, gore dripping from his blade and staining his holy armor in dark, thick spatters. "Hope you didn't think we forgot about you."

Heat from the spreading fires burned against Amadeo's face. He tasted ashes on his tongue when he inhaled, and the screams around him were a symphony of horror and loss. *The Barren Fields*, he thought, his mind reeling. *Damnation. This is what it looks like.*

"Who are you?" he heard himself ask, frozen by fear.

"We're the Dustmen."

"Why?" Amadeo asked, the words catching in his throat. "Why are you doing this?"

The axman shrugged, looking back at his handiwork with a lazy smile.

"It's fun, isn't it?"

"These people haven't done anything to you. They've done nothing to deserve this!"

"They can't stop us," the axman said, giving an indifferent shrug.

Amadeo's hands balled up into fists.

"Then I will."

The axman laughed. "Come on, Father. You're joking."

Amadeo couldn't think, for all the smoke and blood-stench curling inside his skull. His heart jackhammered against his ribs and his fists trembled at his sides, but he wasn't afraid anymore. He was beyond fear. This was fury.

"As far as I'm concerned, I died the night I plunged into the river," Amadeo seethed. "I had no right to ever wake again, but I did. Every minute since, and every breath in my lungs, is a gift. A man who's died once isn't afraid to die twice."

"This time," the killer told him, hefting his ax, "it's gonna stick."

Amadeo took a lurching step forward, spurred by adrenaline, and raised his fists for the first time in his life. "Let's find out. *Come at me!*"

The axman took two steps before a fist-sized rock whipped out of the shadows and cracked him in the side of the head, leaving a bloody gash. He yelped and staggered back, grabbing his wound, and Amadeo turned to see Freda and four of her fellow urchins standing at his back. They clutched sacks laden with stones.

"Why are you still here?" Amadeo shouted. "You should have been on the boat with Livia!"

Freda rolled her eyes. "C'mon, Father. You know she wouldn't leave like that. She's warning people on the other side of the district. Thing is, they got—"

The axman charged, bellowing. A hurricane of rocks drove him back, clanging off his armor and forcing him to drop his weapon and throw up his arms to protect his face.

"They got the Via del Popolo gate open and more knights are coming and we gotta go *now!*" Freda shouted in one pent-up breath. Amadeo didn't need coaxing. The children threw another hailstorm of rocks to cover their retreat and ran, turning down a twisting alley and leaving the carnage behind.

The exodus had already begun. The harbor was thick with boats, casting off from the docks and sailing away from the battle as fast as they could. Most had more passengers than they could manage, desperate survivors dangling from hulls and clinging on for dear life, the weight pushing the rickety boats down to the waterline. It was standing room only on the deck of the *Morning's Glory,* but they didn't cast off just yet, holding their lines until Amadeo and the children clambered aboard.

"Now!" Livia shouted up to the captain. "That's the last of them."

A column of knights rode up to the docks as the *Glory* slid away on black, restless waters. The urchins' rocks fell short, pelting uselessly onto wet timbers, but the knights didn't try to pursue them. They just waited there, watching.

The axman stood in the line. He and Amadeo locked eyes. The axman grinned, flashing blood-stained teeth, and offered a mocking farewell salute.

Behind them, the Alms District burned.

As the sun rose across the waters, painting the sky in shades of pink and tangerine, the refugee fleet sailed south.

#

Livia didn't speak until the Holy City was a speck on the horizon. She stood out on the edge of the fishing boat's deck, staring into the distance.

"How many?" she asked. Amadeo blinked at her, not understanding. "How many did we save?"

He craned his neck, looking across the waves. A flotilla of small and motley boats limped along in the wake of the *Morning's Glory*.

"Hard to tell. Two, maybe three hundred?"

"And how many people lived in the Alms District?" she said.

Amadeo's voice was soft. "You know how many. Livia, don't torture yourself—"

"Two hours," she murmured.

"Hmm?"

Two hours, she wanted to say, *was how long it took me to find the nerve to use Squirrel's spellbook. The sleep-curse was working. I had another trick ready for the guards at the door. That done, I could have freed myself without your help.*

You thought I was some damsel in distress, and you came running to the rescue. And now hundreds of people are dead. They died in my name. But that's not your fault, Amadeo. It's mine. Because I knew what needed to be done, and it took me two hours to find the courage to do it. By then it was far too late. I valued my own soul over their lives, and this is what happened.

Never again.

"It's my fault they died," she said.

Amadeo touched her arm.

"No. It's my fault. I had no idea Carlo's thugs would retaliate like this. If I'd known, I never would have risked it—"

She tugged her arm away and stared at the waves.

CHAPTER FIFTY-ONE

Mari woke with the dawn, lying in the dirt beside the dying embers of the campfire. Birdsong filled the air, drifting down from the treetops and washing over the sound of Werner's heavy snoring.

A folded piece of parchment rested at her side, weighted down by a small handful of gold coins. A cool gust of wind ruffled the paper's edges.

Dante was gone.

Mari sat up, brushed some dead leaves from her tangled hair, unfolded the parchment, and began to read.

"Mari," Dante had written, "*you poor, lovely mad girl. Is it strange to say that I have no desire to live as you do, but I admire you all the more for it? The world needs people like you, to keep people like me in check. But that is exactly why I had to leave.*

"*You seek the truth above all else. Veritas. A fine ideal but one that has no place in politics. Werner, for his part, seeks to protect the church he was raised in. Understandable, respectable, I'll grudgingly admit, but ultimately shortsighted. I can allow neither of you to influence my decision, nor do I have the right to drag you into the danger I'm about to face. There are steep cliffs and deep chasms ahead, and I can only trust that I'm the skilled climber I used to be.*"

Mari looked over at her sleeping partner. His chest rose and fell sharply with every snore and wheeze.

"Werner," she said. "Werner. Get up."

The snoring stopped. He sputtered and rubbed his eyes.

"*I was once a man of influence and power,*" Dante wrote, "*and with the aid of these letters, these blades of paper that can cut sharper than any assassin's knife, I will be so once more. This is my concern. It isn't about the Church, or the truth, or the fallout, or who gets hurt. It's about me, and what I can get for myself. Do you scorn me for that, Mari? I suppose you must. Part of me hopes that* you do. It would be a tragedy if you ever became so corrupted as to understand me."

"Whatsis?" Werner grunted.

"Dante's gone."

That woke him up. Mari pointed to the small pile of gold coins on the ground as she read the ending of the letter out loud.

"'I would ask that you not try to find me, but I know you better than that. Hence, the coins, the last bits of gold from Mayor Barrett's treasure coffer. I am hereby and officially hiring you *not* to hunt me. I am quite certain, Mari, that you would not take a man's money and then break your word. The gold is yours, as is the job. Easiest job you've ever taken.'"

"He's got that right," Werner said, scooping up the coins.

"'Perhaps one day our paths will cross again,'" Mari read aloud, "'and on that day, I hope that time and trouble will have faded none of your zeal, even if it means I must face your wrath. I will sleep easier at night, thinking of you, knowing there is a spot of light in the world to contrast my banal and tawdry darkness. I remain, faithfully yours, Dante Uccello.'"

Finishing, Mari stared at the letter in her hands, head cocked, not quite understanding.

"He knows he's wrong," she said. "He knows he's being greedy and people are going to get hurt."

Werner nodded. "Sounds about right."

"But he's doing it anyway."

"Sounds about right."

Mari folded the letter.

"What now?" she said.

Werner grunted as he pushed himself to his feet, cupping a hand over his weathered brow as he surveyed the clearing.

"Merchant road should be an hour's walk that way. Lots of traffic. We could hitch a ride on a trader's caravan, make our way to a nice big city. Anyplace but Lerautia. Think we'd better steer clear of the Holy City for a while."

"What then?" Mari said.

Werner looked up at the sky and shook his head, smiling.

"All this mess," he said. "Politics, blackmail, popes, and bloodlines...it's not our world, Mari. We're hunters. So we'll do what hunters always do. Live high on what we've earned for a week or two, and then, when the coin runs low, we'll look for a new job."

"It's that simple?"

Werner shrugged. "Life can be simple sometimes, if you'll let it. Job's done. We got paid. Leave it be."

They walked silently through the forest until the tree line broke and they emerged onto the wide and worn merchant road. As the morning stretched into afternoon, when their calves were long past aching, they heard the rattling of a wagon in the distance. They edged over to the side of the road as it approached, drawn by a pair of black horses with shiny, well-groomed coats.

The wagon rolled to a stop. The owners, a man and woman sitting side by side on the driver's perch, looked down at them. The woman had olive skin and braided black hair, and she flashed uncannily white teeth as she smiled.

"Long way to go on foot," she said.

"Wasn't our original plan," Werner said. "Don't suppose you've got a little extra room on your wagon? We've coin to pay for passage."

"Keep your coin. There's plenty of room, and we'd be cruel not to help a pair of travelers in need. Where are you headed?"

"Anywhere but here."

The woman laughed. "An adventurous spirit! I'm Despina, and this is my brother Vassili."

"Werner Holst. This is my partner, Mari."

Mari's eyebrow rose, just a bit, as Despina and Vassili shared a fleeting glance and a knowing smile.

"Why don't you climb in back and make yourselves comfortable?" Vassili said. "As my sister said, we'd be terribly cruel not to help, so come along with us. We insist."

As she clambered in back, finding a place to crouch amid lashed-down barrels and crates, Mari could only think of Dante Uccello.

You have the letters, she thought, *but I still know the truth.*

And I will not be silent.

"We're on our way to see an old friend," Vassili told them, glancing back with a chipper smile as Werner followed Mari up into the cart. "A teacher of ours."

Despina grinned, taking up the horses' reins. "I'm sure she'd just love to meet you."

CHAPTER FIFTY-TWO

The dawn in Mirenze didn't catch Hedy sleeping. The fledgling witch was already up and about in her tiny servant's room at the Hen and Caber, toting a satchel packed with the few items she couldn't leave behind—like her bone mouse mask, tucked safely behind a concealing flap of cloth. She'd remained in the city for one last night, working a double shift at the tavern to earn as much coin as she could for the journey ahead. She was surprised to bump into Renata at the bottom of the stairs, lugging a cheap and overstuffed bag of her own.

"Where are you going?" they both asked at the same time.

"I—I have to leave town for a while," Renata said. "I just need some distance from things."

"I have family," Hedy said. "Sick family. I just got word."

"I'm so sorry. Is it your mother? Your father?"

"Yes," Hedy said. "I mean, both. At once. I liked working with you, Renata. You're a nice person. I hope you find what you're looking for."

The Owl's words swam back to Hedy's mind, unbidden. *Make a friend. Someone you can use as a patsy, just in case anyone sniffs out what you're really up to. You can pin everything on them and disappear.*

"Say," Hedy added, "which way are you headed?"

Renata shook her head. "I haven't decided yet. Anywhere but here."

Hedy smiled. "Come with me, then. To the Holy City. Travel is cheaper and safer for two than it is for one."

"You've got a point," Renata said. "I've never been there, and I hear it's beautiful in the fall."

Hedy took her hand, suddenly giddy, tugging her toward the door.

"You're going to love it. And we're going to have *so* much fun…"

#

A mad impulse seized Renata as the girl pulled her toward the tavern door. Her nightmares had been awash with tangled images of Felix, and she couldn't shake how different he seemed now. Harder. There was a current of darkness under his placid waters, one she'd never seen before.

Passed through fire and fallen into the hands of wolves, she thought, *and he's still trying to protect me.*

Then it hit her, a flash out of the morning sky. People like the Grimaldis made enemies. They had competitors, people with the power and the influence to do them harm, even in the Holy City. She could use that. Make contacts. Trade what she knew.

Felix, she thought, *you're trying to protect me, love, but right now you're the one who's trapped, and I'm free. I have a voice and the courage to use it.*

"I will not be silent," she murmured aloud.

"Hmm?" Hedy said.

Renata shook her head. "It's a line from an old hymn. Haven't heard it since I was a child, but it just…popped into my head. Funny."

Hold on, Felix. I'm coming.

And I'm going to rescue you.

THREE DAYS LATER

CHAPTER FIFTY-THREE

He wears it well, Lodovico thought, seeing Carlo in his ermine robes of office. An amulet bearing the symbol of the Gardener's Tree, the same one his father had worn, dangled at his throat.

In the end, thanks to subtle intimidation from the "knights" and the unexpected last-minute show of support from Cardinal Accorsi, there was no doubt which way the College would lean. White smoke flew over the Holy City, and Carlo was given his throne with very little fanfare. Most of the city was too deeply in shock to pay much attention, after a wildfire—caused, it was widely believed, by an errant cow kicking over a farmer's forgotten lantern—laid half the city slums to waste.

Carlo's first speech had been a eulogy for the brave, tragic dead of the Alms District, and a pledge to rebuild and improve the lives of the scattered survivors.

Lodovico went down on one knee before Carlo's throne. Carlo extended his hand, sullen, and Lodovico brushed his lips against his ruby ring of office before standing once more.

"For someone who just became the most powerful man in the world," Lodovico said, "you seem a bit downhearted."

"I don't get to go out at night anymore," Carlo said. "Too dangerous, they tell me. I don't get any privacy. Have to watch everything I say, mind my language. There are always people...*wanting* things from me. Every time I turn around, another open hand wanting to be filled."

"Well, I'm not one of them, my friend. I only came to congratulate you on a job well done. And to let you know that it's time we moved on to the second stage of our plan."

Carlo's eyes, bleary and bloodshot, narrowed dangerously.

"You're sure about this?" he said. "The orders were dispatched days ago. You can't call an arrow back to the bow after it's been loosed, Carlo. I hope you're not having second thoughts."

"No, no," Carlo said, waving his hand. "Just having a hard time sleeping. It makes my head hurt. I don't...I don't suppose..."

Lodovico smiled at the puppy-dog hope in Carlo's eyes. He reached under his cloak and, with a dramatic flourish of his wrist, produced a bag of crushed purple velvet. Carlo snatched it up greedily and looked inside. Tiny twists of dried root nestled inside, and a musty, earthy smell drifted out.

"The salamander root helps me think," Carlo said, sounding sheepish as he pulled the drawstrings tight.

"I know it does," Lodovico said. "No worries, I can always get more for you. Call it my tribute to our new Holy Father, long may he reign."

Carlo's eyes went distant.

"Whenever I imagined sitting in my father's chair," Carlo said, "I always thought Livia would be here. My whole life, Vico...she's always been right beside me."

Lodovico shrugged. "I'm sorry she was unworthy of your trust. You'll always be worthy of mine."

Carlo reached out and squeezed Lodovico's hand. His expression was lost, lonely, desperate.

"And you of mine," Carlo said.

"Cheer up," Lodovico told him. "You're just getting oriented. Facing a new and exciting change in your life. Soon enough you'll have everything you ever dreamed of and more. I guarantee it. Just stay quiet and stick to the plan."

He took his leave, strolling the marbled halls of the papal estate until Weiss appeared from a darkened doorway and fell in at his side. The knight's polished mail rustled as he walked, and candlelight played on the black and gold curves of his Imperial eagle pauldron.

"Are your men in place?" Lodovico said, not breaking his stride.

"They're ready to move tonight. I thought there were supposed to be three targets?"

Lodovico nodded. "I set my man Simon on the first. He's had a bad run of luck lately, and I need him back on top of his game."

"Long as we're paid the same, means nothing to me."

"Your troops went a little wild in the Alms District," Lodovico said, keeping his tone light.

"They were pent up for too long with nothing to do," Weiss said. "They're excitable boys. Don't worry, it was all covered up. No one's saying a contrary word, at least nobody anyone will listen to."

"I'm not complaining," Lodovico said. "That slum was an eyesore. I just want to be certain everybody is adhering to the master plan. There's too much at stake here."

"Long as your silver keeps flowing," Weiss said, "the Dustmen's blades are yours to command. Speaking of, what about His Highness back there?"

"Hmm? Carlo?"

Weiss nodded. "How long are you actually going to let him keep that fancy throne?"

"Are you familiar with the phrase 'useful idiot'?" Lodovico asked.

"Sounds self-explanatory enough."

"Carlo," Lodovico said, "is the most useful idiot I know. Who knows? He might even live long enough to learn the truth. I doubt it, but people can surprise you."

"I never get surprised," Weiss said. "So. Any plans for tonight? While the job gets done?"

"A tiny celebration. Dinner at a very nice restaurant."

"In front of plenty of witnesses?"

"Of course," Lodovico said. "Let no man say my hands aren't clean."

CHAPTER FIFTY-FOUR

The center table at the Harvest Vine Inn, draped in pristine white linen and adorned with twists of silver wreath, waited for Lodovico's arrival. His company for the evening was a young courtesan who called herself Snowdrop and poured herself into a scandalously short ivory gown with a low-scooped bodice. The servants rushed to pull out their chairs and pour full glasses from a decanter of red wine.

"Only the best and most expensive of everything tonight," Lodovico told Snowdrop, and she knew he was including her in that sum. She flipped a dangling lock of platinum-blond hair and smiled, holding his gaze.

"So what's the special occasion?" she asked.

"The restoration," he said as he lifted his glass, "of my family's good name."

#

Costantini, the aged and withered chairman of the Council of Nine, closed his eyes and slid into his bath. The steaming water soothed his aching muscles and chased away the cares of the day. Minutes slipped by as he happily relaxed, beadlets of sweat breaking out on his wrinkled brow.

"He knows," said a soft voice.

Costantini's eyelids snapped open. Simon Koertig, lean and sharp and dressed to the nines, loomed over the tub. He peered at the old merchant over the edges of his horn-rimmed glasses.

"He always knew."

"Who did?" Costantini demanded. "Who are—how did you get in here?"

"Lodovico Marchetti," Simon said. "Don't yell for your guards. They're all dead. They weren't very good. Then again, neither were you. Word of advice: if you murder a boy's father, make sure you murder the boy. Otherwise, well, it might take decades for your sins to catch up with you...but here we are."

Suddenly the bath felt cold as an icy river.

"No," Costantini said, "you've got it all wrong."

"Luigi Marchetti didn't commit suicide. The Council of Nine murdered him. Not the entire council. It was Basilio Grimaldi, Terenzio Ruggeri...and you. You forced bottle after bottle of wine down his throat, laid him in his bathtub, and slit his wrists, leaving behind a badly forged letter detailing his great regrets at betraying the city and the empire he loved so dearly."

"No," Costantini said, "*no*. You're wrong. It was nothing so simple—"

"Can you even imagine," Simon said, casually rolling up his sleeves as he spoke, "what it's been like for Lodovico all these years? Growing up amid the men who murdered his father and humiliated his family. Rubbing shoulders with them, drinking with them, being *mentored* by them. Pretending to smile and endure their backhanded japes and the way they stared at his widowed mother's ass, knowing that no matter what they promised him, he'd *never* be allowed a seat at the Council's table. Decades of playing the fool. And all the while, planning. Planning for one very special night."

"You don't *understand*. Luigi was mad! He would have dragged our entire city into war with the Empire. I loved that man like a brother, but putting him down was the only way to save Mirenze. *The city had to come first!*"

"And that," Simon said, "is exactly what Lodovico thinks. It's time for Mirenze to come first."

Simon's hands shot into the bath and seized the old man's ankles. He hauled them sharply upward, yanking Costantini back and down, his head plunging under the bathwater. With his feet held high, Costantini couldn't manage to sit up, couldn't find an angle to get a breath of air. He fought and thrashed, and his hands flailed, sending waves of hot water splashing over the rim of the tub. The back of his hand slapped his wineglass, sending it crashing against the ceramic tiles.

#

Red wine spilled into Lodovico's crystal glass. He laughed and raised it in a toast, clinking his cup against Snowdrop's. The servants brought over a feast, laying out dishes of pork in wine sauce, fried wedges of cheese, a fat torte stuffed with chicken and onion, and even a plate of turnips coated in sugar, cinnamon, and cloves.

"Repairing a reputation sounds like a difficult business," Snowdrop said.

"It's a slow and delicate thing, like weaving a spiderweb from silken thread. One snag, one impatient tug, and the whole thing pulls apart. Fortunately, I'm a patient man. Sometimes."

"So how does it begin?" she asked as a servant ladled a fat and glistening slice of pork onto Lodovico's plate.

"Well, first of all, one has to politely explain to some disreputable persons that their rude behavior and loose talk will no longer be tolerated."

Snowdrop nodded at Lodovico's free hand. His fingers danced across the tablecloth, slow and rhythmic. *Tap. Tap. Tap.*

"You seem anxious," she said.

"Just eager for everything to go well," he said with a smile.

Tap. Tap.

#

Tap, went the tip of Basilio Grimaldi's mahogany cane, rapping the cobblestones as he walked the streets of Mirenze by night.

Tap. Tap.

The elder Grimaldi didn't need a cane to walk—he was healthy and fit as one of his prize stallions, but it was an affectation that pleased him.

He didn't need the bodyguards who discreetly trailed him from a respectable distance, either, but he hadn't survived this long without being careful.

He strolled past darkened doorways and shuttered shops, enjoying the lonely night. The air felt cool and clean in his lungs. It helped clear his head and kept him focused on his plans. He was so focused, working out his designs on the Council of Nine, that he almost didn't notice the men coming up the street behind him.

Basilio didn't look back. He didn't need to. Two pairs of footsteps, a fraction too rushed to be a couple of carefree locals out for an evening's pleasure. The second giveaway: they didn't talk to each other. At all.

He cast a sidelong glance at a darkened window as he passed and saw one of the men—now four feet behind and closing fast—slip a dagger from his belt.

"He knows—" the man started to say. That was all Basilio gave him time for.

Basilio twisted the brass hilt of his cane. The thin, lethal sword concealed inside sang as it slid free, whipping through the air while he spun, slashing the knifeman across the face from eye to chin. The knifeman clutched his face, screaming, staggering back. The second, with a stiletto of his own, was smarter. He lunged in close and got inside Basilio's reach, going for his heart. Basilio twisted, snarling, and smashed his forehead down against the man's nose. Cartilage spattered, and while the would-be killer howled like a whipped dog, Basilio grabbed the man's wrist, wrenched it around, and drove the killer's stiletto into his own lung.

He turned just in time to see a third assassin, eyes wild behind his black leather hood, charge from a side alley and thrust his knife like a bayonet. Basilio wheezed as the thin blade went wide and dug into his side, skewering his hip. He dropped to his knees on the street, clutching the wound. The assassin raised his blade high—and plunged backward as a crossbow bolt punched through his throat.

Basilio slumped against the wall, clutching his hip. The first assassin, hands pressed to his slashed face, broke into a blind run. Basilio's two guards, one cradling his crossbow like a baby, jogged up from behind. One pawed at his master's coat, trying to get a look at the wound, but Basilio angrily waved him away.

"I'm *fine*," Basilio snapped as warm blood trickled through his clenched fingers, "I'll live, damn you. Just give me a moment to catch my breath. Go, take him! Bring him back to me. Bring him back to me *alive!*"

As his guards took off in pursuit, Basilio closed his eyes and leaned his head back against the cool stone wall. Blood trickled between his fingers, his life seeping out with every rasping breath, making a faint *tap-tap-tap* on the cobblestones.

#

Lodovico savored a bite of the chicken torte. The caramelized onions added the perfect hint of sweetness to the moist meat and flaky pastry shell.

"Once you've done that," Snowdrop asked, daintily patting a napkin to her wine-moistened lips, "what comes next?"

"Something very special. Something I've been planning for years. Do you know who my father was?"

She shook her head. "No, sorry."

His fingers tightened, ever so slightly, around the stem of his wineglass.

"My father was a patriot. He believed in Mirenze. He believed that this city and its people had a destiny. We were a city-*state* once, the independent and shining jewel of the coast, before the Empire took it all away. Before scared, small men *gave* it all away without shedding a single defiant drop of blood."

"You shouldn't say things like that," Snowdrop said in a hushed whisper, glancing furtively at the other tables. "Someone might hear."

"The Empire thrives on frightened little silences. And I've come up with a way of honoring my father's memory and his dream."

Snowdrop hovered somewhere between curious and nervous as she asked, "What will you do?"

Lodovico held up his glass, studying the ruby wine by candlelight.

"What time is it, past seven bells yet? Ah. I've already *done* it. Can't tell you the details, that'd spoil everything, but trust me."

He grinned at her, baring his teeth like a wolf on the prowl.

"It's going to be a hell of a show."

CHAPTER FIFTY-FIVE

The village of al-Tali stood a day's ride into the desert, nestled in the shadow of a red rock mountain. It catered to the merchant trade, offering a friendly inn and a cool, clear oasis just when western caravans were starting to feel tired and thirsty. Beyond the two-story inn and an open-air market, there wasn't much to the place besides a jumble of crude, white-domed peasant houses that stood out like half-melted salt-licks in the scrub.

"I don't understand the desert," Terenzio Ruggeri said as he squatted on a chair of stretched goat hide and warmed his hands in the glow of a fire. "You burn to death by the noonday sun and freeze to death at night. How do you live like this?"

Gerolt Becker, a Murgardt expatriate in the white robes of an Oerran shepherd, laughed and lifted his glass of mulled wine. "You do what the lizard and the spider do. You adapt."

"Going native," Terenzio said, not hiding the distaste in his voice.

"We're in the no-man's-land, here. Al-Badra marks the edge of the Caliphate's border, and the city stands a mere five leagues to the east. With neighbors such as these, it pays to show you respect their ways."

"Afraid of raiders?" Terenzio asked, quirking an eyebrow.

"Goodness, no! Times have changed since the old Crusades, friend. We have a different emperor, they have a different caliph, and we all know what really makes the world go round."

"Oh? What's that?"

Gerolt rubbed his thumb against his fingertips. "Profit."

"I'll drink to that," Terenzio said. "I'm going to need to hire a guide. Someone who speaks the language and has a head for numbers."

"I know just the lad. He's bright, honest, and works cheap. I'll introduce you in the—"

The heavy hide curtain that dangled over the inn's front door swung wide, and Terenzio's caravan-master dashed in, panting for breath. He pointed, jabbing his flailing finger toward the east.

"War party," he gasped. "Men in Caliphate armor, riding hard, maybe two minutes out. Grizzo was out in the dunes, getting the lay of the land. They cut him down, Terenzio! I saw it with my own eyes!"

Terenzio and Gerolt shot to their feet.

"Impossible," Gerolt said, leading the way to the door. "We've been at peace for a generation. They're our neighbors! My daughter married an Oerran, for the Gardener's grace. She *lives* in al-Badra."

They emerged onto the street just in time to see the first fire-arrows fly.

Shafts arced through the sky like burning hornets, whistling to land in thatch and plaster, spreading flames that sent the peasants screaming from their houses. Muscular stallions kicked up clouds of dust as they thundered into the village, their riders garbed in lacquered armor and helms fit with lion masks of hammered brass. They rode with horsemen's bows and scimitars, firing wild arrows and slicing at anyone too slow to escape. Terenzio saw a villager go down in a spray of blood, cut across the belly with a vicious slash. He tried to pull himself to safety, dragging his bleeding body through the dust, until another stallion's hoof smashed down on his skull.

"My caravan!" Terenzio shouted, running toward the market square. "We'll unhitch the lead horses. We can still get away!"

A stallion whinnied as another rider whipped past, and the caravan-master's head went rolling through the dirt, keeping pace with Terenzio's stride. The dust stung his eyes, and suddenly the flat of a boot hit him from behind. Terenzio hit the ground, but Gerolt kept running in a dead panic, making for the horses.

One of the Oerran soldiers grabbed Terenzio by the back of his tunic and hauled him to his knees, pressing a blade to his throat. Another, still sitting in the saddle, notched an arrow and took aim at Gerolt's back.

"Let that one go," the first masked soldier said in a crisp Murgardt accent. "We need a few survivors, or there's no point."

"Right, right. Gotta tell the tragic tale," said the horseman, lowering his bow.

"I will not be silent."

"Hmm?" the horseman said.

"Line from an old hymn," the soldier holding Terenzio said, frowning. "Weird. It just popped into my head."

"Didn't think you went for that church stuff, Kappel."

"I don't. All right, let's get this one off the street."

They dragged Terenzio past the dead and the dying, the dusty street littered with corpses as the fires of the village houses lit the night sky. The inn still stood. They sat him down on a stretched-hide stool, binding his wrists behind his back with a strap of rawhide.

The soldier—Kappel—took off his helm, revealing the sandy blond hair and ice-blue eyes of a native Murgardt.

"He knows," Kappel said. "He always knew."

Terenzio trembled.

"Lodovico," he whispered.

Kappel nodded, looming over him with a cruel smile on his lips. "He didn't think you'd need much of an explanation."

"I can pay you. I can pay double whatever Lodovico is offering. Triple! Just let me go. Say you killed me. Say I slipped away. Say whatever you want—"

"We are well, *well* past the point of bargaining. Besides, we're the Dustmen. We don't make deals."

"Why do this?" Terenzio said, hearing faint screams outside the inn as the raiders mopped up the last few survivors. "If he wants me dead, so be it, but why a massacre? Why hurt all these people just to get at me?"

Kappel snickered. "He said you'd say that. That you couldn't imagine it wasn't all about *you*. The two or three villagers we let go, they're going to ride for the Imperial borders. And what will they say when they get there?"

Terenzio's eyes widened.

"They'll say," he answered softly, horror in his voice, "that al-Tali was ransacked in an unprovoked attack. They'll say that Oerran soldiers butchered Imperial settlers."

Kappel mockingly clapped his leather-gloved hands. "Now he gets it!"

"That's insane! The emperor's been aching for a crusade since he took the throne! Even without an excuse, it still took Pope Benignus to hold him back..." Terenzio's voice trailed off. He shook his head, understanding.

"You mean, the *dead* Pope Benignus," Kappel said. "The Church is under new management. And the new pope? Let's just say he's not quite the man his father was."

"This...this will mean war. The Empire will march on the Oerran Caliphate. Thousands of people are going to die, on both sides. Tens of thousands!"

"See? You're smarter than you look."

"*Why?*" Terenzio shouted, the word coming out in a strangled cry.

Kappel pulled up a stool, sat down, and offered Terenzio a placid smile.

"For Mirenze."

Terenzio couldn't speak. He tried, but the words wouldn't come.

"The Empire cut off Mirenze's balls," Kappel said, "and you, you and your little friends, you murdered Luigi Marchetti—the last, best hope for his city's freedom. So Lodovico thought it was only appropriate that you be here, right where it all kicks off. His vendetta. A vendetta *against the Empire itself*. This is just the first step. Like I said, he's been planning this for years. When he's finished, *nothing* will be left standing. Nothing but a free Mirenze."

"And me?" Terenzio asked, dreading the answer. "What's my part in all this?"

"Same as your friends," Kappel said.

Terenzio didn't even see the knife. Kappel's hand was empty—then suddenly it wasn't, sprouting five inches of cold steel. He lunged, plunging the blade into Terenzio's heart.

"Same as your friends," Kappel whispered into Terenzio's ear, holding the merchant close as he convulsed and bled out in his arms. "To die in shame, knowing that Lodovico Marchetti beat you. And that his father will be avenged."

Kappel dumped the corpse on the floor and strolled out of the inn, whistling as he wiped his blade clean. It was over now, all but a few frenzied screams as the Dustmen had their fun with the odd straggler or two, but that wouldn't last long. They'd rally, ride out to the marked dune where they'd buried their real leathers, and leave their stolen Caliphate armor hidden deep beneath the sand.

Kappel paused, recognizing the tune he was whistling. He couldn't get that damn hymn out of his mind. It didn't feel like a comfort. It felt like a warning.

CHAPTER FIFTY-SIX

The refugee fleet landed in Itresca on a warm, starry night, making landfall in sight of an olive grove. The weary survivors crashed their leaking boats against the rocky white-sand beach or just abandoned them in the surf, wading through the warm and waist-deep water while hoisting supply crates and sacks over their heads.

Some of the escapees from the Holy City had died on the voyage, taken by their wounds and slipping into the pitiless sea. A hundred and eighty-nine people made landfall, a ragged line following Livia Serafini over the rocks and sand and into the green.

I can't do this, she thought, so exhausted she could barely put one foot ahead of the other. *They're going to want me to speak. To say something to keep their hope alive. I can't do it.*

Then she thought of the dead they'd left behind. She raised her chin and pushed her shoulders back.

You are allowed to be tired, she told herself, *but you are not allowed to be weak. It's your job to be strong, so they don't have to be.*

She turned, facing the growing crowd as they gathered around her in the olive grove. She held out her hands, and when she finally spoke, her voice carried all the way to the water.

"I won't tell you that this happened for a reason," she said. "I won't tell you that it was part of the Gardener's grand design. It was the evil in men's hearts that forced you from your homes, that murdered your families, your friends, your neighbors. It was avarice and hate. I have heard you speak on the voyage. I've heard the calls for violence, for revenge."

Nodding faces all around. Hard eyes and pursed lips.

"My brother has turned his back on love," Livia said, "and that is why *we must not*. Oh, we will fight. We will fight, for even saints have carried swords, but we will fight with a craving for justice in our hearts. A craving that will only rest when my brother's crimes have been set to right.

"We will camp here tonight. Come morning, we march to the Itrescan capital, and I will parley with the king. I wish I could tell you what will happen after that. I wish I knew all the answers. All I know is that I *will not give up*. I will fight to my dying breath. For justice. For our Mother Church. And for you."

There was no fanfare, no grand applause, just a sea of tired faces slowly dispersing among the trees. Little knots of people clung together, families and neighbors, and soon the grove glowed with scattered pinpricks of firelight. Livia sat in the grass and closed her eyes, feeling lead weights pressing down on her shoulders.

"Better than most of my sermons," Amadeo said, crouching beside her.

She didn't open her eyes. "Doubtful."

A few minutes later, the soft sound of a song drifted across the grove. A hymn carried by a handful of refugees gathered around one of the campfires. A ring of survivors at another fire, not far away, slowly took up the song and added their voices. From firelight to firelight, the hymn carried and grew louder.

In chains of iron, in snow-swept night
Wand'ring strange land and sea
I will not be silent, will not hide my light
For thy guiding hand is on me.

"Hymn to Saint Elise, Lady of Deliverance," Amadeo mused. "The voice against tyrants, comforter of prisoners, and speaker of hard truths. Always been one of my favorites."

In cold, in dark, in toil and blight
I may fear, yet shall not flee
I will not be silent, will not hide my light

For thy shielding hand is on me.

"Livia," Amadeo said.

She opened her eyes and met his gaze.

"You know they're not singing to Saint Elise, don't you?"

She squeezed her eyes shut again.

She couldn't find her voice, but her lips moved with the words and she felt a sudden surge of passion, the grim responsibility on her shoulders warring with the fire in her heart.

Saint Elise, she prayed, *lend me your strength. Lend me your sword and your shield, that I might keep these people safe in the tempest to come.*

For I will not be silent.

AFTERWORD

As always, I want to thank my team: Kira Rubenthaler, my editor; James T. Egan, my cover designer; and Michelle Faid, my social-media manager. Even if only one person writes the words of the story, every good book is a collaboration.

And most of all, thank you for reading! If you'd like to find out what happens next, head over to http://www.craigschaeferbooks.com and hop onto my mailing list for announcements about new releases. You can also catch me on Facebook (facebook.com/CraigSchaeferBooks), Twitter (@craig_schaefer), or just drop me an email at craig@craigschaeferbooks.com. I'd love to hear from you.

Printed in Great Britain
by Amazon